Elizabeth Jeffrey was born in Wivenhoe, a small water-front town near Colchester, and has lived there all her life. She began writing short stories over thirty years ago, in between bringing up her three children and caring for an elderly parent. More than 100 of her stories went on to be published or broadcast; in 1976 she won a national short-story competition and her success led her on to write full-length novels for both adults and children.

Elizabeth JEFFREY

The Buttercup Fields

piatkus

PIATKUS

First published in Great Britain in 1993 by Judy Piatkus Publisher Ltd
This paperback edition published in 2012 by Piatkus

A CIP catalogue record for this book
is available from the British Library.

ISBN 978-0-7499-5796-4

Typeset in Sabon by Hewer Text UK Ltd, Edinburgh
Printed and bound by Clays Ltd, St Ives plc

Papers used by Piatkus are from well-managed forests
and other responsible sources.

 MIX
Paper from
responsible sources
FSC® C104740

Piatkus
An imprint of
Little, Brown Book Group
100 Victoria Embankment
London EC4Y 0DY

An Hachette UK Company
www.hachette.co.uk

www.piatkus.co.uk

To my cousin, Jean Millington,
whose memories have coloured these pages.

Chapter One

Becca took one last look at the little thatched cottage before she picked up her faded gingham skirts and ran down the lane, her thick, dark hair tumbling from its pins where George had tangled his fingers in it as he gave her a last kiss before going back to work. She gave a little skip of delight because soon she and George would be married. The date was set for the fourth of October in the year 1890, in six weeks' time, and after that the two of them would be living in the little cottage at the end of Tenpenny Lane they had just visited. She was so happy and full of love for George that she felt her heart would burst.

She slowed to a walk and began to make plans. There were a few sticks of furniture in the cottage – enough to start with – and she could soon brighten up the place with a rub of beeswax and a patchwork cushion or two. She might even manage to find some oddments of material and make curtains, she was good with her needle. And she'd already collected up one or two bits of china . . . She broke into a run again.

1

She reached home, another farm labourer's cottage but in better condition than the one she had just left, and ran down the path and into the brick-floored kitchen, nearly falling over her own feet in her excitement. 'Mr Warner has jest said George and me can have Owd Racky Harris the cowman's cottage, now that Racky's dead and his wife has gone to live with her son,' she said breathlessly. 'Thass not a bad little place, neither. Me and George have jest been to look at it. That want a bit done to the thatch, but George reckon he can do that afore we're wed without a lot of trouble . . .'

Daisy Stansgate, busy at the fire, turned with the kettle in her hand and looked at her twenty-year-old daughter. Becca stood in the doorway, radiant with happiness, her cheeks rosy and her breast heaving from her run down the lane. Daisy's heart flooded with compassion.

'I'm afraid there'll be no harvest wedding for you, Becca, my girl, so you can put that idea right outa your head.' She pursed her lips and banged the kettle down on the hob, emotion making her voice sharper than she had intended.

Becca's jaw dropped as she stared from her mother to her younger sister, who was huddled on the settle in the corner, and back at her mother again. 'What do you mean, won't be no wedding? You know right well George and me's promised.'

'Didn't you hear me, mawther? I said there won't be no wedding between you and George Askew,' Daisy repeated, her tone still sharp. She nodded briefly towards her younger daughter. 'Ellen's put the kibosh on that, good and proper.'

2

'Ellen? What's Ellen got to do with me and George getting wed?'

'She's in the fam'ly way.'

Ellen, sitting next to the kitchen range even though it was a hot, late-August day, broke into noisy tears. Daisy turned to her impatiently. 'And you can shut that row, my girl. You've made your bed and now you'll have to lie on it.'

'In the fam'ly way!' Becca looked at her sister, wide-eyed with a mixture of horror and disbelief. 'Oh, Ellen. You can't be! Are you certain sure?'

'Oh, yes, there ain't no doubt,' Daisy said, her voice weary with worry. 'That wasn't green apples been upsetting her stummick, like we thought.' She brushed a strand of hair away from her forehead. 'Goodness only knows what her father'll have to say when he find out.'

Becca sat down at the scrubbed deal table, her senses reeling at the shocking news. Ellen in the family way, and her only eighteen! What would become of her? The shame of it all – and her not even courting yet! She glanced across at Ellen, snivelling in the corner. She could never be called pretty, with her nondescript fairish hair and pale eyelashes, and skin that freckled and burned at the first hint of sun, but she could look quite pleasant when she didn't wear such a disagreeable expression. In fact, she could look quite attractive when she chose. And she liked the boys, there was no denying that. Unlike her sister she could be quite a little flirt. Becca frowned, the silly little bitch had obviously flirted once too often and it had got out of hand. Now she'd have to get married in a hurry.

That meant she and George would have to wait. All

their plans would have to be put on one side because of Ellen. Becca's expression hardened and she shot her sister a look of pure venom. Why was it that whenever anything exciting happened to her, Ellen always had to go and spoil things? The only time she, Becca, had ever had a brand new dress had been one Christmas and Ellen had somehow managed to be sick all over it. And the nearly new boots that had come from the Manor that fitted Becca like a pair of gloves had had to go to Ellen because she'd kicked up such a fuss. It was always the same. Somehow or other Ellen always contrived to get her own way or else to ruin other people's enjoyment. Even when their brother Tommy was born, when Ellen was only three, she'd gone off and got herself lost in Tulley's Woods and everybody had been too worried about her to celebrate the birth of Daisy and Joe's first – and last, as it happened – son. Well, Ellen wasn't going to ruin this, Becca decided. She was going to marry George on the fourth of October even if it meant a double wedding. But she would have to tread carefully.

She began to trace the grain of the table top with her finger. 'I know thass a dreadful thing, if Ellen's in the family way and her not married,' she said slowly, 'but I can't see why that should stop George and me getting wed. Thass all arranged. We've set the date and the banns'll be called for the first time on Sunday.'

'That they never will. They'll have to be stopped,' Daisy said firmly. The kettle boiled and she turned her back to spoon tea into the teapot warming on the hearth and then poured the water on to it. 'You'd better tell her, you little slut,' she said over her shoulder to Ellen. 'Tell

4

her who you've bin larking around with. Tell her who the father is.'

Ellen sniffed and wiped her eyes on the corner of her apron. 'Thass George,' she whispered.

Becca looked blank. 'George who?'

'Your George.'

'*My* George? George Askew?' Becca's voice rose almost to a scream. She went over and shook her sister until her head rolled back and forth on her shoulders. 'How dare you tell such lies! You're jealous, thass what you are. You've always been jealous of me and you've always had a fancy for George, so you've cooked up this cock and bull story so you can come between us. You little hussy! You little bitch! Thass lies! All lies! You're a wicked, wicked, girl to play such tricks.' Becca's hands dropped and she turned away. 'I don't believe you're in the family way at all. I believe you've made it all up jest so you can get your own way.'

'Oh, yes, she is,' Daisy sighed. 'She's missed twice and she's got all the signs. There ain't no doubt she's in pod.'

'Well, thass nothing to do with George, I know right well. He wouldn't do a thing like that . . .' Her voice trailed off. There was no denying George's hot blood. It was not his fault he hadn't been up under her own skirts before now; her insistence that they wait till they were married was a constant irritation to him. 'Anyway,' she finished lamely, 'when have you ever had the chance?'

Ellen lifted her head. 'That was when we were coming home from the fair after you and George had had a row. Don't you remember? You stormed off and went home with Maudie Edwards and Biddy Grimes. I thought you'd

5

broke up for good so when George asked for a kiss . . .'

'Pity that didn't stop at a kiss,' Daisy said with a scathing glance in Ellen's direction.

Becca sat down again, put her elbows on the table and clasped her hands round the back of her neck. She felt sick. 'You're nothing more'n a little slut! And you only eighteen. You oughta be horsewhipped.' She barely lifted her head to say the words. She was silent for a long time. Ellen's jealousy had never worried her before. With an inherent wisdom far beyond her years she had understood that it was Ellen's defence against growing up in the shadow of an elder sister who had learned to read and write more easily and had grasped the rudiments of arithmetic more quickly, and a younger brother who was made much of simply because he was a boy. Becca knew how Ellen hated having her elder sister continually held up as an example of what she ought to achieve at school. At the same time, Becca couldn't help it if her brain was quicker. She had enjoyed learning and had hated being kept away from school to help on the farm, as all the children often were during their school days, whilst for Ellen and Tommy the reverse was true.

After a while Becca lifted her head. 'So what's going to happen?' she said.

'There's only one thing for it.' Daisy poured cups of tea for them all and pushed Becca's across the table to her. 'She'll have to marry George.'

'No!' Becca's head shot up. 'George and me's spoke for each other. She can't have him. He's mine. Anyway, what would folks say if I let my young sister pinch my intended?'

'No worse than they'd say if you got wed and six

6

months later she had your husband's bastard,' Daisy said brutally. She sat down opposite Becca. 'You wouldn't like to see us all turned out of house and home, now, would you, my girl?' she said more gently. 'Because thass what'll happen if Ellen don't wed the father of her child. You know how strict Mr Green is over that kinda thing.'

'I can't see what thass got to do with Mr Green,' Becca said stubbornly. 'Tenpenny Farm belongs to Mr Warner. He's dad's master.'

'Don't be so pig-headed. You know very well Mr Warner's only the tenant farmer. Mr Green owns this farm and half a dozen others into the bargain. Thass not Mr Warner as'll turn us out, that'll be Mr Green,' Daisy took a sip of her tea. 'An he will, too, make no mistake. I remember what happened when Jabez Goodchild's girl got herself in pod by one of the boys from the fair one autumn. As soon as Mr Green got to hear about it the whole family was turned outa their cottage – I can still see their few sticks of furniture piled up in the road, that was a pouring wet day, too, as I recall. They hadn't got nowhere to go so they ended up in the Spike. Mind you, I don't think they were there for long, Jabez managed to get a place on a farm in Suffolk where they weren't known, but that was a bad business.' She shook her head and gave a great sigh. 'I dessay we shall all come to the work'us in the end, but I'd hoped to keep out of it for a few more years.' She turned away and surreptitiously wiped her eyes on the corner of her apron.

Becca was silent, digesting her mother's words. She knew Daisy hadn't exaggerated in what she had said. Mr Green at the Manor was a just, God-fearing man but he would brook no scandal among his workers. 'Let her find somebody else to marry. She can't have George. Thass me he wants, not her,' she said at last, with a scathing look in Ellen's direction.

Ellen looked up for the first time. 'I wouldn't be too sure about that,' she said with something of a sneer. 'George told me he liked me because I was cuddlesome.'

'A sight too cuddlesome, if you ask me,' Daisy snapped.

Becca's eyes narrowed. 'Jest a minute . . . Was that the only time you and George . . . ? After the fair, I mean?' she asked Ellen.

Ellen shrugged. 'Might have been. Might not.'

Becca got up so sharply that the chair she had been sitting on fell over. She went over to Ellen and began to shake her again. 'Don't you come them tricks with me, mawther. Tell me the truth. How many times?'

'I don't remember.' Ellen began to cry again. 'Five or six. I don't remember.'

'You'll remember time I've finished with you!' Becca pulled her to her feet.

'Oh, leave her be, Becca,' Daisy said. 'If you wanta take it out on anybody I should think George is the one to see. He's as much to blame as she is.'

Becca let Ellen go so suddenly that she fell back on to the settle. 'I will. I'll go and see him right now. He's gone to fetch the cows back for milking. I'll catch him in the pasture if I'm quick. I'll soon find out if you're telling a pack of lies, Ellen Stansgate.'

She ran out of the door and across the lane to the pasture beyond, glad to get out of the house, glad of something to do to release the pent up fury inside her. She shaded her eyes against the brightness of the huge, cloudless East Anglian sky. She could seen the cows making their slow progress across the gentle slope of the meadow, their gait made awkward by the heavy bags of milk they needed to let down. Behind them walked George, whistling happily. She waited by the gate, watching the gentle way he coaxed the cows forward, calling each one by name – Phoebe, Buttercup, Mirabelle, Blossom. George was a good cowman. He was a handsome man, too. Tall, with broad shoulders and well-muscled limbs; his black hair curled thickly over his brow and his eyes were a bright, piercing blue in a face tanned by the sun and the wind to a ruddy bronze.

Ever since they were both at school George had been popular. All the girls had fancied him for his strength and good looks and the boys had been anxious to keep on the right side of him because his father was the blacksmith and could sometimes be persuaded to make iron hoops for them to bowl or runners for the wooden sledges they knocked up in snowy weather. As children, when there was no school and they weren't needed stone-picking or rook-scaring on the fields, the village children would congregate by the pond, between the church and the village pub, known as The Whalebone, the girls on one side with their peg dolls, wooden hoops or skipping ropes, the boys on the other with their spinning tops, marbles or the bows and arrows they made from hazel wands or willow saplings. The smaller children concentrated on their games and were oblivious to the group opposite, but the older ones were covertly aware of every move on the other side of the pond. Gradually, over the years, the older members of the two groups began to converge, at first simply by hurling good-natured insults at each other across the water, then, as the boys began to show off in ever-increasing feats of daring – things like tree-climbing, swinging on a long rope over the water, or walking on stilts – the girls would each choose a champion to cheer, and afterwards, if they were lucky, would be nonchalantly walked home by their favourite. George, being the handsomest and most athletic, could usually take his pick from the girls who had championed him but more and more he had chosen Becca. Becca, proud to know that she was the envy of all the girls had, unlike her flirtatious sister, hardly spared a glance for any of the other village lads but had remained faithful to George. For the past two years it had been accepted that they were 'going steady'.

George gave the last, straggling cow a pat on the rump with his switch as he came through the gate. 'Why, Becca, what's brought you out here? That ain't above half an hour since we parted. Still, thass nice to see you.' He gave her a wide, unsuspecting smile.

There was no answering smile from Becca. She came straight to the point. 'I've come to ask you a question, George,' she said, her voice flat. 'Have you bin tumbling my sister Ellen in the hedge?' She lifted her head and looked him straight in the eye.

He stopped in his tracks, letting the cows amble on to find their own way back to the farmyard a few hundred yards away. 'Becca!' What a thing to ask!' he said reproachfully. 'Whatever made you think I'd do a thing like that?'

'Don't play games with me, George Askew,' she cut in. 'Ellen's already told me what's bin happening.'

A variety of expressions flitted across the young cowman's face before he settled for a look of hurt dignity. He opened his mouth to deny the accusation, then seeing the look on Becca's face he changed his mind, lifted the cap perched on the back of his head and scratched his curls. 'Yes, well, Becca, you know how it is with a chap,' he said with a shrug. 'There's you, always so prissy with your "Wait till we're married, George", after leading a fella on. And then along comes Ellen all eager and willing.'

He tried to put his arm round her but she shrugged him off. He looked at her, waiting for her to say something and when she remained silent he stumbled on, 'But that didn't mean nothing, dear. What happened with Ellen was only a bit of fun. Thass all. That was jest...' He shrugged and spread his hands in a dismissive gesture. 'And that won't never happen again, I promise you that. I shan't never look at another woman once we're married, Becca. But like I said, that was mostly your fault for lead-ing me on. You're a proper...' he searched for an expression that could be used outside the tap room of the Whalebone and settled for 'well, you're a past master at leading a chap on and then leaving him high and dry, so you can't wonder that when Ellen come along... She's a proper little hot-arse, your sister. You wanta watch her, she'll land herself in trouble.'

'She already has,' Becca said.

'What do you mean?'

'I mean Ellen's in the family way, George,' Becca said,

11

slowly and deliberately, her eyes on his face. 'She's having your baby.'

He gaped at her for a full minute as her words sank into his brain. Then he turned away and closed the gate to the pasture carefully and leaned on it. 'Christ,' he said, wiping his forehead on his sleeve, 'thass a facer and no mistake.' A suspicious look came over his face. 'Are you sure thass mine?'

Becca sighed. 'Thass not for me to be sure about anything in this mess, George Askew. Seems thass nothing to do with me. But are you sure thass *not* yours?'

He hung his head and kicked a loose clod of earth with his boot.

'No, I thought not.' She turned away in disgust. 'Well, then, you'll have to do right by her, George.'

'What do you mean?'

She turned back, her voice rising almost to the point of hysteria as she said, 'You'll have to marry her, of course.'

He spread his hands in bewilderment. 'But what about us, Becca? The banns is all ready to be called for us.'

'Thank God they ain't been called yet. We can stop them.'

'But I don't wanta marry Ellen. Thass you I wanta marry, Becca.'

'Then you shoulda thought twice before you started lifting Ellen's skirts.' Tears were running down Becca's face. 'You ain't got no choice, George. If you don't do right by Ellen, Dad'll lose his job and the cottage that goes with it.' She shook her head. 'We shall be turned out of house and home because Mr Green won't allow bastards in his farmworkers' cottages.' She dashed a hand across

12

her eyes. 'I couldn't have that on my conscience, George. I couldn't have my family end up in the workhouse. Not even for you. No, I can't see no other way but that you'll have to marry Ellen and make an honest woman of her.'

'But I want you, Becca. I love you.'

She turned her head away and spoke in a dead voice. 'Ain't no good you talking like that. Thass too late. You shoulda remembered that was me you loved before you interfered with my sister.'

'Seems like you don't want me. Seems like you wanta be rid of me.' He moved to take her in his arms.

She took a step back, her face white with fury. 'How can you say sech a thing, George Askew! Anyone'd think it was my doing that you've got Ellen into trouble. But thass not me thass bin spreading me favours around, thass you! And how do you think *I* feel about it all? The whole village knows we've bin walking out together. How do you think I'm going to feel when you marry my sister? How do you think I'm going to hold my head up in the village? Have you thought about that?

'I'm sorry, Becca.'

'Soft words butter no parsnips. So you damn' well oughta be sorry. But what's done's done and can't be undone. You'll have to marry Ellen and make an honest woman of her, so you'll have me for a sister-in-law instead of a wife.' Her tears began to flow again. 'And it'll be you and Ellen that'll have Racky Harris's cottage, 'stead of you and me. And much joy may it bring you both.'

'But what about you, Becca? What will you do?' Genuine concern creased his forehead.

'Thass a bit late to start worrying about me,' she said

13

bitterly. 'But if thass any consolation to you, I can tell you now that I shall never marry.'

She opened the gate and ran across the pasture to the stile that separated the meadow from the cornfield beyond. Ever since she was a child this stile had been her place of refuge and now she climbed up and sat there, sobbing until she felt drained and empty with all feeling dead and her heart like a lump of lead in her breast. The corn in the field beyond gleamed golden in the late afternoon sun and the poppies spattered through the corn were like brilliant spots of red light. Overhead a skylark sang, hovering high in the air above its nest in the meadow. All this Becca absorbed without noticing. It was as much a part of her life as day following night. The only thing that hammered through her mind was that she and George were to have been married as soon as the harvest was all gathered in but now he was going to marry Ellen and there would be no wedding for her. Not this harvest. Not any harvest. Wearily, she got down from the stile and made her way home, her heart full of misery and despair. She was finished with men, she wanted nothing more to do with them. Anyway, who would want her after this?

The wedding day drew nearer. But now it was Ellen who smugly stitched patchwork cushions and swept and cleaned the cottage that was to have been Becca's home, and Ellen who stood happily for hours while Daisy made over an old dress of Mrs Green's from the Manor for her wedding whilst Becca quietly nursed her broken heart.

Nevertheless, she gritted her teeth and did her share with all the other women to help getting the harvest in. The corn was golden ripe and higher than a man's head, and the men cut skilfully with their great scythes, rhythmically swinging them so that the corn fell evenly in one direction and could be gathered in great armfuls by the women following behind and tied with the traditional binder's knot. Behind them came the younger women and girls, to stook the bound sheaves into traves that had to be spaced evenly down the field and with enough room between each row for the teams of wagons to load and cart them away. There was a cheerful, bantering atmosphere as everyone worked and Becca tried to be cheerful, too, to ignore the pitying glances and the remarks that were occasionally spiteful, but more often well-meant.

'I shouldn't fret, dearie, there's as good a fish in the sea as ever came out of it.' Old Mrs Tadwick spoke from experience, having buried four husbands.

'I should count meself lucky, if I was you,' another remarked.

'At least you found out afore you was wed.'

'Shame it was your sister though. You'd have thought the randy young tup mighta looked a bit further afield.'

'P'raps he didn't hev to look. P'raps he on'y took what was offered.'

A young, pregnant woman straightened up and rubbed her back. 'You wouldn't want him now, though, would you, Becca? Not after what he's done to you?'

Becca lifted her chin. 'No. If my sister Ellen dropped dead this minute and he was the last man left on earth, I wouldn't marry him.' She spoke in a loud, clear voice, certain that George, driving past in the tumbril heard every word. But it wasn't true, and in her heart she knew it.

15

At last the final sheaf was thrown up on to the cart and a great shout went up from the weary workers to think that the hard work was finished. Becca, taking advantage of the jollity as George and Ellen, as Lord and Lady of the Harvest, were hoisted up on to the top of the last load, slipped through the hedge and made her way over the marshes to the river. She had managed to hold her head high and put on a brave front for a whole week but now she was weary, weary to the bone. The tide was full, the water making comforting noises as it lapped the edge of the saltings, and she imagined what it must be like to walk into the cool water and let it close over her head. That way she wouldn't have to keep up appearances, wouldn't have to pretend she didn't care any more. But she turned away, knowing that it was a mortal sin to take your own life.

Slowly, she began to retrace her steps. At the top of the rise the cart was disappearing through the gate amid much shouting and singing. George, she could see, had all too quickly become resigned to his fate and had his arm proprietorially round Ellen, her head resting on his shoulder. As he was so soon to be married he had been chosen by the men as Lord of the Harvest, with Ellen as his Lady. It has been his task to direct the harvest, to tell the men when to work and when to rest, to collect the penny fines exacted for swearing and other small transgressions. Fortunately, the harvest customs had been set since time immemorial and so even though he had never been Lord before George had little trouble in keeping order. And anyway there was always someone on hand to prompt him if he forgot.

The rest of the workers followed the wagon on foot, most of them similarly paired off, ready for the drinking and dancing and general merry-making that would take place in the big barn now that the harvest was safely gathered in. Even young Tommy, who was barely fifteen, had his arm proudly round Tansy Porter, although, equally proudly, over his other shoulder he carried a stick on which hung the six rabbits he had knocked on the head and killed as they raced out of the corn to escape the reapers' scythes.

Becca made her way back up the field, reduced now to stubble, not even noticing that the sharp stalks of the cut corn were scratching her legs till they bled. There was no hurry. There was nobody left to partner her. Not that she wanted anybody. Not now.

Her mother was waiting for her by the 'policeman', the single corn stook left standing in the field to warn the gleaners off. 'Are you going to the barn, mawther?' she asked.

Becca shook her head briefly.

'Thass not the end of the world, my girl,' Daisy said, turning to walk back with Becca. 'That might seem like it now, but in a few years' time, when you've got a husband and family of your own . . .'

'I shan't never marry, Mum,' Becca interrupted. 'Not after this.' She spread her hands. 'Who'd want me?' Her mouth twisted bitterly. 'Who could I trust?'

Daisy stopped and turned to look at her oldest child. 'No, thass a sure thing you won't find a husband, not if you go round all bitter and twisted for the rest of your life. But if you put a brave face on it all folks'll respect you the more.' She laid her hand on her daughter's arm. 'I know you've bin hurt bad, Becca dear, and I ain't tryin' to make light of it, but let me tell you this. That'll either make you into a hard, bitter woman, or that'll soften you and make you understand other people's hurts better. And on'y you can make up your mind which way you'll let it take you.' She put her head on one side. 'Now, don't you think it's time you spoke a civil word to Ellen? She's suffering, too, you know, for what she's done to you.'

Becca made a sound that was half a laugh and half a snort. 'Don't you believe it! Ellen's not suffering. She doesn't care about me. She's always wanted everything I had, she's always wanted George. Well, now she's got him, the sneaky little bitch! And much good may it do her.' She dashed the tears from her eyes. 'I don't think I'll ever forgive her for what she's done to me.'

Daisy glanced at her anxiously. 'Oh, Becky, remember what I've jest said,' she said sadly. 'Remember, too, time is a great healer. And you never know, it could be all for the best. We none of us know what lies ahead.'

'I do. I know I shan't never marry and have a place of me own. Not after this.'

'You're only twenty, my girl. There's plenty of time.'

Becca's only answer to that was another snort of bitterness.

'Now come on, back to the barn with the rest of the folk,' Daisy slipped her hand through Becca's arm.

She shook it off. 'No. I don't feel much like jollificating. I've pretended that I don't care all through the harvest and I've had enough. I'm tired. I'm going home to bed.'

Chapter Two

Becca woke very early on Ellen's wedding day. She leaned on one elbow and peered over the bolster that she had placed down the middle of the bed the night she had learned of Ellen's pregnancy. She didn't want to touch Ellen; she didn't want to talk to her; she wanted nothing at all to do with her. But it had been difficult to share a bed, even a double bed, without some contact and Becca had managed to give vent to her feelings more than once with a vicious kick when her sister's leg had happened to stray beyond her own half of the bed.

Ellen was still asleep, her breathing soft and regular, her hair tightly bound in rags to make sure she would look her best for her great day. Becca couldn't understand her. She should have been eaten up with remorse and shame at what she had done, not lying there sleeping as soundly as if she hadn't a care in the world. But Ellen's argument was that George must have really fancied her more than he fancied Becca or he wouldn't have done what he did. It was just a good thing he found out his mistake before it was too late. She was sickeningly smug about the whole affair. If she hadn't been her own sister Becca would have hated her.

Becca slid out from under the covers and put on her old, grey, everyday dress, giving her sister a look of undisguised irritation and disgust. If it had been her wedding day, as it should have been next week, she wouldn't still have been asleep at half-past five in the morning, she knew right well.

Quietly, so as not to disturb the rest of the house, she crept down the stairs, undid the latch and let herself out into the early morning mist. It was going to be a hot day, she could tell that from the haze hanging over the meadow, spangling the grass and the buttercups with diamonds of dew. Lifting her skirts and letting her hair fall free, she ran across the meadow to the old stile. She sat there for a long time, protected by the tall hedgerows on either side, listening to a blackbird singing and watching the rabbits scuttling about the stubble-field that sloped gently down to the saltings and the thin ribbon of water snaking through the mud banks that was the river at its lowest ebb. Less than two weeks ago she had been tempted to walk into that same river and let it close in over her. Even now it wasn't too late, although common sense told her she would have to wait for the tide to come up and by that time she knew her courage would have failed her.

She clutched the stile until her knuckles showed white. How she had got through the past month was a miracle, trying to ignore the whispers as she went about her work in the dairy, the sly and pitying glances and the cruel gossip. Oh, people had pretended to be sympathetic and kind but she knew perfectly well that they were all laughing at her behind her back because she'd been too green to realise that George had been playing fast and loose with Ellen – her plump, plain, dunce of a younger sister. And that was another thing. Everyone knew the older sister ought to be married first or she'd be left an old maid.

An old maid going to her sister's wedding, that's what she'd be. Only she wouldn't, because she wouldn't be going. She'd made up her mind. She was going to stay away from the house until it was all over and Ellen and George had gone to Racky Harris's little cottage at the end of the lane. The cottage that *she* should have been sharing with George. Not Ellen. And she couldn't help it if Mum had wasted her time staying up till past midnight finishing the pretty blue bridesmaid's dress, because she wouldn't be wearing it. To be Ellen's bridesmaid would really rub salt into the wound. She bowed her head and a tear dropped into her lap.

'Are you going to sit there all day or can a body pass?'

Her head shot up at the sound of the man's voice. 'I'm sorry. I didn't see you coming across the field,' she said, beginning to slide off the stile.

'No, don't s'pose you did. I came along by the hedge, there. No, don't get down, jest shove up a bit and I'll come and sit alongside you for a spell.' The man swung the canvas tool-bag he was carrying down from his shoulder to the ground and hitched himself up on to the stile beside her. 'Thass Becca Stansgate, if I don't miss my mark,' he said, looking at her with a grin.

'How did you know my name?' She dashed her hand across her face, to wipe away any suspicion of tears that might remain.

'I reckon we've played round the village pond often enough, times I came to stay with my Aunt Emma Bradshaw. Not lately, o'course,' he added, screwing up his eyes and squinting into the distance.

'Jethro Miller!' Becca shook her head and looked in amazement at the broad-shouldered, weatherbeaten young man beside her. 'I'd never have reckernised you as Widder Bradshaw's nephew. You've certainly filled out since last I saw you. Wasn't it you that fell in the pond when you tried to skate across on the ice one winter before that was thick enough to bear your weight?'

He nodded. 'That was me. A right tear-away, I was. Always up to mischief. I didn't half get in a row with Aunt Emma for that, though. She was afraid I'd die of pneumonia. She shoulda knowed I was tougher than that.' He gave his infectious grin again.

'I haven't seen you round these parts for years now,' Becca said. 'What's brought you back to Wessingford?' She lowered her voice and looked at him sympathetically. 'Your aunt died six months ago. Didn't you know?'

He nodded. 'Yes, I knew. I've come along to give her cottage the once-over. I don't s'pose anybody else has been high nor by the place since the funeral.'

'Not that I know of.' She looked him up and down, mildly interested. 'Where've you come from?'

'I've walked from the other side of Chelmsford. Called in at the Peldon Rose to mend a couple of chairs and spent last night under a hedge jest outside Peldon.' He took a piece of grey-looking bread and a lump of cheese out of his pocket. 'Might as well have me breakfast,' he said cheerfully and began to eat it.

Becca sniffed. She was going to have to find a different sanctuary if Jethro Miller was going to remain here. 'I'd better be going.'

'Why for? Don't you like settin' here talking to me?' He stuffed the last of the bread and cheese into his mouth.

'I got things on my mind.' She sniffed again as she felt her eyes fill with tears.

He felt in his pocket for his pipe, filled it, then changed his mind and stuffed it away, picking a long stem of grass and chewing the sweetness out of it instead. 'Do you want to tell me about them?' he asked.

'No. I've got to get back. It's my sister's wedding day and I must help with the jellies and things.' Any excuse to get away from him and find another hiding place.

'What, your sister Ellen? She surely can't be old enough to get wed! I remember she always used to tag along when we was playing.'

'She's eighteen. Two years younger than me.'

He nodded. 'Yes, I s'pose she must be. Who's she marrying?'

'George Askew.'

His head shot round and he frowned. 'George Askew? But I thought you was walking out with George Askew, according to last I heard from Aunt Emma.'

She looked up at him sharply. 'You seem to know a mighty lot about Wessingford affairs.'

He shrugged. 'Well, Aunt Emma used to drop a line to my mother now and then and she'd put in news of anybody she thought I might remember.'

'You didn't come to see her after you were grown up.'

'I was 'prenticed to a trade. You can't up chalks and

say "I'm jest going off to visit my Aunt Emma for the weekend." Masters don't take kindly to that kind of behaviour. Then, when I was out of me time, I was moving about and somehow never got round to coming this way. Till now.'

'Till now thass too late.'

'Yes, thass too late to see the old lady, but I thought I might as well come and take a look at her cottage, time I'm in these parts.' He selected another long grass and put it in his mouth. 'So how come George Askew is marrying your sister instead of you?'

'Thass none of your business.'

He nodded. 'No, I reckon you're right. That ain't none of my business. I jest thought that might help to talk about it, 'cause thass a sure thing you ain't happy about the situation.' He was silent for a little while. 'Sometimes it helps to talk to a stranger.'

'You're not a stranger, Jethro Miller.'

'I might as well have been. You wouldn't have knowed me if I hadn't told you who I was,' he said reasonably. He turned and looked her full in the face. 'He must have been blind to turn you down in favour of your sister. She never was much to look at and I'll wager she ain't growed up half as pretty as you.'

Becca coloured and turned her head away. 'I dessay some folks might think she's prettier.'

'I don't believe it.'

'Well, if she ain't prettier she's more free with her favours,' Becca said bitterly.

'Ah, so that's it! I get the picture,' Jethro nodded slowly. 'George was hot for you but you wanted to wait

24

till you was married. Then along comes Ellen, who quite fancies him herself and she ain't so prim . . . Am I right?'

'More or less.' Becca bit her lip. 'Mum and Dad said they weren't having any scandal on their doorstep and George must do right by her. Never mind me!' she finished savagely.

Jethro chewed quietly for several minutes. 'Would you still want him? If you could have him, I mean?'

Becca looked at him in amazement. ' 'Course I would. We'd been walking out for over two years. We was promised.'

He shook his head. 'That's as maybe. But think about it, Becca. Would you really want a man who turned to another girl straight away when you wouldn't give him what he wanted? Would you ever trust him again?'

'He said it was my fault. He said if I hadn't led him on he wouldn't have been so quick to take what Ellen offered.'

'Even blamed you for his sins. I don't think much of a man who'd do that, Becca, do you?'

'Anyway, I didn't lead him on. I had to spend most of my time fending him off.'

'Strikes me you never really loved George Askew at all. Strikes me it's your pride that's suffering, not your heart, if you think about it, Becca Stansgate,' he said perceptively.

'Strikes me you don't know what you're talking about.' She slid down from the stile. 'But anyway, whatever it is that's suffering, I don't want people feeling sorry for me, or laughing at me – I don't know which is worse – so I shan't go to the wedding.' She tossed her thick, dark hair back over her shoulders.

Jethro shook his head slowly. 'Thass no good running away like that, Becca. You've got to face up to things. Hold your head up. Show people you don't care.'

'But I do care.' She bit her lip, her eyes filling with tears.

'Then you must pretend you don't.'

'And how am I going to do that, I should like to know?'

'Take your new beau to the wedding with you. Then folks'll wonder if they'd got it all wrong after all, and that it was you who jilted George and not the other way round.'

'But I haven't *got* a new beau.'

'You can pretend.'

'Don't be daft. Who's gonna believe me if I suddenly come out with the news that I've got a new beau?'

'Thass not what I meant.'

'Then you talk in riddles, Jethro Miller, and I don't understand you.' She began to walk away.

'I'll be your new beau,' he called after her.

She stopped and looked back. 'You?'

'Yes. Why not? We used to know each other when we was kids. I've come back and swept you off your feet, if folks want to know.' He grinned at her.

'Don't be a clump head. I couldn't say that.'

'Why not? You jest said you didn't want folk feeling sorry for you. Well, they won't have any reason to if you've got yourself a new fella.'

She frowned and put her head on one side. 'But you're a lot older'n me.'

'Not that much. I'm twenty-five.'

'Thass five years' difference between us.'

26

He shrugged and grinned at her. 'So I'm cradle-snatching. What of it?'

'Well, I dunno . . .' Undecided, she took a few steps back towards him and looked him up and down. He had two days' growth of beard, his shirt was crumpled and torn and his corduroys were patched at the knee and tied up with string. 'You're not very smart, are you?'

'I will be, time I get to the church. How long have I got?'

'The wedding's at two. But I don't know . . .' She frowned at him.

'Plenty of time.' He gave her another grin. 'Don't you worry. I shan't disgrace you.' He got down from the stile and picked up a length of rope lying beside the stout canvas bag, known as a bass, that held his tools. He threaded the rope through the handles and swung the heavy bass up over his shoulder.

'What've you got in there?' she asked, as they walked across the meadow together.

'Everything I possess. The tools of my trade and a spare shirt for my back.'

'You ain't exactly a rich man, then.'

'Never said I was. But I got plans. One day I'll be rich. Here's my fortune.' He stopped, put the bass down and spread his large capable hands in front of her.

'I can't see any fortune.'

'Daft woman. My fortune lies in the skill of my hands. You'll see. When we're wed.'

She gaped at him. 'I never said nothing about marrying you, Jethro Miller.'

'You said I was to be your beau.'

27

'Only for today.'

He took out his pipe and this time he lit it and took several puffs before saying, 'We'll see about that.' He grinned at her, swung the bass back over his shoulder with an ease that belied its weight and strode away across the meadow.

Becca watched him go, a frown creasing her brow. She didn't quite know what to make of Jethro Miller. His aunt, Emma Bradshaw, had been a widow for as long as Becca could remember, living in a little cottage at the other end of the village. Folk said that both she and her husband had worked for the gentry at one time, and certainly the cottage had belonged to them. But nobody seemed to know very much more about them. Mrs Bradshaw had kept herself very much to herself, hardly leaving the cottage except to go to church on Sunday, when she was always neatly dressed in black, with a black bonnet and carrying a black umbrella. And when Jethro had stayed with her he had always been well looked after, his clothes neatly patched and darned, and he always had to be home for regular meal-times, which the village children envied. Often they didn't know where their next meal was coming from, let alone what time it would be ready. Becca smiled a little as she remembered that Jethro had sometimes had that rare commodity, home-made sweets, and he would always share them with her, even if he only had two. Once, he'd given her an alley, a beautiful, big marble, and she'd treasured it for a long time because of its pretty colours. He'd always been kind to her although she'd never bothered to wonder why.

She shook her head. What Emma Bradshaw would

28

have made of the great shabby, unshaven man that her young nephew had become didn't bear thinking about. She pursed her lips. Jethro Miller had grown up a sight too sure of himself for her liking. Or perhaps he was still being kind. Either way it didn't matter. After today she would probably never see him again.

The household was awake and busy when Becca got back. Her mother was up to her elbows in flour making bread, while Ellen retched into a bucket in the corner as she'd done every morning for the past six weeks.

'Where's Tommy?' Becca asked, looking round for her young brother.

Daisy Stansgate brushed a strand of hair back with a floury forearm. 'Gone to help your dad. He's helping George with the milking. They want to get it done early so Dad can get the trestles up in the yard and George has got to go and get hisself togged up for his wedding. Mr Warner said we could put the trestles up in the barn if the weather was bad but thass going to be a lovely day so we might as well have it out in the open. You can start carving the ham, my girl. It's on the cold slab in the larder, there.'

'Is there any tea in the pot?'

'Yes. It's freshly brewed. You can pour me a cup, too. What about you, Ellen? You ready for a cup o' tea?' Her voice sharpened as she spoke to her younger daughter.

'No.' Ellen sank down on the settle by the side of the fire. 'I'll jest have plain water.'

Becca pured two mugs of tea and put one on the end of the table for her mother, leaving Ellen to get her own water. She hummed to herself as she cut herself a slice of bread and dripping.

'Thass nice to hear you singing to yourself, Becca,' Daisy said. 'I know that'll be hard for you, today.' She shot a disapproving glance at Ellen. 'That won't be easy for any of us, come to that.'

Becca pursed her lips. 'Don't you worry about me. I'll manage,' she said grimly.

Daisy's eyebrows shot up. 'Changed your tune, my girl, haven't you, all of a sudden?' she said. 'But I'm glad to hear it.' All the same, the look she gave her elder daughter was anxious.

Becca shrugged again and walked into the larder to fetch the great ham that had been cooked in the copper the day before. It was the gift of Samuel Warner, the farmer who employed both George Askew and Joe Stansgate – and sometimes the rest of his family, too.

'How many will there be to sit down?' Becca called over her shoulder.

'Twenty-five,' Daisy said. 'And I jest hope there'll be enough food to go round.'

'Of course there will, Mum,' Ellen said impatiently. 'For goodness' sake, stop making such a fuss.'

'You're a bit crotchety considering it's your wedding day, my girl. If you're feeling better you can go outside and see if the faggots in the oven are burned yet. They should be done time the dough on the hearth has risen.'

'Set for twenty-six, then,' Becca said without looking up as she began to carve. 'Jethro Miller's coming.'

'And who invited him, might I ask?' Ellen said.

'I did, if it's any of your business,' Becca said in the

sharp tone she reserved for Ellen when she couldn't avoid speaking to her. The ham began to fall away in thick juicy pink slices.

Ellen opened her mouth to complain but Daisy cut in, 'Here's your dad, back with young Tommy. When they get the trestles up you can go and spread the sheets over and lay the places, Ellen. Sheets'll have to do. I ain't got near enough tablecloths to cover.' She brushed her hair back again, leaving a streak of flour over her face.

'We shall none of us be ready in time to go to church at this rate,' Ellen said. 'That won't look very well if I turn up late to my own wedding.'

'I can't see a few more minutes'll make that much difference. I reckon you're already three months and more late,' Daisy said, glancing at Ellen's thickening waistline. 'All the same, you'd best get a move on with laying them tables. Aunt Docket'll be here with the trifles in half an hour and Miriam promised some of her nice pickled cabbage.' She began to count on her fingers. 'Then Tansy's mother promised spring onions and lettuce and Uncle Will's got nice ripe tomatoes and he said he'd cook a saucepan of beetroot.' She nodded. 'And with nice fresh bread – is that dough finished proving yet, Becca? If it is, go and sweep the ashes outa the oven ready for the loaves to go in. Here, come on, Dolly Daydream, look slippy or we'll never be finished.'

'Yes, all right, Mum.' Becca put down the carving knife and picked up the bowl of risen dough. She had been thinking about Jethro Miller. Whatever would folks say when he turned up in his old corduroys, tied round under the knee with string, even if he did put a clean shirt on?

31

She wished she'd never agreed to his suggestion. Better to be humiliated than laughed at.

The whole village was at the church. This was nothing unusual, the whole village always turned out for weddings, then marked the date up on the calendar and waited for the birth of the first child. And they wouldn't have long to wait for this one, Becca thought grimly, trying to look as if she didn't care that she was the bridesmaid instead of in her rightful place as the bride. She heard the sighs of pity and saw the heads shaking as she followed Ellen up the aisle and she plastered a smile on her face and held her head high. She'd managed to sneak a quick look round the crowd and hadn't seen Jethro Miller's shock of fair hair anywhere, either outside or inside the church. It looked as if he'd changed his mind about coming. She didn't know whether to be glad or sorry. Sticking his head under the pump wouldn't have smartened him up much, but on the other hand if he didn't come she'd have to brazen things out as best she might, on her own. One thing was certain: she was a fool to have let him, with his glib tongue, persuade her to come to this wedding. She should have stayed at home, out of the way, as she'd intended. At least she would have avoided the shame of people's pity.

She glared at the back of Ellen's head, the crimped hair for which she had endured the agonies of rags barely visible behind her veil, and her heart was filled to bursting with resentment and rage. Well, the bitch has got what she's always been angling after, Becca thought savagely, now I hope she'll get what she deserves. I jest hope she'll

32

be as miserable married to George Askew as she's made me. And as for him . . . she looked at George's dark head, bowed to put the ring on Ellen's finger. He was like a straw in the wind, weak as water, following Ellen round like a little dog, and she with a face like the cat that's pinched the cream.

The rage left her and her shoulders sagged. Why? she thought. Why, why, why had this happened to her? Why had George betrayed her like this? To give him his due he had tried to explain, but she had refused to listen. She simply couldn't bear to watch him wriggling like a worm on the end of a hook, trying to justify behaviour for which there was no justification. She still loved him too much to humiliate him in that way. Anyway, what could he say that Ellen's swelling body wasn't already saying?

Of course, deep down inside she had always known that George imagined himself to be God's gift to women with his dark good looks, and she had been proud to think he had chosen her out of all the other village girls to be his wife. In her blissful ignorance it had never once crossed her mind that she couldn't trust him. Now she began to wonder whether Ellen's was the only petticoat he had explored behind her back while they'd been courting. It was a humiliating thought.

The vicar pronounced George and Ellen man and wife and they emerged into the late-September sunshine, Ellen smiling smugly and George with a slightly hang-dog expression. Becca, in her pretty blue dress, hung back. She'd done her bit, her face ached from smiling and her head ached from the strain of it all. She sat down on the stone seat in the church porch and took off the wide-brimmed straw hat trimmed with daisies and laid it on the seat beside her.

'Pity to take your hat off. It suits you.'

She looked up and saw a tall, broad, clean-shaven figure in a dark suit that was a little old-fashioned and a shade too small. His fair hair was thick and springy, in spite of being slicked down with water, and he carried a bowler hat under his arm. There was a large white chrysanthemum in his buttonhole and a wide beam on his face.

'Jethro! Jethro Miller!'

'Don't sound so surprised. I said I'd come and be your beau, didn't I?'

'Yes, but I never thought you would.'

'Then why did you get you ma to lay an extra place at the wedding breakfast?'

'How do you know about that?'

'I asked. Jest to make sure I was welcome.' He offered her his arm. 'Well, come on, Becca, me dear. Come and let people see that I'm your new beau. Ain't no good me dressing meself up like a dog's dinner if you ain't going to show me off, now, is it?'

She looked him up and down. 'I thought you said you'd only got the clothes you stood up in when I saw you this morning?'

'Oh, I guessed Aunt Emma would've kept Uncle Fred's things in mothballs. I knew she wasn't a great one for throwing things away. Mind you, I had to hang 'em out in the sun all the morning to get the smell out. That was chronic! But they don't fit too bad, do they?' He brushed his lapel proudly.

She couldn't help laughing as she stood up and put her hand through his arm. 'You've certainly got a cheek,' she giggled.

'I have that.' He squeezed her hand as it lay in the crook of his arm. 'I shall be making an announcement that you and me's spoke for each other as soon as the wedding cake's cut, if not before.'

She pulled her hand away from his arm. 'You're in a mighty hurry, Jethro Miller,' she said indignantly. 'My father might have something to say about that.'

'He already has. I've asked him and he's said if you're willing to have me, he ain't got no objections.' He grinned. 'Tell the truth, I do believe he like the look of me better than he like the look of his new son-in-law. He don't seem all that struck on George Askew at the moment. Mind you, you can't blame him for that, the way things are.'

'Well, you may have asked my father, but you haven't asked me.'

'I'm asking you now.' He grinned at her expectantly.

She turned her head away. 'But I don't know you.'

'Don't know me!' He slapped his knee. 'God bless my soul, Becca Stansgate, you've known me since we was both knee high to a grasshopper, so don't give me that. Don't tell me you've forgot how I used to give you sweets my Aunt Emma made – the thought of her treacle toffee's enough to make your mouth water even now. And what about the glass alleys I gave you?'

'I didn't reckernise you this morning. You said yourself that you were a stranger,' she pointed out obstinately.

'That was this morning.' He shook his head impatiently. 'A lot o' water has passed under the bridge since then. Anyway, you ain't changed that much and neither have I. I always had a soft spot for you, Becca, when you was a little gal, and you used to like me too, if I ain't much mistaken.' He led her away from the crowd that had gathered to watch the photographer immortalise the day whilst George and Ellen struck poses and stuck artificial smiles on their faces.

He put his hat down carefully on top of a tombstone, carefully brushing the moss first. 'Now, you listen to me Miss Rebecca Stansgate,' he said, sitting her down beside it and standing over her with his hands on his hips, 'I told you I'd come to Wessingford to give my Aunt Emma's cottage the once-over. You never thought to ask me why I should suddenly want to walk all the way from t'other side of Chelmsford to do that, did you?'

She gave a slight, disinterested shrug and shook her head.

'Well, I'll tell you. She left it to me in her will, lock, stock and barrel. Ah, I thought that'd make you sit up and take notice!' He grinned. 'That made your owd dad's eyes sparkle, too, when I towd him. Anyway, thass one hurdle over. I've got a cottage to take you to when we're wed.' He ticked it off on his fingers. 'Two, I've got a trade. I intend to set meself up as a chair mender, so as not to sound too much of a braggart, but there ain't much in the woodwork line I can't turn me hand to, so you need never fear to starve. Three, I think it's time I found meself a wife and I ain't seen anyone in me travels I like better so I'm prepared to settle for you if you're prepared to settle for me.'

Becca was silent as she traced the name that was nearly hidden in the moss growing over the tombstone where she

36

sat. She couldn't believe what was happening. This casual, matter-of-fact, counting off on fingers of points in his favour was not the way a proposal should be made.

'That'll be one in the eye for all them as are saying, "Poor ole Becca, had her man pinched from under her very nose by her own little sister," ' he pointed out.

'Thass true.' She looked up, frowning. 'But I don't love you, Jethro,' she said, 'and thass no good saying I do.'

'Love?' He frowned. 'No, well, I don't know as I eggsackly love you, Becca.' He grinned. 'But I think we'd get along all right. Will that do?'

'I don't know.' She shook her head. After what had happened in the past month she had never expected any man to want her, yet here was this man she hadn't seen since they were both children asking her to be his wife before the wedding bells for George and Ellen had even stopped ringing.

'I think we could make a go of things, you and me, Becca,' he said encouragingly. 'And that'll get you out of a hole and let you hold your head up in the village again.'

She looked up at him, still frowning. 'Thass not much of a reason to get wed.'

'Thass a darn' sight better reason than being in the family way after a quick tumble in the hedge.' He shrugged. 'If you ask me that seem on'y common sense. I need a wife and you could do with a husband.' His expression softened. 'I'll treat you right, Becca, you need have no fear on that score. I ain't a great one for the drink and I'm a hard worker. I'll see you don't go hungry.' He grinned his infectious grin again. 'Anyways, I'm prepared to chance me arm if you are.'

She was silent for a long time, her expression bleak. She looked around the little churchyard, where old grey, moss-covered tombstones leaned at crazy angles whilst the more recent ones stood sentinel over them. How many husbands and wives who were laid to rest together there had enjoyed lives of continual bliss, she wondered? How many had married in haste, like George and Ellen, and lived to regret it? How many had married in love that turned sour with poverty and the struggle to survive? Jethro might not be a rich man but he had a cottage to take her to and a trade at his fingertips. There might not be love between them but at least they would always have a roof over their heads and enough to eat. She had often heard her mother say, when people talked all starry-eyed of love, 'Yes, thass all very well, but you can't live long on bread and cheese and kisses.' Perhaps she was right. Perhaps there were more important things in a marriage than being in love. Love! She'd loved George Askew and much happiness that had brought her.

But what did she know of this man, Jethro Miller, apart from what she remembered of him as a boy and what she had learned of him today? As she recalled he had been a friendly lad, as full of mischief as the rest, taking the punishment his strict but obviously caring aunt meted out to him when he broke her rules with cheerful resignation. He never talked about his own home but it was plain he enjoyed his visits to his aunt. And today he had told her he was a chair mender, and that he had served an apprenticeship. It wasn't much to go on. In any case, how did she know he was telling the truth?

She looked up at him. He was regarding her steadily,

and looking into the depths of his warm brown eyes she could not doubt his sincerity. Instinctively, she knew that she could trust him. Yet still she hesitated. 'When . . . ? How long before you would want to be wed?' she asked, licking her lips.

'Well, as I see it, there ain't no sense in wasting time. I'd reckon to go and see the parson straight away and we'll be married as soon as we can get the banns called,' he said, adding as an afterthought, 'if thass all right with you, Becca?'

She was silent for a minute. Then she took a deep breath and nodded. 'Yes, thass all right with me, Jethro Miller. Like you say, you're looking for a wife and I shall be able to hold my head up in the village again if I've got a husband, so we should do all right together. As long as you understand—' she looked up at him, her blue eyes uncertain. '– I can't say I love you, Jethro.'

He nodded. 'I understand and I'm content.'

She went on. 'But I'll look after you, right willingly. And I'll do all I can to help you build up your chair-mending business.' Her expression hardened. 'We'll show the people of Wessingford what they can do with their pity.'

A shadow passed over Jethro's face. 'Ain't no call to talk like that, Becca,' he chided gently. 'If folks pitied you it was kindly meant.'

She relaxed and gave him a wintery smile. 'Yes, I dessay you're right, Jethro.'

He kissed her gently on the forehead. 'Thass better,' he said, drawing her to her feet. 'Now, hold your head high and we'll go and tell the others.' He picked up his hat and brushed it on his sleeve, then took her hand and led her round to the front of the church.

Ellen and George were just climbing into the waggon that was to take them back to the wedding breakfast.

'If you're going to throw your flowers, the new Mrs Askew,' Jethro called jauntily to Ellen, 'then throw 'em over here towards your sister, 'cause she'll be the next bride. She's gonna marry me! There! Thass a surprise for you all, ain't it?' He grinned hugely as he put his arm round Becca and gave her a squeeze. And as Becca caught Ellen's bouquet any misgivings she may have had were replaced by a sense of smug satisfaction at the gasp of amazement that rippled through the crowd.

Chapter Three

Becca and Jethro were married at eight o'clock one morning towards the end of October when there was a cold, autumnal nip in the air and the bushes that bordered the path to the church were decorated with dew-spangled spiders' webs.

It was a quiet wedding; Becca had insisted that she wanted no fuss.

'Jest the family then,' Daisy said. 'Dad and me. The boy Tommy. Ellen and George . . .'

'No!' Becca's voice was like a whiplash.

'What do you mean, no?'

'I ain't having Ellen and George at my wedding.'

'Why not?'

'Because I don't want 'em. I don't want nothin' to do with 'em.'

Daisy let out a sigh. She'd heard it all before. 'But if we don't ask them we can't nicely invite the rest of the family. Aunts and uncles and sech.'

'Then don't,' Becca said.

41

'But you can't get wed with on'y me and your dad and Tommy there,' Daisy protested.

'I don't see why not. Thass Jethro's and my wedding and nobody else's business.'

Daisy said no more. It was no use arguing with Becca in this new, brittle mood, but at the wedding she wiped away a tear as her daughter made her vows and prayed to God that Becca was doing the right thing. Jethro seemed a decent enough fellow but who could tell? Even the fact that Joe reckoned he was all right hadn't reassured her. After the way George had behaved Joe was likely to think the devil himself was all right. Anyway, the wedding was too soon. They should have waited a bit longer. It wasn't decent . . .

But Becca was quite calm. She wore her blue bridesmaid's dress, though with a woollen shawl over it to keep out the cold, and Jethro again wore his uncle's suit, this time with a sprig of evergreen in place of the chrysanthemum. As he placed the ring on her finger Becca recalled how painstakingly he had measured to make sure it would fit, tying a piece of cotton round her fourth finger and then pushing it as far as it would go on to his own little finger and laughing because it didn't even reach the first knuckle. Then, one drizzlingly wet day, he had walked the five miles into Colchester and bought the plain gold band with the money he had received from repairing a set of chairs for Mr Green of the Manor House – the same strictly moral Mr Green who owned all the farms and most of the land in Wessingford.

'With this ring, I thee wed. With my body, I thee honour. With all my worldly goods, I thee endow.' Jethro spoke the words confidently and the ring was a perfect fit.

Becca looked down at the ring he had just placed on her finger and a shiver of apprehension ran through her. She had just promised to love, honour and obey this man. But she didn't love him, she didn't even *know* him, for goodness' sake. And she had seen very little of him since the day he proposed to her because he had been too busy working and of course it wouldn't have been seemly for her to visit him in his aunt's cottage. But what did it matter that she didn't know him well? After all, she hadn't known George Askew, and she'd grown up with him. She took a deep breath. Jethro had been prepared to take her for what she was and she must do the same by him. She tucked her hand nervously into the crook of his arm as they emerged into the cold morning air and felt it comfortingly covered by his great warm horny palm. Then they walked back to the wedding breakfast Daisy and Becca had prepared and the five of them ate ham and pickles and the young couple's health was quietly drunk in home-made mangold wine.

Tommy said little. As the youngest in the family he knew he wasn't supposed to understand exactly why George had married Ellen instead of Becca. But he wasn't daft. He knew well enough what went on between courting couples – blast, him and his mates had followed some of them into the woods enough times and watched what went on – from a safe distance, of course. He'd never seen Becca go into the woods with George, but he'd seen Ellen – *and* she'd found out and given him tuppence not to tell Becca. He'd seen Ellen with Scabby Wilson, too, only she didn't know that.

He poured himself another drop of mangold wine while the others weren't looking and smiled to himself. He knew what went on all right. You couldn't live on a farm all your life and not know. What's more, he'd tried it with Tansy Porter. And so had most of his mates, come to that. He liked it better than farming.

His father said grace and pushed his chair back from the table. 'Come on, Tommy, bor. Thass time we was back at work,' he said, putting his hand on Tommy's shoulder.

He drained the last of his mangold wine and got to his feet a little unsteadily. 'God blost it, I hate farming!' he said, looking owlishly round the table.

Becca glanced at him briefly. 'You're drunk,' was all she said.

But Jethro leaned forward on his elbows. 'Why do you hate farming, Tommy, bor?' he asked.

'Because I hate getting up at four in the morning to feed and groom the hosses. I hate milking cows – nasty greasy things! I hate raking muck. I hate being out in all weathers and getting wet through.' He glared at his mother. 'And I hate only having sixpence a week outa what I earn.'

'You only get two shilluns, bor. What more do you expect?' Joe said. 'You're a growing lad, you've gotta give your mother a bit towards your keep.'

Tommy blinked at his father. 'I hate only earning two shilluns a week.'

Becca suppressed a smile. 'So what would you like to do, Tommy?'

'Go to sea. And thass what I'm gonna do. Soon.'

'Well, I doubt you won't find life any easier at sea,' Jethro shook his head. 'You'll still have to get up early. And you still be out in all weathers.'

'Oh, don't take any notice of him, he's talking rubbish.' Nervously, Daisy began to clear the table, banging the plates together in her agitation. She didn't like to hear Tommy talk like that. She didn't want him to leave home.

'He'd soon come running back if he did,' Joe said. 'He'd only want to be at sea in a good nor' easter for a few hours and he'd soon find out where he was well off.' He gave Tommy a gentle cuff round the ear. 'Come on, bor, we shall get all behind with the drilling. I want to get six acre sown with carrots today.'

Still grumbling and swaying a little on his feet, Tommy left with his father. Then Becca and Daisy washed up before Daisy went to scrub the flagged kitchen for Mrs Warner up at the farmhouse and Jethro took his bride to her new home at the other end of the village.

George was just coming out of the farmyard with the muck rake and he saw Jethro and Becca leave her parents' cottage. He stood watching them for several minutes, then turned and went up the lane to his own cottage.

Ellen was sitting on a low stool by the fire reading a penny romance. She stuffed the book behind the coal scuttle and got to her feet as he walked in. 'Why, George!' Wass brought you home, this hour of the morning?'

He looked down at her. 'Ain't you got nothin' better to do with yerself than set there with a book in your hand all day?'

'I wasn't feeling too well. I thought I'd set quiet for a

while, till I felt better.' She brushed her hair away from her face.

George looked round the room distastefully. The scrap of bacon rind left from his breakfast was still on the table with the bread board and half a loaf of bread, a jug of milk with a dead fly in it and the two dirty tea mugs. It was obvious that Ellen had been sitting there ever since she got out of bed.

'I jest see Becca and that fella go off down the road together,' he said, cutting himself a hunk of bread.

Ellen shrugged. 'They was supposed to get married today, I believe.'

George paused with the bread halfway to his mouth as a stab of jealousy shot through him. 'What d'you mean, you believe? Why wasn't we told?'

Ellen shrugged again. 'I'spect Becca didn't think it was any of our business.'

His face darkened. 'We ought to have been invited. Why wasn't we invited?' He took a huge bite of bread. 'You're her sister, when all's said and done.'

'Well I wasn't invited, and neither were you. You know very well Becca won't hev anything to do with us. Anyway, would you have gone?'

'No, I bloody well wouldn't.'

'Well then, I dunno what you're making all the fuss about.'

'I'd have liked the satisfaction of refusing. Thass all.' He took another savage bite at his bread. 'Fancy marrying a man she ain't seen for years. That ain't decent.' He cut himself another hunk of bread. ' 'Course, she's on'y doing it to spite me.'

46

'Don't eat all that bread. Thass all I've got till Tuesday when I go down to Mum's and bake again,' Ellen said sharply. 'Anyway, what did you expect her to do? Stay an old maid jest because she couldn't hev you?'

He turned away. 'Where's the cheese?'

'You've eaten it.'

'Well, get some more.'

'I will when you give me the money. I ain't had a penny off you, George, this last week.' She began half-heartedly to clear the table. 'Oh, and look at you. You've put mud all over the place. You and your great boots.' She went over to him and wound her arms round his neck. 'Still, thass nice to see you, George. Nice you've come home in the middle of the morning.' She smiled up at him. 'Did you come for anything special?'

'Yes, I was hungry,' he said, deliberately misunder-standing her. He freed himself. 'But I'd better get back now.'

'I'll hev a nice stew ready for you tonight, George,' she said eagerly. 'I've got a swede and some turnips I found up the top of the garden. Owd Racky was a rare gardener . . .'

But George had gone. Disconsolately, Ellen went back to her penny novel.

Bradshaw's Cottage, as it was known, stood in the corner of a tiny field known as the pightle, its small garden enclosed by a picket fence. Whilst Emma Bradshaw had lived the garden had been a riot of flowers, but since her death it had quickly been overtaken by nettles and weeds. The cottage itself was tiled with thick, red, moss-covered

47

tiles, its whitewashed walls were covered in ivy and there was a little trellised porch over the front door that would be covered in pink rambling roses all through the summer. The porch was bare now and needed a coat of paint.

Jethro had cleared the weeds away from the short path to the front door and Becca didn't even need to pick up her skirts as she followed him nervously through the gate and into the house. He was a tall man and had to duck low to get through the doorway.

There were two rooms downstairs, one on each side of the front door, each with a low, beamed ceiling. A narrow staircase twisted up between them to the two bedrooms above. A bright fire was burning in the living room, giving the place a warm, cheerful, homely look. On either side of the fire stood two stick-back Windsor armchairs, with pretty patchwork blankets thrown over them. A scrubbed table covered with a green velvet cloth was in the middle of the room with four Essex chairs round it and a black horsehair sofa stood under the tiny window. In the corner there was a small table covered in a lace cloth on which an aspidistra was just beginning to come to life again after the six arid months since Emma Bradshaw's death. The mantelpiece, round which was pinned a fringed, green velvet lambrequin that matched the table cloth, was crammed with cheap Staffordshire groups, dominated by a pair of Scotsmen in garish kilts, one with a brown and white dog on his left, the other with a black and white dog on his right. Hand-made rugs helped to take the chill off the bare brick floor.

'It's jest as Aunt Emma left it,' Jethro said. 'Look, china and everything.' He opened the cupboard built in by the

48

side of the chimney breast, revealing willow patterned cups, saucers, plates, dishes – even a teapot.

'All to match, too,' Becca breathed, her eyes wide.

'Come and look in the front room,' he said, taking her hand. 'Thass the best room. Aunt Emma only used it for funerals.'

Becca could believe that. The room had a decidedly damp atmosphere and was as cold as a morgue. Probably there had never ever been a fire lit in the little grate and the spindly chairs didn't look as if they would bear Jethro's weight. There was a round table in the corner, covered with a lace cloth, on which stood photographs of Jethro's family, past and present, and on the wall three samplers bore witness to some poor child's enforced industry. 'God is Love' said one, 'Home, sweet home' said the second and the third, 'The Lord is my Shepherd'. All three were intricately embroidered with flowers and the letters of the alphabet and were stained with damp.

'Did your Aunt Emma have a daughter?' Becca asked, nodding towards them.

'No, she never had no children. Reckon she worked them herself.' Jethro looked at Becca with a trace of anxiety. 'Thass a bit old-fashioned but it'll do like this for now, won't it? You can do different by it presently.'

'Thass . . . beautiful,' Becca said, looking round. 'We ain't got anything like this at home.' She put her hand on the back of one of the spindly chairs. 'These must have cost a rare lot of money.'

'No. Uncle Fred made all his own furniture. He was a handy sorta chap. Like me.' Jethro spoke without arrogance.

'Well, thass all beautiful. Jest beautiful,' Becca breathed, her eyes sparkling. 'And one in the eye for my sister Ellen. She'd be as green as grass if she could see all this. Thass a sight better than the place she's gone to, I can tell you.' She couldn't help a note of smugness creeping into her voice.

Jethro made no answer to that but led the way back into the living room, warm and cosy from the fire he had lit in the little black range. She went over and sat down, stretching out her hands to the blaze.

'There's more to see,' Jethro said, pulling the kettle forward. 'There, time I've finished showing you round that'll be boiled ready for a nice cuppa tea. Look, this is the scullery.' He led the way through to a lean-to at the back of the cottage which served as a scullery and wash house. There was a scrubbed wooden table with an earthenware bowl standing on it and underneath were two buckets full of water, one with a white cloth over it. 'Thass for drinking,' he said. 'I fetched it from the well down the garden. Thass beautiful water, clear and sweet as honey. The other is for washing and the like. That comes from the rain water butt and ain't to be drunk. The copper's in the corner, there. You won't have no shortage of wood to keep it going when you do the week's wash, I'll see to that.' He carried on to the end of the scullery and through a door to a wooden structure, like a large, low shed, which was built on to the end of the cottage. In here Jethro's woodworking tools were laid neatly along the wide bench under the window and three chairs were stacked by another door that led to the garden. A ramshackle lathe stood along the back wall.

'I cleared this shed, soon as I got here. That was full of all sorts of rubbish, but that used to be Uncle Fred's workshop and I reckoned if that was good enough for him that'd do me all right.' He looked round it proudly. 'And so thass proved. I've got everything to me hand.'

'To build up your business,' Becca finished eagerly.

'Thass right.' He picked up a long board that was leaning against the wall. 'Look, Becca, I've got this ready to put up over the gate. I ain't never tried my hand at sign writing before.' He turned it round and on it was written, the letters carefully and painstakingly formed, JETHRO MILLER, CHARE MENDER. 'I've left a gap so that I can put "AND SON" when the time come,' he whispered proudly, adding quickly, 'but there ain't no hurry for that.'

Suddenly, Becca felt tears prick the back of her eyes at the way he'd spelt chair. She smiled at him. 'Thass a lovely sign, Jethro,' she said. 'That must have taken you a rare long time to make.'

He nodded happily. 'I did it o' nights. After I'd done me day's work. Now you've seen it I'll fix it up, but I wanted to show it to you first, afore I did. Mind you, I ain't had no trouble getting work. A couple of evenings down at the Whalebone soon took care o' that. But there's no harm in letting people know I'm here. I dessay there's one or two folks might not have heard.' He laid the board carefully back in its place. 'Oh, I ain't showed you the bedrooms, have I?'

Upstairs the floors were sloping and uneven but every- where was spotlessly clean. 'You must have been busy,

Jethro,' she remarked laying a hand on the white counter-pane that covered the big brass bed.

He shrugged. 'Aunt Emma was rare houseproud. I only had to put a duster round, mostly.' he nodded in the direction of the other bedroom. 'I'll take the dust cover off the bed in there directly. I dessay the mattress might be a bit damp. That must be years since that was slept in.'

'That'll have to come down by the fire then, before ever thass used.'

'Yes, I reckon you're right. We'll get it down directly.' He began to study the bed knob on the big brass bed minutely. 'Thass like this, Becca,' he said, carefully not looking at her, 'I reckon I hustled you into marrying me a bit sharpish.' He glanced up at her. 'Not that I regret it, don't think that, but I realise I didn't give you much time to get to know me.' She said nothing, so he turned his attention back to the bed knob, staring at it and rubbing it with his palm as if it was some kind of Aladdin's lamp. 'That being so, I don't aim to foist meself on you – if you take my meaning – not till you're ready. I don't think that would be fair. Mind you, I'm a man, with a man's needs, but I reckon I can be patient. After all, if a thing's worth having it's worth waiting for.' He went over to the door-way into the next bedroom. 'That being so, I shall sleep in here till you bid me otherwise.' He turned back and smiled at her, his face a little red with embarrassment. 'There, thass that said. Now let's go downstairs and have a nice cuppa tea by our own fireside.'

Becca lifted up her skirts and followed him down the narrow stairway. She hadn't expected that kind of consideration and didn't quite know what to say, so she said nothing at all.

Back in the cosy warmth of the living room the kettle was boiling. Jethro went over to the cupboard by the chimney breast. Becca followed him and took the cups from him. 'I'll do that. I reckon thass my job to look after the house now,' she said. 'And you with it. You'll hev your work cut out with the business.'

Jethro frowned. 'I dunno as I'd eggsackly call it a business, Becca. Not really.' He looked at his hands. 'I'm a tradesman . . .'

'Maybe not yet,' she said briskly. 'But it will be. In time. You'll see.'

He didn't reply to that, but sat down by the fire and took out his pipe. 'Well, anyway, thass very nice being looked after,' he said, watching her make the tea and pour milk into the cups. She went to the bag she'd brought with her. Everything else, which wasn't much, just her few clothes and the odd bits she had collected for her bottom drawer, had been delivered in a box on her father's shoulder the day before. 'I made a few cakes early this morning,' she said. 'Thought they might come in handy.'

A broad smile spread across his face as he bit into one. 'I knew you'd be a good cook, the minute I set eyes on you. I ain't a bad judge, you know. We shall rub along all right together, you and me, Becca. You see if we don't.'

When he had eaten three cakes and drunk two cups of tea Jethro went back to his workshop and Becca pulled her shawl round her and went into the garden. Everywhere was overgrown with nettles but she could see little cushions of herbs bravely clinging to life just outside the back door and there was a narrow pathway leading to a little trellised arbour that contained the privy. Ramblers would cover this, too, in the summer and Becca smiled to herself. It was plain that Jethro's Aunt Emma valued her privacy highly. There was not another house in sight. In fact, the only sign of life was an old donkey standing in the pightle. She went over and leaned on the fence. The donkey immediately trotted over to have his nose scratched.

'Thass a funny old do, Dicky Donkey,' she said, rubbing his silky ear. 'There was me, all set to marry George Askew and live in Racky Harris's little cottage – that weren't a mucha, neither – and now look at me: married to a different man altogether and with a house any woman 'ud give her eye teeth for. You know, Dicky, I never dreamt when I said I'd marry Jethro Miller that he'd got a place like this to bring me to.' She stopped fondling the donkey's ear and rested her elbows on the fence again. The donkey nuzzled her arm for more attention. 'Come to think of it, I don't know what I expected.' She tossed her head. 'Anyway, that'll be one in the eye for all them that pitied me. I can't bear to be pitied,' she added through gritted teeth. 'But I intend to play straight by Jethro. I'll work hard and help him build a good business. I may not hev any partic'lar feelings towards him but I'll stand by him and do right by him. That'll show my sister Ellen she ain't ruined my life. Not completely, anyway.'

The old donkey gave a loud hee-haw, tossed his head and trotted off. Becca watched him go and then turned her attention back to the nettle-filled garden. There were enough nettles to make gallons of nettle beer. She would enjoy clearing them and uncovering the flowers ready for next spring. And behind Jethro's workshop was yet another shed. She tried the door but it wouldn't open so she looked through the window. It appeared to be stacked full of bits of wood and old furniture. No doubt that was where Jethro had put all the rubbish.

When it began to get dark Becca went indoors and lit the oil lamp with its pink fluted chimney. Then she found a table-cloth and laid the table with the willow pattern china. She heard Jethro come in from his workshop and there were sounds of much splashing as he washed himself at the table in the scullery. Then he came in and did more than justice to the pork brawn and vinegar she had prepared.

Afterwards he sat on one side of the fire with his pipe and she sat on the other side with her crocheting, as if they had been married for years instead of only a few hours.

The evening wore on. The pendulum clock on the wall behind Jethro's head ticked steadily, marking every half hour with a pleasant, muted strike, its brass weights gleaming in the firelight and its pendulum swinging rhythmically back and forth. When it struck nine times he yawned. 'I don't keep late hours, Becca,' he said. 'I usually turn in about this time.'

She clapped her hand over her mouth. 'The mattress. We forgot to air the mattress.'

'Never mind. I don't s'pose thass as damp as all that.'

'No, Jethro, you can't sleep on it till it's been aired.

You'll get the rheumaticks and once they get a hold you'll never be rid of them. I know because of my poor owd dad. He's crippled up with them.'

'All right. I'll kip down on the sofa here. That'll be comfortable enough.' He laughed. 'Nice and warm, too. And I can always cover meself with the patchwork blankets off the chairs if I get cold. Oh, I shan't take no harm, don't you worry. I shall be as snug as a bug in a rug down here.'

She looked at the sofa doubtfully but was reluctant to argue too much in case he should think her forward. Because if he didn't sleep there he would have to share her bed, there was nowhere else for him to sleep.

She left him by the fire and took a candle and went upstairs to the bedroom. She undressed quickly and put on her nightgown, then unpinned her hair and brushed it till it gleamed. She twisted it into a thick plait to keep it from tangling and peered at herself in the swing mirror that stood on the chest of drawers, holding the candle near to give more light. She wasn't exactly pretty but she was passing fair, she decided. A bit pale, perhaps, but her eyes were a clear, honest grey and her nose was straight. If she was honest – and she was, as honest as the day was long – her teeth were a shade big, but her mouth was wide and generous and her lips had no difficulty in closing over them; not like Cissie Blackwell, whose teeth stuck out so far that her top lip had never met the bottom one. Woe betide the chap who tried to kiss her, the village girls all laughed, for he'd get chewed to ribbons. She leaned forward and pinched her cheeks with her free hand, unsuccessfully trying to pinch some colour into them.

Then, shivering, she climbed into the big feather bed and found her feet touching the hot brick wrapped in flannel that Jethro had surreptitiously placed there an hour before. It was a very comfortable bed and she snuggled gratefully into its soft depths.

But although she was very tired she didn't sleep. She kept thinking of Jethro, who had been thoughtful enough to put the hot brick in her bed, although knowing he would be confined to the narrow horsehair sofa downstairs, with only two thin patchwork blankets to keep him warm. Once the fire died down it would turn cold and he had nothing else to cover himself with. True, it had been his decision not to share her bed; but she knew that it was purely out of kindness and consideration for her. And what had she done? Shown her gratitude by forgetting to air the mattress on the other bed for him. She lay for a long time, staring up into the darkness. She didn't like to think of him tossing and turning, trying to get to sleep on that narrow plank of a sofa, and him with a hard day's work ahead of him tomorrow. At the same time, she didn't want him to think her forward; shameless; wanton. She was weary, tired with the emotional strain of the day, yet she couldn't sleep for thinking about Jethro, making do downstairs on that hard sofa.

At last she could stand it no longer. She got out of bed and re-lit the candle. Carrying it in one hand and holding up her nightgown with the other she went carefully down the stairs. Jethro was her husband, however unusual the circumstances of their marriage, so there was no shame in inviting him to come upstairs and share the comfort of her bed. Indeed, it was her wifely duty.

57

She reached the bottom of the stairs and pushed open the door into the living room. She could see Jethro by the light of the candle and the last flickers of the dying fire. He was lying on the sofa on his back, one hand flung behind his head, his feet sticking out from under the patchwork blankets, one toe poking through a hole in his sock. He was sound asleep and snoring gently. She stood looking down at him for several minutes, disappointed to think he could fall asleep so easily. He was not an unhandsome man. His eyelashes as they lay along his cheek were thick and dark, in contrast to his fair, almost white hair. Suddenly she had an almost irresistible urge to trace her finger down the long line of his jaw to the deep cleft in his chin. It was a strong, square jaw, revealing a character firm to the point of stubbornness. The jaw of a masterful man. Shocked at herself, she clenched her free hand behind her back and then turned and went back upstairs, accompanied by a strange, hungry feeling inside her that she couldn't put a name to.

The next morning she woke to hear Jethro riddling the ashes in the grate. It was still dark. She lit the candle and dressed herself, putting on her old grey everyday dress and tucking a shawl round her shoulders. Then she unplaited her hair and brushed it before twisting it into a thick bun high on her head. By the time she got downstairs Jethro had the fire well alight and the kettle singing. Beside it a pan of bacon was gently frying.

'Did you sleep well?' he asked, without turning his head.

'Like a baby,' she replied.

'Yes, you looked comfortable enough, an hour ago.'

He shook the bacon in the pan, making it spit and sizzle.

'What do you mean? How do you know that?' She blushed, suddenly embarrassed.

'Oh, I jest crep' up the stairs to make sure you was comfy.' He smiled at her over his shoulder. 'You looked right pretty, lying there with your dark braid on the pillow. I never realised your hair was as long as that. You oughta let it free, like it was the first time I saw you.'

She went to the cupboard and began to get down the plates and cups. 'It'd only get in the way when I'm working. Anyways, married women always have their hair up.' She cut slices of bread and made the tea. Jethro put the bacon on the plates and they sat down.

'You ain't got the mustard out. I always like a little mustard with me bacon, Becca.' He made to get up.

'No, I'll get it.' She went to the cupboard and fetched the blue and white willow pattern mustard pot. 'Your Aunt Emma had everything to match, didn't she!'

'Yes, I only hope you like willow pattern, 'cause you'll be eating from it for a long time.'

'I do like it. It's pretty. This bacon's good, too.' She looked up. 'What do you have in mind to do today, Jethro?'

'First I shall put the sign up,' he said proudly. 'I shall need your help with that. Then I've got the leg to put on a wheelback chair. The old one had been smashed clean to bits. I shall have to turn a new one up. Uncle Fred used to be a wood turner so I fished his old lathe out and rigged it up. I reckon it'll work all right. I hope it will, anyway. You need a lathe to be a chair mender.'

After breakfast Becca went outside with Jethro and

together they fixed up the sign over the gate. Then they went across to the other side of the lane to see how it looked.

'Thass a bit crooked,' Jethro said, eyeing it up. 'That want to go half an inch up on the left.'

'That looks all right to me,' Becca frowned, her head on one side.

'Thass because you ain't got a straight eye.' Jethro climbed the ladder and banged the right hand post holding the sign with his mallet.

'I thought you said it wanted to go half an inch up on the left,' Becca said as he came down and squinted to eye the sign up again.

He looked at her and laughed. 'Oh, Becca! Half an inch up on the left, half an inch down on the right, what's the difference? Anyway, thass level now.'

'That looked level to me before,' she said.

He went back to his work shop and Becca went into the house. When she called him for his dinner he said, 'I'll get that mattress down before I go back to work. We can stand it along the wall there, it won't be in the way, and thass nice and warm in here so it should be aired by tonight.'

Becca hesitated. 'Is there enough bed linen?' she asked.

'Oh, yes. The chest o' drawers in the back bedroom is full of sheets and blankets. Aunt Emma was well set up with everything, as far as I can see.'

'I'll bring some down and hang them on the horse round the fire.'

They ate their meal, a vegetable stew with plenty of dumplings in it, in silence. Becca's feelings were mixed.

Her courage of the previous night had gone. She couldn't bring herself to tell him that if he had been awake when she crept down the stairs she would have been ready to welcome him into her bed. But in some ways he was still almost a stranger to her, and she knew he was wise in giving her time to get used to him.

All the same, as he followed her up the stairs that night and gave her a chaste kiss on the cheek before going into the back bedroom, she couldn't help a pang of guilt mingled with something akin to disappointment, and conflicting thoughts chased themselves round her brain, making it a long time before she slept. She felt she owed Jethro something for the sturdy and well-furnished home he had provided. His Aunt Emma had clearly been a good housekeeper, her sheets were all crisp and white, darned and patched with tiny stitches and his Uncle Fred had made every stick of the beautifully made furniture. And all that lovely willow pattern china! True, some of it was chipped or cracked, but to think it all matched. Just wait till Mum saw! Not that she wanted to make Mum jealous, she thought hurriedly, as she recalled the oddments of china that graced her mother's table.

But, she defended herself, when she'd agreed to marry Jethro she hadn't realised he was going to provide her with the kind of home she – and all the other girls in the village, for that matter – had always dreamed of, had she? And how did she know that he wouldn't have married Florrie Clench or Amy Mason if he'd seen them first? Jethro had made no secret of the fact that he needed a wife, so perhaps almost anyone would have done. And she'd needed a husband to save her pride. It wasn't much of a basis for a good marriage, yet, for all his rough and ready ways Jethro seemed a good, kind man and she quite liked him. But it wasn't love. It wasn't like the way she'd felt about George. The way she still felt about him deep down inside, in spite of the way he had treated her. Perhaps it was all for the best that she didn't love Jethro, because if all you got when you loved somebody was a broken heart you were better off without it.

Chapter Four

Jethro frowned and rubbed his chin as he listened to what Becca had to say. Then he shook his head. 'No, that ain't women's work, Becca. What I do is men's work. Women can't be expected to use a plane or chisels or sechlike.'

Becca looked round the workshop. It was nearly Christmas and there were several pieces of furniture being worked on. 'But there must be something I can do, Jethro. Don't you see? I want to help you. I want to help you get on and make a lot of money.'

He threw back his head and laughed. 'I doubt I'm in the wrong trade to make a lot of money, Becca. Chair menders ain't rich men.' He became serious. 'But we shall get by, don't you fret.'

She banged her fist on the bench. 'But I want to do more than "get by"! I want to help you to get rich. I want to show people . . .'

He caught her by the wrists, suddenly serious. 'Now, we'll hev no more talk like that, Becca,' he said sternly. 'What I do for my living is my business, and for my satisfaction, not to make an impression on other people. We shan't starve, I promise you that. But you needn't think you'll go swanking round the village in a carriage, neither, so you can get that idea right outa your head.' He let go of her wrists. 'Now, you've got quite enough to do in the house, without worrying about helping me, so let's hear no more about it.'

Becca said no more; it hadn't taken her long to realise that Jethro was a stubborn man and not easily swayed. So she waited until she saw him poring over the books with inkstained fingers, trying to work out prices and labouring over writing out bills one evening. She said casually, 'I could do that for you, Jethro. I was top of the class in arithmetic and handwriting.'

He looked up, chewing his pen, but she was concentrating on her sewing. He went back to his calculations in silence, the only sound in the room the ticking of the clock and the sound of a log shifting in the fire. At last he threw down his pen. 'All right,' he said, 'come and see what you make of this, Becca, I can't make the blamed thing come right. And when you've worked it out you can write a bill for Mrs Green at Brookfield House.'

She drew her chair up to the table, careful not to smile, and looked at the books. 'How much an hour do you charge?' she asked after a little while. 'And how many hours did you spend on this? And this?' She scribbled for a few minutes. 'And then there's materials . . . Now, is that about right?'

Jethro scratched his head. 'I've been all the evening trying to work that out,' he said, with a touch of resentment.

She shrugged. 'I told you I was top of the class for arithmetic.'

But after that she did all the book keeping. And when he went into the cold, unused parlour one day and saw how brightly polished she kept the furniture there he said, 'There's a little table I've just finished working on for owd Mrs Green, up at the Hall. That needs a good waxing before I take it back. You can see what you make of it, if you like.'

'I'll do it when I get a minute,' she said, so as not to appear too eager. But she smiled to herself. As her mother often said, there were more ways of killing a pig than choking it on strawberries. And she hadn't finished.

Once a week both Becca and Ellen went to Daisy's house to bake bread. Becca didn't want to go on the same day as Ellen; she avoided her as much as she could and would cross the road rather than have to speak to her, much to Ellen's amusement. But Daisy refused Becca's suggestion that she should bake on Thursdays. Tuesday was baking day. It was enough trouble getting the faggots and heating up the oven once a week, let alone twice. And there was always the hope that the two girls would be reconciled.

A forlorn hope. Trading on Ellen's sloth, Becca made a point of going early and she gathered the faggots to heat the oven and would often have finished baking and gone home, her three crisp loaves wrapped in her apron, before Ellen arrived. So Ellen was left to gather more faggots or bake her loaves in a cooling oven. She usually chose the latter option, which meant that her bread was inclined to be heavy.

Goodness knows how she'll manage with a baby to look after, if she don't buck her ideas up, Daisy thought grimly. She couldn't help contrasting her two daughters, now that they were both married. Becca was brisk and business-like, never one to gossip, attending to the work in hand and then going on to the next thing. Once her bread was baked she was off home, not even stopping for a cup of tea and a chat. Sometimes Daisy wondered if Becca kept on the move because she was afraid she might be asked awkward questions – like was she happy, married to Jethro Miller? It was a question Daisy would dearly have loved to ask, given the opportunity, because Becca gave no sign of what her feelings might be. Ellen, on the other hand, was always ready to stay and chat till long after she should have been at home making a meal for George. But Daisy excused her because she was becoming big and awkward so she needed plenty of rest. Sometimes Daisy wondered if she was carrying more than one . . .

She was right. Ellen's twins, Albert and Henry, were born one stormy day early in April.

Daisy attended the birth along with Mrs Plackett, the village midwife and layer-out of the dead. When it was all over and the babies neatly swaddled, Mrs Plackett and Daisy each solemnly picked up a child, and to make certain that it would 'rise in life', took it in turns to stand on the only chair in the room, an age old superstition that had rarely shown much proof. Then, when that little ritual was over and Ellen had been settled for a well-earned sleep, Daisy set off to give Becca the news, picking her way carefully through the puddles in the lane that led past Mr Warner's farmhouse, past her own cottage and then on between blackthorn hedges to the road, where she turned right to go another half mile or so to the other end of the village, past the church and the pond and the spaced-out clusters of cottages in pairs, known as 'double-dwellers' along the road to Bradshaw's cottage, where Becca and Jethro lived. Bradshaw's Cottage stood alone on the corner where Ferry Lane, which ran down the hill to the river, joined the road. At the end of this lane the river could be forded at very low tides by the coal and carrier's carts. 'Owd Sharpie' the ferryman carried passengers back and forth in a creaky old rowing boat at a penny a time, regardless of the state of the tide.

Daisy reached Becca's house and paused at the gate. It was raining again and her old black umbrella had too many holes in it to keep much of the downpour out. But she had been determined to carry the news to Becca herself, although she knew she must curb her own natural excitement because she was more than a little apprehensive about what her elder daughter's reaction would be.

It was unenthusiastic. 'That'll keep Ellen busy,' was all Becca said, not even asking after her sister's health. She made tea in the willow pattern teapot and got out a tin of gingerbread she had made that morning, her face wooden.

Daisy sat wearily down at the table opposite Becca and drank the tea she was given, dunking a piece of gingerbread between whiles. She'd had a hard night although the birth had been easy for a first confinement. 'She'll birth as easy as shelling peas,' had been Mrs Plackett's opinion and she'd been right. All the same, Daisy had had little sleep and she was tired.

'Thass good for a man to have sons,' she said at last, to break the silence. 'Although naturally enough a woman always like to think she'll have a daughter.' She eyed her own daughter up and down. 'I should have thought to see you big by this time, my girl. Thass six months and more since you was wed.'

Becca bent over the teapot to hide the colour that spread over her face. She could just imagine what her mother would say if she were to be told that Jethro had never yet shared her bed. 'There's plenty of time,' she said briskly. 'We got more'n enough to worry about at the minute, getting Jethro's business 'stablished. More tea, Mum?'

Daisy pushed her cup across the table and watched as Becca poured her a second cup. 'Hmm,' she said as she drew it back, 'from what I know of it, babies ain't all that famous for waiting till thass convenient afore they put in an appearance. 'Fact, they generally manage to pick the worst time possible. But when they come they bring their love with them, so folks mostly find they manage.' She looked round the room. 'Anyway, I can't see what you and Jethro got to worry about. You look very comfortable here. And the cottage is your own, so you can't be turned out. Strikes me you don't know how lucky you are, my girl. I wish me and your father were placed as secure.' She shrugged. 'But perhaps you don't want littl'uns to mess up such a neat and tidy place?'

'Oh, it's not that, Mum,' Becca said quickly. 'Really. It's not that. But there's plenty of time.'

Daisy sniffed but said nothing. She sipped her tea noisily for a few minutes, then tried another approach. 'When you go to see Ellen you'll take a little something for the twins, won't you? I dessay you've knitted her a few bits, mittens or bonnets or sechlike.'

'No, that I certainly ain't.' Becca banged her cup down on its saucer. 'And you needn't think I'm going to *visit* her, neither. I've never been near Racky Harris's place since the day she moved in and I don't intend to start now, babies or no babies. Not after what she did to me.'

'Oh, Becca, thass no way to talk. Can't you let bygones be bygones?' Daisy said sadly.

'But what if George Askew should walk in? Don't forget *I* was the one he was walking out with, *I* was the one he was supposed to be marrying, not Ellen. And the cottage where they live was supposed to be *my* home.' Becca emphasised her words by jabbing her chest with her forefinger. 'How do you think I'd feel, going there and seeing them together as cosy as love birds?'

'You ain't got a lot to be jealous about, Becca, I can tell you that,' Daisy said, looking round the comfortable living room. 'You know very well their cottage ain't a patch on this one.'

Becca digested this, waiting for her mother to say more, but she was disappointed. She shook her head. 'I still shan't visit.' She shrugged. 'I don't s'pose I'd be welcome, anyway.'

'I reckon you would.' Daisy got up to go. 'Ellen'll have her hands full, right enough, with two babies to look after. I reckon she'd be glad of help from any quarter.'

'Well, she needn't look in my direction,' Becca said bluntly.

'This 'ud be a good time for both of you to make up,'

Daisy persisted. 'You'd have a good excuse to visit. That ain't every day you're made aunt to twins.'

'That ain't every day your sister pinch your sweetheart, neither.'

Daisy sighed. 'Oh, Becca, thass all over and done with.'

'Not as far as I'm concerned, thass not.'

'Would you want George back?'

Becca turned her head away without answering.

'Well, would you?'

'That was Ellen's fault. She led him on.'

'He was quick enough to follow.' Daisy sighed. 'Well, I've done what I can, Becca. If you won't forgive and forget I can't do no more.' She gathered her belongings and went to the door. 'But I never thought you was one to bear a grudge. After all, you ain't done bad for yourself. There ain't many got such a comfortable home as this. And you ain't got a landlord breathing down your neck all the time, neither. You want to think yourself lucky, my girl. I would, if I'd got a place like this.' She glanced round enviously, then opened the door. 'I must get back. I've got to call in home and get a good fire stoked up afore I go back to Ellen's. I dessay your father'll be wet through when he get back tonight, with all this rain about, so that'll be a job getting his clothes dried ready for the morning if there ain't a good fire.'

'How is Dad?' Becca said with more interest than she'd shown before. 'I know this wet weather is bad for his rheumatics.'

'Yes, his owd screws play him up something cruel. Sometimes he's hard put to get about, what with the pain in his knees and his owd back. But Mr Warner is very good, he'll always find him a job in the dry if he can and he don't push him too hard, not like some masters.' She sighed. 'Truth to tell, I don't know how much longer your dad'll be able to carry on working. Sometimes thass as much as he can do to get hisself moving in the morning, he's that stiff and sore. If that wasn't that he'd worked on Tenpenny Farm all his life, for the present Mr Warner and his father before him, I reckon he'd have been laid off long before now. And living in a tied cottage like we do . . .'

She broke off, shaking her head, her shoulders sagging with the burden of her anxiety. At the sight of it a shaft of pain shot through Becca with the realisation that her parents were no longer young and she put out her hand to her mother. But Daisy straightened up and shrugged off her thoughts. 'Still, there's no point in meeting trouble halfway, is there?' she said with something of a smile. 'Your dad can still manage to hoe a field of turnips, and there ain't a man around these parts can plough a straighter furrow, even if that do take him longer these days. And he can still milk a cow, so we've got a lot to be thankful for.' She changed the subject. 'You get on all right with Jethro, don't you, Becca? Even though he ain't the man you'd have chosen? He seem like a good, hard-working man to me.'

'Yes, Jethro's a good man,' Becca agreed, her expression giving nothing away.

'You never know, perhaps Ellen did you a good turn, then.' Daisy couldn't resist a parting shot as she gave her daughter a peck on the cheek and left, putting up her old black umbrella against the rain that still fell. This was not the first time she had tried, and failed, to effect a reconciliation between the two girls. It saddened her beyond words to know that there was animosity between her children.

After her mother had gone Becca piled the tea cups on the tray and took them out into the scullery, ready to be washed. She didn't want to go and see Ellen. As far as she was concerned the twin nephews that were the result of George and Ellen's clandestine meetings made no difference at all to her feelings towards her sister. She still hated Ellen for what she had done; she couldn't forgive her for playing fast and loose with George behind her back, and if the marriage was a disaster it served her right. In her mind she had come to blame Ellen entirely for what had happened, reasoning that George was only a man and easily led.

She put down the tray and stood looking out at the garden. There had been some warm and sunny days in March and she had spent these clearing the nettles and weeds. There were two gallons of nettle beer in the cupboard under the stairs that she had made from the crop of nettles. She had discovered that there were primroses and polyanthus bordering all the paths and they were just coming into flower, holding up their heads gratefully in the rain that was falling. In the herb garden just outside the back door she had found two kinds of thyme, a bush of sage, a clump of chives, and some marjoram. Soon, she was sure the mint would show through. And there was quite a big parsley bed. There was an old saying that in a garden where parsley thrived the woman wore the trousers in the family. It would be interesting to see how much came through.

She carried on through to the workshop to tell Jethro the news about Ellen. She loved the smells of Jethro's work place. Newly planed wood shavings mingling with methylated spirits, beeswax, the warm Scotch glue that he heated every morning on the back of the living-room stove, and the dust of old upholstery gave out a distinctive, somehow comforting smell that seemed to cling to Jethro even when he came through into the house. This afternoon he was standing at his bench by the window, anxious to catch what light there was in the grey April day, cutting tiny dovetails for a bureau drawer he was repairing.

'Look at this,' he said, holding up what was left of the little drawer. 'Thass one of the little fitments from inside a bureau and that look to me as if a hammer's been took to it.' He turned it over in his hand. 'Thass no way to treat good furniture.'

Becca went over to the bench. The little drawer did indeed look for all the world as if it had been smashed with a hammer. 'Who does it belong to?' she asked.

'Young Mrs Green. She brought it in last week and she's bin back twice already to see if thass done. Some people ain't got a mite of patience.' Jethro continued measuring and cutting the tiny dovetails.

Becca stood watching him. Young Mrs Green was the wife of Edward Green, son of the Greens at the Manor House. They lived at Brookfield House, a pleasant, Georgian building that had views down to the estuary. Mrs Green was a dark-haired beauty, a bit of a mystery and what Daisy Stansgate termed 'a reg'lar fashion plate'. Rumour had it that she had come from a titled family and from her manner this could well be true, but nobody in the village knew for certain. There was one son from the marriage, a spoiled boy of six called Teddy. 'You're always at her beck and call, ain't you?' she said, after a long silence.

'Whose beck and call? I dunno what you're talking about.' Jethro didn't look up, but Becca noticed a flush reach his neck.

'Young Mrs Green's. If she ain't calling you up to her house to look at something, she's fetching bits down here. She must think you ain't got nothing better to do than cart about after her.'

Jethro straightened up. 'Thass all work, Becca. I can't afford to turn jobs away.'

'Don't look to me you've got any shortage.' Becca sniffed and looked round the workshop. There were four chairs married together in the corner, a chest of drawers with no handles in front of them and beside this a round table tipped up and waiting for Jethro to remove a large white heat mark and replace the veneer where it had bubbled.

'No, I've got plenty work, thank the good Lord.' He grinned at Becca. 'I see your mum called. Is there a cup left in the pot for me?'

'Yes, I'll fetch you one.' Becca turned to go.

'What did she want? Must have been something special for her to turn out on an afternoon like this.' A clap of thunder gave weight to his words.

'Yes. She came to tell me Ellen's been brought to bed with twins.' Without waiting for his reaction Becca went back into the house and felt the teapot. It was still warm. She added more water from the kettle and filled the half-pint mug that Jethro preferred to a cup and saucer. Then she cut a slab of gingerbread and went back to the workshop. She reached it just as the door from the garden opened and the young Mrs Green they had been speaking about came in. Becca noticed that she walked straight in, without knocking, and made a great play of shaking the rain from her umbrella, and even more of shaking it from her skirts. Suddenly, the homely smells of the workshop were overladen with Felicity Green's heavy perfume, making Becca feel slightly sick.

'Why, Mrs Green, what brings you out on such a day?' Jethro said in surprise.

'It's my poor Teddy's hobby horse. He's terribly fond of it, plays with it all the time, and now it's broken.' She laid the wooden hobby horse on Jethro's bench. 'Look, his ear's broken off. Teddy was broken-hearted till I said I knew a nice, kind man who would mend it for him in no time.' She dimpled at Jethro and perched herself on the sawing horse, spreading her skirts round her. 'I said I was sure you would do it while I waited.'

'Yes, of course, ma'am. That won't take a minute. I've got some Scotch glue on the hob here, all ready.' He left what he was doing and picked up the hobby horse.

If either of them noticed Becca, standing by the door into the house with the mug of tea in one hand and the lump of gingerbread in the other, they took no notice. Quietly, she went back into the scullery and tipped the tea into the slop bucket. Then she went back into the living room and put the gingerbread back into the tin and sat down by the fire, staring into it and hugging her arms close as if she would never be warm again.

75

She didn't like that young Mrs Green. She was all powder and paint with her raven-black curls and peaches and cream complexion. Becca had never had much to do with her, but people who worked at the Manor gossiped that Old Mrs Green and Young Mrs Green didn't see eye to eye over a good many things and that Young Mrs Green was very fond of the gentlemen. Becca didn't know about being fond of the gentlemen but it was as plain as the nose on your face that she was making a dead set at Jethro. And him, silly fool, couldn't see it. Or could he? Did he fancy his chances with that painted, scented beauty, all dressed up to the nines like she was? Mutton dressed up as lamb, too. She must be all of ten years older than him. Becca rocked back and forth. This was a pretty kettle of fish and no mistake. Married barely six months and Jethro with another woman setting her cap at him; a well-to-do woman, at that. It wouldn't be surprising if his head was turned. And the way she was acting she'd have his breeches off as soon as look at him. The thought was like a knife twisting in Becca's breast.

'I'm a man, Becca, with a man's needs.' Jethro's words suddenly came back to her. They were six months married and she'd never yet been a proper wife to him. Would it be any wonder if his head was turned by that painted trollop? Becca closed her eyes. Oh, if only he had been awake that first night when she had gone downstairs they wouldn't be in this pickle now. For apart from giving Jethro his due rights, most likely she'd have had a baby lying under her heart by this time so there wouldn't have been any reason to be jealous of Ellen. She had been shaken by the intensity of sick longing that had come over

76

her when her mother brought the news of the twins, a longing that could only be hidden from Daisy by sharp words towards her sister. Before today she hadn't realised how much she longed for a child of her own.

Not that she was unhappy with her lot. In fact, she considered herself very lucky. When she had agreed to marry Jethro it had been almost an act of bravado – to show the people of the village, and perhaps more importantly to prove to herself, that she wasn't going to be left on the shelf after Ellen taking George the way she had.

But although she had known so little about Jethro when she married him, things weren't working out badly. They rubbed along all right together. As she had told her mother, Jethro was a good man. He treated her kindly, and was generous when he could afford to be – which wasn't often – encouraging her to buy anything she fancied: lengths of material, tin trays, buttons or ribbons, when the pack man called laden with his wares. Not that she ever bought much. She preferred to save what she could for the business, as she liked to call it, and nothing gave her more pleasure than putting a few coppers in the box under the bed that she kept for the purpose. A box Jethro knew nothing about.

Yet, although she felt easy and comfortable with him most of the time, after nearly six months of marriage she still couldn't bring herself to invite him into her bed. She was far too shy. And for some reason the longer they were married the more shy she became and the more impossible she found it to tell him that she wanted to be a proper wife to him. She felt almost ashamed to admit, even to herself, that they had not been married many weeks before she had longed to take him by the hand and lead him to the big bed as they reached the top of the stairs. But each night, as he placed a chaste kiss on her cheek and turned to go into the little back room, she had let him go, disappointed, yet lacking the courage to call him back, hardly realising that the ache inside her was only in part a need for a child of her own. The other part, the part that left her empty and restless, the part that wished he would take what was his by right and not wait to be asked, she tried to hide – even from herself.

Recognising all this, how could she blame him if he had turned to another woman – even that Jezebel?

She turned round to the table and put her head in her arms and wept.

George was like the proverbial dog with two tails. Down at the Whalebone that evening everybody was anxious to help him 'wet the babies' heads', and there being two babies, twice the amount of beer was consumed. The landlord was well pleased with his evening's takings as his customers rolled home at closing time and only 'Owd Grimble', the oldest inhabitant, who spent most of his time in the corner of the tap room, was heard to wonder what cause there was for celebration in these hard times over two extra mouths to feed? But nobody ever took any notice of Owd Grimble.

Ellen was not so pleased when her husband woke her up, standing bleary-eyed and swaying at the foot of her bed. 'I told 'em,' he said proudly, 'I told 'em, that ain't everybody can manage to knock two off the shelf in one go. You need plenty lead in your pencil for that.' He blinked owlishly at her. 'They all stood me a drink on the strength of it.'

'Oh, George. They stood you a good many, by the look of you,' Ellen whispered, annoyed that he was drunk, yet secretly pleased that he had found cause to celebrate in the birth of his sons. 'Look now, find yourself a blanket and get to bed and let me get some sleep. And keep quiet, or you'll wake Mum up. I don't want her waking and seeing you like this.'

'I want to have a look at me sons.' George tiptoed elaborately over to the drawer that held the babies, one at each end, his boots creaking loudly. 'The image of their owd dad, the pair of 'em,' he said proudly, nearly falling on top of them.

Ellen giggled. 'Oh, go downstairs, George, you'll wake them up. Can't you let me get some sleep? I'm tired out.'

'Go away? Ain't I comin' in beside you?' He peered at Daisy's still form lying beside Ellen. 'Wass your mum doing there? Thass my place.' He sat down heavily on the bed.

'No, George.' She got up on one elbow and shook her head. 'You know you mustn't. You know very well a man don't sleep with his wife for six weeks after she's bin confined. You'll jest have to roll yourself in a blanket and lay down in front of the kitchen fire. Here, you can take a pillow with you.'

'Thank you for nothin'. I don't think much of that idea. I didn't reckon to sleep on me own tonight. You know I always feel a bit fresh when I get a bit of drink inside me and I was looking forward . . .'

'Hush, George. Mum'll hear,' Ellen warned, trying not

to giggle again. 'Anyway, I reckon you've had too much beer tonight. You know you can never manage it when you're too drunk, even if you do think you fancy it.'

'Hmph!' Grumpily, George left the bedroom and staggered downstairs to the kitchen, falling over the table when he got there. After a good deal of grumbling and swearing he rolled himself in the blanket as he had been told and lay down in front of the dying cinders. His good mood returned. He felt inordinately pleased with himself. He'd done better than bloody Jethro Miller. Knocked two off the shelf at once, he had. Didn't look as if Jethro Miller had even managed to knock one off yet. Smug bugger. Pinching my girl, he thought in his fuddled state.

He began to smile again. He'd lay a penny to a pound Jethro Miller wouldn't be able to get twins on Becca, not like he'd managed to on Ellen. He grinned in the darkness. Not that it had been a lot of trouble. He dessay he could manage it on Becca, too, given half a chance. The thought of getting twins on Becca was very pleasant. Christ, he'd been a bloody fool. She wouldn't even look at him now. What did she want to go and marry that wood butcher for? If that bugger hadn't come along she'd have come crawling back, given time, whether or not he was wed to her sister. He'd have had her eating out of his hand inside six months, if it hadn't been for Jethro bloody Miller. Well, perhaps he still could. Only it might take a little longer. It was a happy thought. He began to snore.

Daisy stirred.

'Sorry, Mum,' Ellen whispered. 'George ain't got much thought. But he'll be quiet now so you can go back to sleep.'

'I'll jest get out and take a look at the babes, now I'm awake.' Daisy crept out of bed and tucked the blankets round the sleeping babies before getting back in beside Ellen.

Daisy sighed. The birth of the twins had given George an excuse to get drunk but she suspected he would have done that, anyway. From what she could gather George spent more evenings at The Whalebone than in his own home these days. She stared up into the darkness. Ellen was fond of George, Daisy didn't doubt that, but she wasn't so sure about George's feelings towards Ellen. Marry in haste, repent at leisure, the old saying had a lot of truth in it and George had been hustled into marriage with Ellen as much by his own family as by her and Joe. George's father, Brad Askew, the blacksmith, was a huge brawny man who sang in the church choir on Sundays and had an unshakable conviction of what was right and what was wrong. George had been wrong to get Ellen in the family way and he had to do right by marrying her. If either of them suffered in consequence, then that was just punishment for their wrong-doing. Brad believed in punishment for transgressions but sometimes he didn't know his own strength and the whole village remembered the day he had nearly killed his own wife because she had burnt his favourite rabbit stew. After that he had managed to keep his temper under control. Daisy suspected that George had a temper, too. Either that, or Ellen tended to walk into doors and give herself a black eye a sight too often.

She shifted her position beside her sleeping daughter. That was just one more worry to add to all the others. Joe had come home soaked to the skin tonight, just as she had expected, and she wondered how many more soakings his poor swollen limbs would take before they seized up altogether. And then what would they do? Would Mr Warner turn them out of the cottage if Joe couldn't work and so couldn't pay the rent? She herself was getting past stone picking, although she still did it at times. But stone picking wouldn't pay the two shillings a week rent and feed them into the bargain. And if Tommy carried out his threat and ran away to sea . . . He was for ever talking about leaving the farm and joining the navy. And him barely sixteen. Daisy didn't think he would ever pluck up the courage to do it, but there was always the nagging fear that he might. A nagging fear that had given her more than a few sleepless nights. And Becca. There was something wrong with Becca, but Daisy couldn't put her finger on quite what. And the girl was as close as a clam. She'd never say. Perhaps there was another case of marry in haste, repent at leisure, although Jethro seemed a level-headed, hard-working young man. And Becca had got a home a good many people would envy, with her matching china and the posh furniture in her front room.

Daisy turned uncomfortably again. Bother George Askew, coming in and waking her up like that. Things always seemed worse when you couldn't sleep. Her thoughts turned back to Joe. She hoped his clothes would be dry by the morning. Perhaps the sun would shine tomorrow. His joints were always easier when the sun shone and he could get a bit of warmth into them.

Chapter Five

'Have you bin to see your sister yet, Becca?' Jethro asked as he sat at the dinner table, his mouth full of mutton stew. He knew perfectly well what the answer would be.

She shot him a glance across the table. 'No, nor don't intend to,' she said briefly.

'I think you oughta go and see her, dear. That ain't every day twins are born in the family. How old are they now?'

'A week. They were born a week ago today.' Becca pushed the food around on her plate under pretence of eating it.

Jethro finished his last mouthful and rubbed his stomach. 'That was a rare good drop o' stew, Becca.' He leaned back in his chair and picked his teeth. 'Albert and Henry, did you say they was to be called?'

'Thass right.' Becca got up from the table and collected the plates and took them out to the scullery. 'There's a bit of rhubarb pie left. Do you want it?'

'Why, yes. I wouldn't want it to go to waste. Thass the

83

first rhubarb we've had this year, and we shouldn't have had that if you hadn't put that owd bucket over it to force it.' Jethro watched Becca as she fetched the pie and served it to him. She hadn't been herself for a week or more now. He scratched his head, frowning. There was a maggot biting her over something, and he could give a pretty good guess as to what it was, but he was blamed if he could figure out the best way of getting her to tell him.

Becca went over to the kettle boiling on the stove and made the tea. She poured a cup for herself and a half-pint mug for Jethro and sat down in her own place again, all without speaking.

Jethro finished eating and looked at the clock on the wall. Seeing the time, he took a quick slurp of hot tea and got up from the table all in one movement. 'I ain't got time to drink that now. I'll have it cold later on.'

'You're in a mighty hurry today,' Becca said in some surprise. 'You can have half an hour for your dinner, surely to goodness!'

'Yes, well, I do as a rule, but I promised young Mrs Green I'd get her table back to her this afternoon. I've got the heat mark out of it and I jest want to iron the veneer back down then I can put it on the hand cart and take it back while the weather's fine.'

Becca banged her own cup back on to its saucer. 'Thass all I ever hear these days. "I've got this job to do for young Mrs Green." "I've got that job to do for young Mrs Green." "Yes, of course I'll drop everything and glue the ear back on Teddy's hobby horse, Mrs Green." "Yes, sir, yes, sir, three bags full, Mrs Green." Do you ever do work for anybody else? Or are you too busy kowtowing to that woman to have time? She may be a titled lady, but can't you see what the hussy's up to? She's only got to crook her little finger and you go running.' She got up and went over to the window, where the geraniums on the sill were just beginning to bloom, and stood looking out. 'Oh, go back to your workshop,' she said over her shoulder. 'I dessay if you asked her nicely Mrs Green 'ud find you a shed to work in up at her house, so you'd be even more handy to dance attention on her.'

Jethro went over and put his hands on Becca's shoulders. 'There ain't no call for you to take on like that, Becca,' he said gently. 'If young Mrs Green put work in my way I'd be a fool to turn it down, now, wouldn't I? I ain't that 'stablished that I can pick and choose where I take work from. And I do get work from other places. Why, I fixed the leg of Owd Granny Appleyard's table only last week.'

'That wasn't work. You never charged her a penny.'

Jethro gave her a little shake. 'Be reasonable, Becca. That was work. While I was doing that I couldn't be doing anything else, could I? But how could I charge a poor owd lady like Granny Appleyard? She couldn't afford to give me a shillun to mend her table. But young Mrs Green didn't notice the extra shillun on the bill for her bureau drawer and the other bits I'd done for her, did she? Thass all wheels within wheels, Becca, my girl, surely you can see that.'

She bit her lip. 'Yes, you're right. I'm sorry, Jethro. I shouldn't have said what I did.' There was a catch in her voice as she spoke and he turned her round to face him and saw the tears running down her cheeks. He looked at

85

her closely. 'Come on, now, Becca. This ain't like you. This ain't like you at all. What's wrong now?'

'Nothing. Nothing's wrong.' She gave a little shrug and tried to turn away but he held her firm. She stayed rigid for a moment then suddenly she crumpled and began to cry, her shoulders heaving with huge, despairing sobs.

'Here, here, what's all this about?' He drew her to him and held her close. 'Ain't you happy, Becca? I thought you and me was making out all right together. You've seemed contented enough, with the garden and the house and all the bits you do for me. What's suddenly got into you to make you so miserable?' He closed his eyes and stroked her hair. She smelled fresh and sweet and womanly, and faintly of the lavender bags she kept in her clothes cupboard. Holding her like this he wasn't sure how much longer his self-control would hold out, especially with having to contend with that Mrs Green breathing her thick, heady perfume all over him and giving him blatant 'come hither' looks, which he had so far managed to resist. 'Perhaps you'd feel better if you was to go and see your sister, Becca,' he suggested, his voice not quite steady.

'No!' She twisted away from him violently. 'I don't want to go and see Ellen. Nor her silly babies!'

'Aaah!' Jethro nodded to himself. So he'd been right. Becca had turned her back on him and was looking into the fire, her head bowed and her shoulders hunched. He took a long drink of tea and then filled his pipe from the pouch in his pocket. He got it drawing to his satisfaction before he said, 'So you don't want to go and see your sister's babies, Becca. Do you reckon that might jest be because you hanker after one of your own?'

She didn't answer but he was watching her closely through eyes narrowed against the haze of smoke and didn't miss the almost imperceptible nod of her head.

'Well, I reckon we can soon remedy that, matey.' He said no more but patted her arm as he made his way back to his workshop.

That night he waited until she had blown out her candle and then came into the bedroom and climbed into bed beside her. 'Are you sure this is what you want, Becca?' he asked gently.

'Yes, Jethro, quite sure.' Her voice dropped till it was barely a whisper. 'I'm sorry I've kept you waiting so long.'

'If a thing's worth having, it's worth waiting for, dear. I didn't want to come to you till you was ready for me.' He kissed her with a rough gentleness and stroked the long dark braid that lay over her breast. He was glad he'd been patient and that his self-control had held out until she had come to him of her own accord. He never believed in forcing the issue.

She put her arms round him and drew him close, understanding at last that this was what she had wanted to do for a long time.

The next day she went about her work singing and that night Jethro didn't even wait for her to blow out the candle but followed her into the bedroom.

Before long Becca knew without any doubt that she was pregnant.

'I'll have to get the sign down ready to print in "AND SON",' Jethro straightened up from fixing glue blocks

87

on the underside of a chest of drawers, a broad beam on his face.

'Best wait and make sure it's a boy before you do that,' Becca said happily. She carried on waxing an oak coffer Jethro had just finished repairing.

'How long have I got to wait?' He looked at her with sudden concern. 'Hadn't you better stop doing that, Becca? You don't want to do yourself harm.'

'Don't be silly. Polishing won't hurt me.' She pushed a strand of hair back into its place. 'It's not due till after Christmas. End of January, I reckon.'

'Thass another six or seven months!'

Becca laughed, a sound Jethro was both pleased and relieved to hear. 'That won't take long to go. You'll see. 'Time you've made a cradle . . .'

'I'll make a pram, too, so you can push him up to your mother's, save you carrying him on your arm. How does your sister Ellen get on for a pram, with two of them to cart about all the time?'

Becca's mouth hardened. 'I don't know. I've never asked.'

Jethro looked at her and frowned. There was only one reason, as far as he could see, for Becca to remain so bitter towards her sister: George Askew. For all she said about not wanting him after what he'd done to her she must still hanker after him, deep down. He couldn't understand it. The bugger wasn't worth it; he was all mouth and trousers. But of course, Becca hadn't seen him swaggering into The Whalebone on pay night, chucking his weight around and spending money that should have gone on his wife and children. It was a wonder somebody hadn't punched him on the jaw before now. He jabbed the brush into his glue pot and went back to the chest of drawers.

Some of the best weather of the summer came towards the end of September when the harvest was at last gathered in. It had been a poor, late harvest, after weeks of rain, and Tommy had become more and more miserable and bad-tempered.

'I don't know what ails the boy,' he heard his mother say as he stamped off up the stairs to his bedroom.

'Ah, leave him be. He's at a funny age. He don't know whether he's colt nor horse,' his father replied.

Tommy shut the bedroom door carefully. Ever since the girls had left home he had had their bedroom all to himself. A whole room of his own with a double bed instead of having to make do with a truckle under the kitchen table. He threw himself down on it and stared up to the ceiling.

'Tommy! Thass time we was getting back,' his father called up the stairs. 'We've still got Moses to rake.' Nobody knew why that particular field was called Moses, but nobody could remember it being called by any other name.

Tommy rolled off the bed and went over to the window where there was a loose brick in the sill. He pulled it out and put his hand in the hole and took out a little canvas bag. He emptied the bag on the bed. There were several shillings and one half sovereign, which had been his share of the harvest money. He counted it carefully and put it back in its hiding place. He'd been saving for a long time, now. He'd stayed away from The Whalebone and the Fair and even Tansy Porter once she'd wanted sixpence every time. But soon he would have enough for his plans and then all the feather beds in the world wouldn't keep him in Wessingford.

'Tommy! Come on, bor!'

'All right, Dad. I'm coming.' Tommy slammed the bedroom door and stamped down the stairs.

A week later, Becca was in the garden early, picking beans before the heat became too fierce. Summer had come late but now it had come with a vengeance and a thick haze hung in the valley between Wessingford and Wyford, completely obscuring the river, a sure sign that it would be another hot day. She gathered enough beans for her needs in her apron and some extra to salt down for the winter and walked up the garden path to the front gate. She loved to savour the early morning scent of the roses that rambled round the little trellised porch and bloomed in the patch between the cottage and the picket at the back, and she had done it all, anxious that the garden shouldn't waste Jethro's precious time.

She leaned on the gate and noticed in the distance a figure with an awkward, ungainly gait trying to make haste along the road. She waved, surprised and apprehensive at seeing her father out of the fields at this time of the day.

'Is anything wrong, Dad?' she called, when he was within hearing distance.

He didn't answer, concentrating on efforts to increase his speed, but the years spent out in all weathers, following the plough over heavy, boot-clogging land had taken their toll and his pace was set. Becca opened the gate and stood aside and then followed him into the house.

He took off his cap and wiped beads of sweat from his forehead. 'Have you seen the boy Tommy, Becca?' he asked, sitting down with a sigh of relief.

'When? Today? No, he ain't been high nor by. But he wouldn't be at this hour, would he? Why?'

'He's gone. Left home.' Joe's mouth worked as he gave the news.

Becca sat down on the nearest chair and put her hands protectively over her swelling belly. 'Gone? What do you mean, gone? Where's he gone to?'

'That we don't know. But I reckon he's gone to sea. Thass what he's always been a-threatening to do.'

'Didn't he leave a note?'

Joe shook his head. 'You know Tommy never took to scholaring. He can't hardly write his name, let alone leave a note. But he's took all his clothes.' Joe sniffed. 'You can't blame him really, I s'pose. There ain't much of a life in farming these days. Mind you, he couldn't say he was bad off. Three shilluns a week he got, and his mother mostly reckoned to let him keep one. She always reckoned to pay the rent with Tommy's money,' he added, half under his breath.

Becca got up from her chair and went through to the workshop, where Jethro was busy sharpening his panel saw. 'Dad's here,' she said. 'Tommy's gone off. They reckon he's run away to sea.'

Jethro put down the file he was using and carefully removed the saw from the vice before following her through to the living room. 'What's this, then Joe?' he said. 'You say Tommy's run off?'

91

He nodded, too upset to speak.

Jethro sat down. 'Are you sure, bor?'

Joe nodded again. 'Thass a sure thing he ain't got up and gone to make an early start at work. He's never been one to get out of his bed afore the last minute,' he said with a pathetic attempt at humour. 'Anyway, he's took all his clothes. What few he'd got,' he added as an afterthought.

'D'you want me to go after him?' Jethro asked.

Joe spread his hands. 'How would you know which way he went?'

'Well, I'd give a good guess that he went across the river and caught the train out of Wyford,' Jethro said, rubbing his chin, the stubble making a rasping sound on his horny palm. 'Either that or he's walked into Colchester.'

'You won't ketch him if he's caught the train,' Joe said.

'No, but I might find out where he's making for. If thass what he's done.'

Joe nodded. 'That might comfort his mother a little if she knew where he'd gone.'

Jethro untied the canvas apron he wore for his work. 'I'll go and see what I can find out. You never know, he might have told Owd Sharpie where he was bound for when he rowed him across the river.'

'I'll come back with you, Dad,' Becca said, after Jethro had gone. 'I dessay Mum could do with a bit of company.'

Joe nodded. 'Yes, she took on something awful when she found he'd gone. Worse than . . .' He hesitated, nodded again and glanced briefly at Becca. 'Well, you know, worse than the business with young Ellen.' He got carefully to his feet, gingerly balancing his painful limbs. 'But thass all water under the bridge. She's got her hands full with the twins and you seem well enough set up with Jethro. He's a hard-working man, so I'm told.'

'Yes. Jethro's a good man.'

'Thass a rare nice place you've got here, too.' Joe looked round appreciatively.

'I ain't complaining.'

'No more you should. I reckon you're wunnerful set up, here.' He turned and looked at Becca. 'Well, come on, if you're coming. I've got to get to work. I want to finish ploughing Moses today afore the weather breaks. I've left owd Boxer in the shafts. He'll be a-wondering where I've got to.' He sniffed. 'Young Tommy was s'posed to be giving me a hand, but I 'spect I'll manage on me own.'

'I don't know what makes you think it's going to rain, Dad,' Becca said as they walked the mile to the cottage where the Stansgates lived. 'I reckon we're in for another scorcher, today.'

'There was a ring round the moon last night,' Joe said. 'Thass always a sign o' rain.'

'I know. But they say, "near circle, far rain" so I don't reckon it'll rain today. Anyway, I should think we've had enough this summer to last all winter.'

'That don't always follow,' Joe said darkly. 'We could still get a hard winter.' He turned off into the field called Moses, calling to his horse as he went, and Becca carried on, past the church, past The Whalebone, past the village pond and along the lane to her mother's house.

Daisy was scrubbing the kitchen table. She always scrubbed the kitchen table when she was distressed, and if every now and then a tear dropped onto the scrubbing brush Becca pretended not to notice. 'He was always threatening to go but I never thought he would,' Daisy said, venting her feelings on the table.

'He'll be back, Mum, don't worry,' Becca said, putting her arm round her mother's shoulders.

Daisy shrugged her off. 'Pull the kettle forward. We'll have a cup of tea,' she said, in an effort to conceal her feelings. 'No, he won't be back. Not if he's gone to sea. He'll find out what a drudge of a life farming is and that'll be that.'

'I don't think it's all that much of a feather bed at sea, from what I hear of it,' Becca said from the stove. She grinned round at her mother. 'Don't you worry, Mum, once he starts missing your suet dumplings he'll come running back.'

Daisy sniffed. 'He won't come back. You mark my words.' She brushed her sleeve across her eyes. 'I wouldn't have minded so much if he'd only said goodbye to us. But going off like that, without so much as a fare-thee-well . . .' She bit her lip.

'I reckon he was afraid you'd cut up rough.'

Daisy shrugged again. 'Is that tea ready yet?'

'Yes.'

The two women drank their tea in silence. Then Daisy said, 'Ellen must be told. I want you to go and tell her, Becca.'

'Me?' She looked up, almost frightened.

'Yes. Why not? She's still your sister, even if you haven't spoken to her for nearly a year. And Tommy's her brother as well as yours.'

Becca shook her head. 'I don't want anything to do with her.'

'Oh, God, what have I done to deserve all this!' Daisy said, her voice despairing. 'A man who's nearly too crippled to work, two daughters who have nothing to do with each other and a son that's run away to sea.' She pressed her knuckles to her chest and bowed her head.

Becca watched her mother for a few minutes, noticing with some surprise that her hair was almost completely white. A wave of compassion washed over her. Whatever her own feelings she couldn't refuse her mother's request. Reluctantly, she got to her feet. 'All right, Mum. I'll go and tell Ellen, if it'll please you,' she said with a sigh.

Becca went along the lane from her mother's house to Owd Racky's cottage. It had been almost this time last year, when the blackberries and sloes were ripening, that she had tripped along this same lane, full of excitement. Excitement that had turned so sour.

Her step slowed. She had never been to the cottage since and she didn't want to go now. She didn't want to see how George had prettied the cottage up for Ellen. He was a handy man and Becca knew what plans he had had for it – plans they had made together. It would be like twisting the knife in the wound to witness the cosy domesticity Ellen was enjoying with George. Didn't her mother realise that?

She rounded the bend in the lane and saw the cottage and stopped dead in her tracks. Far from being cosy it looked more derelict than when she had last seen it. Nothing had been done to smarten it up. The gate swung crazily on one hinge, the garden was overgrown, with a few self-sown vegetables fighting a losing battle with nettles and weeds. Weeds were even growing in the thatch and the paintwork was peeling. Odd bits of curtain were strung haphazardly across most of the windows. She could hardly believe her eyes. Where were George's plans for the neat rows of vegetables and a few chickens scratching round the back door? If there were chickens here they'd be lost in the long grass. And what of his ideas of bright blue paint against freshly whitewashed walls?

Shocked at the sight she picked up her skirts and made her way carefully round to the back door, which stood open. A baby was crying inside.

'Oh, shut your row, can't you?' she heard Ellen's sharp voice. 'I'll see to you in a minute. I've only got one pair of hands.'

Becca knocked and stepped inside. Ellen was sitting on a low chair by the kitchen stove, dressing one of the babies. The other one lay in a drawer on the floor, crying. The remains of George's breakfast, a crust of bread and a few dregs of tea, were on the bare table and there was a heap of dirty washing on the floor by the door. The room looked bare and comfortless and had a faintly sour smell.

Ellen looked up as Becca's shadow fell across her, pushing a strand of hair back from her face. 'Oh, my, look what the wind's blown in,' she said, with a lift of her chin. 'What do you want?'

Becca didn't answer, she was trying to examine her feelings honestly. She had carried bitterness towards Ellen in her heart for so long that it had become part of her, but could she really hate her now, seeing all this? Would this have been her lot, if she'd married George as they'd planned? Had she had a lucky escape? And perhaps more to the point, did she really care any more? Jethro Miller had proved to be a good, kind – she was almost going to say loving – husband. And he had provided her with a home that would be the envy of a good many and his chair-mending business was growing – slowly, it was true, but it was growing. Unexpectedly, a wave of genuine pity for her young sister washed over her.

She went over to the drawer and picked up the baby, crimson in the face with screaming. 'You've got a fine pair of lungs, my lad,' she said, rocking him. She smiled at Ellen. 'Which one is this?'

Ellen scowled uncertainly at her sister. 'Albert. He's a bad-tempered little sod. Here, give him to me and take this one. If you hold him on your shoulder he'll be asleep in no time.'

Becca gave Albert to Ellen and took Henry from her. At least he smelled sweeter. The boys were not a bit alike. Henry's face was full and round, where Albert's was pinched and sharp, even at this tender age. She held the baby as Ellen had suggested and he snuggled into her neck and fell asleep. She felt a warm glow spread through her at the thought that soon she would hold her own son like this.

'Well?' Ellen looked up from feeding Albert. 'Have you seen all you want to see? Or have you jest come to gloat?'

Becca sat down on the only other chair in the kitchen, careful not to disturb the child on her shoulder. 'If you ain't happy, Ellen, thass your fault, not mine,' she said evenly.

'I never said I wasn't happy,' Ellen was quick to reply.

'No? Well, you don't look it, thass all I can say.'

'And if thass all you've come to say, you can go as quick as you come!'

'Thass not all I've come to say. I've got a message from Mum. She asked me to come and tell you the boy Tommy has gone off.'

Ellen looked up. 'Gone off? What do you mean?'

'He's gone off and taken all his clothes with him. Mum and Dad reckon he's gone to sea.'

'He was always threatening,' Ellen said thoughtfully, 'but I never thought he would.'

Becca got to her feet. 'Well, I've come and told you, like Mum asked me to, but I can see I'm not welcome, so I'll be on my way.' She bent over to lay Henry in the drawer. 'Ain't much room for the two of them in this drawer,' she said.

'No, George says he'll make a cradle for them before long.' Ellen finished feeding Albert and buttoned her dress. 'Don't put him down. I'll come along with you to mother's house. You can carry him.' She eyed her sister up and down. 'It'll be good practice for you. Jest wait while I change this little perisher's nightshirt.'

They set out to walk down the lane in cool silence. Becca spoke first. 'How do you usually manage, carrying two of them?' she asked at last, as she transferred the sleeping Henry to her other arm.

'I manage all right.' There was a hint of truculence in Ellen's tone. 'I've got a big shawl and I carry one on each arm.'

'Hm. Thass not too bad while they're little, but I don't know how you'll manage when they get a bit older. Thass a good job thass not too far to Mum's. Can't George make a little cart for you to wheel them about in?'

'He could if he wasn't too busy. What with the farm and the garden, and the thatch – he's never had time to mend the thatch yet.'

Becca said nothing. The near-derelict look of the place told its own story but she let Ellen keep her pride.

Jethro was in the kitchen with Daisy when Becca and Ellen arrived. Daisy automatically took Albert from Ellen and Ellen pulled the kettle forward.

'Mum and me had a cup before I came to see you,' Becca said as Ellen ladled tea into the teapot.

'I 'spect you can drink another,' Ellen said. 'And thass a change for me to have tea made with real tea leaves. Tea made with toast crumbs don't taste near the same.'

'You're welcome to take the tea leaves to brew up again,' Daisy said, 'I've told you that, many a time. They've come straight from Mrs Warner's, so they've only been used twice.'

'I could save you mine . . .' Becca began, then bit her lip as Ellen's face darkened. 'Not that I have that many,' she added quickly. She sat down and turned to Jethro. 'You're back quick,' she said. 'How did you get on?'

'I never even had to cross the river,' he told her. 'That was at low ebb, and I only had to walk to the bottom of the hard on this side and I could shout across. As soon a I saw Owd Sharpie he said – and he mimicked the old man – ' "I reckon I knows who you're a-lookin' for, bor. That young brother-in-law o' yourn, Tommy Stansgate." I said that was right and he told me Tommy had crossed the river afore five this morning, jest as the tide was on the turn.'

'Where was he bound for?' Becca asked anxiously.

'London town, jest like I surmised,' her mother said, taking the cup of tea Ellen had poured.

'So he did ketch the train?' Becca said.

'No,' Jethro replied, 'he didn't, as it happened. He got a lift on a stackie, out from the Hythe on the ebb, bound for London.'

'What's a stackie?' Ellen said dully.

'Oh, Ellen, you know what a stackie is,' Becca said impatiently. 'You've seen them enough times on the river. The big stack barges – they look like floating hay stacks – that take the hay up to London for the horses and bring the muck back to spread on the fields.'

'Oh, yes, I forgot.' Ellen sat wearily down at the table. 'So we needn't have made all this fuss 'cause he'll be back in a few days.'

'No, he won't,' Jethro said. 'He told Owd Sharpie he was going to sea. He won't have no trouble finding hisself a ship once he get to the London docks, don't you never fear.'

'More's the pity,' Daisy said. 'I don't know what his father'll say when he find out.'

'I've already told him. I saw him ploughing in Moses as I come past, so I called in and let him know,' Jethro said. 'He told me his owd screws ain't so good today, even though the sun's a-shining.' He got up from his chair. 'Well, I must get back to work. I hope you'll be able to rest more easy in your mind now you know for certain where Tommy's gone, Mrs Stansgate. I'm only sorry I couldn't bring you better tidings.'

Daisy nodded. 'Yes, thank you, Jethro. I'm obliged to

you.' She looked at the clock on the wall. 'And I must make my way up to Mrs Warner's. Today's my day for scrubbing out her kitchen and there ain't no point in jest settin' around mopin'. You two girls can stay here as long as you like, I shall only be gone an hour or so, unless she's got any other jobs for me.'

'I'll come and give you a hand, if you like, Mum,' Becca said. 'Oh, I shouldn't want paying for it, but I know you're upset over Tommy, so I thought . . .'

Daisy hesitated. She would have preferred to leave the two girls happily talking together but it was plain that their reconciliation was both cool and reluctant, to say the least. Better to be thankful for small mercies and not try to force the issue any further. She nodded. 'Thank you, Becca, I'll be glad of your company.' She put a blanket on the settle and laid down the baby she held. Becca followed suit with Henry.

'You'd better watch they don't roll off, Ellen,' Daisy warned. 'I've put a chair up agin the side.'

Ellen looked up from the battered penny weekly she had found to read and glanced across at them. 'Oh, they'll be all right,' she said, without much interest. 'Pour me another cup of tea before you go, will you?'

Chapter Six

The days lengthened into weeks but there was no word from Tommy. It was as if he had vanished off the face of the earth. Becca tried to spend extra time with her mother, but she herself was always busy. She loved her little home and appreciated it even more now that she had seen the squalor her sister lived in. She made sure it was always well swept and polished, telling herself she owed it to Jethro. He had a healthy appetite, too, so there was always cooking to be done. Then there was the coming baby to prepare for and she liked to help Jethro as much as he would let her. Although she wouldn't admit it to anyone, sometimes she was almost too tired to walk to her mother's house and take her a few eggs or a cabbage.

'You're a good girl, Becca,' Daisy said, not for the first time. 'But you shouldn't trek up here nearly every day. Thass a tidy step, and you the way you are.'

'I like to make sure you're all right,' she said, sitting down wearily. 'I don't s'pose you've heard . . . ?'

Daisy shook her head. 'Not a word.'

'You're bound to get a card for Christmas,' Becca said, with more optimism than she felt.

'Yes. Bound to.' Daisy was silent for a few moments. 'I was thinking, would you all come here for Christmas Day?' she asked. 'I've got an owd hen gone off the lay. I'll get your dad to kill it. And we'll ask Ellen and George . . .'

'I'll have to see what Jethro says.'

She waited until they had finished their evening meal and Jethro had got his pipe stoked. He listened, watching her through a haze of sweet-smelling tobacco smoke. 'We mustn't impose on your mum and dad, they ain't got all that much to spare, 'specially now Tommy ain't there,' he said after some thought. 'But I reckon they'll be glad of a bit o' company now the boy Tommy's gone and I dessay we can take a few vegetables with us, and if you make one of your treacle puddens . . .' He licked his lips and rubbed his belly, grinning at her.

Becca didn't return his smile. 'She's asking Ellen and George as well.'

Jethro's smile died. 'Well, she's got every right. Ellen and George are as much to her as we are,' he said reasonably. 'And if they don't make no trouble, we shan't.' He looked at her intently. 'Shall we, Becca?'

She shook her head impatiently. 'No, of course we shan't.'

Becca spent the days before Christmas helping her mother with the preparations. The hen was plucked and drawn and the giblets stewed ready for the gravy, while Joe brought branches of holly and mistletoe in from the hedgerow to poke behind the pictures Daisy had bought over the years by paying tuppence a week to the tally-man.

'Don't you stretch to put that up,' Daisy warned, as Becca picked up a holly branch, 'you've only got a month to go. You'll do the baby a mischief. Here, give it to me.' Red-faced with exertion and excitement she clambered on a chair and stuck bits of holly round the pictures and the mirror that hung over the mantelpiece. 'There. Now we're all finished,' she said happily. 'Mind you and Jethro ain't late, tomorrow, Becca.' She got down from the chair. 'And thank him for the vegetables. They're all ready and waiting to be put in the copper to cook, 'longside the treacle pudden.' She sighed. 'All we need now is for the boy Tommy to walk in.'

Jethro was up late on Christmas Eve putting the finishing touches to the present they were giving to the twins. There was no question of the adults giving presents to each other and Becca had been dubious at Jethro's idea for the babies' gift but she had to admit that it would be a very useful present.

'Hev you got time to do it?' was her first question. 'You can't let your own work get behind. The business is coming along nicely now . . .'

'I shall fit it in with me other work, Becca.' Jethro's voice had an unusual sharpness to it. He didn't like the way Becca always referred to his work as 'the business'. He was a simple chair mender and didn't pretend to be anything else – although he knew other people valued his work far more highly than he did himself. But he sometimes felt his wife was trying to push him along in a direction he didn't much want to go. As long as he had work to do, a roof over his head and enough to eat, he didn't ask for more.

'All right, then.' Becca knew better than to protest further. 'But wait till after dinner before you get it out, Jethro. Just in case . . .'

'In case what?' he frowned.

'In case there's any trouble.'

'Why should there be any trouble? We're giving the boys a little push cart I've made for Ellen to trundle them about in. What's wrong with that?'

'Nothing.' Becca shook her head. Jethro was too open-hearted and generous even to begin to understand how easy it would be to destroy the fragile peace that existed between her and her sister.

Becca and Daisy tended the old hen, roasting in the faggot oven, while the rest of the family went to church. When they returned the fire was lit in the best front room, the kitchen table was set and everything was ready for the most substantial dinner of the year.

'I'll fetch the bird, Becca. You go and bring in the vegetables,' Daisy said. She had a spotless white apron over her grey Sunday-best dress and she had put on her best embroidered cap for the occasion.

Becca went out to the wash house, where the vegetables were boiling in the copper, scoured out in readiness. She began fishing about in the boiling water and brought out potatoes, turnips and swedes, all merrily dancing round the pudding, which was tied up in a bag and floating on the surface.

'I thought I might find you here, Becca. Do you want any help?'

At the sound of George's voice she nearly dropped the pudding basin full of vegetables and turned round sharply. 'No, thank you, George. I can manage very well,' she said, managing to keep her voice even.

'We ain't really had a chance to talk lately, have we?' He was blocking the doorway so she couldn't slip past him.

'I don't see we've got a lot to talk about, George,' she said. 'You've got your wife and family and I've got . . .'

'Yes, I see you'll soon have a family, Becca.' He looked her up and down approvingly. 'I must say that suits you, being in pod. You're a rare bonny girl.' He put his hand on her arm.

'That's enough of that, George. Now let me pass. All these vegetables'll be cold before I can get them to the table.' In spite of herself she felt a warm glow spread through her at his words.

'We can soon remedy that.' He took the bowl from her and tipped them all back into the copper.

'Oh, now what did you want to go and do that for!' she said. 'They'll all go to mash.'

'Well, at least they won't get cold.' He grinned. He looked at her with his head on one side. 'I really mucked things up between us, didn't I, Becca?' he said sadly. 'It was always you I wanted, you know. If Ellen hadn't been such a little hot-arse and trapped me into marrying her . . .'

'Thass over and done with, George. I don't want to hear any more talk like that. You've made your bed and I've made mine.'

'Oh, thass a pity that ain't the same bed, Becca, gal,' he said with feeling. 'I still fancy you something rotten.'

'You should have thought of that before,' she said.

'Well, what about a kiss, for owd times' sake?' he took a step towards her.

'George, I thought you'd only come out here to get your beer?' It was Ellen's voice from across the yard.

'Yes, all right. I'm bringing it.' He turned back to Becca but she was busy fishing about in the copper again. He hesitated, took a step towards her, then thought better of it and picked up the beer keg and went into the house.

Becca was subdued during the meal. She saw that George took little notice of Ellen and none at all of his two sons, although Ellen hung on every word he uttered. Their marriage was a disaster, it would seem, although it was plain that Ellen was pregnant again.

'Fill up your mug again,' George said to Jethro, 'this is a drop o' good, although I say it meself. Here, hold out your mug, Joe. There's plenty more where this comes from.'

'Thass a pity you don't put as much effort into digging the garden as you do into making that beer of yours,' Ellen was at last stung to remark.

'Oh, shut your trap, mawther. You're always on the nag.'

Becca looked at Jethro, busily doing justice to his dinner. He would never speak to her in that fashion. For all his rough and ready ways he was a gentle man. She felt an unaccustomed rush of tenderness towards him and sudden tears pricked her eyes, though she couldn't have said why.

By the time the treacle pudding was eaten the men were

107

all slightly tipsy and even the women had a rosy glow to their noses.

'We'll put the dishes in the copper,' Daisy said. 'There's plenty of nice hot water in there and thass only had the vegetables and pudden cooked in it.'

'Us men'll do that, Mrs Stansgate,' Jethro said, getting to his feet. 'I reckon you and Becca deserve a rest. You cooked it all, and very nice it was, too.'

The three women went through into the front room, only used at Christmas and funerals, and sat down by the fire, shivering slightly although they wouldn't for the world have admitted that the room had a slightly damp feel about it. Ellen unbuttoned her dress and began to feed her babies. Much raucous laughter came from the wash house as the men tackled the unfamiliar task of washing dishes. After half an hour they came back. 'Look at my hands,' Joe laughed, holding them out, 'they ain't never been so clean and soft.'

'You're welcome to do the washing up all the time,' Daisy said amid laughter. 'Don't let me stop you.'

'Becca and me have got a little present for the twins,' Jethro said, coming in behind him. 'I hope you won't take it amiss.' He pushed the little carriage into the middle of the room. 'I've made it wide enough to take the pair of them. I thought it might make it easier for you to get about,' he said as silence descended on the room.

'What's all this?' George elbowed his way in to see what was happening. He stood looking down at the beautifully made little wooden cart. 'We don't want your charity, Jethro Miller,' he said sullenly.

'That ain't a case of charity, George.' Jethro kept his

108

voice reasonable. 'I'd got these few bits of wood going spare . . .'

'And you thought you'd show off to your poor relations what you could do with 'em? Well, you can keep your charity and show it off somewhere else. When my boys need a chariot, *I'll* make one for 'em, not you.'

'They could do with one right now, George,' Ellen pleaded. 'They're getting very big to carry. Especially with me the way I am again. And you don't have a lot of spare time, George, do you? All the hours you work on the farm, and then with the garden . . .'

He sighed. 'Yes, you're right. I don't get a lot of time for fiddlin' and fart-arsin' about with bits o' wood. I got more important things to occupy my time with.'

Becca shot a glance at Jethro and saw his face darken at George's insult. 'Well, then,' she said quickly, 'perhaps you'd like to make use of this – until sech time as you have a few spare minutes to make one for yourself,' she added with a trace of sarcasm, knowing the hours of work Jethro had put into it.

'Oh, thass a good idea, ain't it, George?' Ellen was determined not to let the little carriage out of her possession. 'We'll jest borry it till you get one made. How's that?'

He shrugged. 'All right. But I don't want charity.'

'That wasn't meant as charity, George. Me and Jethro ain't that well off. That was meant as a Christmas present for the boys,' Becca said. 'But if you take it amiss we'll have the thing back when you don't want it, won't we Jethro?'

'I'll take the blamed thing home with me right now,' he

exploded. 'I'd never have made the bloody push cart if I'd thought it was going to cause so much aggravation.'

Ellen's eyes filled with tears. 'No, don't do that, Jethro,' she whispered. 'Please don't do that.'

'How about a tune on your jew's harp, Jethro?' Daisy said, in an effort to calm the situation. 'You tell us what you're playing and we'll all sing.'

Jethro got his jew's harp out of his pocket, trying to suppress a smile of pride. He liked to be asked to play. He began to tap his foot. 'This one's "Oh, Dear, What Can the Matter Be",' he said and began to play.

Daisy and Becca began to sing. They both had pleasant, low voices. Joe joined in in a quavering tenor and George in a tuneless bass. Ellen quietly laid Henry and Albert in the controversial carriage and wheeled them back into the kitchen where they wouldn't be disturbed. Then she began to sing, too. By this time they were singing 'Bobby Shaftoe' at Jethro's command, although he was still strumming the same tune on his jew's harp. And so it went on. He would call a tune and the others would sing it while he played the same few notes over and over again and they ate the chestnuts that Daisy had roasted in the fire.

'Hark, I believe thass one of the twins hollerin',' Ellen said when there was a lull for Jethro to eat a chestnut.

'I'll go, since I'm nearest the door,' Becca said. She slipped out into the kitchen and looked down at the babies, lying side by side in the pram Jethro had made for them. Henry had stirred but he had settled again and was sleeping quietly. Albert was wide awake, staring up at her with disconcertingly bright blue eyes. Becca stared back at him and a thought suddenly struck her. She didn't like Albert. She shrugged the thought away. It was ridiculous to dislike a baby.

'Are they all right, my boys?' George said from behind her.

'Yes, they're quite all right.' She turned to go back into the front room but he stood in her way. 'Why are you following me about, George?' she said with a sigh. 'You followed me into the wash house, now you've followed me in here.'

He held up a piece of mistletoe. 'I want my Christmas kiss, thass why I've followed you, Becca.' He took a step towards her. 'I used to enjoy kissing you, Becca, and you used to enjoy kissing me, as I remember. We used to get quite hot for each other, didn't we?'

She took a step backwards. 'Thass all over and done with, George. There's no going back. Anyway, look at me, eight months gone . . .'

'And all the more fetching, to my mind.' He caught her by the arm and whispered in her ear, 'A slice orf a cut loaf is never missed. You and me could slip upstairs . . .'

She shook him off. 'Don't be so damned silly, man. Do you think we shouldn't be noticed?'

'But you'd like to, wouldn't you, Becca?' His arms slid round her and he pulled her to him. 'You can't deny that.' He looked down at her, rousing the old, familiar feelings in her that she had thought dead. 'No, George,' she said weakly, 'let me go.'

'Not till you've given me my Christmas kiss, Becca,' he whispered, breathing heavily in her ear.

111

'All right, jest the one.' She gave him a swift peck on the cheek.

'No, not like that. Thass not what I had in mind at all. This is what I want, Becca.' His mouth came down on hers, forcing her lips apart, so carried away by his feelings that he didn't even notice her struggle to escape.

She was frightened. She had never seen him like this before. Always, in the days when they were walking out, he had controlled his feelings but now he was behaving like some wild animal. She was powerless against his strength and afraid both for herself and for the child she carried, for the more she struggled the worse he became.

Suddenly, the door burst open and Jethro came in. 'You leave my wife alone, you lecherous bugger!' he roared, dragging George away from her. George, taken by surprise, staggered back and Jethro caught him a punch on the side of the jaw that sent him crashing to the floor, taking the table with him and sending the pram with the twins in it spinning over to the other side of the room. 'And you leave my wife alone in future or I swear I'll thrash the living daylights out of you, George Askew!'

But George didn't hear. He was out cold.

'It was the drink,' Ellen said, when George was upstairs in Daisy and Joe's bed and the room put back to rights. 'He wouldn't have done a thing like that if he'd been sober.'

Everybody nodded but nobody really believed her.

She glared at Becca. 'And I dessay you led him on.'

'That I never did,' Becca said hotly. 'Thass not my fault he's bin following me about. I told him to leave me alone.'

'Are you sure you're all right, Becca?' Daisy asked anxiously. The day she had planned so carefully in the hope that it would effect a real reconciliation between the girls and their husbands had gone as sour as week-old cream. 'That to-do was enough to bring you on before your time.'

Becca nodded, glad to be sitting safely in the circle of Jethro's arm. 'A bit shook up, thass all.'

Jethro examined his knuckles. 'I hope I ain't caused no damage out in the other room, Mrs Stansgate,' he said. 'I know I oughta say I'm sorry for what I did, but I can't, because I ain't. I'm glad I did it and I'd knock the bugger down again if I caught him after my wife.'

Becca looked up at him. 'I think perhaps we should go home, Jethro,' she said. 'I don't want to be here when George comes to.'

'Oh, I don't think we shall have any more trouble with him, Jethro said grimly. He gave her a companionable squeeze. 'But I'll take you home if thass what you want, dear.'

'Yes, I think you should. I don't want you here when George come round, neither,' Ellen snapped, her jealousy getting the upper hand. 'I know you still hanker after him, thass why you led him on, but I'll hev you remember thass me he's married to, not you.'

'Oh, Ellen, as if I'm likely to forget,' Becca said wearily. 'But thass over and done with. Why can't we forgive and forget? I'm willing to, if you are.'

Ellen gave a sharp little laugh. 'Fat chance of forgetting if every time you get near George you start kissing and cuddling with him.'

'Ellen, I *told* you it wasn't my fault . . .' Becca was near to tears.

'You were as much to blame as he was. You led him on,' Ellen insisted. 'You must have done. He wouldn't have touched you, else.'

'Thass not true. I didn't lead him on. Jethro . . . ?'

'Come on, dear, I'll get your coat, I've had enough of this.' Jethro put a stop to the argument. 'Thank you for your hospitality, Mrs Stansgate,' he said formally. 'I'm sorry that had to end this way.' Firmly he took Becca's arm and led her out of the door.

Ellen gave a shrug and pulled her chair nearer to the fire to wait for George to pull himself together. She didn't have to wait long. Becca and Jethro could hardly have reached the road before he came lumbering down the stairs, rubbing his jaw.

'Where is he?' he said thickly. 'Where's the bugger that knocked me down?'

'He's gone,' Ellen said. 'And we're going now.' She put on her hat and coat and went over to the pram.

He stared at her. 'You ain't taking my kids home in that push cart! I o'nt be beholden to that man,' he roared.

Ellen lifted her chin. 'When you make me a push cart I'll give this one back. I've on'y borried it. Now, come on, thass nearly dark. Time you got the milking done.'

Daisy and Joe stood at the door and watched them go. Daisy said nothing but she feared that Ellen would pay dearly for that show of authority. As for Becca, she seemed to have landed on her feet in spite of everything. Jethro was a fine man and treated her with genuine affection. Daisy wondered if Becca appreciated how lucky she was. It was difficult to tell. Becca was never one to give her feelings away.

Later that evening, when Joe returned from helping a taciturn George with the milking, he said, 'The boy George has got a rare bruise on his chin.' He chuckled. 'That Jethro can pack a punch when he's a mind to. He'd be a good'un in a boxing booth at the fair.' He stared into the fire for some time, then he shook his head. 'I never thought to see fighting under my roof, Daisy.'

'No more did I, Joe. P'raps I done wrong to try and bring the family together again. But I thought I'd try and make Christmas as nice as I could, seeing as how Tommy wasn't here.'

'I don't reckon you'll ever make George and Jethro take to each other. George is as jealous as fire is hot because Becca belongs to Jethro, and Jethro don't trust George.' Joe drew on his pipe. 'And you can't blame him for that, judging by what happened today.'

'George ain't got nobody to blame but himself. I ain't got no sympathy with him,' Daisy said primly. 'And young Ellen knew what she was a-doing, too. Though I feel a bit sorry for her, because I doubt she's found she's bit off more'n she can chew.'

Joe was silent for some time gazing into the fire and puffing on his pipe, then he said, 'Yes, I reckon Becca's better off with Jethro than she would have been with George, chance how quick they was wed. Young Jethro seem a good, level-headed sorta chap.'

'Yes. He's got a kind heart, too. In fact, the best part of the day was seeing Ellen wheeling the twins home in their new pram,' Daisy said, smiling at the memory. 'Though even that caused trouble.' She sighed. 'I'm disappointed over Christmas, Joe. Apart from anything else, I did think we might have had word from Tommy. I even thought as how he might come home, it being Christmas, and I've listened for his step all day. But he's never come.' She sniffed. 'I dunno, Joe. Whichever way we turn there seem to be trouble.'

He leaned forward and put his hand on her knee. 'Don't talk like that, wife. We've still got a lot to be thankful for. We've still got a roof over our heads and our bellies are full. Things could be a lot worse.'

As if in reply to his words there was a knock at the door. He got stiffly to his feet and went to open it. 'Shorty!' he said. 'Thass Owd Shorty, from next door,' he called over his shoulder to Daisy. 'Come you in, bor. What brings you out on a cold Christmas night like this? Have you run outa beer at your house?' Shorty was the pigman at the farm. He lived in the other half of the double-dweller where Joe and Daisy had their home.

Shorty didn't return Joe's smile. 'No, nothing like that. It's bad news, I'm afraid, Joe.' He snatched off his cap as he stepped over the threshold. 'I was jest shutting the pigs up for the night when I see Mr Warner's brother-in-law – him and his wife what have come to spend Christmas with the master and missus. He was a-saddling up his horse to go and fetch the doctor from Wyford. He told me that master's bin took bad. They reckon he's had a stroke.'

'Oh, my Lor. How bad is he?' Joe asked.

'Pretty bad, as I understand it. The brother-in-law was in a right stew in case he didn't get the doctor back in time.'

116

The three of them were silent for several minutes, each busy with their own thoughts. 'Well, thankee for coming and telling us, Shorty,' Joe said at last.'

'Thass the least I could do, Joe.' He shook his head. 'Thass a bad day for us, because I reckon thass the end of farming for him. And he was always a good master to his men.'

'Aye, Shorty, you're right there, bor.' Joe accompanied the pigman to the door and then went back to his place by the fire.

Daisy wiped a tear from her eye. 'You said things could be a lot worse, Joe, not five minutes ago. What's to become of us now, with the master took bad?'

'We shall have to wait and see, Daisy, my girl, shan't we?' he said with a brave attempt at a smile. But his heart was heavy.

Samuel Warner died three days after Christmas. He had no children to follow him on the farm so his wife went to live with her sister and brother-in-law in Sudbury. Mr Green, at the Manor House, decreed that his son Edward should take over the running of Tenpenny Farm.

'It's time you did some real work, my boy,' Old Edward said over the after-dinner port. They were sitting in the spacious dining room at the Manor, the ladies having retired to the drawing room. 'You're supposed to act as my agent, but Cooper virtually runs the estate while you spend most of your time gambling and riding to hounds. You need something to get your teeth into; something you are totally responsible for. Tenpenny Farm will fill the bill very nicely. It needs pulling round a bit – Sam Warner was inclined to suffer from a kind heart, which you can't afford if you're going to make things pay. But by and large it's not bad. It's well stocked, the milkers yield well and there's plenty of good pasture. Young Askew's good with the cattle, I'm told, and what's-his-name? Shorty Johnson, he's the pigman. A good fellow. I'm not so sure about Joe Stansgate – he used to be very good, by all accounts, but he's pretty crippled up now from what I hear. But be that as it may, you shouldn't have any trouble making the place pay – as far as any farm pays these days.'

'Wouldn't it be better to sell, sir?' Edward asked, twisting the stem of the expensive, heavily engraved wine glass between his fingers. 'There's precious little profit in farming, you've said so yourself. So what's the point of slaving ourselves to death flogging the proverbial dead horse? In any case, Felicity and I are very happy where we are, in Brookfield House.'

Old Edward stroked his whiskers and regarded his son over the decanter. 'I dare say you are,' he said, 'but Brookfield House is the one I'm prepared to sell.'

'But it's a fine house!'

'Yes,' old Edward nodded. 'It should make a good price.'

'But I'm not sure that I want . . .' Edward began.

The old man banged his fist down on the table, making the glasses shiver and the silver and china rattle. 'I don't care what you want, Edward,' he said, his voice deadly quiet. 'It's what *I* want that matters. And I want to see what you make of Tenpenny Farm.' He leaned forward. 'One of these days you'll have the entire estate to manage.

118

I want to be sure you can manage a piddling little farm before I entrust you with it. Remember, I can always leave the lot to the dogs' home.'

'Oh, you wouldn't do that, Guv'nor.' Edward laughed nervously.

'Don't be too sure.' Old Edward drained his glass. 'Now, shall we join the ladies? And you can tell Felicity you'll be leaving Brookfield House so that she can start packing.'

'I'm afraid she won't be very pleased.'

The old man stood up. 'Good!'

Two days later Teddy, Edward Green's seven-year-old son, crouched outside the door of his father's study, clutching his rag doll and with his thumb in his mouth, listening to his parents quarrelling. It was nothing unusual, they often quarrelled but it seemed worse today. They were saying something about leaving Brookfield House, which made him feel sick because where would they go? And would he be left behind? He didn't like the idea of staying here with only Nanny to look after him. And supposing they took Nanny and left him here all alone? He clutched Billy, his doll, tighter and tried not to cry.

He hated it when Mama and Papa quarrelled. They said such awful things. Things he didn't understand. But mostly the same sort of things. Mama would say, 'You told me you would inherit a big estate. But you forgot to say that it was at the back of nowhere and that I should be expected to live shrouded in fog for half the year and each time I ventured from the house I should be ankle deep in mud . . .'

119

At that point Papa invariably interrupted to say that *she* should talk of deception. Hadn't she deceived him enough, letting him believe she was a titled lady? And so it would go on, their voices getting louder and louder, until Papa crashed out of the room, nearly knocking him over and telling him he had no business to be listening at doors. Whereupon Mama would sweep him up in her arms and call him her heart's darling and what had dreadful Papa said to him? He knew this was what would happen, he always experienced the same sick feeling as he listened at the door, yet he couldn't help staying there. It was as if he was glued to the cold marble floor outside the door.

'I won't go!' His mother's voice rose almost to a scream. 'I won't go and live on some stinking farm. What do you think I am?'

'I think you're a scheming, lying bitch, if you want the truth,' his father shouted back, 'but if you don't want the whole village to know what you are, you'll come and live at Tenpenny Farm and make the best of it. That's all I have to say on the matter.'

Before Teddy could move away from the door it was flung open and his father came out, his handsome face set and his eyes black with rage.

'What are you doing here, boy? I've told you before not to skulk at keyholes.' He snatched Billy away. 'And what are you doing with dolls? A boy of your age should be playing with soldiers, not cuddling stupid dolls.' He looked down at Teddy, crouching at his feet. 'Oh, for goodness' sake, stand up and stop snivelling like some silly girl. What have you done with the box of soldiers I bought you, eh, boy?'

120

'They're in the toy cupboard,' Teddy whimpered.

'Speak up, boy, don't mutter. In the toy cupboard? Well, next time I come to the nursery, make sure they're ranged for battle and I'll show you how to have a good old war.' He flung Billy into a corner. 'I'll get Thomas to put that stupid doll on the kitchen fire.' He stalked off.

Teddy scrambled after Billy and hugged him very tightly as his mother came through the door and swept him up in her arms. 'What is it, my heart's darling?' she asked, kissing his tears away. 'What did that dreadful Papa say to make you cry?'

Teddy gulped. 'He said he was going to put Billy in the fire,' he sobbed.

'He'll do no such thing, my darling. Oh, don't cry all over Mama's dress, Teddy, you're making wet patches on it.' She relinquished her hold on him and gave him a delicate square of lace to dry his eyes on.

'Are you going away, Mama?' he mumbled, half afraid to ask the question.

'What makes you ask that?' she said sharply.

'I heard Papa say . . .'

'You shouldn't listen at doors, poppet. You hear more than is good for you. Now, run upstairs to Nanny and ask her to wash your face. I've got to go and see a man about mending my jewel box.'

'Is that the box you wrenched the lid off, Mama?' Teddy asked innocently.

'Never you mind. Just run upstairs to Nanny.'

Teddy went slowly up the stairs, clutching Billy. He was a clown doll, with orange wool hair, a purple spotted waistcoat and blue-and-white striped trousers. He had a wide, red felt grin and long black eyelashes round bright green eyes. Teddy loved Billy as the only thing in his life that was always the same. Billy was always there, always ready to be loved and cuddled. At night, in the darkness – because his father wouldn't allow even a glimmer of a nightlight – Teddy would be comforted by Billy's presence and would go to sleep with his finger on the funny little glass bead that was stitched to Billy's cheek. Teddy didn't know that it was meant to be a teardrop.

Chapter Seven

Becca's baby was born on the last day of January in the year 1892. She looked down at the little downy head nestled in the crook of her arm and then up at a beaming Jethro. 'I'm afraid you can't put "and son" up on your sign yet, Jethro. I'm sorry.'

'That don't signify,' he said with a proud smile. 'Thass nice to have a little maid first. She'll be company for you, dear. Anyway, I dessay the next one'll be a boy.' He touched the baby's soft cheek with a horny finger, marvelling that this tiny being had come from his union with Becca. 'What shall we call her?'

'Kate's a nice name,' Becca said.

He nodded. 'My sister what died was called Kate. I like the name. So Kate it shall be.' He dropped a careful kiss on little Kate's forehead and another on Becca's cheek and tiptoed from the room.

She relaxed against the pillows, her little daughter beside her. She was lucky and knew it. Jethro was a good husband and would be a good father to their children, they had a comfortable home and his chair-mending business gave them enough for their wants. What more could she ask? Yet she often wondered what it would have been like if she hadn't been married in such haste. If Jethro had courted her the way of all young people and they had fallen in love. But would they have fallen in love? That was something she would never know because they were married before she had the chance to find out. As it was, they had thrown in their lots together and must make the best of whatever came along. Love didn't come into it. In fact, she wasn't even sure what love was any more. But perhaps it didn't matter. Jethro was a kind, comfortable man to be with and she in turn did the best she could by him. Maybe that was enough. And if he wasn't quite as ambitious as she could have hoped, well, as she'd told herself before, there were more ways of killing a pig . . . and there was plenty of time. She closed her eyes and drifted content-edly off to sleep.

The first time Becca carried Kate to her mother's house Ellen was already there.

'I dessay you'll want the push cart back now,' she said, her mouth pursed primly. Her new baby was due in a little over two months and she looked tired and drawn.

'No, I reckon you need it more than I do,' Becca said, trying to ignore her sister's somewhat sour tone. She wondered if Ellen would ever forgive her for George's behaviour at Christmas. 'Although I don't know how you'll fit three into it.'

'Oh, time the new one comes I'll be able to prop the twins up one end and lay the baby across the other.'

Ellen's expression relaxed a little. She had obviously been worried at the thought of being deprived of the pram.

'I s'pose you don't need Ellen's back because Jethro's made you a new one,' Daisy said innocently, nursing her new grandchild in the rocking chair by the fire.

Becca looked uncomfortable. 'Well, no. To tell the truth he's been too busy. He's been doing a bit of work repairing a set of Chippendale chairs for Mr Letch, of Headgate in Colchester, and when the cart came to fetch the chairs back Jethro went as well. I didn't know what he had in mind, but when he came back he said he'd been paid more'n he expected so he went along to Dyer's second-hand shop and bought a proper pram for the baby.'

Her words were greeted with silence. Daisy, seeing the look of naked jealousy on Ellen's face, realised she had unwittingly said the wrong thing. But a pram was not something that could be hidden for long. 'How did he get it home?' she asked, for something to say.

'Why, he pushed it home, of course. How else?'

Ellen gasped and shook her head. 'Oh, he shouldn't have done that,' she said in a voice of doom, relieved to have something negative to latch on to. 'Didn't you know it's unlucky to push an empty pram? That means the baby won't . . .'

'Why didn't you bring little Kate in it today?' Daisy cut in quickly, knowing exactly what Ellen had been going to say.

'Because Jethro's painting it up and trying to make it smart.' Becca shrugged her shoulders, still uncomfortable under her sister's unconcealed envy. 'Thass not all that special. That was only a second-hand pram. I don't think he paid very much for it. He's got quite a bit to do to it.' She hated herself for sounding so apologetic. After all, why shouldn't she have a proper pram? They could afford it. The trouble was, she was torn between pride in her comparative affluence plus loyalty to Jethro, who had been so proud when he wheeled the pram home, and anxiety that her sister shouldn't feel outclassed. It was a feeling that was to dog her for years, although for the life of her she couldn't imagine why she should suddenly start feeling guilty over Ellen when it was her sister who had made the choice in the first place.

Ellen got up to go. 'Well, your pram might not be much cop, but at least thass a proper pram and I don't doubt thass got proper springs so *your* little dear won't get the living daylights jounced out of her,' she said, her voice heavy with sarcasm. 'Not like my poor little beggars, bumped about like peas in a drum whenever they ride in their box on wheels.'

'Which they wouldn't have had if it wasn't for my Jethro,' Becca said sharply. 'You'd still be trying to carry them on your arm.'

'George would have made them a proper pram, with springs, only he didn't want to fly in Jethro's face,' Ellen snapped.

Becca tossed her head. 'And the band played believe *that* if you like! But there's nothing to stop George putting springs on the one Jethro made. Jethro wouldn't mind.'

'I dessay George will. When he get the chance.' The two sisters glared at each other across the kitchen table.

'Sit down, Ellen.' Daisy's voice cut into the quarrel.

'Becca, make another cuppa tea and both of you stop yelling at each other.'

'No, I can't stop any longer,' Ellen said, looking out of the window. 'I've left a line of washing out and that look like rain again. I'll come and see you tomorrow, Mum. When *she's* not here.' She left without so much as a glance in Becca's direction.

Becca watched her go, pushing the little cart Jethro had so carefully made up the uneven path to the lane. Already the paint on it was scuffed and scratched and one of the wheels wobbled ominously. George hadn't even bothered to tighten it, Becca thought sardonically, so Ellen didn't stand much chance of getting him to fit springs on it. 'Poor old Ellen,' she said, under her breath, 'strikes me she doesn't have much of a life with George.'

Her mother looked up from rearranging the shawl round little Kate. 'Perhaps you should think yourself lucky, then. If things had gone different, *you'd* have been in her place.'

'No, I wouldn't. George wouldn't have treated me the way he treats Ellen. I reckon he takes it out on her because he had to marry her.'

'Well, that was nobody's fault but his own. He was the one that got her in the family way. So he's as much to blame as she is. Stands to reason.'

Becca gave a wry smile. 'I don't reckon reason comes into George's reckoning all that much,' she said with a sigh.

'You don't still hanker after him, Becca, do you?' Daisy said sharply.

Becca shrugged. 'What's the use? There's nothing to be

gained by moping over what might have been. I reckon what you have to do is make the best of what you've got.'

'Thass easy enough for you to say that, my girl. You ain't got a lot to complain about. Maybe you did marry Jethro Miller in a bit of a hurry, but you've fallen on your feet, all right. He seems a good man and you're well provided for.' Her voice took on an anxious note. 'Even the house you live in is yours.'

Becca sat down and took her mother's cue. 'So what's going to happen up at the farm?' she asked, nodding her head in the direction of the farmhouse.

'Haven't you heard?' Daisy sighed. 'Mr Green's son Edward is to take it over. I believe they move in next week, and from what I hear thass not going down too well with the Lady Felicity.' This was the half-disparaging way in which Edward Green's wife was referred to among the villagers. Some didn't believe that she really was a titled lady although there was no doubt she acted the part, sweeping imperiously among the villagers at fêtes and expecting men and boys to doff their caps and women and girls to curtsey when her carriage rolled by.

'Well,' Becca said thoughtfully. 'I suppose it will be a bit of a come-down for both of them after the life they've led at Brookfield House. From what I hear of it the hardest work Mr Edward does is organise the Hunt. And as for her . . .'

Daisy nodded. 'Tenpenny Farm's a nice house. And even if it's not quite as big as Brookfield House, there's still plenty of room in it. And thass a rare big kitchen. I should know, I've scrubbed the flags there often enough.' She sighed. 'But I dessay it'll come a bit hard on her, taking on the job of farmer's wife. Thass a bit of a come-down, her being who she is and all that.'

'Hmm.' Becca sniffed. 'I jest hope she won't expect Jethro to be at her beck and call all the time when she gets there. I hope she'll find herself something better to do than keep running after him to repair things that I'll swear she's smashed on purpose.' She put her elbows on the table and leaned forward. 'Do you know, Mum, she even came along when Jethro was making Mr Warner's coffin to see what sort of handles he was going to put on it. She said they didn't want anything too fancy. But that wasn't anything at all to do with her. That wasn't as if she'd got to pay for it.' She leaned back in her chair. 'You want to watch out for her, Mum, she's a reg'lar nosey parker.'

'I reckon she'll have better things to do than nosey parker in my direction,' Daisy said with a grim laugh. 'And I'm certain sure I shall have more things to worry about than her.' She shook her head. 'I'm told Mr Edward is likely to be a hard master. I don't know where that'll leave your dad, I'm sure. I doubt Mr Edward won't be so fussy about finding him a job in the dry as Mr Warner was, however bad his owd screws are.'

'How is Dad?'

'He'll be better when the warm weather come. He ain't up to much at the minute. And worrying his insides out about it all don't help any.'

Becca was quiet for a few minutes. Then she asked, as she always did, although she knew what the answer would be, 'Any news of the boy Tommy?'

Daisy shook her head, biting her lip. 'I shoulda thought he might have got someone to write us a line to let us

129

know he's in the land of the living,' she said sadly. 'But we've never had so much as a postcard since the day he left.' For Daisy this was the hardest thing of all to bear.

Becca kissed her mother. 'One of these days he'll turn up and surprise us all, I shouldn't wonder.'

Daisy looked up. 'With his pockets full of gold?' she said dryly.

'Yes, and wearing a smart suit and carrying a cane.'

'I wouldn't care if he was in rags, as long as he came,' Daisy said.

Becca walked home under grey skies. The rain hadn't materialised but the clouds were low and heavy and the hedgerows were still dripping from the previous night's downpour. It was the worst kind of weather for her father's rheumatism.

She looked down at the baby, tucked warmly in her shawl and sleeping soundly. She was growing, as Jethro said, 'like a little hop'. She was a pretty baby too and Jethro was inordinately proud of her, even though she wasn't the son he so desperately wanted. Becca smiled down at her and walked on. But when she got within sight of her own cottage her contented mood left her because Felicity Green's carriage stood at the gate. Her jaw hardened. Why did that woman keep coming after Jethro and spoiling everything?

She slowed her step and went into the house by the front door instead of through the workshop as she usually did. She didn't want to have to speak to that woman.

Jethro knocked the dottle out of his pipe on the chimney back and filled it from his tobacco pouch. When he had got it drawing well he leaned back in his chair, well satisfied with a good day's work done and a good meal inside him. He looked at Becca, sitting on the other side of the hearth, busy with her darning in the light from the oil lamp, and at the cradle – his own handiwork – on the hearthrug between them. He gave the cradle a little push with his foot to set it rocking and nodded happily. Things weren't working out so badly. Becca was a good wife. She kept the house spotless, cooked well and never refused his attentions in bed. He smiled a little to himself. Truth to tell – although she would be mortified to admit it – she had been more than ready for him when he returned to her bed after Kate's birth. A long six weeks that had made him hungry for her, too.

Added to that, he had plenty of work, especially now that Mr Letch had said he would put jobs in his way. Mr Letch was likely to give him the trickiest, most fiddly things to repair; things he was reluctant to trust to his own workmen, good though they were. It was a real feather in his cap. In fact, Mr Letch had wanted him to go and work for him but Jethro had refused, saying he preferred to remain his own master. Well, he liked to make things as well as repair them. And one day he might even get round to sorting out all the old rubbish in Uncle Fred's shed behind the workshop. There was no end of junk in there.

In fact the only cloud on the horizon that he could see was that damned Green woman. She was a nuisance, but he couldn't be rude to her because he owed her something for putting work in his way before he got properly established. He gave a deep sigh.

131

'What did the Lady Felicity want today?' Becca asked, without looking up, as if she had read his thoughts.

'Oh, she brought along some chairs. Or rather Dick, her coachman, brought them in, but she came too, to tell me what she wanted and bring the material.'

'And what did she want?'

'She wants the colour of the velvet on the seats changed, if you please.' Jethro made an impatient gesture. 'I never head anything so damned stupid in all my born days. There's nothing wrong with the velvet on the chairs, except that it's green and she wants it red. Got more money than sense, if you ask me.'

'Will you do it?'

He took a deep breath. 'Well, she's left them, and she says if she likes the look of them when they're done she'll have the armchairs done to match.' He scratched his head with the stem of his pipe. 'But I don't know. I don't like upholstery work and thass no good saying I do. I prefer to work with wood, not with fancy materials. I ain't happy to take the job on – 'specially the armchairs – because they'll have to be stitched.'

Becca lifted her head. 'I reckon I could help you do that.'

'What, stitch?'

'I reckon I could help you re-cover the chairs.'

'Have you ever done anything like that?'

'No, you know very well I haven't. But you could teach me.' She grinned. 'And I might as well learn on Lady Felicity's furniture as anybody else's, since she ain't short of money.' She became animated. 'You know only too well I'd like to do more to help you, Jethro.'

'You already do all the book work and most of the polishing. What more do you want?' His eyes twinkled as he spoke.

'I reckon I could learn to do upholstery. I reckon I've only got to watch the way the things are taken apart and build them up again the same way.'

'Thass not quite as easy as that, dear.' He smiled, humouring her.

'Well, you could show me.' She saw the expression on his face and shrugged. 'But if you don't want me . . .'

He was silent for a very long time, puffing on his pipe and looking into the fire. Then he said, 'All right, Becca. I'll show you and you can see what sort of a job you make of it. But I reckon I'd better find an old chair in Uncle Fred's shed for you to practise on first.'

The next morning Becca helped him to sort through the bits and pieces his uncle had accumulated over the years. There were table tops with no legs, legs with no table tops, chairs with one, two or no legs or no seats, cupboard fronts with no backs, the carcasses of chests of drawers, and drawers that didn't fit anything; and underneath them all a stack of unrecognisable remnants that had once been items of furniture. Everything was covered with years of dirt and dust.

'I should think the best thing to do with all this is have a good bonfire,' Becca said, pushing a strand of hair back with a grimy hand. 'Whatever did you uncle want with keeping such a lot of rubbish?'

Jethro straightened up and shook his head. 'Same thing as me, Becca. When I want a piece of wood to repair something I can usually find a bit that I can use out here.'

133

He grinned. 'And you never know. Some of this might be worth a lot of money. One day.'

'Pigs might fly. One day.' She brushed a thick black cobweb off her apron. 'But where's this old chair you're going to teach me to cover?'

'Here. I've just got to glue a leg back on. Do you know, I think there are half a dozen of these chairs? Might even be eight.'

'They're a bit old-fashioned, aren't they?' Becca put her head on one side.

'Yes. They're what you might call in between, so they ain't worth much. They're not new enough to be modern and not old enough to be antique. Still, they won't eat nor drink anything where they are. One of these days we'll have a good old sort out.'

'But not today. I want to learn to cover a chair today.'

Becca learned quickly. She was naturally quick and neat, and if she hit her own thumbnail more often than the tacks she was putting in, she didn't complain. She did exactly as Jethro told her and when the chair was finished he had no fault to find.

The next day he went into Colchester with the carrier's cart. There was a Sheraton what-not to be returned to Mr Letch and Jethro didn't trust the carrier to handle the delicate piece with sufficient care. 'I don't want him knocking off all that fret-work I've put on those little shelves,' he told Becca, 'and anyway, I need to match up the locks for Mr Atkinson's bureau.'

Becca waited until he'd gone and Kate was fed and laid in the now-smart pram and then she went into the workshop and took down one of Felicity Green's chairs. She knew

Jethro. He'd humoured her by letting her cover that old chair but he would keep finding excuses so that she didn't do what she called 'proper' work. She took the chair seat out. It didn't look very different from the one she had covered the day before; it was what Jethro had called a drop-in seat. She was confident she could re-cover it without his help.

Once her mind was made up it didn't take her long to remove the green velvet cover and she used this for a pattern on the new red velvet. Then she took her scissors in one hand and her courage in both and cut the new cover and tacked it on to the seat, being careful to stretch it tightly as Jethro had shown her. By the time he came back she had finished two chairs, the second one nearly ending in disaster when she found she had cut the material with the pile going the wrong way. She hid this and cut a third, learning from her mistake.

Jethro's reaction was not what she had expected. His face darkened with anger. 'What the devil do you think you've been doing?' he said, rounding on her. 'Do you realise how much that material cost?'

'I cut into it very economical, Jethro.'

'You might have spoiled it.'

'I know. But I didn't, did I? I was very careful to do it exactly as you showed me.'

He didn't answer, but lifted the seat out of first one chair and then the other. 'You need more tacks in here.'

'I couldn't find any more. If you give me some more I'll put them in.' She kept her blackened thumb behind her back. 'Oh, Jethro,' seeing his stern, unsmiling face, 'I was only trying to help. And you didn't want to do it, you said so yourself.'

135

'No,' he said, still not smiling. 'And I don't want to do the other four, either, so you'd better see how you get on with them. It'll be a little pin money for you.'

She flung her arms round his neck in an unusual show of affection. 'Oh, thank you, Jethro. I'll make a good job of them, you'll see. And I don't want pin money. I want to be part of the business.'

He shook his head solemnly. 'No, I ain't putting "Jethro Miller and Wife" up on the sign, not even for you, Becca.' His face broke into a grin. 'But I reckon we're partners, all the same. Next thing I'll show you is how to do rush seating and cane chairs.'

The Greens moved into Tenpenny Farm. Young Teddy had watched apprehensively as the furniture was all loaded on to the big horse-drawn van and taken the two miles from Brookfield House to the farm. His mother and father were both stern and unsmiling and he realised without being told that they hadn't wanted to move. But Teddy thought Tenpenny Farm was a nice house. The rooms weren't as vast and unforbidding as in Brookfield House and his bedroom and the schoolroom – he must remember not to call it the nursery any longer because Mr Long had been engaged as his tutor and would come every day to give him lessons – were on the top floor and looked out over the farmyard where the hens scratched and the pigs snorted and the cows mooed. Sometimes he saw other children, too. Johnson the pigman had two girls and Askew the cowman had twin boys that he sometimes brought along to see the cows being milked. It was nice to see other children, even if his mother said he wasn't to mix with them or speak to them because they were common. He didn't know what 'common' meant. They looked quite ordinary to Teddy.

Two things he didn't like about Tenpenny Farm. One was the fact that he had to keep Billy hidden upstairs. His father had insisted that he was too old for dolls now and if he found that clown doll kicking about once more he'd put it on the boiler fire. He meant it, too, this time, so Teddy had to keep Billy hidden in a cupboard all day behind the dreaded box of soldiers. But he cuddled him under the bedclothes every night and told him what had been happening during the day. Sometimes he even let him take a surreptitious peep out of the window, too, when there was nobody about.

The other thing Teddy didn't like was that he couldn't get away from the noise of his parents quarrelling in this smaller house. His mother was forever complaining that they had 'come down' in life and that she couldn't put a foot outside the door before she was up to her ankles in mud. But Teddy noticed that she had gone right to the farm gate with the man who brought the chairs back. He hadn't recognised them at first because they were red now instead of that pretty green. Teddy couldn't understand why the colour had been changed. They'd looked all right the way they were, to him. In fact, he had liked the green best, and so had his father, it seemed, because he had shouted at mother for a long time when he saw them and ended up shutting himself in his study. All the same it wasn't long before the armchairs and the sofa had been covered to match. When Teddy saw Mr Miller deliver them on his hand cart he hurried upstairs and hid in a cupboard with Billy until tea time and he judged that the row would have died down.

By haymaking time the Greens were well – if not happily – settled in at Tenpenny Farm. The haysel went without incident. The hay crop was good and the weather stayed fine for it to be gathered in. Joe and the other men began to think that perhaps Mr Edward wouldn't be such a bad master, after all. He didn't even complain when the men took time out to drink a toast to George's new daughter, Dolly, born during the haysel.

But Mr Edward was not keen to take advice, especially from his inferiors, and when Joe respectfully pointed out that the hedge between middle and bottom fields was none too secure, he brushed him aside, telling him to put a few sticks across where it was broken and leave it till after the hay was all in and stacked. This, the men agreed, discussing the matter afterwards, wouldn't have been so disastrous if he hadn't then let the sheep through from top field into middle field, where they could get through the hedge without a lot of trouble to the succulent clover in bottom field. Everybody knew that sheep shouldn't be allowed to stuff themselves on clover – everybody except the sheep and Mr Edward, that was – and by the time Harry Cook, the shepherd, found them they'd got in among the clover and had a feast. The result was, they were lying on their backs with their legs in the air, their stomachs blown up like balloons, helpless with bloat.

Of course, Harry knew what to do. He had to pierce the stomachs of the poor distended animals to let the wind from the fermenting clover out, and this he did, knowing just where to put the knife so as to avoid other vital organs. But he had to work quickly – some of the sheep were in a bad way – and whether he was just too late with the treatment or whether he didn't quite get the knife in at the right angle on some of the sheep, several of the flock died and Harry was blamed. And sacked.

This caused trouble among the other farm workers, who professed no knowledge at all about sheep and presented blank, stupefied expressions when asked to tend them. Mr Edward had no choice but to reinstate Harry, even providing a cart to return his few bits of furniture from his mother-in-law's house to the tied cottage he'd been forced to leave only days before. It was a triumph for the men but did nothing to improve Mr Edward's relations with them and they had the feeling that it wouldn't rest there.

They were right. But all was quiet until after the harvest was gathered in and the land was ready for winter plough-ing. It was a cold, dreary day. A steady drizzle was falling and Joe and George and a couple of other men were in the stables, where it was warm and dry, with its own distinc-tive, not unpleasant smells, oiling and checking the harnesses. They were exchanging tales at the expense of other farm workers at other times, tales that lost nothing in the telling and generated a good deal of chuckling and banter between them.

Mr Edward came in. He was not in the best of moods. The bill from that chair mender fellow had just come in and he had taken it straight to Felicity to demand an explanation. He had agreed to the chairs being recovered; going along with her argument that green was too dull for

139

an east-facing room, because although he didn't think it was important, it mollified her a little for having to move out of Brookfield. But the other things were downright extravagant – there was nothing wrong with the polish on the little side table, and the handles on the chest of drawers in the spare room were perfectly adequate. She didn't seem to be able to get it into her head that somehow he'd got to make this bloody farm pay and he wouldn't be able to if she ran up all these unnecessary bills.

It didn't escape him that the men were sitting down although they got to their feet pretty quickly when they saw him approach. All except Joe Stansgate, whose rheumatism wouldn't allow quick movements.

'I don't pay you men to sit around yarning and laughing the day away,' he barked. It was the way he asserted his authority. He hadn't wanted to take on the farm and he almost wished he'd taken more notice when Cooper, his father's estate manager, had taken him round and tried to teach him. But it didn't do to let those fellows think they knew it all, it made them too cocky, so he'd pretended indifference and hadn't listened. And it didn't help that Felicity complained from morning till night about the farmhouse being cold and draughty, dark and poky. He squared his shoulders. 'Askew, the cow shed's filthy. Cook, your work's with sheep, not horses. Stansgate, you were supposed to be making a start on Tringle today, not sitting on your arse in a warm stable. We're already behind with the ploughing.' Tringle, thought to be a corruption of triangle, was a three-cornered field.

'Tringle won't take no harm for another day or two,

140

sir,' Joe said, in his slow, almost drawling voice. 'There ain't no sense getting wet through ploughing on a day like this. The ground'll be that heavy that'll clog everything up.'

'You're soft, man. It could rain for a week. Get Boxer and Beauty harnessed up and get yourself out there. I want that field ploughed ready for winter sowing.'

'I'll do it, if you like, sir,' Shorty the pigman said. 'I can plough as good as the next man and that won't do . . .'

'No, thass my job and I'll do it,' Joe said quickly. 'I'll get up there right away, Gaffer. But I doubt that'll take a bit longer, with the rain making the ground sticky.' He turned to Shorty after Mr Edward had gone. 'Thank ye kindly, Shorty, I know you meant well, but I dursen't let the gaffer think I can't do my share.'

'Well, put this owd sack over your head and shoulders, bor. That'll keep the worst of the rain off.' Shorty looked out through the open door at the sodden landscape and then turned and spat in the sawdust of the stable floor.

'That ain't fit to turn the pore owd hosses out on a day like this, let along the man behind the plough,' he said. 'The Gaffer don't know what he's a-talking about. And he ain't got no thought for us pore sods. No thought at all. The Owd Gaffer wouldn't have treated us men the way he do, I know right well.'

Joe had always enjoyed ploughing and he knew he was good at it. But not in the rain, when the heavy, wet soil stuck to the plough share, and clogged his boots till they were three times the size, and so heavy it was as much as he could do to lift his foot off the ground to scrape the great clods away. Painfully, he tramped up

141

and down the long straight furrows, stopping every now and then to scrape the clods of glutinous mud from his boots, a lonely figure in the bleak, grey landscape behind the two great, patient horses, every step he took increasing the agonising 'screws' in his legs and shoulders. It was a bitterly cold, raw day, but the pain from his limbs made him sweat and it poured off his brow and mingled with the rain to drip off the end of his nose. By the end of the day he was wet to the skin, despite the heavy sack he'd worn over his head and shoulders. As he trudged home up the lane he could hardly put one foot before the other. When he got indoors Daisy made him sit by the fire while she rubbed his joints with liniment. But it was no use. When he tried to get out of bed the next morning after a painful, sleepless night, his body rebelled and he couldn't move.

Joe struggled back to work after three days but his movements were painful and slow. Shorty, Harry Cook, even George, who was not the farm's most conscientious worker, did what they could to hide his infirmities from the Gaffer, taking his tasks on with their own and giving him the lightest work to do. But farm work is never light or easy, especially in the depth of winter, and it wasn't long before Edward Green realised what was going on.

'You're past it, Stansgate,' he said, brutally. 'I can't pay you to hang about while the others do your work. Anyway, I can't trust you any more. Look what happened when I asked you to mend the fence between middle and bottom field. You only half did the job and all the sheep got through. I let it go at the time, but I haven't forgotten.'

Joe's face darkened. 'You can't blame me for that, Gaffer. You didn't give me time to mend it proper,' he said. 'You said lay a few sticks acrost, which I did, thinking I'd go back to it later. But I'd have laid a proper hedge there and then if I'd known you was aiming to put sheep in the field, even if it did take me best part of all day.'

Edward brushed him aside. 'It's all very well to be wise after the event. I lost half my flock through your carelessness.'

'Here, come on, Gaffer...' Harry Cook stepped forward to defend Joe, but his courage failed him when he saw the look in Edward's eye and he contented himself with shuffling his feet and clearing his throat. He'd been sacked once; he didn't want to repeat the experience.

Edward turned to go. 'You can work – if you call it work – till the end of the week, Stansgate. But I can't afford to pay men who can't pull their weight.'

The others were all shocked into silence and gaped at one another. Shorty got his voice back first. 'But who's going to take Joe's place, Gaffer? There ain't another ploughman like him hereabouts.'

Edward looked at him coolly. 'Well, no doubt some of you will learn. Since you've been doing most of his work between you, I don't see the need to employ another man. You can all continue to do a bit extra. Times are hard. We all need to haul in our horns a bit.' He glanced at Joe. 'If you see the doctor and get yourself put right, I might consider having you back seeing as you've worked on the farm all your life,' he said, 'but you'll need to look sharp about it.' He turned to go. 'And don't forget it's a tied

143

cottage you live in, Stansgate. It goes with the job. And while you're there, there's rent to be paid.'

The men were silent after Edward had gone. Joe stood, his head bent and his jaw clamped tight against the tears that grown men never shed. The men, one after another patted him on the shoulder, the best way they knew to show they cared.

Chapter Eight

'See a doctor? How in tarnation can he expect me to see a doctor? Where does he think I can get the money from for doctor's bills?' Joe, huddled in his chair by the fire, seemed to have shrunk in size, whether from pain, disappointment, worry or defeat was difficult to say. It was probably a mixture of all four.

'If you can't work any more, what'll happen about the house, Dad?' Becca asked. She and Jethro, Ellen and George were sitting round the kitchen table, their own differences forgotten in their shared concern, although Becca had been careful to sit as far away from George as she could. 'Thass a tied cottage.'

'We know thass a tied cottage, you don't need to remind us,' Daisy said sharply. She was standing in front of the fire, warming a piece of flannel to put on Joe's swollen knees.

George breathed in on a long, slow sniff. 'I reckon you should sit tight and keep quiet,' he said. 'The Gaffer did say he won't be going to replace you, Joe, I heard him with me own ears, so if you ain't here this place'll only stand empty. As long as the rent's paid . . .'

'And how do you think we're going to manage that?' Daisy snapped, anxiety making her short-tempered with everyone. 'The few coppers I can pick up scrubbing and stone picking won't keep us in vittles, let along put a roof over our heads.' She turned her back to wipe a tear away with the corner of her apron. 'I can't see nothing else for it. We shall hetta go to the Spike.'

'Oh, no, Mum. You can't do that.' Agitated, Ellen picked Dolly up out of her pram and rocked her on her knee.

Daisy glanced at Joe's woe-begone face. With an obvious effort she lifted her shoulders and tried to smile. 'That won't be as bad as all that. There's plenty people ended up in the work'us before now and they do say the one at Colchester ain't half bad.' She looked at Joe again and her eyes once more filled with tears. ' 'Course, they separate the men from the women . . .'

Joe reached out and patted her arm. 'Ain't no call to upset yourself, Daisy, gal. Jest give me a few days in the warm and I shall be as right as ninepence again,' he said. 'I shall be back at work, this time next week, you see if I ain't – the Gaffer said he'd have me back if I got meself fit.' He moved his leg slightly and winced at the pain. 'Your liniment's already done me a power o' good, mate, so let's have no more talk about the Spike. I ain't ready for that yet.'

'You shan't go to the Spike,' Becca said fiercely. 'You shall come and live with Jethro and me afore I see you go there.'

'I ain't going nowhere,' Joe said, shaking his head. 'I'm a-going' back to work next week.'

They all smiled at him and nodded but they all knew he would never work again.

Going home some time later, Becca pushed the pram down the lane and Jethro walked beside her. 'I think I'll jest take a trip over the river and have a word with Dr Squires about your dad. He might be able to give me something for him,' he said thoughtfully. 'He might even come and pay him a visit if I offered to pay.'

Becca sighed deeply. 'I doubt that wouldn't be any good, Jethro. Didn't you see how twisted and swole up Dad's knees and feet were? Poor owd chap, he can't hardly walk. He'll never work again.' She shrugged. 'I s'pose you could say he's been lucky to be kept on at the farm as long as he has, crippled up like he is. And it's all very well for George to say they should sit tight and not think about moving from the house – Mr Edward ain't that generous! I'm sure he only kept Dad on when he couldn't work quite as quick as the rest because he's always been so good with the horses, but he'll put him out on the street as soon as look at him if the rent's not paid.'

Jethro was quiet for some time, walking beside Becca and puffing on his pipe. Presently he said, 'P'raps you're right, Becca. P'raps thass no good me going to see Doctor Squires. P'raps thass Mr Edward I oughta go and see.'

'I don't see what good that'll do. He ain't likely to take much notice of you, is he? Two shillun a week is two shillun and ain't to be sneezed at.'

'Is that what the rent is? Well, it won't do no harm to go and explain the situation, will it?'

147

'I don't reckon that'll do much good, neither,' she said gloomily. 'The crafty owd devil know very well Dad won't work again. If the rent's not paid he'll turn them out afore you can say knife.'

'I shall still go.' Jethro said no more and Becca knew better than to argue further once his mind was made up. But when he returned from his visit to Tenpenny Farm the next day she could see by his face that the interview hadn't gone as he might have hoped.

Yet, three days later when she went to do her weekly bread baking, Becca was amazed at the transformation in her parents. Joe was still practically immobile by the fireside; but he was contentedly puffing away at his pipe, smoking the tea leaves that could no longer hold any colour in the teapot, and Daisy was humming to herself as she got out the big dough crock and set it on the table.

'I've already gathered the faggots and lit them in the oven,' she said happily.

'Goodness me, you must've got up before you went anywhere,' Becca laughed.

'Well, to tell the truth, we were so excited that neither of us slept a wink last night.' Daisy disappeared into the cool larder for the flour and placed it on the table. 'Oh, thass no good,' she sat down, beaming at Becca, 'I shall have to tell you afore we start work, don't I shall burst!' She leaned forward. 'The Gaffer came to see your dad last night. He say we don't have to leave the cottage! He say we can stay here as long as ever we want to!' She sat back in her chair to see the effect of her words on Becca. 'There, what do you think of that?'

'And we ain't got to worry about the rent, neither,' Joe

added, shaking his head. 'I can't hardly believe it. That ain't like the Gaffer. He don't gen'lly give much away.'

'No, he wouldn't give you the drippings off his snout as a rule,' Daisy said with a trace of her old bitterness. 'I don't know what's come over him. But that don't matter. He's said we can stay here as long as we want and not pay any rent, so with what I can earn and the vegetables I can grow, we shall be able to manage nicely after all.'

A shadow passed over Joe's face. 'Thass me what should be providing, not you, Daisy.'

She laid her hand on his shoulder. 'I don't see that signify who does the providing as long as we have a roof over our heads and food in our bellies,' she chided him gently.

Becca looked round the warm kitchen. The kettle was singing on the hob and the carefully ironed linen was hung to air on a line strung across the room, so low that even Daisy, who was not tall, had to duck when she passed underneath it on her way to the larder or dresser. The dresser held all the crockery, the best of which was displayed on the open shelves. None of it had ever matched, and Becca felt a pang of pride mingled with something akin to guilt as she thought of her own willow-pattern china. The settle stood in its place by the wall adjacent to the fire and her father sat as he had always done in his high-backed elbow chair on the opposite side of the hearth. The three chairs stood round the scrubbed table and the two stools that Ellen and Tommy had used stood one each side of the back door. The room with its peeling white-washed walls was exactly the same as she had ever known it, the only change over the years being

149

that when one rag rug had worn out it was replaced by another using different coloured scraps of material. Tears pricked her eyes as she realised just what it meant to her parents to be able to stay here in this shabby little cottage that had been their home ever since they were married some twenty-five years before. She closed her eyes and prayed silently that they would never have to leave it.

'Mind you,' Daisy said, getting up and fetching the flour and salt for the bread-making, 'I don't know what come over Mr Edward that he should offer for us to stay. I shouldn't be surprised if his father had a hand in it, meself. Owd Mr Green's a real gentleman. I saw him talking to one of the gardeners when I went up there yesterday to see about the job in the laundry.'

'Oh, the Gaffer ain't sech a bad 'un,' Joe said. 'He ain't had the experience, thass all.'

'Joe Stansgate, you'd find good in a rotten apple, you would,' Daisy said, exasperated.

Becca said nothing until she got home. Then she put her still-warm loaves to cool before storing them in the crock in her larder and went through to where Jethro was working on a sabre-legged chair that had had both its front legs smashed off halfway down. She stood watching him for several minutes, her hands planted firmly on her hips. She knew better than to disturb him at this point. He had trimmed both the broken legs to an angle of about thirty degrees and planed them smooth; then he had roughly trimmed to shape the two pieces of mahogany he was using for the repair and planed them to the same angle so that they would fit exactly on to the prepared legs. He was at that moment applying Scotch glue and bonding the two joints so tightly that when he had finished shaping the new pieces to the distinctive sabre shape that gave the chairs their name and coloured them to match the old wood, there would be nothing more than a hair crack to show that the legs had ever been repaired.

He applied a last bit of pressure, wiped a tiny bubble of glue away and examined both joints minutely. Then, satisfied, he straightened up. Only then did Becca speak.

'Can we afford it?' she said.

He looked round. 'Oh, hullo, dear, I didn't know you was standing there.' He smiled at her, his face a picture of innocence. 'Can we afford what?'

'To pay the rent on the cottage for Mum and Dad.'

He grinned. 'How did you know?'

'Didn't take much working out. Mr Green ain't exactly one for giving much away. If he told them they could stay there without paying any rent, then somebody else must be paying it for them. You went to see him the other day . . .' She gave an eloquent shrug and spread her hands.

'Well, don't tell your mum and dad, Becca. I wouldn't want them to feel beholden to us.'

A worried frown creased her forehead. 'But are you sure we can afford two shilluns a week? Every week, Jethro? Thass a lot of money. And there's me trying to put a bit by . . .' Her voice trailed off as she saw the reproachful look on his face.

'The money you put by wouldn't give you much pleasure if your mum and dad were in the Spike, would it, Becca?' he said. 'But you ain't got no call to worry. I've got plenty o' work. And I can always make a start a bit earlier in the morning if I need to.'

151

She stood on tiptoe and kissed his cheek. 'You're a good man, Jethro.' It was with a feeling approaching humility that she went back into the house.

He wiped the sweat off his brow with his forearm and turned back to his bench. He picked up the second chair in the set of six. This one wasn't so badly smashed. He began work on it, glad Becca hadn't asked any more questions because what he could never tell her was that finding the two shillings a week was the least of his worries.

He picked up a piece of wood and began planing it as his mind went back over the events at Tenpenny Farm the day he had gone to see Mr Edward Green.

Mr Edward had been out when he called to see him so Jethro had been forced to speak to Felicity. She had insisted on giving him tea in silly little cups that only held a thimbleful and were so thin you could see through them. His great hands, so deft and skilful that they could replace pieces of inlay so small that they could only be picked up on the point of the razor-sharp knife with which he had cut them to shape, were clumsy and ham-fisted in the presence of this green-eyed, cat-like woman whom he knew enjoyed watching his discomfort; silently taunting him because he wouldn't give her what she wanted most.

She'd picked up the silver teapot, leaning over the tray so that her breasts nearly fell out of the low-cut dress that was almost the colour of her eyes. 'More tea, Mr Miller?'

'No, thank you, ma'am.' He'd put his cup carefully on the tray, looking everywhere except to the spot where his eyes were inevitably drawn. 'Would you be knowing' when the Master'll be back? Thass quite urgent that I should see him.'

'I've no idea. I shouldn't think he'll be returning yet.' She'd hitched up her dress ever so slightly so that he couldn't fail to watch as she crossed one delicate ankle over the other. She smiled winningly at him. 'Would you like to wait? I'll be happy to entertain you till he comes. Or is it something I can do for you?'

Bitch! Jethro thought, remembering the scene. Every word she'd spoken had held a double meaning. He recalled how he'd got to his feet, twisting his cap in his hands. 'I don't know as there's anything you can do, ma'am,' he'd said. 'I've come about my father-in-law, Joe Stansgate. He's laid o'one side on account of rheumaticks and ain't likely to work again. Your . . . Mr Edward said he could stop in his cottage as long as the rent was paid. Well, I've jest come to offer to pay it every week, if thass all right by him.'

'That's very noble of you, Mr Miller.' She'd looked up at him, her eyes dancing. 'Would you like me to pass the message on to my husband? I will, if you like, although I dare say he might take a little persuading.'

'I don't see why he should,' Jethro had said honestly. 'As long as the rent's paid every week, I don't see that make any difference where the money come from.'

She'd stood up and smoothed her dress, some silky, satiny kind of material that gleamed and emphasised her big breasts and tiny waist. 'I'll see what I can do, Mr Miller. But you must understand that my husband can sometimes be quite a difficult man to deal with. If he is persuaded, it's me you'll have to thank.' The meaning behind her words had been unmistakable.

153

He had chosen to ignore it. 'I always give the work I do for you my best attention, ma'am, and I assure you I shall continue to do so.' With a brief nod he had left, sweating slightly, anxious that she should pass on his message, but worried at what she might make him pay for the favour.

Now, three days later, it was plain she had done her part. And a cabinet stood in the corner waiting to be delivered to Tenpenny Farm.

He let it stand there a whole week more before he plucked up the courage to deliver it. Then he laid a cloth on the hand cart and with Becca's help lifted the cabinet carefully on to it. Then he pulled the cloth up to cover it completely so there was no danger of it getting scratched and set off for Tenpenny Farm.

Felicity was waiting for him in the drawing room. The dress she was wearing today was worse than the one she'd been wearing the last time he'd seen her. It was pale blue, all loose and silky, with a gold girdle thing round the waist and was far too low in the neck for decency to his mind. He tried to keep his eyes averted, but try as he might they would keep straying to the lacey ruffles that barely concealed her nipples. He didn't know what Mr Edward was thinking of to allow his wife to wear such things. He knew right well he'd never let Becca parade herself like that. Not that she would ever want to.

'You've brought my cabinet back, Mr Miller? Yes, I was expecting you. I can't imagine how it got that awful scratch right across both doors. Yes, I think I'll have it there, between the windows, then if there's a teeny mark left it will never show, will it?' She wrinkled her nose conspiratorially at him.

'You won't find any trace of the scratch, not now I've finished it,' Jethro said stiffly, noticing the huge, cruel-looking diamond ring on her finger. Ah, he thought, so that was how it was done . . . 'I'll go and fetch it.'

He went out to the cart and manhandled the cabinet up the steps and through the front door.

'Oh, can you manage, Mr Miller? I'm afraid my man Job isn't here to help you. My goodness, aren't you strong?' She fussed him along to the drawing room and watched as he put the cabinet in place. 'No, a teeny bit to the left, I think . . . Yes, that's right. Oh, it does look beautiful. You're so clever, Mr Miller.' She laid a daintily manicured hand on his arm. 'You'll stay and have tea? It's all ready on the tray.'

'No, thank you kindly, ma'am. I've more work to be done today, and time is money.'

'Ah, yes. I'll get my husband to send you a cheque, Mr Miller.'

'Then perhaps I might ask you respectfully, ma'am, to add on the cost of the foot stool I made for you, the table I repolished and the lady's chair that was re-covered in pink brocade? I ain't been paid for them yet.' Becca had recovered the chair but Jethro didn't see the need to tell Felicity Green that. He stood stiffly by the door, studiously avoiding looking in her direction lest his eyes should stray to the ruby pendant nestling in her cleavage. 'And now, ma'am, if there's nothing more, I'll be on my way.'

'There is one more thing, Mr Miller.' She dimpled at him. 'You're not in such a terrible hurry, are you? After all,' she wagged her finger, 'I did you a favour only the other day, so you owe me at least a few minutes of your time, don't you?'

'Well, I ain't . . .'

'No, of course you haven't got all day. But I'm sure you've got just a tiny minute to look at the door on my wardrobe. It sticks and I have difficulty in shutting it. This way.'

Without giving him a chance to refuse she swept past him in a cloud of heavy perfume and led the way upstairs to her bedroom. Jethro followed reluctantly. He didn't care for the situation, and it was made worse because there didn't seem to be anybody else about. He glanced uneasily behind him. Whatever would people say if they knew he'd been in Mrs Green's bedroom? Whatever would Becca say?

The bedroom looked out over the newly ploughed fields, wheeling gulls witness to the fact that the horses were still at work at the far end of Tringle. He craned his neck to see if he could recognise the man following the plough. It looked a bit like George.

'Oh, it's all right, Mr Miller. We can't be seen.' She gave a low, gurgly laugh.

He turned a deliberately blank gaze on her. 'That don't signify either way, ma'am,' he said, 'since I've only come to look at a wardrobe door.' He turned to the heavy wardrobe and began opening and closing it. 'The trouble with this is you've got too many clothes crammed in it,' he said after a few minutes. 'Take some of 'em out and you won't have no more trouble with it.' He picked up his bag of tools and went to the bedroom door.

'Do you think you could do something with the mirror, then?'

He turned. Felicity was half lying on the bed, smiling invitingly at him.

156

He took a deep breath. 'If you ask your man – Job, isn't it? – to bring the mirror to my workshop, I'll have a look at it, Mrs Green, but for now I bid you good day.'

'No so fast, Mr Miller.' Like a cat Felicity was off the bed and standing in his way. 'I said I should expect you to pay for the favour I did you, but I didn't expect to have to grovel for it.' Her green eyes were sparkling with fury. She leaned towards him, her lips parted seductively. 'You're trying to tell me that you don't find me attractive, but I know it's not true. You're trying to escape because you can't trust yourself not to take what I'm offering you.' She slid her arms round his neck. 'What you want just as much as I do . . . Jethro.' The last word was whispered into his ear as she began to nibble at his ear lobe.

He tried to free himself but she clung like a limpet, her body pressed hard against his, and he knew she must be aware of the shameful response his own body was making to her advances.

Then, suddenly, she went limp in his arms, her knees buckled and her head fell back. Alarmed, he looked down at her. She didn't appear to have lost any colour, but it was impossible to tell under the thick layer of powder and paint. She must have fainted, there was no other explanation that he could see.

He picked her up and carried her over to the bed and laid her carefully down, at the same time looking round for a bell to summon someone. Anyone. But before he could straighten up her green eyes flew triumphantly open and she renewed her vice-like grip round his neck and pulled him, off-balance as he was, down on top of her. Cursing himself for a fool at being taken in by such

157

a stupid trick, he wrenched her hands away and released himself so that he could stand upright. The pure animal lust that, to his shame, she had managed to arouse in him was gone, replaced by a cold fury that he felt less able to control.

'My God, woman,' he said, his face blazing, 'you may be a titled lady but you behave worse than a bitch on heat. What you need is a damn good thrashing to cool your courage, and I'm buggered if I don't give it to you!'

Before she realised what he was about he had sat down on the bed and dragged her across his knee. The silky thing she was wearing hampered him, but such was his fury that he tore it away as if it was no more than a rag, exposing her petticoat. He tore this away too, but stopped for decency's sake when he came to her drawers. Then, holding her down easily with one hand despite her humiliated struggles, he unfastened his belt with the other and began to thrash her. Six times the belt came down on her backside, protected only by the thin cotton of her drawers, before he threw her away from him and stood up.

'Now, perhaps you'll leave me be . . .' he paused, fastening his belt back round his trousers before adding, with more than a touch of insolence, '. . . ma'am.'

He looked briefly down at her, a crumpled snivelling heap on the bed, and then turned away in disgust, picked up his tool bag and headed for the door, wiping the sweat from his collar as he went.

He didn't get far. His way was barred by Edward, Felicity's husband, who was standing in the doorway watching the scene.

Jethro stopped in his tracks and the two men stared at

each other for a full half minute. Jethro broke the silence first. 'I'm sorry Mr Green,' he said with a lift of his head. 'I don't know how much you saw of what I've jest done, but whatever you saw, I'm sorry. What I ain't sorry about is that I done it, because she may be your wife but, by God, she deserved it. And thass the truth.'

Edward was a tall, slim man, always immaculately dressed, with black hair sleeked back and a neatly trimmed moustache and sideburns. He had obviously been riding and surveyed the scene, white to the lips, tapping his riding crop against his breeches. Without moving his head he glanced over Jethro's shoulder to where Felicity still lay weeping on the bed and then at Jethro himself. 'I'd like you to come to my study, Miller,' he said, his voice expressionless. He glanced once more at Felicity, then turned and led the way.

Jethro followed him, sick with fear and apprehension now that his fury was spent. Now he'd done it. Now he'd really buggered things up. Oh, it didn't matter that he would never have any more work from the Greens, that didn't bother him in the least – in fact, he was glad. He had more than enough without it. He was much more concerned with the fact that he'd let Joe and Daisy down. Through his hot temper they would have to leave their cottage and go to the workhouse. After arranging it all so carefully he'd gone and ruined everything, because Edward Green would never go on accepting rent from the man who'd thrashed his wife.

All this went through his mind as he followed Edward noiselessly down the thick red turkey-carpeted staircase and across the polished hall to the study. It never once occurred to him that he could land in gaol for what he'd done.

The study was not a very big room and the bay window overlooked the yard where hens scratched and clucked among the cow pats left as the cows made their way to and from the byre opposite. It was quite a come-down from Brookfield House for Young Mr Green and his lady wife, Jethro recognised. He could feel almost sorry for him. But not for her, the bitch! He felt his temper rising again at the thought of her.

He looked round the room, apprehensively waiting for Edward to speak. The desk stood opposite the door and was cluttered with papers and bills. The carpet had obviously seen better days and it looked as if this room was a repository for things that weren't wanted elsewhere. There was a large, shabby armchair in the corner, and along one wall were two wooden Essex chairs and a heavy oak chest. On the other stood a glass-fronted bookcase only half full of books and too big for the room. A tray holding two decanters and glasses stood on a table in the bay and it was to this that Edward went.

Jethro watched the other man as he stood with his back to him, pouring himself a shot of Dutch courage. Poor bugger, Jethro couldn't help thinking, you couldn't blame him for drinking with a wife like his. But he wished Edward would say something; the silence was unnerving, especially as the thought had suddenly entered Jethro's mind that men had swung for lesser crimes. God, he thought, as the thought trickled like icy water down his spine, if he'd ruined his life for that bitch he'd never believe in justice again.

160

Edward was a long time at the table. When he'd finished pouring his drink he stood looking out of the window for several minutes before turning back into the room. To Jethro's amazement he was holding two glasses, and he walked over and handed one to Jethro. He gave a twisted smile that held little mirth as he held up his own. 'Here's to the man who's done what I should have done myself. Months – no, years – ago,' he said bitterly. He swallowed his whisky in one gulp and went straight over and poured himself another.

Jethro took a draught of the fiery liquid and savoured it as it slid down his throat. He had never before tasted such good whisky and this, coupled with the words he had just heard, made him wonder if he was taking leave of his senses. He had expected to be called everything under the sun, to be hauled up before the magistrate and even possibly to swing from the end of a rope for the way he treated this man's wife. Instead of that he was being given whisky and congratulated! It was beyond belief.

'It was a wrong thing for me to do, sir. I know it and I'm sorry.' Jethro looked down at the glass in his hand. 'At least, what I mean is, I'm sorry that it had to be done, but I'm not sorry that I did it, if you can understand me, sir, because I'm bound to say she asked for it.'

'I do understand, Miller.' Edward gave his mirthless smile again. 'And I have to tell you that I'd a bloody sight sooner have found you spanking her than riding her.' He compressed his lips. 'I know what's in her mind. It's her way of trying to strike back at me because I haven't given her the lifestyle she expected. It's nothing personal to you,

161

Miller, so don't go imagining she'll pine with unrequited love for you.' He made a dismissive gesture with his hand. 'Anyone would have done, as long as he was big and brawny and totally unlike me. It just so happened that you came along.'

'I never thought anything different, sir,' Jethro said with dignity. 'But if I may say so, the lady's caused me a deal of worry and embarrassment over the past year or so.'

'Well, she won't embarrass you any further.' Edward went to his desk. 'Can you tell me what I owe you for the work she's contrived for you?'

Jethro scratched his head. 'I reckon that must come to near on ten pound,' he said with a frown, 'but I can't give you the exact amount. Not till I ask Becca . . . er, my wife.'

'We'll make it a round ten, then.' Edward sat down at his desk and scribbled a cheque, blotted it carefully and handed it to Jethro. 'You understand, of course, that there will be no further work for you from this house.'

Jethro nodded. 'I understand, sir. But if there's anything you yourself want done, I assure you of my best services.' He drained the last of the whisky and set the glass down on the edge of the desk. 'There's jest one more thing, sir.'

Edward looked up, his eyebrows raised. 'Yes?'

'Thass about the matter of the rent for the Stansgates' cottage . . .'

'As long as it continues to be paid I shan't turn them out. I don't need the cottage for anyone else.' He got up and went to the table by the window.

'Even if it's paid by . . .'

'I don't care who pays it as long as my man receives it every week, Miller.'

Jethro inclined his head slightly. 'Thank you, sir. I'm much obliged to you.'

Edward had his back to him, pouring himself a third whisky. 'Is that all?' he asked.

'Yes, thank you, sir.'

'Very well, you can go.' He half turned, studying the light through the amber liquid. 'I'm sure you'll agree that this afternoon's events are best not spoken of, Miller. Not to *anybody*.'

'My feelings entirely, Mr Green, sir.' Quietly, Jethro left the house.

Edward stood looking out of the window for a long time after Jethro had left. It was not until he had finished his fourth whisky that he turned and went slowly up the stairs to the bedroom where Felicity was lying on the bed clad in a negligee with a lacey scrap of handkerchief soaked in eau-de-Cologne on her forehead.

'Is that you, Edward?' she said in a weak voice as he entered the room.

'Yes. It's me.' He walked over to the window and stood looking out over the fields, the rich brown earth raw and bleak now in the mist rising up from the river.

She sat up. 'Oh, Edward, my dear, thank heaven you came when you did!' She put her hand to her head. 'Oh, that man! What he would have done to me if you hadn't come in, I can't bear to think.' She shuddered. 'He was . . .' she searched for the word '. . . depraved! Absolutely depraved! One hears about such . . . perversions . . . but

163

one never expects . . .' she shuddered again. 'An animal, that's what he is, an animal.' She lowered herself gently back on to the pillows.

Edward smiled grimly to himself. So that was the way she was choosing to play it. Very well. He narrowed his eyes and watched the figure – it could have been George Askew – plodding home across the field with the two plough horses. 'Perhaps you can tell me what he was doing in your bedroom in the first place, my dear? And you in *dishabille*, too,' he said with the merest hint of sarcasm, without turning round.

She sat up again. 'I simply asked him to look at my wardrobe door because it was sticking,' she said self-righteously.

'I could have told you what was wrong with it. I fact I have. Many times. You try to cram too many clothes into it.' He still didn't turn round.

'That's what *he* said. But then – without any provocation from me – he turned on me!' She got off the bed, wincing from the pain in her buttocks, and went over to Edward. She clutched his arm. 'Edward,' she whispered dramatically, 'do you realise he might have raped me if you hadn't returned when you did?' She closed her eyes briefly. 'Thank God you got back in time.' She put her head on his shoulder. He let it rest there but made no reciprocal movement but remained as he had been, gazing out into the gathering dusk.

At last she put her hand up and turned his head so that he was forced to look down at her. 'Job has taken Nanny and Teddy into Colchester in the dog cart and it's Marjorie's afternoon off,' she said softly. 'There's nobody here but you and me, Edward.' She began to caress his neck, allowing the negligee to fall away and expose her white shoulders.

For a moment he held back. She had engineered an empty house in order to seduce Jethro Miller and because that had failed she needed someone else to take his place. Even her own husband would do. His lip curled in something of a sneer. Well, why not? It was not often she invited him to share her bed these days.

Without a word he began to unbutton his riding breeches. When he left her she was crying.

Chapter Nine

Becca was standing at the table cutting bread for tea when Jethro returned from delivering the cabinet to Tenpenny Farm. As he came in she noticed an odd, preoccupied look about him.

'You've been gone a long time,' she said.

'Have I? I didn't notice. How long before tea? I've got a little job to do in the workshop. Shouldn't take more'n half an hour.'

As he went past her she caught a whiff of heavy perfume. So that was what was the matter with him! Her head shot up. 'For Felicity Green, I suppose?' she said acidly. 'No wonder you didn't realise you'd been gone nearly all the afternoon. You've been too busy dancing attendance on that hussy to notice what the time was.'

'Now, Becca, I've told you before, we've been glad to do work for the Greens.' He didn't look at her as he spoke. 'But there won't . . .'

'For *her*, you mean?' Becca interrupted. 'Do you think I don't know what she's up to? Do you think I haven't seen how she makes up to you with her: "Oh, Mr Miller, how strong you are . . . what a clever man you are to mend the jewel box that clumsy little me wrenched the lid off for an excuse to come and see you again." ' She gave a fair imitation of Felicity Green's little girl voice. 'Bah, she makes me sick!' She hacked off another slice of bread and then straightened up. 'And so do you, coming home reeking of her expensive scent and then trying to tell me you haven't been near her.'

'Be reasonable, Becca, and stop waving that bread knife about, do,' Jethro said. 'You know as well as I do that you only hev to get within a mile of that woman for her scent to cling. Thass so strong you could cut it with a knife.'

'Well, you smell to me as if you've been nearer than a mile today. You stink like a . . . like a . . . brothel.' She was nearly beside herself with fury. 'You'll be the talk of Wessingford, Jethro Miller. That is, if you ain't already. And I shall be the laughing stock 'cause I bin deceived not once, but twice. Oh, I can see now what a fool I was. I should never have married you. I wouldn't have done, neither, if I'd known you was a womaniser.'

'Becca! Stop that talk this minute! You know thass not true and I won't hev you speak of me like that!' Jethro's face was black with rage. He stepped forward and caught her by the arm but she shook herself free and turned away so that he shouldn't see the bitter, furious tears in her eyes. He put his hand out again to pull her round but she pushed him away and suddenly he felt a searing pain as the bread knife sliced across his palm.

'Oh, God! My hand!' He sank on to a chair and cradled

167

it in his other hand. In seconds blood was running through his fingers on to the floor.

'Oh, Jethro! I'm sorry, I'm sorry. Oh, dear Lord, what have I done?' Becca dropped to her knees, overcome with remorse, her temper forgotten.

'That wasn't your fault, Becca. I forgot you was still holding the knife, blamed fool that I was.'

'Let me see.'

'No. I dursen't open my hand. Jest bind it up with a towel to staunch the bleeding, then we'll take a look at it presently.'

'P'raps I should fetch Mrs Plackett.'

He gave the ghost of a grin. 'I ain't dead, Becca. I don't need laying out. Thass on'y me hand.'

'I know.' She was too agitated to return his smile. 'But she'll know what to do. Maybe it needs a stitch in it.'

'I don't need her to tell me that. That feels as if it's cut clear through to the bone. Me right hand, too.'

'At least the knife was clean.'

'Yes, thass one good thing.' He rested his head on his left hand for a few minutes, the colour gone from his face. 'Make me a cuppa tea, Becca, there's a dear. And when I've drunk it I'll make my way across the river to Wyford and get Dr Squires to give it the once-over. I think that'll be the best thing to do. I can't afford to neglect me hand. Thass where me living is.'

'I'll come with you. You'll never walk all that way on your own. Thass best part of a mile and a half.' She poured a mug of tea, laced it liberally with sugar and pushed it over to him. 'While you drink that I'll run up to Mum's with Kate. She'll be all right there till we get back.'

'There ain't no need . . .'

'I'll be the best judge of that.' Becca put on her hat and coat and bundled Kate into the pram.

She had never made the journey to her mother's house as fast. There, she dumped Kate with a brief, breathless explanation and started to run back. She remembered passing Dixon's coal cart on the way there. With any luck Mr Dixon would be on his way back to Wyford. She caught up with him and asked him.

'Thass right, dearie.' The old man smiled, his teeth showing yellow in his black face. 'Tide is low now, so I shan't hev no trouble getting acrost.'

'Could you stop by my place and take me and Jethro with you? he's hurt his hand bad and we've got to get to Dr Squires.'

' 'Course I will, dearie. You fetch him out. We'll soon hev him over the water.'

It was a good thing the coal cart had come by. When Becca got back to the cottage Jethro had lost a lot of blood and his face was ashen. 'Come on, dear, Mr Dixon's waiting to take us over to Wyford,' she said, trying not to let him see how worried she was. 'We'll hev you in front of Dr Squires in no time.'

She wrapped the hand in more clean towels and helped Jethro on to the back of the cart with the empty coal sacks and got up beside him. It seemed an age as the old horse plodded down the hill and forded the river through the muddy shingle and then on through the little narrow streets. 'I'll take you right to the doctor's door,' Mr Dixon said over his shoulder. 'Your man don't look in no fit state to walk anywhere.'

169

'Thank you. Oh, thank you. I don't know what I'd have done if you hadn't come by, Mr Dixon.' By this time Becca was supporting Jethro as the cart lurched along.

Dr Squires was a man of few words, added to which he didn't much like being disturbed out of surgery hours. But he moved quickly when he saw the hand and even insisted on giving Jethro a tot of brandy after he'd stitched it up. 'I'm afraid you won't use that hand again in a hurry,' he warned as he bound it with thick bandages. 'Come back and see me in a fortnight. I'll see how it's progressing.'

'A fortnight!' Jethro exploded.

Dr Squires looked at him over the gold rim of his spectacles. 'Yes. I may be able to take the stitches out then. But it'll still have a long way to go before it's better. It's a bad cut. How did you do it? Are you left-handed?'

'It was an accident.'

The doctor nodded. 'Well, take a couple of aspirin for the pain. Have you come far?'

'Wessingford.'

'Hmm, Well, take it steady on the way back. You've lost a lot of blood.' He watched them prepare to leave. 'By the way, how do you earn your living?'

Jethro turned a bleak gaze on him. 'I'm a chair mender. I earn my living with my hands.'

Dr Squires nodded. 'Then go down on your knees and pray I've made a good job of stitching you up,' he said quietly.

It was dark and cold with a grey fog rising over the river as Becca and Jethro left the surgery and made their way back to the ferry. The tide was beginning to rise and Owd Sharpie the ferryman complained bitterly at having to leave his warm fire to put them across to the other side. Jethro tried not to lean too heavily on Becca but the hill seemed interminably long and they had to stop several times for him to gather his strength to continue. But at last they were home and he was settled by the fire with his hand resting on a cushion and a mug of soup beside him. By the time Becca had fetched Kate from her mother's he was dozing, his bad hand cradled in his good one.

Quietly, Becca put Kate to bed and then sat down opposite him, looking at the thick bandage on his right hand. 'This is my fortune,' he'd said, that day on the stile, as he'd spread his big, capable hands out to her, 'my fortune's in my hands.' And now his hand, his right hand, was crippled and it was possible he would never be able to use it properly again. All the plans she had made for helping him to build up a business came crashing down round her ears, but she knew she'd got nobody to blame but herself. It was all her fault, because she had been eaten up with jealousy over that woman. As if Jethro would ever . . .

Now, in a more rational mood, the very thought was ludicrous. A wave of something – she didn't know what – washed over her as she looked at her big, capable, vulnerable husband and she wanted to take him in her arms and smooth away the worry lines that were creasing his forehead even as he slept.

'I married you for better or for worse, Jethro,' she whispered under her breath, 'and it's bin for better up to now. But if things get bad, we'll manage, don't you fret. You're a good man.' Even as the thought came to her her heart swelled again with that overwhelming emotion that

171

she couldn't name. It never occurred to her that it might be love.

But Jethro did fret. He fretted because he couldn't use his hand. He fretted because there was work to do and he couldn't do it. He fretted when the few shillings Becca had saved were gone and she had to leave her work in the house to re-cover chairs in a hurry to find the rent for Mr Green.

'We could manage well enough for ourselves,' she said as she finished in the workshop and filled Jethro's pipe with dried tealeaves before beginning the ironing, 'we've got plenty vegetables in the garden so we shouldn't starve for a week or two. It's the two shillun a week for Mum and Dad's rent that's bothersome. Mr Green won't let us get behind with that. And then there'll be the bill for Dr Squires.' She sighed. 'And there ain't that much more in the workshop that I can turn me hand to, neither. You ain't taught me how to do wood repairs yet.'

Jethro stopped, with a spill halfway to his pipe. 'Wait a minute, Becca. You talking about Mr Green jest reminded me. That day I cut my hand he'd jest paid me a cheque for ten pound! And to think I'd clean forgot about it.'

He got to his feet and went over to his jacket that still bore faint blood stains that Becca couldn't get out and felt in the pocket. 'There! Ten pound! See?' He smacked the side of his head with his good hand. 'How could I have let you work your fingers to the bone, Becca, when there was all that money layin' there?' He put his arm round her. 'I'm sorry, dear. But you don't need to pinch and screw any more. This'll last us for some time.'

'It might have to last us for a long time, Jethro, if your hand don't heal,' she warned.

'That'll heal. Look, I can already move me fingers about. That'll heal, never you fear. And thass surprising what I can do with me left hand. Tomorrow I'm gonna try and see if I can french polish that little table in the workshop.'

'For Mrs Green?' Becca could have bitten her tongue out the minute she'd said it.

'No, Becca, not for Mrs Green. I shan't be doing any more work for Mrs Green.'

'Oh? Why not?'

'Why not? I thought you'd be glad, not asking why not. You were forever complaining about the work I do for her.'

She laid her hand on his arm. 'I shan't never complain again, Jethro. I've learned my lesson. I know I can trust you. I always knew it. And I shouldn't never have said the things I did.' She looked into the fire. 'I reckon I was jest plain jealous.'

He covered her hand with his own. 'I reckon you were, Becca.'

She looked up at him. 'So if you want to do work for her . . .'

'I don't. I'm fed up with all her shilly-shallying ways.' Jethro longed to tell her the full story but he had made a promise to Edward Green that he could never break. 'And thass all there is to it,' he said.

'Very well.' Becca had too much sense to press the point.

Jethro's hand improved slowly. The stitches came out

just before Christmas and he was able to use it to a limited degree, as long as he wore the cotton glove Becca had made him to keep the dirt out, although it irked him that it remained slightly curled and that it ached if he used it for too long at a time.

As for Becca, her heart bled as she watched him struggling to learn to use his left hand, especially when he swore because jobs took twice as long or else bodged work that would normally have given him no trouble at all.

Meanwhile, she continued to do all she could to help him. He taught her to french polish and she did all the upholstery work, as well as the caning and rushwork. But this was only a small part of the business and there wasn't enough of it to keep them, let alone continue to pay the rent on her parents' cottage. Gradually, the ten-pound cheque dwindled.

A further blow came just after Christmas when Becca discovered she was again pregnant. At first she said nothing to Jethro because she knew he would stop her from working in the workshop. But when she fainted for the second time she could no longer hide it from him.

'I'm sure this one'll be a boy,' she said as she dragged herself about, trying to continue as she had before. She smiled. 'At least there's one good thing about it – we're saving on food. I feel that sick I can't eat a morsel.'

'Don't make jokes about it, Becca,' Jethro said, his voice rough with worry. 'You know I can't abide to see you like this.' He held up his maimed hand. 'And me so bloody helpless.'

'You're not helpless, Jethro, your hand is getting

stronger every day, even if you can't work such long hours as you used to. And you don't need to worry about me. I'll be all right once he's born. I was lucky with Kate, but babies don't all carry the same.' She sat back from the chair seat she was caning and brushed her hand across her eyes.

He left the bench where he was laboriously trying to cut tiny pieces of inlay with his left hand and came over to her and stroked her hair. 'You mustn't set your heart so on a boy, Becca,' he said, his face anxious. 'You always call it "he" and it might be another little maid. I wouldn't want you to be disappointed.'

She smiled wearily and bit into an apple – apples, it seemed, were the only things she could eat without being sick. 'He'll be a boy. You'll see. Then you'll be able to finish off your board – JETHRO MILLER & SON – like you've always wanted.'

He made an impatient gesture. 'I don't care whether this one's boy or girl. I jest don't like to see you so poorly, Becca. I'll be glad when it's all over and you can get your health and strength back. I never thought to see you this way. And leave that chair. I dessay I can manage to do that. Go and put your feet up while Kate's asleep.'

'No, I'd rather do this.' She looked up at him with a trace of her old smile. 'At least it takes my mind off feeling sick.'

Becca was brought to bed on the last day of September and her son was born in the early hours of October the first. It was a long and hard birth but despite all the difficulties that had accompanied the pregnancy and his birth

175

little Ashley was a beautiful baby, with a shock of fair hair, neat regular features and large gentle brown eyes. She was delighted to have given Jethro the son he so dearly wanted and she would smile as he bent over the little boy and told him of the things 'You and me'll do together, boy.' She was happy. Jethro's hand was healed as much as it would ever be and he could use it almost as well as he could before. Added to which he had become quite dextrous with his left hand, so that now anything he couldn't manage with his right hand he simply did with the other one. The quality of his work hadn't suffered and Mr Letch of Headgate in Colchester was still happy to bring him the most intricate of his repairs – and, almost as important, to pay him promptly.

To Becca's surprise, her sister Ellen came to see her as she lay propped up in the big bed with the week-old baby at her side. It was the first time Ellen had visited Bradshaw's Cottage.

'Mum said I oughta come and see you, seein's you had sech a hard time,' she said, standing awkwardly at the foot of the bed. 'I must say you don't look too bad.'

'No, I'm all right.' It was true, but Becca knew that if she had felt like death she wouldn't have admitted it to Ellen. 'Well, now you're here, you might as well sit down.' She gestured towards the little rosewood lady's chair that Jethro had discovered in Uncle Fred's shed. Jethro had repaired it and Becca had covered it in some of the green velvet she had saved when she re-covered Felicity Green's furniture. There had also been enough of the material to do the sofa in the living room and two chairs in the front room, but the little lady's chair had been the most tricky and although the intention had been to sell it, Becca was so proud of her efforts that Jethro had said she could keep it. Three months ago, when finances had become really tight, she had been afraid it would have to go after all, but they'd managed to get by without selling it and so it still had pride of place in the bedroom.

Ellen perched herself uncomfortably on the edge of the chair. Becca noticed that her dress was none too clean and had a tear in the sleeve. Her boots were in worse condition than the pair Becca had discarded less than a week ago. She resolved tactfully to pass them to her mother to give to Ellen. It would be less embarrassing. 'Where are the children?' she asked, for something to say.

'I've left them with Mum. She said they'd be all right with her for an hour.'

Mrs Simons, the woman from the village Jethro had called in to look after Becca, put her head round the door. 'Anything you want, Mrs Miller? The kettle's on the boil if you'd like a cuppa tea.'

'Oh, yes, a cuppa tea'd be nice, Mrs Simons. I'm sure my sister could drink one, too.'

Ellen stood up. 'No, I ain't got time for fancy tea parties,' she said, 'I got work to do.'

'Oh, sit down and shut up, do,' Becca said irritably. 'You said Mum was looking after the children. Mrs Simons'll be back in a minute with the tea. You've got time to drink a cup.'

Ellen perched herself back on to the chair, glancing round the room, unable to hide her envy. Becca said nothing but watched her, her face expressionless, until Mrs Simons brought the tea. Ellen accepted a cup and a biscuit, unable to take her eyes off the tray with its lace tray cloth and willow-pattern china.

'Looks like I done you a good turn,' she said with something of a sneer when the woman had left the room. 'If I hadn't married your George you'd never have had a place like this, with your posh furniture and your cups all to match.'

'*My* George is it, now?' Becca said dryly. 'Ain't things going so well between you two these days?'

'I never said that. All I meant was you wouldn't have had a place like this on farm labourer's wages.'

'I wouldn't have had it on a chair mender's wages if Jethro's auntie hadn't left it to him in her will.'

'Fell on your feet, then, didn't you!' Ellen's lip curled. 'Got a bit above yourself, too, if you ask me. A woman in from the village to see after you, indeed. What's wrong with asking Mum, like I do?'

'Jethro said I was to call Mrs Simons in because we reckon Mum's got enough on her plate, what with looking after Dad and working at the Manor and at Tenpenny Farm. She's only got one pair of hands, when all's said and done.' Becca's eyes flashed. She didn't feel inclined to admit to Ellen that it was Mary Simons way of paying Jethro for mending two kitchen chairs her husband had smashed in a drunken rage. It was what Jethro called a 'bodged job', done before his hand was even half healed, and he hadn't wanted to charge her. But Mary had been so delighted with them that she had offered her services at Becca's lying-in.

Becca's voice softened. 'But is that all you've come here for, Ellen?' she said with a trace of sadness. 'To make trouble and carp at me? It's not *my* fault if things ain't right between you and George.'

'Who said things weren't right between us? I never said anything of the sort. All I said was you've fell on your feet. And so you have.'

'I've never denied it. I didn't need you to come here and remind me. But now you're here, ain't you even going to take a look at little Ashley?' Becca picked the baby up from beside her and cradled him in her arms.

Ellen stared at Becca, her cup halfway to her lips. '*Ashley*, did you say? You're never gonna give the child a name like that?'

'And why not? Me and Jethro agreed on it.' Becca was furious with herself for being on the defensive.

Ellen turned up her nose. 'Ashley, indeed. Thass a name for the nobs, I shoulda thought, not for the likes of us.'

'That was Jethro's auntie's maiden name, if you must know,' Becca lifted her chin. 'We thought it would be very 'propriate.'

Ellen wasn't quite sure what the last word meant. 'Well, like I say, I think you're getting above yourself, Becca Stansgate. Pride come before a fall. Remember that.' Her eyes nearly blinded by tears of jealousy, Ellen put down her half-finished cup of tea and stumbled from the room.

Becca laid the baby carefully down beside her again, her face set. It was no use, she and Ellen always seemed to be at loggerheads these days. One day, she supposed, her mother would give up trying to heal the breach.

Ellen collected the three children from her mother's

with a brief: 'Oh, she's all right,' in answer to Daisy's questions about Becca.

'And is the boy Jethro's hand all right now? Do that give him any trouble?'

'I dunno. I never asked.' Ellen hurried off to her own house.

Daisy, busy making damson jam with the last of the fruit picked from the tree at the end of the garden, stopped stirring the thick bubbling liquid on the stove and looked across at Joe. He was sitting as he did all day in the wooden elbow chair that Jethro had fixed on to a low wheeled platform so that Daisy could move him about the house or wheel him outside to sit in the sunshine. 'Suthin's upset milady by the looks of things,' she said, shaking her head.

Joe watched his wife without speaking for several minutes. Then he said, 'Thass time you realised that trying to bring them two girls together after what happened is like trying to mix fire and water, Daisy, my girl.'

She rounded on him. 'But they're sisters! Thass my Christian duty to try and bring 'em together.' She shook her head. 'I can't abide to see them daggers drawn all the time. That ain't right. Our two girls, who sat swinging their legs under our kitchen table, shared what food there was, shared the same bed . . . they should be close, Joe. They shouldn't be always at each other's throats,' she finished sadly. Adding, 'Although that Ellen's a sight worse than Becca these days.'

Joe reached for his pipe in the big pocket Daisy had made and tied on the arm of his chair to hold all the things he might need. 'I know, Daisy. But if they don't want to act friendly all your good intentions on't make it so. The days are gone when they'll do as they're bid. They're grown women.'

Daisy stopped stirring her jam and pulled the pan to one side. She sat down at the table, wiping sticky hands on her apron. 'Where did we go wrong, Joe, boy?' she asked, shaking her head. 'Six childer I've birthed. Three of 'em cold in the churchyard and of the others the two girls can't speak a civil word to each other and the boy's bin gone to sea these two years with never a word to say whether he's alive or dead. That ain't much of a comfort for our old age, is it?'

He leaned forward painfully and patted her hand. 'I've got all the comfort I need between these four walls, Daisy. Every day since the Gaffer came and told me we could stay here 'ithout worriting about the rent, I've thanked the good Lord for his mercy. If I can stay here till I die I shan't ask nothing more. I don't feel I've got the right to, seeing how good God has already bin to me.'

Humbled, Daisy turned her own hand to clasp his and nodded. 'Yes, Joe, you're right, bor. We got a lot to be thankful for.' But the words did nothing to ease the pain in her heart.

Ellen trundled the push cart home with the twins squabbling up one end and Dolly kicking them from the other. It was no good, George would have to do something about the back wheels; one of them was buckled and the other wobbled dangerously. She eyed the push cart with disgust. It could do with a coat of paint, too, it was all scratched and chipped. She didn't even notice how filthy

181

it was inside, nor that the stinking scrap of blanket the children had been sitting on had been replaced by a clean piece cut from one of her mother's threadbare store.

She set the children to play in the corner of the kitchen, giving them a crust of bread and dripping each, while she coaxed some life into the fire and set yesterday's potato stew over it ready for George's tea. She cut herself a thick slice of bread and spread it liberally with pork dripping. She was starving and she knew what that meant. She'd felt hungry when she'd started with Dolly, and with the two that had miscarried. But she hadn't managed to dislodge this brat, drat it, and it was too late now, she was over three months gone. With a sigh she set the flat iron on the stove to heat and fetched the blanket from hers and George's bed to spread on the table, stopping only to take a nip from the gin bottle that she kept hidden under the bed. She picked up a sheet that she had washed for a ha'penny and began to smooth the iron over it. It wasn't a very good colour. Mrs Hardy had said when she took the last lot back that if she didn't get them a better colour she'd have to get someone else to wash her sheets. But it was all very well for Mrs Hardy. She didn't have to carry every drop of water she needed from the pump in the farmyard nearly a quarter of a mile away, did she? You had to be sparing with what you used. She took the sheet over to the open doorway and held it up to the light. Perhaps it wasn't such a bad colour now it had had a good boil in the copper. She'd seen plenty worse. She folded it carefully and placed it in the basket on the table.

Ellen had ironed six sheets by the time George came in. Six sheets. That was threepence – and she'd managed to save tuppence from last week's batch. That was fivepence she'd have to spend when the tally man came round tomorrow. If she gave it to him towards what she owed for the secondhand boots she'd bought for Dolly he might let her have the picture of the dear Queen she so wanted. Oh, not the big one, that was far too expensive, but the little one. It was sixpence and would look handsome over the mantelpiece between the two china cats Mrs Hardy had given her because they were chipped and one of them had lost an ear. She looked round the bare little room. She tried hard to make it homely. She'd made cushion covers just after she and George were married, but there hadn't been any cushions to put in them and they looked silly laid over the seats of the wooden chairs. Anyway, the children kept taking them to make beds for the peg dolls their grandmother had made for them.

She brushed her hair away from her forehead with the back of her hand. What a difference there was between this hovel and Becca's smart little place! And George never doing a hand's turn to make it any better, the lazy sod. Of course, it might look better if the floor was swept. And she'd have to do that herself. She didn't have Mary sodding Simons to run about after *her*! She took the peg rug up and relieved her temper on it outside the back door, then took the besom and swept the baked earth floor. Only slightly mollified, she put the rug down by the hearth again, surprised at the difference it made.

She went across to the corner, where a bench holding a chipped enamel bowl stood under the window, with a bucket half full of water underneath it. A cracked mirror hung on a hook between the window and the door and she peered into it, biting her lip. She never had been very pretty, she knew that, but what looks she had had were gone now, leaving her gaunt and tired-looking. She peered a little closer. She wasn't even very clean. With a sigh she poured a little water into the bowl – not too much because she didn't want to have to make another trip to the pump today – and splashed it over her face, then dragged a comb through her faded fair hair and tied it back with a piece of rag. She felt better after that and had another little nip of gin. By the time George came home she was sitting hunched over the fire reading a dog-eared penny romance. The children had each been given a spoonful of potato stew and a smack – this last for no particular reason, but it helped to relieve her feelings – and put to bed, tucked up on the mattress in the back bedroom, in the corner furthest from the damp wall where the roof still leaked.

She looked up and smiled as George came through the door, his handsome face tanned dark brown except for the white crow's feet round his eyes where they were continually screwed up against the sun.

He didn't return her smile. 'What you lookin' so pleased with yerself over?' he said, slumping down on the chair by the table.

'I'm pleased to see you, George, thass all.' She put the book down and doled him out a good helping of stew, scraping the pan for herself. She could smell the beer on his breath.

She sat down opposite and picked up her spoon. 'Thass Sat'dy, George,' she said hopefully.

'I know thass Sat'dy. What of it?' He began to shovel the stew into his mouth.

'Pay day, George.' She kept her voice light.

'Oh, I see. Is that why you've spruced yerself up? Well, you won't get any more by doin' that. You can't hev what I hevn't got.'

'Didn't you get you pay, then?'

'I got it. But I ewe most of it to Brock, so I called in and paid him.'

'Brock' Badger was the landlord of The Whalebone. Ellen's lip tightened. 'An' I s'pose you thought – as you ewe him so much – you might as well tip what little was left down your throat while you was there?' She pushed her empty plate away. 'But I dessay you'll still want your bread and cheese every day, even if you don't give me no money to buy it? And what about the childer? What am I s'posed to fill their bellies with? Answer me that.' She got up to take the plates over to the bench in the corner and he reached over and pinched her bottom. 'An' you can stop that as soon as you like.' She brushed his hand away.

'Oh, I beg yer pardon, I'm sure. But I thought . . . seein' as you'd smartened yerself up . . . I'm always ready, you know that.'

'Well, you thought wrong. And you're a damn' sight too ready sometimes,' she sniffed.

He eyed her with suspicion. 'You up for another brat?'

She nodded.

'I thought so. I could smell the gin. Ain't it done the trick?'

She shook her head. 'Thass too late now. I'm three months gone.'

185

He pushed back his chair and got up. 'You fall a damn' sight too easy, if you ask me. I've only got to chuck me trousers on the bed and you're up for another one.' He spat in the fire.

'I can't help it, George Askew. If you was to leave me alone . . .'

'Leave you alone? Why should I leave you alone? You're my wife. I'm entitled to take you whenever I like. God knows, I get precious little else out of you – except more mouths to feed,' he added savagely.

She sat down by the fire. 'I do love you, George. I've always loved you. Don't you love me?'

He turned and looked at her, his arm resting on the mantelpiece. 'No,' he said after some time, 'I don't love you. I married you because I didn't have no choice.'

She closed her eyes briefly against his cruel words. 'Thass not what you said before we was wed,' she said quietly. 'You said I was pretty. And cuddly. And you was only too ready to take me under the bushes.'

'And you was only too ready to come with me! You led me on!'

'You didn't take much leadin'!' Suddenly her eyes flashed. 'I reckon I did Becca a good turn, marryin' you, you lazy, lecherous lout!'

He turned away, but not before Ellen had seen a suspicious glistening in his eyes. 'Your sister's worth ten o' you, Ellen Askew. She's the one I wanted, and if I hadn't bin so damned randy and impatient, she's the one I'd have had.' He turned a scathing look on his wife. 'If you hadn't gone and buggered everything up by gettin' yerself in pod!'

Ellen got to her feet, white with fury. 'Well, I went to see your precious Becca today,' she said, thrusting her face into his. 'She's bein' looked after by Mrs Simons from the village, would you believe! Lyin' there like Lady Muck, with her new baby – his name is Ashley, if you please – in her smart little place. She's done a sight better for herself marryin' Jethro Miller than ever she would have done if she'd married a great pillock like you.' She turned away. 'When I think what Jethro Miller's done for her and what you've done for me I could . . . I could . . . spit!'

He shrugged. 'Well, you ain't got nobody to blame but yerself.' He picked up his coat. 'And if all the comfort I get when I come home is you moanin' an' carryin' on, I'm goin' back to The Whalebone where the company's more cheerful.'

He slammed out of the house, leaving Ellen gazing tearfully into the fire.

As he walked down the lane to The Whalebone George thought over Ellen's words. So that Miller fella had even got a woman in to see after Becca at her lying in, had he? Must be doing all right with his chair mending then, even though he'd had that bad hand for months. Funny business, that. He said he cut it on a chisel, but you'd think a craftsman 'ud be a bit more chary of his tools. That was a rare bad cut though, by all accounts. Pity the bugger hadn't cut his throat instead of his hand!

He thought about Becca. Pretty, happy Becca, whom he had loved so much, in spite of her 'Wait till we're married, George' every time he wanted to do more than kiss her. Come to think of it, he respected her, which was more than he could say for Ellen, the slut. He had loved

Becca. Damn it, he *still* loved Becca. And he hated Jethro Miller because he'd married her. And then the bastard had had the gall to knock him down when he wanted to give her a Christmas kiss!

By the time George pushed open the door of The Whalebone his mood was ugly. It was not improved by the sight of Jethro Miller across the smoke-filled bar.

Chapter Ten

Becca had insisted that Jethro should go to The Whalebone and 'wet the baby's head'. 'It's your first son, Jethro. Folks'll think it's odd if you don't go and celebrate,' she'd said with a smile.

'I don't like leaving you on your own,' he'd protested.

'Oh, don't be daft, man. I shan't take no harm jest lying here, now, shall I? And Mrs Simons left everything I need close to hand afore she went home.' She nodded towards the crib in the corner. 'Jest take a look at little Kate afore you go, make sure she's asleep.'

'Sound as a house and snug as a bug in a rug.' He dropped a kiss on Becca's forehead and another on the little downy head lying beside her. 'I shan't be gone long.'

The Whalebone was thick with noise and the smoke that over generations had stained the walls and ceiling a gingery brown. Jethro sidestepped an overworked spittoon on the sawdust-covered floor and made his way over to the settle in the corner where Owd Grimble, the oldest inhabitant, had taken root over the years. A quick game of dominoes with the old man, the obligatory round of drinks for every-body, and then he'd go back home. Jethro was not a man to waste his time, or his money, drinking the evening away.

He had finished the game of dominoes and had just given the order to Brock, the landlord, when George Askew pushed open the door.

'Drinks all round to wet Jethro's new boy's head!' Brock shouted over the general buzz of conversation.

Glasses were immediately pushed forward for refilling; domino and cribbage games were suspended and arguments left unresolved.

'You're jest in time, George, bor,' someone shouted to him. 'The drinks are on Jethro, here.'

George shouldered his way to the bar. 'I don't want none o' his charity,' he muttered. 'I'll buy me own drink.'

'D'ye hear that, all of ye?' Shorty Johnson said with a laugh. 'George Askew'd rather buy his own drink than wet his new nephew's head. Well, I never!' He turned to Joe, whom he pushed up the lane to The Whalebone in his wheeled chair for a game of dominoes every Saturday night. 'I never thought to hear your son-in-law say that, Joe. But you'll hev a drink with the rest of us, on't ye?'

'Indeed I will,' Joe nodded. 'And thank ye kindly, Jethro, bor.' His voice dropped. 'But don't pay no heed to George. He can be a rum'un when he feel like it. Best not take any notice of him.'

'Give George a drink with the rest,' Jethro said quietly to Brock. 'Add it in with all the others.'

'I said I'll buy me own drink.' Jethro hadn't realised that George was at his elbow and turned to find him glowering at him.

Jethro shrugged. 'Jest as you like, bor.' He turned back to the bar.

'I'll hev me usual,' George said to Brock.

'Not tonight, you on't,' Brock said, leaning over the bar and speaking quietly. 'Not unless I see the colour of your money. You won't accept your brother-in-law's charity and I ain't offering you mine. I told you when you was in earlier that you'd got to keep the slate clean for a week. Thass taken you three months to pay off what you ewe me. I gotta live, same as everyone else.'

George flushed to the roots of his hair at being so humiliated in front of his brother-in-law. 'I don't want your bloody charity and I don't want your bloody beer! I'll make me own!' He put his head down and barged his way to the door.

For a moment there was silence, then Brock shouted. 'Well, has everyone got a drink? Then here's to Jethro Miller's firstborn son! And a bonny lad he is, from all accounts.' They all raised their glasses and one wag shouted from the back. 'An' make the most of it, bors, 'cause by the time he git to number ten he on't feel quite so much like celebratin'!'

Outside The Whalebone George kicked a stone into the pond. He didn't want to go home to Ellen's nagging and there was nowhere else he could go for a drink. He turned and began to walk aimlessly along the road, his shoulders hunched and his hands in his pockets, going over again in his mind the scene in the pub. Then suddenly he straightened up and began to walk purposefully along the road.

* * *

191

The house was very quiet. Becca lay contentedly dozing, her little son making gentle baby snuffling noises beside her. Away in the trees an owl hooted and once the old donkey in the pightle hee-hawed with his ugly, whistling moan. In some ways it irked her to lie idle in bed when there was so much to be done, but at the same time she was glad to rest and regain her strength. The fire flickered in the little grate and a coal dropped, sending a shower of sparks up the chimney. Jethro had insisted on lighting a fire and carried the coals up the narrow stairs every morning. Becca gazed thoughtfully across at the red embers and smiled to herself – birth or impending death, bedroom fires were never lit for anything less.

She gave a gentle, contented sigh. She had fallen for Ashley while Jethro's hand was bad. They had often taken comfort from each other in the big bed during the long weeks wondering whether Jethro would ever use his hand again. It had been worse after she knew she was pregnant again, because what with his hand and her feeling so poorly, neither of them had been able to work much. It was a good job she'd managed to put those few shillings by. Even so, goodness knows how they'd have managed without that ten pounds from Mr Green, especially with Mum and Dad's rent to pay as well. She smiled to herself. If Mum had known! But she was convinced that Old Mr Green was responsible for them living rent-free and Becca had never disillusioned her.

Anyway, it didn't matter, things were better now. Jethro could use his hand nearly as good as ever and it hardly pained him at all. And he'd got plenty of work. Only last week Mr Letch sent him six Sheraton chairs to repair and recover. She aimed to be back on her feet herself in time to do that, she knew how Jethro hated upholstery work. And added to their blessings was the little boy lying beside her. Dear Lord, she murmured, what more can I ask?

The baby whimpered and she picked him up and, unbuttoning her nightgown, began to suckle him. In the silence she heard the familiar creak of the wicket gate and a moment later the back door latch. Jethro was back. She turned her head as she heard his step on the stairs. He hadn't been gone long.

'You're soon back . . .' she began, but her voice died as not Jethro, but George came into the bedroom. Embarrassed, she pulled her shawl round her to conceal her exposed breast. 'George! What you doing here?'

'I've come to see my new nephy.' He stood looking down at her, an unfathomable expression on his handsome face.

As discreetly as she could she released the child and held him so that George could see him. The baby made little sucking noises and looked bewildered but didn't cry. 'He's a fine boy,' George said without interest. He turned and sat down on the chair his wife had occupied earlier in the day and sat, his shoulders hunched, staring at the floor.

'What's the matter, George?'

He scratched his head and gave a great sigh. 'I've made a right bugger-up of things, Becca, ain't I?' he said, without looking at her.

'What do you mean?'

'Well, you and me was all set to marry . . .'

'George! Thass all in the past.'

'Not for me, that ain't. Thass no good, Becca. I still wish I'd had you 'stead of Ellen. She's a right tartar and thass a fact.'

'You ain't all that good to her, by all accounts.'

'She trapped me into marryin' her.'

'She never got in the family way by herself, George, did she?'

He shrugged. 'A quick tumble . . .'

She made an impatient gesture. 'George, men who are about to marry don't hev quick tumbles with their future sister-in-laws!'

'I've paid for it.'

'And you'll go on paying for it. You've made your bed. You've gotta lie on it.'

'Don't you ever hev no regrets, Becca?' He looked at her for the first time and she saw that his eyes were wet.

She sighed. 'Thass no good having regrets, is it, George?'

'I still love you, Becca.' The tears spilled down his cheeks.

'Oh, George. Thass no good. Ellen's your wife and Jethro's my husband.'

'I could kill him for marryin' you,' he said viciously.

'Oh, I see.' Becca's voice was dry. 'You didn't want me but didn't want anybody else to have me, either. You'd rather I stayed a dry-as-dust old spinster, hankering after you for the rest of my life.'

'I made a fool of meself with Ellen, but that wasn't because I didn't want you, Becca,' he insisted.

'No. Well, we won't go into that again.' She laid the baby down beside her and wagged a finger at him. 'Listen

194

to me, George Askew. If you've come here seeking some kind of comfort or sympathy you've come to the wrong place. My advice to you is to forget the past and make the best of the present. Ellen loves you – oh, you might not think it, and if you don't mend your ways you'll kill that love – but she loved you all right when she wed you or she wouldn't have done what she did. If you was to show her a little affection you two could make a go of things. But not while you keep feeling sorry for yourself, you great soft pudden.'

'Don't you still love me? A bit?'

She hesitated for a long time, then shook her head. 'Not like I did, George. You broke my heart when you married my sister and it took me a rare long time to get over it.' She frowned and bit her lip, choosing her words carefully. 'But I'd still be quite fond of you if you was to stop all this nonsense about hankering after me. Thass dangerous talk and don't do anybody any good.'

George digested this, then thrust his head forward belligerently. 'Do you love him? Jethro Miller? You married him in a mighty hurry.'

'That suited us to get wed in a hurry. He needed a wife and I . . . well, that suited me, too.'

'But do you love him? Thass what I asked.'

She thought for a minute. 'Jethro's a good man. He's a good husband to me and I try to be a good wife to him. We rub along all right together.' She hesitated. 'As to loving him, I don't know whether I do or I don't. I ain't even sure I know what love is any more. But I wouldn't want to see him come to any harm and I shall be content to look after him and bear his children.' She looked up.

'And whether I love him or not, he's my husband and I shall be faithful to him till the day I die. Has that answered your question?'

He got up from the chair. 'I reckon so.'

'Then look to your own marriage and stop trying to spoil mine. I made the best of a bad job and so must you.'

'I'd have bin a different man if I'd married you, Becca. I'd have worked . . . The roof wouldn't leak still if you'd bin living under it with me . . .'

'Then it'd do you more credit if you was to go home and mend it, 'stead of coming whining to me.' She waved him away. 'Oh, go away, George. I'm tired. I've had enough listening to you. And Jethro'll be back in a few minutes. He won't be very pleased to find you up in my bedroom.'

'I ain't laid a finger on you!'

'And you'd better not, neither.'

He shuffled to the door, then turned back and dropped a kiss on her forehead. 'Thass for owd times' sake, Becca.'

She smiled and reached up and patted his hand. 'Remember what I said, George. Make the best of what you've got. If you treat Ellen right she'll be a good wife to you. I reckon she's as disappointed in your marriage as you are. After all, you got yourselves into the mess so it's up to you both to help each other out of it.'

'And what about you, Becca?'

'Don't worry about me. I got a good husband and two bonny childer. I don't ask for more.' She looked down at little Ashley, sleeping contentedly beside her in spite of his supper being interrupted, and a wave of contentment washed over her as she realised the complete truth of her words.

George left, determined to take Becca's advice, for her sake if for no other reason. He walked back along the road full of good intentions, listing in his mind all the things he would do to make life better for Ellen. First he would mend the thatch, then he would put new wheels on the push cart. Ellen would need that if there was to be another baby. It was a good thing she'd got that push cart, she'd never have managed without it. It had been good of Jethro Miller to make it, too, he couldn't have made such a good job of making one himself.

His magnanimous mood left him. Bloody Jethro Miller! Why should he have the best of everything? He was a good tradesman, one of the best, everyone said so; his old aunt had left him that comfortable little cottage; and he had Becca. There was no justice. The bugger had humiliated him in The Whalebone tonight, too. George spat on to the road. He hated bloody Jethro bloody Miller. All his pent-up frustrations and disappointments focused on Jethro Miller and as if his hatred had conjured him up out of the darkness the man himself appeared in the moonlight, coming along the road towards him.

George slid silently into the ditch, waited until Jethro had passed, whistling, then leapt out and jumped on his back, knocking him to the ground. Defenceless in his surprise, Jethro could do nothing but try to protect his head with his arms and roll over and over as George rained furious blows on him and kicked him with hobnailed boots. Then, seizing his opportunity he shot out his hand and grabbed George's foot as it was poised to kick him in the ribs again. George overbalanced and came crashing to the ground and the next minute Jethro was sitting astride him, panting, with blood streaming from his nose and a deep cut on his forehead.

'George Askew!' Jethro recognised his brother-in-law for the first time. 'What in tarnation's got into you, you blamed fool? You mighta killed me!'

'I thought you was somebody else,' George mumbled, suddenly ashamed at his uncontrolled burst of fury.

'Well, God help whoever you thought it was, thass all I can say. If you go about doing that to people you'll find yourself on the end of a rope afore you're finished. Are you drunk?'

'You know damn' well I ain't drunk.'

'Well, come on then, back to The Whalebone with me and I'll buy you a drink.' He got to his feet and held out his hand to help George up.

'I don't want . . .' George's temper began to rise again. Then his conversation with Becca came back to him and he knew it was up to him to check his impetuosity and make an effort. 'All right, bor. I'll come and wet your baby's head.'

Jethro helped him to his feet and the two men solemnly shook hands. 'You can't go in looking like that, bor.' George peered into Jethro's face by the light of the moon. 'Folks'll think you've been in a fight.'

Jethro put his hand to his brow and felt the sticky blood. 'So they will. I'll have to clean meself up in the pond afore I go in.' He nodded at George. 'You'll have to wipe your coat, too. Thass covered in blood.'

They went to the pond and cleaned each other up as best they could. Then they went into The Whalebone. It was very late when they left. They had their arms round each other and were pleasantly drunk.

Becca had never seen Jethro drunk before and deemed it prudent not to mention the fact that George had paid her a visit, especially when her husband stood swaying at the foot of her bed telling her some rambling tale about George washing him in the pond when he gashed his head on the doorpost.

As for Ellen, she was equally puzzled by George's behaviour. He crawled into bed beside her, swearing that he would be a better husband to her in the future. Tomorrow he would mend the thatch; tomorrow he would fix the push cart; tomorrow he would fetch water from the pump before he went to do the milking. Tomorrow. Ellen had heard tales of what he would do tomorrow before but as he took her in his arms and began to fumble under her nightgown her main concern was for tonight. She just hoped that the amount of beer he had consumed wouldn't affect his prowess.

Ashley was a contented baby. He rarely cried and would lie quietly in his cradle or pram playing with his fingers or watching the little woolly ball Becca had made and hung nearby. But he grew apace and Becca was glad he was a placid child because she liked to spend as much time as she could helping Jethro. Later, she was to wonder if she had spent too much time helping Jethro and that was why she hadn't noticed. Hadn't realised that Ashley was not quite like other children.

But Daisy noticed. And sometimes as she nursed her latest grandchild she would look at him and wonder if perhaps he was a little slow to grasp the finger she held out for him or to take the hard crust she had baked to help his teeth through. But she confided her anxiety to no one, not even Joe, and when, later, Ellen's new baby, Rosie, seemed more alert and active at six months than Ashley was at a year she tried to tell herself that some children came on quicker than others. In any case, he was a happy, placid child. Always ready with a smile, he loved nothing better than to sit on her lap and be rocked while she sang him nursery rhymes. Perhaps it was because he was so docile and affectionate that she worried over him so much and sometimes felt she loved him best of all her grandchildren. In any case, Becca and Jethro had such plans for their son, she didn't want to worry them with her fears.

But just before Christmas, when Ashley was a little over a year old, something happened that drove all other fears and worries from everybody's mind.

It was bread-baking day. The bread was cooling on big wire trays on the kitchen table and Becca had taken Kate to gather holly from the hedgerow across the field. Ash was sitting on his grandfather's knee by the fire cuddling Nip, a knitted dog with only one ear that accompanied him everywhere.

Ellen arrived to fetch her loaves, the three older children trailing behind her, and Rosie in the push cart that George had not only mended but also given a coat of the brown paint that had been left over when the stables were painted. She had long since given up coming to bake her own bread, saying it always seemed to turn out heavy, so Becca and Daisy baked enough between them to keep her supplied.

'I see Becca's over on the field,' she said as she pushed

open the door. 'She's late going home, else I'm early today.' It was Ellen who tried to avoid Becca these days, Daisy noticed.

'I think you must be a bit early. She's jest taken Kate to pick some holly ready for Christmas. There's a lot of berries in the hedgerow this year by the looks of it.' Daisy automatically went to pick Rosie out of the push cart and nurse her.

'Sign of a hard winter,' Joe remarked. 'The Lord in his mercy always provides food for the birds. I always reckon it'll be a hard winter when there's a lot of berries and I ain't bin proved wrong yet.'

Ellen went back to the door. 'Who's that with Becca, then?' Ellen asked. 'I can see somebody else there, 'sides little Kate.'

'Where? There wasn't nobody with her a minute ago.' Daisy came and looked over her shoulder. 'Why, yes, so there is. Can you see who it is, Joe?' She stood aside to give Joe a view.

He lifted his head from talking to Ash. 'Nobody I know.' He turned back to the child.

'Well, we shall know soon enough. They'll be here in a minute.' Daisy turned back inside and pulled the kettle forward to make a pot of tea, crooning to Rosie as she did so.

But Ellen still watched, frowning. She didn't recognise the girl with Becca but she noticed that every now and then they stopped and waited for a few minutes before continuing. Suddenly, Kate broke away and came running ahead.

'Mum says can you come and help, Aunt Ellen?' she shouted as soon as she was within earshot. 'And quick.'

Too puzzled to argue, Ellen hurried up the garden path, through the gate and across the field towards the two women. As she got nearer she could see that the girl, whoever she was, was heavily pregnant. Daft bitch, Ellen thought unsympathetically, fancy going for a walk so near her time. If she ain't careful she'll birth in the ditch.

'Quick, Ellen, help me get her into the house,' Becca called. 'Her baby's nearly here.' She had her arm round the girl, supporting her. She was a tall girl but thin as a wraith and clearly half-starved. Her clothes, which were made of good stuff, were dirty and ragged and her boots were tied on to her feet with rag. She looked half frozen with cold.

'Well, what's she doing out in the middle of a field then?' Ellen went to the other side and took the girl's arm, supporting her or she would have fallen as another spasm of pain washed over her. 'Who is she, for goodness sake? What's she doing here? You can't expect Mum . . .'

'Shut up and help.' Becca bent towards the girl. 'Come on now, only another few steps . . .'

'I . . . can't . . . go any further.' The girl's voice was weak but even those few words shocked Ellen with the realisation that this was no country girl. Her speech was precise and clear with no drawn-out Essex vowels.

'You must.' Becca's voice was sharp with anxiety. 'Come on. We'll help you.'

Between them Becca and Ellen half dragged, half carried the girl over the last yards to the house. 'Can we get her upstairs?' Becca said breathlessly.

'What, that mawther? She's not going up my stairs!' Daisy said, horrified. 'Who do you think I am? I'm not harbouring any old trollop in my house. Put her in the wash house. Let her birth there. I won't turn her away but I'm not . . .'

'Mum!' Becca said urgently. 'This is no trollop. This is Tommy's wife. Now will you help me get her upstairs.'

'Tommy's wife? My boy Tommy?' Daisy's face lit up. Then her expression hardened as she shifted Rosie from one arm to the other and eyed the girl in disbelief. 'Never. I don't believe that, and neither you nor Father Peter'll make me. If she's Tommy's wife, what was she doing in the middle of the field? And where's the boy? I never heard such a cock and bull yarn.' She sniffed. 'But whoever she is, thass a sure thing she can't go no further. She'll hev to birth in the wash 'us. Never let it be said that I turned away a poor creature needing help.'

'Please . . . it's true. I'm Jenny Stansgate. Tommy's my husband. It's his child.' The girl sank to her knees, clutching Becca's skirts, and bit her knuckles to prevent herself crying out with pain. 'Look. Here.' She dragged a scrap of paper out of her pocket and thrust it into Daisy's hand, then keeled over unconscious. It was as if she had willed herself not to give in until she had achieved her purpose.

Daisy frowned at the document in her hand. 'Thass marriage lines, ain't it?' she said handing it to Becca to read for her.

'Thomas Joseph Stansgate and Jane Elizabeth Rowlands,' Becca ready slowly. 'Yes, they were married on July the second, 1894, thass this year, in Barking. Look, she signed her name and Tommy marked his cross.'

'He never was no scholar,' Daisy said inconsequentially.

The girl screamed and arched her back in agony. Becca bent to hold her.

'We'll never get her up the stairs. Not in the state she's in,' Ellen said, looking down at her.

'No, we shan't, an' thass a fact.' Daisy, still holding little Rosie, gave her back to Ellen. She pulled the girl's clothes aside. 'We ain't got many minutes, by the looks of her. Quick, now. You go and fetch blankets and the feather bed off your old bed, Becca, and bring them down into the parlour. We'll hev to get her in there. Look slippy or we shall be too late. Put the baby down and you go and help her, Ellen. I'll set a pan of water to boil.'

'Should I fetch Mrs Plackett?' Ellen asked.

Daisy pursed her lips. 'No, we'll manage on our own. This is a private fam'ly matter.'

In fact the birth took longer than they expected. In the end Ellen took all the children home with her, and Becca and Daisy stayed by the girl's side as she lay alternately wracked and incoherent with pain but with moments of exhausted lucidity in which the two women endeavoured to piece together her story, and Daisy anxiously gleaned what news there was of her lost son.

It was not until the early hours of the morning that the child was born, in an explosion of pain that took the last ounce of strength from its mother.

'You have a son,' Becca leaned over the girl and held the child for her to see. 'He's a fine boy.'

The girl's eyelids fluttered open and she gave the ghost of a smile. 'Thank God it's over. Will you take him, Becca?'

Her eyes were moist. This was no time for pretence.

The girl was dying and she knew it. 'Yes, Jenny, as God's my witness I'll take him and bring him up as my own.'

'Thank you. I shall rest easy now.' She closed her eyes and Becca could see her slipping away. She put the baby gently into the crook of her arm and Jenny's eyes opened again. 'Call him Timothy,' she whispered. 'Timothy James. Tell Tommy I . . .' Her eyes closed and she never spoke again.

Two days later Jane Elizabeth Stansgate was buried in a shady corner of the churchyard. It was not a pauper's funeral where the coffin was loose-bottomed so the body could be slid to rest and the coffin be used again; Jethro made it from good seasoned elm. While he worked Becca nursed the baby and told him the tale which they had managed to glean from the child's dying mother.

'It seems Jenny was the daughter of a parson somewhere in Kent. Tommy had got a gardener's job there to earn hisself a bit o' money between ships. Well, they fell in love – young Tommy always was a fine-looking boy and I reckon she was a pretty girl, once – and wanted to get married. Her father wasn't heving any and said she wasn't to have any more to do with him but by that time it was too late, she was expecting his child.' Becca's lip twisted. 'Her father might hev been a parson but he didn't show much Christian love. He turned her out without a penny.'

'Poor gal,' Jethro said, shaking his head. 'I expect the father couldn't face the shame. He thought more of himself than of his daughter, thass for sure. Was she the only child?'

'No, I believe she had an older brother. Yes, she did,

because she said he threatened to kill Tommy if he got his hands on him. Thass why Tommy had to find a boat quick and go back to sea . . .'

Jethro looked up. 'He didn't marry her, then?'

'Oh, yes, he did. She went to him and told him what had happened and they walked for miles till they found a parson willing to marry them. Then the day after they were married he took a ship to China. She knew he would be away for two years but she was anxious that he should go because of what her brother had said.'

'And what about her?'

'Well, he'd left her some money and found her a room and he said he'd send her more when he could. But he never did.'

'Did he tell her to come to Wessingford?'

'No, but she'd heard him speak of it once or twice and guessed that was where he'd come from.' Becca frowned. 'From what I can make out he didn't hev much good to say about the place. But when she couldn't pay the rent on the room and got turned out she hadn't got anywhere else to go so she decided to walk here – she knew it was near Colchester so she only had to ask and she got put in the right direction. She'd been on the road for nigh on a month, sleeping in barns and picking up food where she could.' Becca looked up, her eyes wet with tears. 'She said she was desperate to get here because she didn't want Tommy's baby born in a work'us. Oh, Jethro, to think that my brother's wife should come to that! What must Tommy have been thinking of?'

He sighed. 'At least he married the girl. I reckon her father is more to blame.' He worked thoughtfully for several minutes, then rested his elbows on the bench. 'No, Becca, whatever the shame that might bring upon the family I don't believe I could turn a child of mine outa house and home. I should never forgive meself for such an act. How that man can stand up in the pulpit every Sunday and preach the Gospel with his own daughter lying cold in her grave through his unforgiving, I can't think!'

'He doesn't know she's dead.'

'Nor care neither, that seem to me.' He finished planing the wood and carefully fitted the coffin together.

'I said we'd bring Timothy up as our own, Jethro. There was no time to ask you . . .'

'You did right, Becca. He shall be as much a child of ours as any of our own.' He came over and touched the baby's cheek. 'He'll be a little mate for Ash to play with. Two sons we'll hev now.'

Becca smiled. 'So you can put JETHRO MILLER AND SONS instead of AND SON on your board.'

He scratched his head and grinned. 'Better wait till they both get a little bigger, don't you think?'

Chapter Eleven

There was very little speculation in the village over Timothy's appearance. It wasn't even associated with the early morning funeral in the windswept churchyard, attended only by Jethro and George, who brought the coffin on Jethro's cart and carried it through the church-yard between them to where the vicar and his sexton waited. Not that there was anything unusual about this; funerals were an everyday sight and Wessingford women rarely attended; it was not the custom. It seemed that knowing that Becca herself had not been pregnant, the villagers assumed that the child had been born to Ellen and that the Millers had taken him to bring up as their own out of charity. Becca let them believe what they chose. If nothing else it saved her brother Tommy from being shown up in a bad light and it did no harm to Ellen, isolated in her cottage at the end of the lane.

In spite of the unhappy circumstances of his birth, Tim was a contented baby and thrived. As he grew old enough to crawl about the floor he and Ash were constant companions, chasing each other between the table legs and squabbling amiably over the building bricks Jethro had originally made for Kate. But it soon became obvious that it was Tim that took the lead in all their play, even though he was over a year younger.

'He's as bright as a button, young Tim,' Jethro said as he watched them together. 'Look how he's trying to pull hisself up agin the leg of the chair already. Come on, Ash, bor, don't let your brother get the better of ye.' He ruffled Ash's fair hair affectionately.

Becca frowned, watching the two boys: Ash pale and thin, his fair hair curling over his forehead, his wide blue eyes holding a puzzled, faintly uncomprehending look; Tim by contrast a well-built, muscular child with quick, intelligent brown eyes and thick dark hair that was, as Daisy put it: 'straight as a pound o' candles'.

A finger of fear, little more than half-formed, was beginning to probe at her mind. Ash was indeed very slow. He made no attempt to walk or talk or even to feed himself, whilst Tim roared for the spoon and shovelled his groats in the general direction of his mouth and shouted words that Becca, if no one else, understood. But she said nothing to Jethro, concentrating instead on thoughts of the new baby that would be born in the autumn, near Ash's third birthday. By that time she was sure he would be walking and talking and all would be well, her worries unfounded, their family complete.

The child, a girl, was stillborn and two years later another little girl lived only two days. By this time it was quite obvious that Ash, staggering around on spindly legs, with his puzzled wide blue eyes, was not like other children. He was a loving and gentle boy and took great pleasure in watching the birds and wild creatures and spent hours talking to the old donkey in the pightle beside the house, but he was slow to grasp even the simplest of ideas and what he learned one day he had forgotten by the next.

Daisy came to see Becca, lying-in after the second confinement.

'I don't know what's wrong with me,' Becca said bleakly, her face to the wall, her tears spent. 'Why can't I hev babies like Ellen? Look at the pigsty they live in, yet she hev babies like shelling pears, and they all seem to thrive – well, most of 'em anyway.'

'Thass jest the way of it, Becca, my girl. Thass not for us to question the way of the Lord,' Daisy said, in a clumsy attempt at comfort. 'At least you've got three, and they're all healthy. Well . . .'

'Yes, you might well say "well" . . . seeing as I never bore Tim and Ash is . . .' She bit her lip and sniffed. 'Ash is . . .'

'Yes, I'll grant you, Ash is a bit on the slow side,' Daisy finished for her.

Becca shook her head. 'He's more than that. He's . . .'

'He's a bit simple, thass all.' Daisy tried to gloss over the fear that had lived with her since Ash was a tiny baby. She had realised long before his parents that Ash was not a normal child. 'But look how young Tim watch over him. He'll see Ash don't come to no harm.' Her eyes softened as she spoke of Tim. She was convinced that he looked exactly like Tommy, his father. The rest of the family said nothing to contradict her, happy that she should think that way if it gave her comfort even though they considered it nothing more than wishful thinking on her part. 'Anyway,' she went on briskly, 'I dessay he'll grow out of it.' Daisy spoke with too much conviction for her words to ring true.

Becca shook her head wearily. 'No, Mum, Ash won't never be no different, you know that as well as I do. And I shan't never hev another baby. Not one that'll thrive, any road.' She closed her eyes and a tear trickled down on to the pillow.

Daisy got up to go. 'Well, then, you must jest be thankful for them you hev got,' she said with the stoic acceptance of her breed. 'At least you ain't been left childless altogether. You've still got a lot to be thankful for.'

After her mother had gone Becca lay looking up at the ceiling. Her mother was right, of course, she should be thankful for the three children round her table, but to her mind there was a reason for everything and she couldn't help feeling that in Ash's inadequacies and her own inability to bear another living child she was being punished by God for some sin she had committed. But she didn't know what the sin was. She went to church on Sundays, helped arrange the flowers at Easter, said her prayers every night. 'Be sure your sins will find you out' was one of the vicar's favourite texts. But what sin? She tried to live a good, Christian life and she was faithful to Jethro, just as she had promised in the marriage service. She chewed her lip. She had made a lot of promises that day; promises she shouldn't have done, because she didn't know whether she would be able to keep them. What must God have thought of her, standing before him and promising to love, honour and obey a man she hardly knew? Yet things had turned out all right. She had been married to Jethro for close on eight years now and there had been hardly a cross word between them – barring the time she had slashed his hand with the bread knife. She rolled her head from side to side, the tears flowing. She didn't know why she should be so punished, she could only think that God was being cruel to her for something she didn't know she'd done.

'Why, Becca, don't take on like that, my lovey.' She hadn't heard Jethro come tiptoeing up the stairs. He sat down beside her and smoothed the hair away from her brow. 'You mustn't grieve so for the little maid. I've made a little white coffin for her and lined it with rabbit skin to keep her warm. She look right cosy, lying there. Would you like to see her?'

Becca shook her head. 'No, I couldn't bear it. Oh, why does it happen, Jethro? What hev I done that God should punish my wickedness in such a cruel way? One baby I could understand, every woman hev stillbirths from time to time – even Ellen. But *twice* . . . And this one was sech a pretty little thing.' She turned her head and looked up at him. 'Perhaps we shouldn't hev married the way we did, Jethro.'

He frowned. 'What do you mean?'

'Well, we both made promises before God . . . you didn't know me and I didn't know you . . . perhaps we shouldn't hev promised to love and honour when we didn't know if we'd be able to.'

Jethro picked up her hand and gave it a little shake. 'I never heard sech rubbish in all me born days,' he said

212

sharply, 'so stop making yourself ill with silly thoughts like that. The promises we made we've both kept. You've looked after me and I've done my best to see you hevn't come to any harm.' His voice dropped. 'I can't speak for you, but if I didn't love you when I married you, Becca, thass growed within me as the years hev passed and I can truly say I love you now.' He blushed at such unaccustomed baring of his heart. 'I like to think you ain't entirely without feeling for me neither, Becca,' he added quietly.

She put her free hand over his. 'No, Jethro, I ain't. You're a good man, a good husband to me and a good father to my children.' More than that she couldn't bring herself to say.

He bent over and kissed her. 'Then let me hear no more nonsense about losing the babies through wickedness. Don't you think the little mites are safe in the arms of Jesus now?'

She nodded. 'Thass the only thing I take comfort in.'

'Then take comfort in it and don't worrit yourself any more.' He smiled at her. 'You're only twenty-eight, Becca, there's plenty time. You'll hev more children, you'll see.'

'But will they live?'

'That'll be as the good Lord wills.'

After Jethro had gone downstairs Becca lay looking at the wall. She didn't honestly know whether her feelings for her husband were love or not. She had never had for him the quickened heartbeat, the surge of emotion, that George Askew had so often roused in her; feelings that were as dead as yesterday's mutton now. If George roused anything in her these days it was irritation. But what she felt for Jethro was unexciting – steady, warm affection and concern for his well-being. With a sudden jolt she realised that she couldn't imagine life without Jethro now; it would be like having her right arm cut off. Perhaps that was what real love was.

After a few days Becca was up and about again, performing her household tasks automatically but without enthusiasm, caught in the grip of a depression that coloured the whole of her life grey. Jethro watched and worried over her, and one day when he arrived back from a visit to Mr Letch to fetch a Sheraton sideboard to be re-polished, he put a carefully wrapped package down in front of her.

'What is it?' She looked at him with dull eyes.

'Open it and you'll see. I think you'll like it. You like pretty things, don't you?'

She unwrapped the layers of paper and found the lid of a china fish paste jar with a picture of Pegwell Bay painted on it. 'Thass pretty,' she said, holding it up to the light. 'Where did you get it?'

'I saw it in Mr Letch's window and thought you'd like it. People collect them, you know. They call them pot lids and they hang them on the wall. I'll turn you up a wooden frame to put it in if you like. Then you can hang it up over there.' He nodded to a space by the window.

'No, I think it would look better opposite the window, Jethro, then it would ketch the light.' She put it against the opposite wall. 'There.'

'You oughta come with me sometimes and look for another one to go with it. Mr Letch hev some pretty china in his emporium.' Jethro was watching her, anxious to encourage her to take an interest in something new.

'Yes. Yes, I might come and take a look one day.'

'You can come in with me when I take the sideboard back.'

'But what about the children?'

'I've bin thinking, Becca. Why don't we keep young Polly Jakins on? She's near fourteen and she's been good with the littl'uns while you've been lying abed. I know her mother'd be glad for us to keep her, 'specially as we'd on'y need her in the day, so she could go home to sleep. Widder Jakins don't like being alone at night. What do you say?' He looked at her, his bushy eyebrows raised eagerly.

She frowned. 'Can we afford it, Jethro?'

'I reckon we can afford a few coppers and her keep and thass all she'll want. I've already spoke to her mother.'

'Oh, Jethro, you shouldn't. Not without you asked me,' Becca said sharply.

He shrugged. 'I didn't want no argy-bargy, since I'd already made me mind up.'

'Then why bother to ask me, if I ain't to hev any say in what goes on in me own house?' She began to fold the paper the pot lid had been wrapped in, her disapproval showing in every movement.

Jethro laid his hand over hers. 'I shall be glad of you spending more time giving me a hand, thass the truth of it,' he said. 'I've got more work than I know what to do with. There's a whole suite o' furniture from Abberton Hall to be re-covered and you know how much I hate re-covering things.' He grinned at her. 'Come on now, Becca, you like Polly, don't you?'

She nodded grudgingly. 'Yes, she's a willing little thing.

And like you say, I dessay her mother can do with a few extra coppers every week.'

'Well, then.' He grinned at her, willing her to smile back, and after a minute he was rewarded. 'Thass better, Becca. Thass the first time I've seen you smile for weeks.'

Ellen was sitting with her foot propped on a stool nursing nine-month-old Joey while Rosie and little Arthur played round her feet. Dolly and the twins were squabbling outside the back door.

'Ain't that foot any better?' Daisy asked. She had called to see Ellen on her way home from her morning's work at Tenpenny Farm and had brought a can of soup with her for the children's dinner.

'Thass all right if I rest it,' Ellen said, wincing as she moved it.

Daisy sniffed. She had no illusions about her younger daughter. Ellen would use any excuse not to get off her backside and do a bit of work. 'Thass three weeks now. Time you was about again.'

'That pain me if I walk on it too much,' Ellen sighed.

'Wouldn't hurt you to walk on it a little.' Daisy looked round the room, at the dirty platters still on the table and the everlasting heap of washing in the corner. 'Look at the place! And the children are filthy. I shoulda thought you'd got a bit more pride in yerself, Ellen Askew.'

She brushed her lank hair back from her face. 'Thass all very well for you to talk, Mum, but I had a bit of a bad do of it this time. Left it a bit late . . .'

'Then drank half a bottle o' gin and sprained your ankle when you jumped off the table because you was

216

three sheets in the wind. Oh, I know. You don't need to tell me.' Daisy pulled the kettle forward and began collecting up the platters.

'Well, anyway, that did the trick, thank the Lord,' Ellen said. 'Even if I did begin to think I'd done meself in. Even George got the wind up and wanted to send for the doctor. And you know George on't rightly waste his money on doctors.'

'You'll do it once too often, my girl.' Daisy pursed her lips. 'If you ask me thass time you started sleepin' with your bum to the wall, then that wouldn't happen. Now, I'm going to put the copper on and when the water's hot I'll give these children a bath. I can't hev my grandchildren looking for all the world like little climbing boys. And hev you got clean clothes for 'em?'

'Yes, in the drawer there. But they might want a bit o' mending.'

'Well, thass something you can do while you set there. Where's your sewing basket?'

'I ain't got one.'

'Ain't got a sewing basket! Gracious me, you oughta be ashamed. Ain't you got a needle and thread somewhere.'

'Yes, on the mantelpiece there. And there's plenty buttons on the floor. The children like to play with them.'

'You wanta be careful they don't swallow them.' Daisy dumped a pile of clothes on Ellen's lap. 'There. That'll keep your head out of your penny novelettes for a little while.' She went outside to the wash house to fill the copper and light the fire under it. When she came back she poured water from the kettle into the bowl in the corner and began to wash the dishes. 'Your sister

Becca wouldn't let her place get in a pickle like this, I know right well,' she said as she banged a saucepan down on the table.

'Don't talk to me about my sister Becca 'cause I don't want to hear. That strike me she's getting above herself. I dessay my place 'ud be as neat and clean as a new pin if I could afford to hev the likes of Polly Jakins in to do for me, same as she can.' Ellen spoke grumpily as she bent her head over the mending she'd been forced to do.,

'You might spare a little pity for her. She's in a rare way because this last baby died.'

Ellen looked up, her eyes cold. 'Me? Pity Becca? Whatever next, I should like to know? It's her that's always had the best of everything, not me.'

'At least none of your littl'uns are ninepence in the shillun,' Daisy reminded her sharply. Her shoulders drooped as she finished the washing up and she shook her head sadly. 'You've always been jealous of Becca, Ellen, ever since you was no bigger than young Dolly. And I don't know why. Your dad and me never treated any of you children different. We loved you all. Still do. I pray young Tommy be kept safe every night of my life.'

She was silent for a few minutes. Then she turned to Ellen. 'You spoil yourself, my girl. Instead of keeping carping on about Becca why don't you count your own blessings? Remember, she's got her troubles, too.' Daisy said no more, and neither of them spoke again as she swept the floor and fetched the tin bath in from the wash house and put it before the fire. But as she bathed the children and washed their hair, putting them in the bath two at a time, leaving the oldest – and dirtiest – till last, Ellen had the

218

grace to get up from her chair to dry them and dress them in clean clothes, most of which had been passed on via Daisy from Becca.

Becca had to admit that she enjoyed her trip to Mr Letch's emporium in Colchester in spite of her reluctance to go in with Jethro. They went in on the carrier's cart, Becca sitting up with Mr Wyatt the carrier and Jethro in the back, keeping an eye on the sideboard he had re-polished for Mr Letch. It was a fine piece of furniture and he had carefully wrapped it in a blanket against the jolts of the unmade roads, but he preferred to travel with it to make sure it came to no harm.

They reached Colchester, the streets busy and noisy after the quiet village roads Becca was used to. She put her hands over her ears against the noise of the motor cars, amazed that neither Major, Mr Wyatt's old horse, nor the numerous other horses that pulled wagons and carts along the busy roads, bolted at the sound of all those horns blaring out and the trams rattling rigidly along on their iron tracks. There was the smell, too – not that she was any stranger to smells, there were plenty enough in the village – but here in the town they were magnified and overladen with petrol fumes until she was ready to choke. But the people hurrying along the pavements didn't seem at all concerned with either the noise or the stink; they called to each other and stood blocking the way as they chatted, or hurried along looking neither to left nor to right, taking their lives in their hands as they wove between the traffic if they wanted to cross the road. Becca didn't care for it; after the spaciousness of the fields of

Wessingford she felt hemmed in by the tall buildings on either side of the road.

They reached Mr Letch's Emporium, an imposing building three storeys tall in the High Street. At ground level there were large windows set out with his best stock, brand new furniture in one and antiques in the other; on the first floor he kept a stock of good quality secondhand furniture and on the second floor were all the oddments that he had picked up in job lots at auctions, or house clearances. Here, as well as broken chairs and tables there was an assortment of china, some in heaps, some in boxes, that had never been sorted. Whilst Jethro was unloading the sideboard and talking to Mr Letch Becca went up to the top floor and spent a happy hour poking around. When Jethro came to find her he was surprised to find that there was a whole boxful of china waiting for him to take downstairs.

He exploded with laughter. 'I expected you to buy a plate or two, not a whole dinner service,' he said, picking the box up.

'Oh, there's not a dinner service in there. It's all oddments,' she said seriously, leaving a black streak across her forehead as she pushed a strand of hair back. 'There's some pretty pieces – all dusty and dirty, of course, but when they're washed . . .' She looked at him anxiously. 'Hev I got too much?'

'Thass all right, dear. You hev what you want. I'm on'y too pleased to see you interested. And I got a good price for doing the sideboard, even though that did get a bit of a scratch bringing it back . . . but I've put that right . . . so I can spare a shillun or two for your china. We'll see how much Mr Letch'll take for it.' He went whistling down the stairs and with a final look round she followed him.

Javis Letch wasn't interested in china. He took it if it happened to be going cheaply, or if it was included in a house clearance, but he knew little about it and cared less. He was glad to let Jethro take the whole boxful for two shillings. It was probably the best two shillings Jethro had ever spent.

Later, as he watched Becca unpack her box of oddments, humming under her breath, Jethro nodded to himself. A new interest was just what she had needed after the loss of her babies. He went back to his workshop thanking God he had found something that would make her happy.

Two hours later she called him and he was amazed at the sparkling array of plates, dishes and ornaments that were spread over the table. He picked up a plate with a centrepiece of roses and a pink rim edged with gold and took it to the window. 'This look to me like real gold round this edge,' he said, looking at Becca in amazement. 'I shouldn't be surprised if this plate is worth a lot of money.'

She came and looked over his shoulder. 'Do you reckon? That was smothered in dust when I found it. 'Well,' she turned back to the table, 'everything was smothered in dust. Thass surprising what a good wash has done for it. Look, this is pretty, too.' She held up an ornament, faintly arcadian, of a shepherd with a lamb under his arm.

Jethro frowned. 'Strikes me I better get you a book, Becca, so you can find out a bit about china. There's all sorts, you know, Derby, Chelsea, Wedgwood . . .'

'Yes, and they all hev different marks, don't they?

221

Look, here's a little red anchor on the bottom of this plate. I wonder what that is?' She put her head on one side. 'I think I shall come into Colchester with you next time you go, Jethro, and take one or two of these bits with me. I might be able to sell them. There's a secondhand china shop in Eld Lane. If the man there wouldn't buy them he might be able to tell me what they're worth.'

'Then you could sell them to Mr Letch,' Jethro laughed.

She shook her head seriously. 'Oh, no, Jethro. I don't think that would be right.' Her face broke into a smile. 'Anyway, if I did he might realise what he's got in his attic and I might not be able to buy any more cheap from him. Mind you,' she picked up a plate that had most of the pattern worn off and a large crack right across it, 'some of it ain't worth much.'

'But then again,' Jethro said looking round at the assortment on the kitchen table, 'some of it might be worth quite a bit.'

Chapter Twelve

Polly proved a good reliable girl. The children loved her and she worked hard and cheerfully. What particularly endeared her to Becca was her kindness and patience with Ash. She was always ready to listen to his halting words and when he brought in a little bunch of wild flowers or berries she would leave what she was doing and find an egg cup or a little pot to put them in.

Polly, for her part, was happy working for the Miller family and sang as she went about her tasks.

'You're always singing, Polly,' Becca said one day when she came in from the workshop to look for an old sheet to tear up for rag.

'Oh, I'm sorry, Mum. I didn't realise . . .' Polly looked up from the chair she was dusting and blushed scarlet.

'Mercy me, Polly, I didn't mean no complaint.' Becca smiled at the girl. 'I like to hear it, that mean you're happy.'

'Oh, I am, Mum, indeed I am. Thass like heving me own brothers and sisters, looking after young Kate and Tim and

223

Ash.' She twisted her duster in her hands. 'I olwuss wanted brothers and sisters, Mrs Miller, but I never had none, me dad being drownded when I was a babby and me mum never marrying again.' She hesitated for a few seconds, then said in a rush, 'I hope I shall olwuss be able to stay here with you, Mum. Till the day I die.'

'I reckon you'll want to leave before that, Polly,' Becca said, still smiling. 'You'll want to get wed and hev a family of your own.'

Polly shook her head. 'No, I shan't,' she said matter-of-factly. 'Nobody won't ever want me. Not with my foot.' She looked down at the heavy boot that concealed a club foot and gave her a lopsided limp. She grinned, an impish grin that lit up her rather plain face. 'But I don't care. I don't want to get wed. I'd rather stay here with you and Mr Miller.'

'And I'm sure we'll be happy for you to stay. As long as we can afford it, that is,' Becca added cautiously.

Jethro didn't share her caution. Business was good. He had begun to visit the salerooms and found that he could buy furniture in worse condition than anyone else because he had the skill to repair it. When it was done Mr Letch was usually happy to buy it from him, and if not it could always be returned to the saleroom to be sold at a good profit. Added to that there was the work that Mr Letch entrusted to nobody but him.

'I bin thinking, Becca,' he said, looking up from fixing the ornate escutcheons back on to a bureau he had just finished repairing, 'I reckon thass time I bought a hoss and cart.'

Becca straightened up and rubbed her back. She was

recovering the final armchair from Abberton Hall and was beginning to feel she wouldn't care if she never saw another length of blue brocade. 'A horse and cart? Whatever next! What do you want a horse and cart for, man?'

'Because I reckon I pay for the keep o' the carrier's hoss, the amount I pay Owd Willy Wyatt for carting things for me. And if I had a hoss of me own I could cart things about when *I* want and not hev to wait till Willy was ready to do it.'

'Well, I don't rightly know . . .' Becca shook her head. 'Where would you keep it?'

'Why, in the pightle, with the owd donkey. They'd be company for each other. I'd knock him up a shelter and I could keep the cart there as well.'

'You seem to hev it all worked out.'

He grinned. 'You know me. I don't do things on the spur of the moment.'

'I don't know about that.' She gave him a sly smile. 'You offered for me on the spur of the moment.'

'And how do you know I hadn't come looking for you?'

Her jaw dropped. 'Had you? Were you looking for me that day?'

He left what he was doing and came over to her. 'Ah, Becca Miller, thass given you suthen to think about, hasn't it?' He kissed the tip of her nose. 'And thass suthen you'll never know.' He grinned at her again and went back to his work.

She rubbed her nose where he had planted the kiss. 'Well, I never. I never thought . . .' She shrugged and picked up her needle again. 'You're an old spoofer, Jethro

Miller. I don't believe you'd come looking for me at all, you're jest making it up.' She watched him closely as she spoke but his expression was bland.

'Well, what do you think of my idea of buying a hoss and cart?' was all he said.

'If thass what you want to do, then you'll do it,' she said, vaguely annoyed because she couldn't read his mind to know whether he had been teasing her or not.

A week later Jethro came home from the market with a mare, Blossom, bought cheaply because she had proved to be barren, and a farm cart that had been in a fire and been badly scorched. He was cock-a-hoop.

'I can soon put the cart to rights,' he said excitedly. 'I'll jest hev to replace a few of the worst burnt timbers and then when thass had a coat of paint, that'll be as good as new. And the mare was a bargain. I shall set to work on a stable for her right away.'

'I come, too, Dad,' Ash said. He rolled his words round his mouth as if they were marbles. 'I like horses.'

'Come on then, bor. You can hold the nails for me.' Father and son went off to the pightle hand in hand, whilst Polly took the other two to pick primroses in the wood and Becca washed the box of china she had bought whilst Jethro was busy with his horse-dealing.

She washed the pieces carefully. She was getting to know a little about china now. When she had first visited the shop in Eld Lane she was surprised to find that it was run by a woman, Meg Parsons, who told her she had kept it going after her husband died some years ago. Meg wasn't interested in furniture; she liked what she called 'small stuff', china, glass, silver, little boxes, tea caddies.

She also dealt in embroidery and lace – tablecloths, babies' gowns, collars and cuffs. Becca found Meg's shop a fascinating hotch-potch of interesting things. And Meg seemed to know what she was talking about and taught Becca how to sort the saleable from the dross.

'But even the rubbish is worth a bit,' she had told Becca on one of her visits. 'Look, I put mine outside the shop on trestles and sell it for a penny a piece, a ha'penny if it's chipped. It all mounts up, you know. And it's surprising what people will buy.'

Meg was well-spoken, in spite of the fact that she wore a man's cap, turned back to front, over her sparse grey hair, and smoked a clay pipe. 'You can put a few of your bits out there, if you like.' She had sorted through the box Becca had brought. 'No, not that dish, that could be worth a bit and so could that jug – see, the jug has got a mark a bit like a new moon on the bottom so it could be Worcester, and it's a good shape, too.' She'd held up a dinner plate with an ornate green rim and roses in the centre. 'Pity you haven't got a dozen of these. But one might sell. I'll stick it in my window, if you like.' She'd laid her pipe on the table. 'Five per cent of whatever I sell for you. Is that fair?'

Becca had nodded. 'Very fair, I should think.'

And now Meg had put a new proposition to Becca. Every two months Meg took a stall at Colchester Market, selling her china and glass.

'Folks'll buy just about anything at the market,' she'd told Becca. 'And they think just because it's on a market stall it must be cheap.' She laughed. 'I can often charge more – and get it – at the market than I can in my shop. If you'd like to bring a few bits and sell them, what profit you make's yours. I could do with an extra hand.'

Becca had hesitated. She knew only too well that Jethro wouldn't approve of her standing behind a stall at the market – especially with an old woman who wore a man's cap and smoked a pipe – yet the thought excited her. Meg had said she could make more money in a morning than she often made in her shop in a week. The thought of presenting Jethro with . . . she plucked a figure out of thin air . . . five pounds! Surely he wouldn't complain to think she'd earned that much all in one go? So she had taken up Meg's offer and next Saturday was the day. All the china she hoped to sell was carefully washed and packed, and safely stored in Meg's shop, waiting to be transported to the stall with her own. Becca had already told Jethro she intended to go to the market on Saturday; if he didn't want to go she would go with Willy Wyatt. No, Jethro had said, he didn't have it in mind to go to market this week. Becca had heaved a sigh of relief at that. She smiled as she sorted a few more pieces to take with her on Saturday. If Jethro had been going she wouldn't have changed her mind; she would just have kept a sharp look-out to make sure he didn't see her standing behind the stall. A pin prick of guilt wiped the smile off her face. She didn't like deceiving Jethro. But it would only happen this once, because when he found out how much money she could make he wouldn't object to her going again. She was sure he wouldn't. Anyway, it would only be once every two months.

Saturday came and Jethro was up even earlier than

usual because he wanted to work on the new cart. Before she set off Becca went into the pightle, where he was sawing planks to length to replace the burnt ones.

'Don't you go buying everything you see,' he warned with a laugh. 'I know what you women-folk are like when you get round a market stall – everything's a bargain, even if it cost double the shop price.' Still laughing to himself, he went back to his sawing.

'You'll be surprised what I might come back with,' she replied. She was as excited as a child at Christmas at the adventure of it all.

Willy Wyatt, the carrier, set her down at the top of Head Street. 'There's no chance of me getting along the High Street on a Sat'day, not with all them stalls and cattle pens and sech right down the road,' he said.

'Thass all right, Mr Wyatt. I can wander along and look at all the stalls as I go,' she said, climbing down from beside him.

The cattle pens were at the Head Street end of the main thoroughfare, after which the market traders' stalls ranged down by the edge of the pavement to the other end, almost to the castle. There were vegetable stalls; stalls with lace and ribbons, buttons and cottons; butchers' stalls, where the blood ran unheeded in the gutter; sweet stalls, already festooned with fly papers to catch the flies as they escaped from the meat stalls; there was an old clothes stall; and there was Meg's china stall, nearly opposite St Nicholas's Church.

Meg was already there, with her stall laid out and a smaller, empty table beside it.

'I've managed to get an extra trestle so you can have

your own table,' she said. 'It's not as big as mine but it'll hold all you've got to sell.'

'Thank you, Meg.' Becca didn't know whether she was trembling with excitement or nervousness now because she had never done anything remotely like this before. Carefully, she unpacked her own boxes, copying Meg in the way she set the china out. When she'd finished she looked round, frowning. There had been a little Staffordshire money box in the shape of a house amongst her things but it didn't appear to be there now. Yet she was sure she had put it in. She groped about under the stall, going through the packing in the boxes to make sure she hadn't missed it, but it wasn't there. Then, as she straightened up, she saw it, right at the far corner of Meg's display. She hesitated. How could it have got there? Surely Meg wouldn't steal from her?

'Your display looks well, Meg,' she said. 'Hev you sold much?'

'Not a lot. You have to wait till people's purse strings are loosened by a trip to The Red Lion. But they'll come, don't you fear.' Meg lit her pipe and stood with her hands on her hips, waiting for the customers she was so convinced would come.

'That little Staffordshire money box over in the corner there,' Becca said diffidently. 'I had one like that, but I can't find it.'

'Can't you? Well, you must have made a mistake. You must have left it at home. They're common enough.' It was impossible to see Meg's expression behind the cloud of tobacco smoke.

'I don't think I did,' Becca said uncertainly. 'Are you sure . . . ?'

'Well, if you can't find it you must have done.' Meg turned away quickly as a potential customer hovered by the stall.

Becca frowned. She didn't think Staffordshire money boxes shaped like houses were that common, but she didn't yet know enough about china to be sure. She pressed her lips together. Perhaps Meg Parsons wasn't such a good friend as she appeared.

The day wore on. Becca, who was used to hard work, had not realised how tiring it could be simply to stand still in one place. Her legs and feet ached as she shifted from one foot to the other and her head pounded from the incessant noise of the traffic rumbling up and down the High Street behind her. But she tried to keep a smile on her face as she scanned the throngs of people, willing them to come and buy.

And they did, although not so much from Becca as from Meg. As soon as a potential customer stopped to browse over Becca's stock, Meg would point out something of hers that was 'better quality', or 'not quite so expensive, dear', and the customer would move on to be expertly cajoled into making a purchase. It was all quite cleverly done, so that it was some time before Becca, inexperienced as she was, realised what was happening. Disillusioned at how little she was selling and Meg's devious methods, Becca began to wish she had never taken up the older woman's offer.

She was to regret it even more before the day was out.

In the middle of the afternoon, Meg went off to get a sandwich and a pint of porter from The Red Lion, leaving Becca in charge with instructions to 'price according to what you think the customer'll pay'. Becca wasn't happy with this. She had carefully worked out what each of her pieces was worth in relation to what she had paid and her prices were set. Nervously, she watched the thronging crowd, looking for likely buyers.

Suddenly a voice behind her said, 'So, this is what you mean by going to hev a look round the market!'

She spun round. Jethro was standing there, his face like thunder.

'Jethro! What are you doing here? Is the cart mended already?'

'No, the cart isn't bloody well mended already. I've left it and come all the way on Blossom's back.'

'Why?' But she knew the answer.

'To bloody well fetch you home, thass why! To think a wife of mine should stand selling things in the market place like some common hawker. I never heard the like in all me born days.'

'I was only selling a few bits of my china. Thass respectable enough, Jethro,' she protested.

'Not in my book that ain't.' As he spoke, he picked up Becca's table and threw it into the road with a crash of broken china. 'There. Now you know what I think of you standing behind a stall in the market place.' He moved across to Meg's table.

'No, Jethro, don't touch that china!' Becca screamed, tears running down her face. 'That don't belong to me.'

'No, it's mine. And if you so much as touch it I'll have the police on to you.' Meg had returned from The Red Lion, her pipe in her mouth, her cap on the back of her head and porter on her breath. Her walk was not quite steady.

232

'You mean to tell me you've bin sharing a stall with this . . . with this owd . . .' Jethro's mouth hung open as he searched for words.

'This is Meg Parsons. She's got a shop in Eld Lane,' Becca said, miserably aware of the crowd that had gathered to see what the commotion was about.

'Well, she can keep her bloody shop. And her bloody stall. You're coming home with me. I'm buggered if I'm having my wife mixed up with the likes of sech folk.' He caught her roughly by the arm and began to drag her away, pushing his way through the people who were still jostling for a better view. Becca knew better than to resist. She had never seen him so angry in her whole life.

'What about all this mess?' Meg shouted after him, shaking her first.

'You can clear it up and hev anything thass whole for your pains,' Jethro called over his shoulder, knowing full well that everything had been smashed.

'You can let go my arm, I shan't run away,' Becca said, trying to shrug off his vice-like grip as he hurried her down St Botolph's Street to The Plough Inn, where he had left Blossom in charge of the ostler there. He took no notice, so she tried to twist round to face him, breathless from the pace he had set. 'But how did you know? How did you know I was there?'

'Brock Badger's wife had come into the market and she saw you,' he said, her face like stone. 'When I went down to The Whalebone to wet me whistle at dinner time she said that was the first she knew you'd got a market stall. I pretended I knew all about it, but by God, I was savage to think you'd go off and do a thing like that behind my

233

back.' He gave her arm a shake that sent a pain up into her shoulder.

'The only reason I didn't tell you was because I didn't think you'd let me go,' she said between her teeth.

'You're too bloody right I wouldn't. But you knew I'd find out in the end. You couldn't be such a damn fool as to think you'd get away with it for long.'

'No. But I thought when I showed you how much money I'd made with my china you'd be pleased . . .' her voice tailed off.

'Then you don't know me as well as you thought you did, my girl. I'm bloody savage and no amount of money'ud make me feel any different. To think a wife of mine should stand in the street like a common hawker selling cups and saucers. And to do it behind my back . . .'

'Well, you've proved it wouldn't hev bin any good me trying to do it in front of your face,' she flashed. She was as furious as he was. 'Anyway, why shouldn't I find somewhere to sell my china? I'd sell it in me own shop if you'd let me hev one.'

'Where do you think I should get the money for a shop, woman? Anyway, you sell some of it back to Mr Letch at a fine profit, ain't that good enough for you?' They reached The Plough and Jethro went to fetch Blossom. 'Here, get up behind me and hold tight. She ain't used to carrying one person, let alone two.'

'I'll walk.'

'You'll do as I say and get up behind me, or I *will* make you walk, and thass a bloody long way. I know, 'cause I've done it.' He held out his hand and reluctantly she took it and allowed him to pull her up behind him.

They journeyed home in silence. When they got back he left her to go into the house while he took Blossom back to the pightle and rubbed her down and fed her. Even then he didn't come in but stayed out there working on the new cart until it was far too dark to see what he was doing.

Becca gave the children their tea and helped Polly to put them to bed, then she sat down and waited for Jethro to come in, sure that when his temper had cooled he would apologise for humiliating her by making such a scene in the market place.

But when he eventually put in an appearance his face was still set and there was no word of apology. He ate the meal she set before him in silence and it wasn't until the pendulum clock in the corner struck nine and they began to make ready for bed that he spoke.

'Well,' he said, 'hev you sulked for long enough? Are you ready to say you're sorry for making sech an exhibition of yerself?'

She was on her knees, raking out the last embers of the fire. Amazed, she sat back on her heels and looked up at him. 'Me?' She pointed to herself. 'Me? Say *I'm* sorry? Why should I be sorry? It wasn't *me* that made the exhibition. *I* didn't overturn the stall and draw everybody's attention to what was going on. I was quietly tending the stall and trying to turn an honest copper for meself.'

He sniffed. 'All right, my girl, if thass how you see it there's no more to be said.' He went off up the stairs and by the time Becca got into bed beside him he was lying on his back and pretending to be asleep.

She lay rigidly beside him, gazing up into the darkness.

There was fault on both sides, she was ready to admit that. She should have told him where she was going. But he needn't have humiliated her. And if he wasn't going to give in and admit he was partly to blame, then neither would she.

Chapter Thirteen

For over a week Becca and Jethro didn't speak to each other unless it was absolutely necessary. Jethro spent most of his time in the pightle mending and then painting his new cart, and when it was finished it was Tim, not Jethro, who came to tell her.

He stood and looked at her with his head on one side. 'Ain't you coming to look at it, Mum? Thass a rare smart cart now Dad's finished it. Thass bright blue, and he's painted the wheels red. He's right proud of it.'

'I dessay I shall see it afore long,' Becca didn't look up from the table she was waxing in the workshop, venting all her temper on it so that the surface was beginning to resemble glass.

'He's going to harness up Blossom and take us all for a ride,' Tim persisted. 'Ash is already in the cart with Polly and Kate. I've come to fetch you.' He tugged at her skirt.

Becca stopped polishing and straightened up. 'Did your dad send you to fetch me?' she asked suspiciously.

Tim nodded and answered innocently, 'Yes. I said shall I fetch Mum and he said you can if you like.'

'Like that, was it?' Becca returned to her table. 'Well, you can tell him I've got better things to do than go parading all over the village jest to show off a new cart.'

Tim's face fell and he turned away. For all his boyish, boisterous ways he was a sensitive, affectionate lad and hated to think there was something wrong between his beloved parents although he didn't know what. He had tears in his eyes as he went back to his father to be lifted on to the cart. 'Mum's too busy,' he said, biting his lip.

'I thought she might be,' Jethro answered grimly. 'But never mind it, Blossom's all ready so we'll go for our ride. Where would you like to go? Abberton?'

Becca heard them set off but resisted the urge to watch them pass the house and when they came back, an hour later, she made herself busy sorting china in the front parlour.

The children sought her out. 'Oh, Mum, you should hev come. We had a lovely time. We waved to everybody and they all stopped and waved back,' Kate said, her cheeks rosy with happiness.

'We waved,' Ash said, demonstrating. 'And Blossom went clip-clop.' He galloped round the table.

'I'm glad you enjoyed it, dearie.' Becca ruffled his curls and smiled at him.

'We'd have liked it better if you'd come, too,' Kate said seriously.

'Yes, we would.' Tim's brown eyes held a sad, almost accusing look.

'I'll come another time,' she promised. 'Now, get Polly

238

to give you your tea, then off to bed. It's past your bedtime.' She smiled at them all but as she turned back to her china, her heart was like lead in her breast.

The cottage only had two bedrooms so the two boys, Ash and Tim, slept in a little room that Jethro had built over the workshop for them. The boys loved this room with its tiny dormer window. They called it their attic and kept all their treasures in it. It was quite separate from the other two bedrooms and they felt very grown up scrambling up and down the ladder in the corner of the scullery to reach it.

As Becca sat with her knitting and Jethro smoked his pipe in what was becoming habitual silence after their evening meal, there was a noise from the region of the scullery. Becca pricked up her ears, noticing that Jethro also put his head to one side, listening. It was the sound of crying. It was Tim, up in the attic, sobbing as if his heart would break.

Becca got to her feet, but before she could reach the foot of the ladder, Jethro was halfway up it. 'What's the matter, Timmy, bor?' he was saying as he emerged into the attic. 'What's got into you, my boy?'

But Tim could only hold out his arms and sob, trying to hug both his parents at once. 'Don't go away,' he hiccupped at last. 'I don't want you to go away.'

'I ain't going away, Timmy boy.' Jethro said gently. 'Whatever should give you that idea?'

'You and Mum . . . you don't love each other no more.' At that, Tim's sobs were renewed and he buried his head in Jethro's chest. He stroked the boy's dark head. 'What should make you think that, my boy?' he asked gently.

239

'You don't talk to Mum and she don't talk to you,' he said wretchedly. 'I know what that mean. That mean you'll be going away. Like Billy Crickmore's dad. Thass what happened to him. Billy told me. He said his mum and dad stopped talking to each other and then his father went away and he ain't never bin home since.'

Jethro rocked the boy back and forth. 'I ain't going away, Timmy boy,' he repeated. 'You need never fear that.'

Tim looked at Becca, his face stained with tears. 'Are you going away then, Mum?' His face began to crumple.

'No,' Jethro answered for her firmly. 'Your mother ain't going nowhere. Are you, Becca dear?' He looked at her, his face wistful.

Becca sank to her knees, her own face wet with tears. 'No, 'course I ain't going away, Tim. I shall always be here and so will your dad, don't you never fear it.'

Tim looked up with a watery smile. 'Are you sure?'

Jethro held out his hand to Becca and she took it. He pulled her into the circle of his arm. 'Quite sure,' he said firmly. 'Your mum and me may hev our differences from time to time, but I couldn't do without her, and thass the truth. We shall always be here, Tim.'

Becca nodded in agreement, too full to speak.

Tim looked uncertainly from one to the other. Then, satisfied with what he saw, he gave a great sigh of relief. 'Oh, thass all right, then,' he said, his face clearing. He gazed at them for a moment longer, as if to make certain, then gave them each a great bear hug and rolled back into his bed. Before Becca and Jethro could reach the top of the ladder he was asleep.

Downstairs they sat down on either side of the fire, staring into it without speaking. After a few minutes Jethro stood up and went over to Becca and pulled her to her feet.

'I think this has gone on long enough, Becca,' he said gruffly, still holding her by the arms. 'I won't hev the children upset like this.'

She tossed her head. 'I . . .'

He put his finger over her lips. 'There was fault on both sides, Becca. You should never hev done what you did and I should never have lost me rag over it. I'm sorry for that and I beg you to forgive it.'

Becca opened her mouth to speak but he held up his hand. 'That said, I hev to ask, didn't you *know* what company you were keeping? Didn't you *know* what an owd rogue Meg Parsons is? She's the talk of the district, with her sharp, thieving ways.'

Becca hung her head. 'No, I didn't know. She seemed kind and helpful when I took things to her shop. I learned a lot from her.'

'Pity you didn't learn what an owd swindler she is.'

'I did. She pinched a money box from me and had the gall to put it on her stall and swear it was hers.'

'There y'are, then.' His hands slid up to her shoulders. 'Jest imagine, heving your name linked with an owd rogue like that. You wouldn't want that, Becca, would you?'

'No, I wouldn't.' She lifted her head. 'But would it hev bin any different if it had bin Mr Letch's stall, Jethro?'

He half smiled. 'But Mr Letch don't see the need to hev a stall in the market place, Becca. Thass the difference. Don't you see? He offers his goods in his shop at a fair

241

price, he don't try to rook people left right and centre selling rubbish in the market.'

Her shoulders sagged and she nodded. 'Yes, Jethro. I see.'

His arms went round her. 'We was both at fault, Becca, so we'll say no more about it, 'cept I want to tell you that I don't know about you, but I've had a miserable week. I don't like this coldness between us. And all because we was both too stubborn to give in.' He laid his head against her hair. 'Fancy us, two grown people, upsetting a young shaver like Tim because of our silly pride. Funny that should have bin Tim, too, and him not really ours.'

'That jest goes to show we ain't made no difference between him and the others. Funny, I never think of him as not being ours now.' She was quiet for a moment, rubbing her cheek against the rough tweed of his waistcoat. 'I promise I shan't never do anything again without talking it over with you first, Jethro,' she said at last. 'I bin as miserable as sin these past few days.'

He stroked her hair gently, then put his finger under her chin and lifted her face to look at him. 'My owd Aunt Emma always used to say, "Never let the sun go down on your anger". I don't reckon thass a bad rule to work by.' He gave her a little grin. 'If I'd remembered it afore we might hev saved ourselves a miserable week, Becca, don't you think?'

She gave him a watery smile and nodded her head.

'I'll tell you this, I shan't forget it again.' His arms tightened and he held her close. 'Now, I think thass time we had a bit of bread and cheese and went to bed, dear, don't you?' He gave a chuckle. 'And I warn you here and

242

now, Becca, my girl, I shan't be sleeping on the edge of the bed tonight.'

'Oh, Jethro!' Even after nearly nine years of marriage the implication behind his words brought a blush to her cheeks, but later, in the warm, featherbed darkness, she was as eager as he was to complete their reconciliation.

Nine months later, Lucy was born.

From the very beginning Becca tried to ignore the fact that she was pregnant as far as she possibly could.

'Don't get too excited. You'll see, I shall miscarry afore three months,' she prophesied when Jethro showed signs of pleasure at the prospect of another baby in the house. But she didn't.

'Well, I doubt it'll be born live,' when her first prediction proved false.

Jethro watched over her and held her close, knowing that her pessimism was nothing more than a wall she was building against disappointment, because she wanted this child so desperately.

But against all Becca's fearful predictions, everything went well, it was an easy birth and Lucy thrived. She was a pretty child, with a mop of fair curly hair and enormous blue eyes framed by long, dark lashes. Polly revelled in being nursemaid to her and the other children idolised her, pampering and petting her until Becca laughingly told them they must stop or they would turn her into a spoilt little monster.

Every Thursday Becca went to her mother's cottage for the weekly breadmaking. She could have done it at home in her own oven but she maintained that bread baked in a faggot oven tasted better than any other and Jethro, who loved nothing better than fresh bread with a lump of cheese and an onion, didn't disagree with her. Sometimes one or more of the children went with her, sometimes she went on her own, leaving them in Polly's capable hands.

It was a hot, dusty day in early June. The three older children had elected to stay at home; Kate was going to help Polly turn out a cupboard and Tim had found an old tin bath and filled it was water and he and Ash were having a high time splashing about in it with their shoes and stockings off.

Becca pushed Lucy along in the pram Jethro had bought new when she was born sixteen months earlier. Twice before he had got out the old pram and prepared it to receive a new baby and it had gone unused. After the second disappointment the sight of it so upset Becca that she had given it to Ellen to replace the old push cart. The new one was high and well-sprung, with a satin lining, which had made Ellen sarcastic with jealousy when she first saw it.

It was as well it was well-sprung. Tenpenny Lane, named because it led to Tenpenny farm, was corrugated with deep ruts from Edward Green's motor car, which churned up the rough track and made a muddy quagmire in wet weather that baked solid when it was hot and dry. On either side of the lane white campion and yellow toadflax rioted in the hedgerow and buttercups and dandelions carpeted the bank. Becca stopped to pick several handfuls of dandelions for her mother to make into her potent brew of dandelion wine, knowing that when it was ready there would be a bottle to take home for Jethro.

Daisy's kitchen had changed very little over the years,

except that the settle had been moved away from the fire to accommodate Joe's chair on its wheeled platform. But today Daisy had pushed him outside and he sat by the back door, drinking in the sunshine and watching the birds enjoy a dust bath in the cabbage patch Daisy kept cultivated.

'You're a bit late today, mawther,' Daisy said from inside the house as Becca appeared. 'I've already got the oven hot. Ah, dandelions. Thass good. I'll see after them when the bread's made.'

Becca left Lucy asleep in the pram beside Joe and sat down just inside the door, fanning herself. 'Yes, I am late. I couldn't seem to get meself together, somehow. And then the baby was sick all over her clean dress and I had to stop and change her. But never mind, I'm here now. And how are you, Dad?'

'Fair to middlin',' Joe said from his chair. 'I don't know which is worse for me owd screws, the wet weather or this heat. But I like to be outdoors time I can.' He sighed. 'I hate it when I hev to be stuck indoors all the time. I was always used to the fresh air and the wind in me face.'

'Yes, and right bad-tempered he get when he can't set outside,' Daisy said, up to her elbows in flour.

'Well, I've always bin used to it,' Joe repeated. He shifted painfully in his chair.

'His knees are bad,' Daisy said, watching him. 'And he's getting that fat! He hev a job to get from the bed to his chair these days.' She turned to Becca. 'Are you ready to make your dough? Or do you want me to do it, seeing as I've already got me hands floury?'

Becca got to her feet. 'No, I'll do it, Mum. You've got

245

quite enough to do, making yours and Ellen's.' She rolled up her sleeves. 'Mind you, I think thass high time Ellen baked her own bread, instead of leaving you to do it all the time. You work too hard, Mum, slaving up at the farm all hours like you do, and seeing after Dad and the house and garden into the bargain.'

'Shh.' Daisy shot a warning glance in Joe's direction, but he was busy feeling in the capacious pocket on the arm of his chair for his pipe and wasn't listening. 'Don't you think your dad feel bad enough that he can't work and I hev to go out to bring in a few coppers? she said fiercely, her voice low. 'Without you making a song and dance about it.'

'I wasn't making a song and dance. I only said . . .'

'I know very well what you said. Jest don't say it again.' Daisy thumped at her dough to vent her feelings. 'Goodness knows where we'd be if we didn't get the rent paid for us.' She straightened up. 'You know, I've often wondered about that, Becca,' she mused. 'I can't see Mr Edward letting us live here rent free, he ain't that type of man. I reckon thass his owd dad, Mr Green at the Manor House. I reckon that was his doing. I reckon he pay it.' She nodded, the matter solved to her satisfaction.

Becca said nothing. Jethro was more prosperous now. He hardly missed the money he paid to Edward Green's bailiff each week, even though the rent for the cottage had gone up to half a crown.

Becca and Daisy finished making the dough, then sat in the sunshine while it was left to prove. When it had risen they kneaded it again and shaped it into loaves and had a cup of tea and a slice of Daisy's fruit cake while it proved again. The loaves were in the faggot oven to cook when Ellen came along the lane, trailing her brood. Thursday was the only day she and Becca saw each other, and not then if Becca had finished early and gone home and Ellen was late arriving.

'Mm, smells nice,' she said as she passed the old brick oven. 'I could jest do with a new crust and a nice hunk of cheese. I got a craving for bread and cheese with this one.'

'Well, you'll jest have to crave, then,' Daisy said, 'thass not even outa the oven yet. But we can all hev another cuppa tea. Pull the kettle forward, Becca.'

She did as she was asked and then sat down again.

'Hmm. No children round *your* skirts, I see,' Ellen said, lowering herself on to a chair. Her hair was lank and she was as thin as a rake except for where her skirt, gaping at the placket, strained across her huge belly. She obviously hadn't taken her mother's advice.

'Lucy's out there in her pram,' Becca said briefly. 'The others didn't want to come today, it was too hot. So they've stayed behind with Polly.'

'You've still got your servant girl, little cripple Jakins, then? Ain't you the lucky one!' There was a sneer in Ellen's voice.

'Don't call her cripple. Polly's a good girl,' Becca said sharply.

'A servant girl *and* a horse and cart, too. Must be coining the money in.'

'Jethro works hard.' Over the years Becca had learned to ride her sister's barbed remarks although they still hurt.

'So do George, but he can't afford a horse and cart.'

247

'He might if he . . .' Becca bit her lip at the warning glance she received from her mother.

But Ellen didn't appear to notice. 'If you go on at this rate with your airs and graces, I dessay the next thing'll be a motor car.'

Becca shrugged. 'When we do I'll let you know and you can come for a ride in it.'

'What, me! Ride in one of them noisy, smelly things? No, thank you! I'd rather walk.' Ellen pursed her thin lips.

'Thass a good thing, because your George is never likely to own one,' Becca said unkindly.

'Oh, you two, stop your everlasting bickering,' Daisy said wearily. 'Whenever you get together all you do is carp at each other.'

'Thass not me,' Becca said hotly. 'I got no quarrel with Ellen. But she will goad . . .'

'Make the tea, Becca, there's a good gal,' Joe cut in, 'I couldn't spit a farden.'

Becca made the tea and poured it out. She nodded to a bundle on the settle. 'I brought a few bits Lucy's already grown out of for the new baby. Thought they might come in handy.'

'Thanks.'

'How much longer? Not much, is it?'

'About a fortnight, I reckon.'

Becca hesitated. 'I dessay you'll be glad of a bit of help when the time come. Would you like me to send Polly . . . ?'

'Don't be daft. How could I afford to pay a servant girl?' Ellen wriggled round on her chair till her back was turned to her sister.

'I wasn't suggesting that you should pay her. She gets her wages from Jethro every week.'

'I don't want Jethro Miller's charity.'

Becca sighed. 'Very well. Would you like *me* to come?'

'No, I wouldn't. You're only saying that because you think you might be able to get round George . . .'

'Get round George!' Becca's jaw fell open. 'Do you really think that? Hev you looked at George lately? Really looked at him, I mean? Great drunken lout that he is.' She gave a mirthless laugh. 'You don't need to worry, Ellen, I wouldn't touch your George with a barge pole.'

'You ain't going to get the chance! I don't want you in my house when I'm lying-in. Mum'll come and see after me.' Ellen rubbed her side as she spoke.

'Mum's got enough to do . . .'

'I can manage,' Daisy broke in, 'you don't need to worry about me. The Lady Felicity is going off on her holidays about the time Ellen'll be brought to bed so that'll all work out very well.'

'What about the others? Mr Green and Master Teddy?' Becca asked.

'The Master won't trouble whether I'm there or not. He'll be out hunting nearly every day. And as for Master Teddy, well, he's a funny lad and no mistake. All he think about is his painting and drawing.'

'How old is he now?' Becca asked.

'Oh, must be fifteen, I should think. And a real trial to his father.'

'Why?'

'Because he won't take no interest in the farm. I think Mr Edward hoped young Teddy would be a born farmer

249

like his grandfather, then Mr Edward could leave him to run things while he went off on his hunting and shooting parties. But Teddy ain't heving any. He don't care for farm animals and ain't interested in crops – except to paint them. And he won't get his hair cut.' Daisy made a clucking noise with her tongue as she poured herself another cup of tea. 'There's a carry-on there sometimes, I don't mind telling you. Mr Edward shout and holler at Teddy and the Lady Felicity shout and holler at Mr Edward . . .'

'And what about Teddy?' Becca asked. 'Does he shout, too?'

Daisy shook her head. 'No, he jest go off to his room and paint. There's a row going on now because Milady wants to employ an art teacher for Teddy. She say he's talented. Mr Edward say he can't afford it and anyway the boy oughta be learning about farming, not daubing paint on canvas all day.'

'So what do you reckon'll happen?' Becca asked.

'Oh, I dessay he'll get his teacher. Teddy's a past master at playing one off against the other. He'll get round his mother and the Lady Felicity usually manage to get her own way with the Master, by hook or by crook.'

Ellen rubbed her side again. 'George say young Teddy don't know one end of a cow from the other, and if he get a bit of cow muck on his boots you'd think he'd bin shot. He say he's a rare namby-pamby mother's boy. George wouldn't want to work for the likes of him.' Suddenly, she stiffened. 'I think I'd better be going home. I think me time has come,' she said, her voice more anxious than she realised.

Becca glanced at her mother. She looked very tired. 'Mum, could you wheel Lucy home? And call in at Mrs Plackett's on the way and tell her she's needed at Ellen's. I'll take Ellen and the children home. Tell Jethro I don't know when I'll be back.'

'I don't want . . .' Ellen began, but bit her lip as another pain struck.

'You may not want but you ain't in a position to choose,' Becca said briefly. 'Come on now, let's get you home.'

'Leave the littl'uns with me,' Joe said. 'I can watch them from my chair. They won't take no harm with me.'

'I shan't be gone long,' Daisy said. 'I'll give them their tea when I get back.'

Becca got Ellen home with difficulty and half an hour to spare. The baby, a boy, slipped easily into the world, small and pale and the image of his brother Albert. A hope flashed through Becca's mind that he would be a more likeable child. She left her sister to the care of Mrs Plackett and went downstairs.

The door stood open. Everything had happened in such a hurry that she had had no time to do more than light the fire and set a pan to boil and it was clear Ellen had done nothing for several days. As Becca set about cleaning the room she couldn't help musing on the fact that this would have been *her* home if things had been different. She pursed her lips grimly. If this had been her home it wouldn't have looked as bare and grubby as it did now!

When Mrs Pluckett had gone Becca took Ellen a cup of tea and sat with her for a while.

'Thass no good you looking round the room and turning your nose up at the state of it,' Ellen said as she watched Becca. 'I know thass like a pig sty. I don't need you to tell me.'

'I was only thinking I'd give it a good turn out tomorrow,' Becca said as she sipped her tea. 'That'll be company for you while I do it, too. Stands to reason you couldn't do it while you were so big. There ain't room to swing a cat.' She smiled at her sister. 'That won't take me long.'

'Thank you, Becca.' Ellen's face crumpled. 'I'm sorry I was bitchy and said I didn't want you near. That was only because I didn't want you to see what the place was like. Your place is so much better.'

She put her cup down on the coverlet and lay back on the grey-looking pillow. 'I do try, Becca, but thass an uphill job. I started to take in washing people's sheets so I could buy a few bits to brighten the house up from the tallyman, but more often than not that money hev to go to pay the butcher. George is as tight as a duck's arse with his money. Sometimes I get fed up so I sit and hev a read. I like reading. That take me outa meself.' She sighed. 'But that don't get the work done.'

Becca patted her hand. 'Well, you can hev a good read while you're lying-in. And I'll give the house a good clean so that'll give you a fresh start when you're up and about again. I'll bring you some books when you've had a good sleep. Thass what you need more'n anything at the minute.' She went downstairs and looked round. It was difficult to know where to begin. The kettle was singing on the hob so she began with the dirty dishes.

To her surprise George came home early. Shorty

Johnson the pigman had told him he'd seen his wife and it looked as if her time had come, so he wasn't surprised to find he had another son. In fact, he'd called in at The Whalebone on his way home for a drink on the strength of it.

'Becca!' His face lit up. 'What you doing here?'

'What does it look as if I'm doing?' She dried the last of the dishes she had washed and reached up to put them in the cupboard by the side of the fireplace. 'You've got another son. Ellen's asleep,' she said over her shoulder.

She didn't know George had come up behind her till she felt his arms slide round her and his hands cover her breasts. She knocked them away and spun round. 'Thass enough of that, George Askew. I want no hanky-panky from you or I'll slap you across the chops.'

He grinned. 'You're still a comely wench, Becca. A little kiss and cuddle wouldn't do no harm. For owd times' sake.' He stepped forward again.

She moved round till the table was between them. 'My God, George, don't you ever think of anything else?' she said. 'There's your wife upstairs, worn out with bearing your children, not to mention the number of times she's miscarried, and now you're trying to get round me! You oughta be ashamed of yourself.'

He looked surprised. 'Ashamed? Why should I be ashamed because I got plenty lead in me pencil?' He grinned. 'There's several women out in the fields more'n happy for me to mark their card with it, too, I don't mind telling you.' He sniffed proudly. 'I don't go short, you don't wanta worry.'

She looked round the room. 'No, you don't go short of

what you want. I can smell from here that you've already got tanked up at The Whalebone. It's your fam'ly that goes short, you selfish great oaf!'

He flushed a dull red as his temper rose. 'Don't you speak to me like that in me own house, Becca Stansgate,' he said, reverting to her maiden name. 'Jest because you've come up in the world, with your servant girl and your horse and cart, don't give you the right to tell me what to do. Coming here with your airs and graces . . .'

'George? Is that you, George?' Ellen's voice sounded from upstairs.

'You'd better go and see your new son,' Becca said, jerking her head in the direction of the stairs.

'But I ain't had me tea yet.' He looked surprised.

'There's a bit of cold pork and pickle in the cupboard. You can get it for yourself when you come down. Tell Ellen I'm off to fetch the other children from Mum's.' She eyed him coldly. 'I shall be staying the night but that needn't trouble you. You can sleep down here in the chair.'

'Miserable bitch,' she heard him mutter as he lumbered up the stairs.

My God, she thought, I've come a long way since I was promised to that selfish brute. My sister's got no need to be jealous. I'm only thankful I never married him. She shook her head. In a way she felt sorry for him. Sorry for them both. The trap they'd fallen into had been of their own making but it was still a trap and she wondered, as she had many times before, what kind of a man George would have been if he hadn't been caught in it.

Chapter Fourteen

The new baby was called George, after his father, but anything less like a George Becca had never seen. The baby was pale and pinched-looking and cried a lot. He seemed to know he was unwelcome but hung on to life with a tenacity that surprised everyone.

Becca stayed with Ellen for over a week, only going home for short periods to see her own children and to make sure that Polly was managing. She knew her sister was grateful for what was being done for her although she couldn't bring herself to admit it. She knew, too, that Ellen was ashamed of her situation and hid this behind sarcasm and sharp words. Understanding that made it easier to bear when she made snide remarks about Becca's lifestyle.

But when Ellen was up and about again she did make an effort to maintain the level of neatness and cleanliness that Becca had worked long and hard the whole week to achieve; for a few weeks the floors were swept regularly and the children were kept washed and their clothes mended. But Georgie was a miserable baby and continually demanded feeding, and while Ellen fed him she read a novelette, and when he was asleep she continued reading and got behind with Mrs Badger's washing so Dolly had to help her with it. And the smaller children got into the field and got their clothes muddied and torn because Dolly wasn't there to watch them . . . And so it went on. Life was so much more pleasant in a cheap novelette.

Back in her own home Becca's life resumed its routine. Kate was a long-legged nine year old now, growing more like her mother with each year that passed. She was bright and quick and always near the top of the class at school. Unlike her brother Ash. Poor Ash struggled but could never grasp what he was being taught and the other children called him 'Daft Ash' or 'Nooncey Miller', and would dance round him, calling him names until he was fuddled and giddy, not understanding that they were making fun of him. Tim came home with many a bloody nose received trying to protect his older brother from the taunts of the other children, because the way Ash was treated upset him far more than it did Ash, who quite enjoyed being the centre of attention and thought the other children laughed at him because they thought he was funny.

Polly had grown plump with contentment. She had a plain, honest, smiling face and asked nothing more in life than that she should be allowed to do Mrs Becca's bidding. Becca had taught her to cook and she kept the house clean and looked after Lucy while Becca worked with Jethro and went with him on his expeditions into Colchester, buying and selling her china whilst he collected or delivered furniture to Mr Letch or visited the auction rooms on sale day.

But just as Ellen envied Becca, so Becca envied Mr Letch. She would dearly have loved a shop – oh, not so big as Mr Letch's, but a shop of their own.

This was something Jethro had no interest in. 'We do all right as we are, Becca,' he said, whenever she broached the subject. 'With a bit of buying and selling – and I can buy cheaper than most others because I can do me own repairs – and the work I get from Mr Letch, we hev enough to get by, don't we?' He looked at her closely. 'Do you go short of anything you want, Becca?'

'No,' she had to admit. 'We're quite comfortable. But there's my china . . .'

He nodded. 'Yes, you've got a lot of china, Becca, and you're getting to know quite a bit about it. I was surprised at the way you told Mr Letch the other day that the Derby figure he'd got in his window was a copy. How did you know that?'

She shrugged. 'You learn by handling the stuff. It wasn't delicate enough . . .' She stamped her foot in frustration. 'Don't change the subject, Jethro. If we had our own shop I could sell my china there.' She gave him an innocent look and said wickedly, 'Of course it would be cheaper for me to take a market stall, I grant you that.' She waited for his reaction.

He said nothing for several minutes, chewing his beard thoughtfully. 'I think the least said about market stalls the better, Becca,' he said at last, not rising to her bait. 'But I'll tell you what you could do. You could ask Mr Letch if he'd let you hev a corner in his shop. I'll pay the rent for you.'

'I don't *want* a corner in Mr Letch's shop.' She stamped her foot again. 'I want a shop of our own.'

'And who's going to tend it? Hev you thought of that? I can't be out buying furniture and repairing it in the workshop and look after a shop as well,' he pointed out. 'And you can't be out buying china and see after things here in the house and look after a shop. We can't halve and quarter ourselves, Becca.'

'We could take it in turns to be in the shop.'

'And where is this wunnerful shop to be, may I ask? It wouldn't be any good here in Wessingford.' He eyed up the piece of wood he had been planing, then placed it carefully back on the bench.

'I don't know. Colchester? Across the river at Wyford?'

'Colchester's too expensive. And you're dependent on the tides to get across to Wyford. No, thass not worth the candle, Becca. We do all right as we are.' He went back to his planing.

'The trouble with you, Jethro Miller, is you ain't got no ambition.'

'I'm contented with my lot, Becca,' he said, without looking up. 'There's a difference.'

Becca said no more. The argument always ended like that and she could see no way round it. Since her interest in china had begun she had collected so much that ornaments and fairings covered every surface in the front parlour and plates were hung on every available space on the walls upstairs as well as down. Then there were boxes full stacked in odd corners and in the cupboard under the stairs. Becca could resist neither a bargain nor a likely-looking box where there might be something interesting.

258

And she could never bring herself to throw anything away. If she didn't think it would sell she packed it away in case it might one day be useful. She could afford to indulge her passion because now and again she would recognise something of real value as she unpacked a box and it would sell for a good price at the sale, and Mr Letch was always happy to buy a pretty plate or jug to decorate the furniture he had on display.

Becca had been appalled at the chipped and cracked oddments of china at her sister's house and a few weeks after her stay with Ellen she pulled out some of her boxes and began to rummage through them to see what she could find. As she began unpacking, she was excited at what she was doing but a little apprehensive as to how Ellen would receive it.

Becca always packed her china carefully, everything was wrapped in newspaper, and before long she had a stack of china on one side and a heap of crumpled paper on the other. But she had found what she was looking for. In amongst all the oddments was enough matching china to make a complete tea service, teapot and milk jug included. It was nothing special, cheap cream-coloured earthenware with little green flowers round the edge, but at least it was all the same and wasn't chipped or cracked. She also found seven dinner plates, all white with blue rims, and a vegetable dish with a cracked lid to match and there were eight pale-blue soup bowls and two pretty dishes that didn't match anything, not even each other. She sat back on her heels. She had been going to sort those boxes for ages to see if she could match anything up ready to send to the sale room but she had never got round to it.

Well, perhaps it was a good thing. It would do Ellen far more good to have it all. She got Polly to leave what she was doing and help her to wash the china, then she packed it in a box so that when Jethro was out with the cart she could get him to drop her off at Ellen's house with it.

She was so excited she could hardly wait but she had to contain herself until Saturday, when Jethro had a cabinet to return to Mr Green at the Manor House. 'Thass a bit outa my way to take you up Tenpenny Lane but I dessay that won't take long,' he said good-humouredly. 'Are you coming along, Katie?'

'Yes,' she said. 'The boys have gone to play in the woods and Lucy's asleep so there's nobody here for me to play with. I'll come and talk to Dolly.'

'I see the gate's still off its hinges,' Jethro said as he put Becca and Kate down at Ellen's cottage. 'I should hev thought George could hev put a few screws in it. But there, I reckon thass taken root in that long grass.' He shook his head. 'The whole place is in a tidy pickle and no mistake. There, can you manage the box, Becca? Thass a bit heavy.'

'Yes, I've only got to get it up the path. You go off and deliver your cabinet. We shan't be long. I dessay we'll be home by the time you get back.' Becca staggered up the overgrown path with the heavy box and round the side of the cottage to the back door, with Kate skipping on ahead of her.

Dolly was trying to teach the little ones to play hop-scotch in the dust in front of the back door. Ellen was sitting inside, a book in her hand, Georgie at her breast to keep him quiet.

'I've brought you a little present,' Becca said, placing the box carefully on the table.

Ellen looked up, eyeing the box suspiciously. 'What is it?'

'Jest a few bits of china I ain't got no use for. You know I collect china, don't you?'

Ellen put down her book and fastened her dress, ignoring Georgie's howls. She put him outside in his pram, still yelling, and came over to the table. 'Thass no use you bringing me ornaments. That'll only be something else for George to chuck at me when he come home drunk,' she said resignedly.

'I haven't brought you ornaments. Hev a look.' Becca shrugged. 'You may not want what I've brought.'

Gingerly, Ellen began to unpack the box, her hands trembling slightly from the excitement she tried hard to conceal. 'Plates,' she breathed. 'Cups and saucers . . .' Her eyes widened. 'And they match, too!' She turned to Becca. 'But don't you want them? I mean, there's a whole set . . .'

'No. I've got plenty of china,' Becca said, then added in order to save Ellen's pride, 'I've got all that owd willow-pattern stuff that belonged to Jethro's aunt. Thass too good to throw away.'

'Well, if you're sure you don't want it . . .' Ellen looked longingly at it. Then she squared her shoulders. 'That'll do for every day. Save me getting the best stuff out all the time.'

'Thass what I thought.' Becca went along with the face-saving lie. 'Well,' she looked round the untidy room, 'I can see you're busy so I won't hinder you. We'll be on our way. Come on, Kate, time we were off. We'll call and see Granny and Granpa on the way home.'

Kate poked her head in at the door. 'Me and Dolly thought it would be a good idea if we went for a picnic in the woods. Can we do that, Mum?'

'Not today, dear. But next Saturday, if Aunt Ellen don't mind.'

Ellen shrugged. 'That'll get them out from under my feet.' She turned to Dolly. 'You'll hev to get up early, mind, and get your jobs done first.'

Dolly nodded eagerly. 'Yes. I don't mind that.'

After Becca and Kate had gone Ellen called Dolly in to show her all the new china before she began packing it away. Dolly thought she had never anything so pretty. 'We'll keep it for best, Mum. We don't want it to get broke, do we?' she said, her eyes shining.

'No, we don't want you father getting hold of it, either,' Ellen said. 'So I'll put it on the top shelf, where he won't see it. While I'm doing that you can go up the garden and get Mrs Oliver's sheets off the line. You'll jest about hev time to get them ironed before tea.'

'All right, Mum.' Happily, Dolly went off into the garden, seeing nothing strange in a nine-year-old girl being expected to handle heavy sheets, while Ellen began to stack her new china lovingly away. She had always envied Becca her cupboard full of matching blue and white willow-pattern china. She thought it was the height of luxury to have not only cups and saucers that matched, but milk jug and sugar basin and best of all a matching teapot. She picked up the cream teapot with the little green flowers round the lid and put it carefully on the shelf. That would only be used on very special occasions.

She had had no time to put anything else away when

262

George came in. It being Saturday and pay day he had finished work at dinner time and called in at The Whalebone to clear his slate. As usual, by the time he left he had drunk himself back into debt, with the result that the children scattered when they saw his unsteady progress up the garden path.

'Where's me dinner?' he greeted Ellen.

'You'll get your dinner when I get some of your wages,' she answered without turning round.

'What's this, then?' He stood swaying and blinking as his eyes became accustomed to the dimness of the room after the bright sunlight outside. 'You had the bloody tallyman round here again? Buying all this trish trash?' He peered frowning at the crockery on the table.

'No. That didn't come from the tallyman. That didn't cost you a penny piece,' Ellen quickly began to stack the dinner plates and tea plates in the cupboard.

'Where did it come from, then?' He picked up one of the dishes.

'Put it down, George Askew, afore you break it. Thass a pretty dish.' Hurriedly, she gathered the rest of the china and stacked it away. 'Becca brought it this afternoon. You know she collects china. Well, she said she didn't want these bits and I could hev them.'

'Did she, by God!' George dragged his sleeve across his mouth. 'Well, we don't want her bloody charity. You can tell her what she can do with her bloody crockery. Where's the box?'

'Under the table.' Ellen caught his arm to try and take the dish from him. 'Don't be daft, George. You can't take it all back to her. She meant well. We can't fly in her

263

face. Anyway, we ain't got a sight of china to eat off – even if we ever had a sight of food to eat,' she added under her breath.

He groped under the table and brought out the box. 'I'll tell your precious sister what she can do with her bloody china,' he shouted, flinging the dish at the wall. 'There, put that in the bloody box and the rest of it can go the same way.' He lurched across to the cupboard.

Ellen caught his arm to stop him, desperate to protect her beautiful china. He tried to shrug her off but she hung on and he stumbled over the stool she had been standing on. Still off-balance, as he wrenched the cupboard door open he hit himself in the face with it. He took a step back, swore, tripped over the stool again and fell to the ground, cracking his head on the corner of the table as he went. Ellen stood looking down at his senseless figure with her hands on her hips. 'Serve you right,' was all she said.

Dolly came staggering in, hardly able to see over the heap of sheets in the linen basket. 'What's the matter with Dad?' she asked as she put it on the chair, seeing his inert figure. 'Is he drunk again?'

'He started to smash all my pretty china,' Ellen said, her lips pursed.

'Oh, Mum, you didn't knock him down!' There was admiration in Dolly's voice.

'No, I didn't hev to. But I woulda done if he'd broke any more. Come on, mawther, help me to get him up the stairs. He hit his head but he's more drunk than knocked out, he'll walk if we help him. You get the door open, Doll. Come on, you great drunken sot.' She heaved her husband to his feet and half-pushed, half-dragged him across to the stairs. Then she sat him on the stairs. 'Go on, up you go, you great lout,' she said and he automatically began to heave himself up from stair to stair with her hauling from behind and Dolly pushing his feet. Together they managed to get him on to the bed with a deftness born of long practise and Dolly went back down the stairs.

Ellen sat on the end of the bed to get her breath back and looked at George, spread-eagled and snoring now. To think that this was the man she had been so desperate to marry! Could it be that this coarse-featured, bloated man with untidy whiskers and unkempt greying hair was the same handsome George Askew, who had been the heart-throb of all the girls? And was this the man she couldn't wait to lift her skirts for? She turned away and leaned her head on the dented iron bed rail.

Oh, what a fool she had been to think she could take Becca's place in his affections. She had wanted George, oh, there was no denying that she had been in love with him, but if she spoke the truth she had wanted him as much because he belonged to Becca as for himself. And she had been determined to have him, little realising that he would never forgive her for trapping him. Trapping both of them. She looked round the squalid little room and back at him sprawled on the bed. And by God what a trap it was. She stood up and turned her back on him. 'Well,' she said aloud, 'you ain't smashing my china, George Askew. I'll see you in your grave first.' With that she left him and went down the stairs, to help Dolly fold the sheets.

The following Saturday dawned with a haze over the river, heralding a hot day. Kate was excited over the picnic and managed to persuade Polly to bake a cake for her to take. Becca made a pile of sandwiches and a bottle of lemonade and at two o'clock Kate set off to meet Dolly.

'I've put plenty of sandwiches in the basket because I dessay Tim and Ash'll find their way to where you are if they know there's food about, and I've no doubt Dolly'll hev to bring the littl'uns with her,' Becca said as Kate set off.

Becca was right. As Kate got near to the path through the wood where they had agreed to meet she saw that Dolly was trailing Rosie, Arthur and Joey in a ragged procession behind her. But they all looked happy and excited and Dolly had obviously made an effort to smarten them up because their faces all shone with soap even though Arthur had no boots and Joey's hand-me-down trousers were several sizes too big. The hem of Rosie's dress had been cobbled up with wool but her pinafore was clean and her hair had been brushed. Kate recognised Dolly's dress as one she herself had outgrown. It was a little short for Dolly too, and her black stockings were full of holes.

A flood of conflicting emotions rushed through Kate's mind; pity for her cousin who struggled so hard in an impossible situation; a feeling of irritation towards her aunt, mingled with something she only dimly recognised as disgust; and a warm gratitude, not completely devoid of smugness, for her own comfortable family life.

'Can we go to the stream?' Arthur asked. 'There might be tadpoles.'

'They'll have turned into frogs and hopped away by now, Arty,' Dolly said, laughing. 'You'll hev to come earlier in the year if you wanta find tadpoles.'

'Well, we can still go to the stream, can't we?' Rosie pleaded.

Kate frowned. She had the picnic basket so she was naturally in charge. 'No. I don't think we'd better. You know how deep that is. One of the littl'uns might fall in and get drownded. I know where there's a nice open patch among the trees. We'll go there. Look, Mum's even put a checked tablecloth in for us to spread on the ground.' She led the way through the cool green paths to the clearing and they all sat down, their eyes wide and hungry as Kate unpacked the basket although it was barely three o'clock.

Kate didn't eat much, Becca had made sure she'd had a good dinner before she left, but the Askew children did more than justice to the pile of sandwiches and the fruit cake that Polly had made that morning. Then they passed the lemonade bottle round. Every last crumb had been finished and Kate was just folding the red checked tablecloth when there was a crashing through the undergrowth and Tim leapt out on them, closely followed by Ash who fell over as he tried to copy his brother.

'Where's the picnic, then?' Tim demanded.

'You're too late. We've eaten it all,' Kate said.

'But it's only jest gone three!'

'I know.' Kate smiled sweetly. 'We were hungry.'

The boys' faces fell. 'What are you gonna do now, then?' Tim brightened up. 'Shall we play hide and seek?'

Kate looked worried. 'I'm afraid the littl'uns might get lost.' She turned to Dolly. 'What would you like to do, Dolly?'

'Don't mind.' Dolly smiled, a little shy of her two boy cousins. In truth she so rarely had time to herself that she would have been happy simply to sit in the sunshine and make daisy chains.

'I want to paddle in the stream,' Rosie said. She was nearly seven, a thin-faced child with big brown eyes. When she grew up she would be beautiful.

'Thass too dangerous, 'Dolly said. 'I've told you that afore.'

'Thass cold, too, even in the middle of summer,' Tim said. 'I dunno why.'

'Because that come straight from the spring,' Ash said in his funny rolling tone.

'How do you know?' Kate's eyebrows shot up in surprise.

'Mr Teddy told me. He showed me.'

'I don't believe you. Don't take any notice of him, he's making it up,' Tim said, showing off by turning a cartwheel.

'When did you see Mr Teddy, Ash?' Kate asked.

'I often see him. Here in the wood. He paints squirrels and fings.'

'And he *talks* to you?' Dolly breathed, impressed.

'Yes. About the animals and fings. He's nice.'

'I bet you couldn't show us where the spring is.' Tim was breathless from doing several somersaults, one after another.

'Oh, leave him be, Tim,' Kate said.

'I could so,' Ash said, scrambling to his feet.

'Come on, then. Let's go and find it.'

They all stood up and Dolly brushed the crumbs off her younger brothers and sister. Ash stood for a moment with his head cocked to one side. Then he plunged off through the bushes. 'Wait for us,' Kate called. She left the basket by the trunk of an oak tree and grabbed Joey's hand. 'I'll look after Joey, Dolly. You bring Arthur. Rosie, you stay with us.'

Kate hurried after Ash. Tim was with him, trying to pretend that he was in the lead, Rosie was a little behind and Dolly brought up the rear. Her progress was slower. Every time the going got rough she picked six-year-old Arthur up and struggled along with him in her arms, mindful of his bare feet. Before long they reached the stream. It was in a deep culvert between banks that in springtime were covered in primroses.

Kate was nervous. 'Did we hev to come this way?' she called to the boys. 'I'm afraid the littl'uns might fall down the bank.' But the boys were too far away to take any notice so she had no choice but to follow them, keeping a tight hold on Joey's hand. Every so often they had to make a detour and push through quite dense undergrowth in order to get round a clump of trees or a thick patch of bramble growing on the edge of the bank. Once there was a fallen tree right across their path and hanging out over the stream, a jagged crater beside it where it had been uprooted in a storm. Then Kate waited for Rosie and made sure that Dolly and Arthur weren't too far behind.

The stream began to narrow and by the time they came to the edge of the wood the bank either side was little more than a gentle slope leading out on to the meadow beyond. Here, Ash led them to the place where it began, fed by a steady trickle from an old piece of earthenware drain pipe around which a patch of bright green swampy grass showed the presence of a spring.

'This is where the spring is,' he said importantly. 'You can drink the water coming outa that pipe, Mr Teddy showed me.' He knelt down and cupped his hands under the trickle and the older children did the same, shivering a little in the bright sunshine as the pure, cold water ran down their chins.

Dolly cupped her hands and gave Joey a drink. 'Careful now,' she said, 'thass cold as ice.'

'We could stay out here in the meadow for a little while,' Kate said. 'The littl'uns can pick some buttercups and daisies. They'll like that.'

'No, Me and Ash are going back into the wood. We're building a tree house, ain't we, Ash?' Tim said.

Ash nodded. He felt important. He had shown them all something he'd known and they hadn't.

'Come on, then Ash. Let's leave them here.' Tim went whistling off, Ash shambling along behind him.

The two older girls went further down the meadow, where they could see Farmer Green's cows grazing on the marsh and beyond them the fishing smacks coming up river on the tide. They sat down and Kate took off her straw hat and put it on the grass beside her. Arthur and Joey went off with Rosie to pick daisies.

Dolly stretched out on the soft grass and closed her eyes. 'Ooh, this is lovely,' she breathed, 'but I mustn't be away too long. I promised Mum I'd be back in time to deliver the washing to Mrs Hamford. I ironed it all afore I came out, so thass all ready.'

'Do you hev to do all the ironing, Dolly?' Kate asked, chewing on a piece of grass.

Her eyes flew open. 'Yes, 'course I do. Don't you?'

Kate shrugged, suddenly feeling for some reason inadequate. 'I iron the hankies sometimes,' she said.

'Hankies? We don't hev hankies.' Dolly closed her eyes again.

Rosie brought a handful of buttercups and gave them to Kate. 'Can I wear your hat?' she asked, picking it up.

'Yes, if you like. Go and fetch some daisies now and I'll make you a nice long daisy chain.' Rosie went off and Kate began to thread some nearby daisies through each others' stems. It was very quiet except for the two boys shouting to each other as they raced round the meadow and the occasional lowing of a cow on the marsh. Dolly had gone to sleep.

She finished threading all the daisies she could reach and looked round to see if Rosie had collected more. The boys were crouched down, watching a grasshopper now, but Rosie was nowhere to be seen. Kate shaded her eyes. 'Arthur, where's Rosie?' she called.

He looked up. 'Dunno.'

Kate stood up. 'Rosie!' she called. She could see right across the meadow, across the marsh to the water's edge, but there was no sign of Rosie in her faded pink dress and white pinafore. 'She was wearing my yellow hat, too,' Kate said to herself, 'so I'd be bound to see her.' She knelt down and shook Dolly. 'Wake up, Dolly, I can't find Rosie,' she said anxiously, 'she must hev gone off somewhere. We've lost her.'

Chapter Fifteen

Dolly sat up, blinking in the sunlight, immediately wide awake. 'I'll bet the little perisher's gone to try and find Ash and Tim,' she said. 'She's a rare one for the boys, if she get the chance.'

They called the two little boys and hurried back into the cool wood. 'Do you know where the tree house is?' she asked urgently. 'I reckon she's gone to find that.'

Kate shook her head. 'No, I don't, but I reckon she'll follow the stream back, don't you?'

Dolly made a face. 'Paddling in it, as like as not. There's no telling with that little perisher, she's up to all manner of tricks. Roseee!' She cupped her hands and called again, 'Roseee!'

There was no reply. The two girls looked at each other, alarm reflected in each other's eyes. 'Do you know the woods?' Dolly asked.

'Not very well. Not as well as Tim and Ash. I think we'd better keep together,' Kate said uncertainly.

Dolly nodded. They began to go back the way they had

come, stopping every few steps to call to Rosie and getting no reply. Arthur was a little ahead. Suddenly, he came back. 'Look, I found these daisies. Do you think they're Rosie's?'

Kate took them. 'Yes, I reckon they are. That means she must hev come this way, so we're on the right track. Roseee!'

'Can me and Joey walk along in the stream?' Arthur asked.

'No, that get very deep a bit further along where the bank is steep,' Kate said, 'you stay with us.'

'Look, Kate, there's your hat,' Joey called as they reached the place where a tree had fallen across the stream. 'Thass caught in a branch, there.'

'Rosie was wearing it. I said she could. So she must be somewhere near. Oh, come you back. Never mind the hat,' as Arthur got a stick and began to crawl along the trunk of the tree to try and reach it. 'You'll fall in if you try to stretch over there and get swept away. You can see, the water runs quite fast jest here.'

'Oh, Kate, do you reckon thass what Rosie did?' Dolly said, running further along the bank. 'Roseee!'

'Help! Oh, Dolly, come quick,' a little voice cried.

There was a crashing through the undergrowth and Tim appeared, followed closely by Ash. 'What's all the row about?' he called. 'We heard you from our tree house.'

'Thass Rosie. We couldn't find her but we can hear her calling now,' Kate said, running along the top of the bank and looking down into the stream. 'Oh, I can see her, she's down here in the water, all caught up in that branch there. Can't you get out, Rosie?'

'No, I'm stuck. My hair is all tangled in this branch and my skirt's all caught up, too. I can't get move and this water's freezing. I think I'm gonna drown. Oh, Katie, I'm frightened.'

'It's all right, Rose, you won't drown. We'll get you out, don't worry,' Kate called, sitting down and unlacing her boots.

'It's OK. I'll go. I can easily slide down the bank and get her.' Tim had his boots and stockings off. Arthur, already barefoot, tried to follow.

'No, Arty, you can't go too, you'll fall in,' Dolly shouted, grabbing him. 'Oh, do be quick, Tim. She'll ketch her death, and her with her chest, too.'

They watched as Tim slid down the steep grassy bank on his backside and waded into the icy water to where Rosie was still floundering about, caught up in the branch by her hair and skirts and held down by her boots. Arthur, forbidden to go with Tim, was leaning over the edge of the bank with Joey, trying to reach her with a long stick.

Dolly caught the two little ones just before they over-reached themselves and joined Rosie in the water and they all watched as Tim got to her and began to untangle her from the branch. 'Ow, my hair!' she yelled as he tried to pull her free. 'And my boot's got stuck. Oh, I'll never get out. I shall die.'

'Oh, don't be such a ninny, of course you won't die,' Tim said yanking at her hair and grappling with her skirts and the strings of her pinafore. 'I'll get you out in a minute if you keep still. Golly, this water's cold. There. You're free now. But hold my hand, there's quite a swift current jest here. Come on, it's not far to the bank.'

'My boot. I've lost my boot.'

'You'll hev to do without it.'

'No. Mum'll kill me if I go back without it. Arthur's got to hev them next.'

'Oh, hang on then.' Tim fished in the clear water and brought out the boots. The water ran out from a hole in the sole as he handed it to her. 'Now come on.' He dragged her over to the bank and pushed her unceremoniously on to it. Dolly and Kate pulled her up the bank. She was suffering more from cold and shock than anything. The stream was not very wide and the water had only come up to Tim's waist, but Rosie was almost fainting from fright and cold and was helpless to do anything for herself.

'We'll take her home to our house, it's nearer,' Kate said wringing out her pinafore and dress as best she could with Rosie still inside. 'It's all right, Dolly, the boys and me'll look after her. You take Arthur and Joey home and tell your mum what's happened. My mum'll find her some dry clothes. Come on, Rosie, now. We'll take you to Aunt Becca's. Can you walk?'

Rosie was blue and shivering. She nodded, her clothes clinging cold and wet round her legs. 'I lost your hat, Kate,' she said, through chattering teeth. 'And when I reached over to try and get it, I fell in the stream and couldn't get out.'

'Oh, never mind about my hat. I've got another one,' Kate said, without thinking. 'Quick now.' She put her arm round her cousin and began to help her along. 'She'll be all right, Dolly, don't you worry,' she called over her shoulder. 'Mum'll look after her.'

'Mum'll look after her,' Ash said, shambling along behind the little party with Kate's hat on his head. Anxious to be useful but not quite knowing how, he'd crawled out along the tree trunk and rescued it while the others were busy rescuing Rosie.

Becca was just finishing the chair she was caning. Jethro had gone into Colchester but she had declined to go, saying this was the last of the set of six and she wanted to get them finished and out of the way. She looked up as the bedraggled little party came down the path and went to the door to meet them.

'What in the name of goodness . . . ?' She didn't wait for explanations but fetched the tin bath from the scullery and put it down in front of the fire that was kept alight whatever the weather. 'Get those wet clothes off, child, and get in the bath, quick. A sunny day that may be but you look ready to ketch your death.' As she spoke she was filling the bath from the kettle on the stove and cooling it with water from the bucket. She laced it liberally with mustard, all the time listening with half an ear to Kate's story of Rosie's fall in the stream, and the way Tim had rescued her.

'You can get in after Rosie, Tim,' Becca said over her shoulder as she began helping the shivering child to strip off her wet things. 'You're a big lad, you won't take no harm for another five minutes. Come on, now, get in this bath, Rosie, then I'll make you a nice hot drink. You're frozen half to death, child.' Once Rose was sitting in the tub, still shivering, Becca wrapped a hot brick from the side of the hearth in a piece of flannel and gave it to Kate. 'Here, child, take this and put it in your bed. We'll put Rosie in there when she's bathed and dried. She's in no fit state to go back to her own home. I'll make up a bed on the floor for you for tonight.' She turned back to Rosie and began to chafe her hands and feet. 'Look at you, blue with cold. And your teeth haven't stopped chattering yet.' She went to the foot of the stairs. 'Bring one of your nightgowns down for Rosie, Kate, and warm it by the fire.'

Half an hour later she was sitting by the fire in Kate's flannel nightgown, with a patchwork blanket tucked round her, drinking hot milk. She was still shivering, her little face looking even more pinched than usual and her brown eyes wide over the rim of the mug, nervously taking everything in.

Becca pushed the girl's freshly washed hair away from her forehead. 'You don't need to worry, dearie, you'll stay here till I'm satisfied you're none the worse for your soaking,' she said kindly. 'It's a wonder you didn't ketch your death, falling in that stream. That water's like ice, even on the hottest day. Now, hev you finished that milk? Then up to bed with you. We'll see what you're like after a good night's sleep.'

So Rosie was put to bed in Kate's room. Shivering and sweating in turns, she snuggled down between the crisp white sheets and thought she was in heaven.

She very nearly was.

For two days and nights Becca sat with her, holding her against the dry, rasping cough that wracked her thin body, bathing her face and changing her sweat-soaked nightgown. But on the third day the fever left her and Becca was able to tempt her with a little broth.

Kate tiptoed into the room to see how the little girl was.

'She'll do.' Wearily, Becca brushed the back of her hand across her forehead and got up from the chair she had hardly left. 'She's sleeping properly now. You can sit with her for a little, Kate, if you like, but don't wake her. Sleep's what she needs.'

'Uncle George is downstairs,' Kate whispered, taking her mother's place. 'He comes up at least twice every day to see how she is.'

Becca nodded. 'I'd better go down and hev a word with him.' She went slowly down the stairs. Over the years her relationship with George had settled into a faintly irritated acceptance. He worked hard, Edward Green boasted that he was the best cowman in Essex and Suffolk, and he drank hard – he had a reputation for that, too. Now he was sober, sitting by the table twisting his cap between his knees and talking to Jethro. He was still a handsome man although his features had coarsened somewhat and there were grey flecks in his hair and whiskers. He looked up as Becca came into the room, his eyes very blue in his weatherbeaten face. 'How is the little maid now?' he asked anxiously.

'She'll do. She's asleep now. But I think she'll be better here for a few more days, George. Ellen's got enough to do . . .'

'I'd be glad,' he interrupted. 'There's a sight more comfort here than at home. And she'll be better looked after.' He sniffed. 'Young Rosie was always the delicate one, y'know. That would be her as fell in that damn' stream. But thank God – and thanks to you, Becca – she's getting over it.' He got up to go.

'Do you want to go up and see Rosie, George, before you go?' Becca asked.

'Will I disturb her?'

'No, she's fast asleep.'

'Well, I'll jest take a little look, then.' He crept up the stairs behind Becca as quietly as his lumbering frame would allow and stood looking down at his little daughter. 'Poor little owd gal, she ain't no bigger'n a minute, is she?' he whispered. He dropped a kiss on her forehead and turned away. 'I know I shouldn't hev me favourite but she's always bin the one I got on best with. She'd always come to meet me from work and set on me lap while I was eating me dinner. Even when I'd had a bit to drink she wouldn't be afeared.' Surreptitiously he wiped away a tear. 'Tell her her owd dad come to give her a look, will you, Becca?'

' 'Course I will, George.' She patted him on the back as a sudden surge of emotion – pity? love? compassion? she couldn't put a name to it – flowed through her.

After George had gone, leaving a strong smell of the farmyard behind, she sat down on the chair he had left, shaking her head. 'George is a funny bloke, ain't he? With all his faults, do you know I believe he think the world of his children.'

Jethro spat in the fire, unimpressed. 'Well, all I can say to that is he's got a funny way of showing it, most of the time.'

Rosie's recovery was slow. She was only a tiny scrap of a thing, and the rasping cough her illness left her with seemed to shake her whole frame. Becca fed her nourishing broths and stews, which she ate with relish, but it made no difference – she remained skinny and frail.

'I don't feel I can send her home while she's got that awful cough,' Becca said to Jethro, 'but she's been here nearly a fortnight now. We can't keep her for ever.'

He stoked his pipe and leaned back in his chair, replete after his supper. 'She can stay here as long as she like as far as I'm concerned,' he said. 'She ain't a mite of trouble, is she?'

'No, she's no trouble.' Becca frowned. 'But I don't want to upset Ellen.'

Jethro chuckled. 'I shouldn't think you need to worry about that. She ain't even bin to see her yet, hev she?'

'Well, she's got a lot to do. She don't hev much time,' Becca said defensively.

'I don't s'pose she's got any more to do than you hev, Becca. And that reminds me, that owd wooden box full of china you left a bid on at the sale room – I brought it home, thass in the workshop.'

'Oh, was it knocked down to me? Thass good.' Becca's face lit up. Than she became serious again. 'My sister's got the idea that I never lift a finger to do anything. She think I live the life of a lady.'

'Why should she think that?' Jethro's eyebrows shot up.

'Why, because I've got Polly Jakins.' She was quiet for a minute. 'Mind you, I don't work young Polly half as hard as Ellen work her own daughter, I know right well. That Dolly hev to slave from morn till night in that house.'

The next day while Rosie helped Becca to unpack the china Becca asked her if she was ready to return to her own home?

'No, I'd rather stay with you, Aunt Becca.' She coughed as she always did after speaking.

'Don't you miss Dolly and the others?'

'Not much.' She pulled out a Staffordshire dog. 'Oh, look, Aunt Becca, this is nice. Is it Crown Derby?'

'No, dear, it's Staffordshire,' Becca said absently. She was nonplussed. She didn't want to seem to be turning the child out but it was plain that Rosie was in no hurry to go home.

As if in answer to her thoughts there was a knock at the door and Ellen stood there, her arms folded across her scrawny chest, her faded fair hair dragged back into a thin knot at the back. 'Where is she, then? Where's my Rosie?' she demanded.

'She's here, of course, with me. Come in, Ellen.' Becca stood aside for her sister to enter. 'Rosie, here's your mum come to see you,' she called over her shoulder.

Ellen remained on the doorstep. 'I ain't come to see her, I've come to fetch her home. I think you've had her quite long enough.'

'I didn't want to send her home till she was well again,' Becca said, puzzled at Ellen's tone. 'Oh, do come in, Ellen. The kettle's on the boil, I'll make a cup of tea.'

'I don't want no tea. I'm taking her home and you needn't try to stop me.'

'Try and stop you? Why should I do that?'

'Oh, I can see your drift, there's no need to play the innocent.' Ellen stepped inside. 'You think now she's

281

getting to be useful, you can 'tice her to stay with you.'
Rosie was carefully unwrapping another piece out of the
box as her mother walked into the room. 'Yes, jest as I
thought. You've already set her to work. Well, I'm not
heving it. She's not slaving here for nothing, jest because
she's fam'ly.'

'Ellen, for goodness' sake! I never heard sech rubbish.
Sit down while I make the tea, do.' Becca was angry.
'Rosie's bin very ill. George can tell you that. He's bin
here every day, sometimes twice, to see how she was.'

'Hm. Yes, well, he would, wouldn't he?' Ellen snapped.
'He wouldn't miss an opportunity to come and see you.'

'Oh, for heaven's sake, woman, don't rake that up
again,' Becca said, exasperated. 'He didn't come to see
me, he came to see Rosie. Which is more'n you ever did.
You've never come high nor by till now. But now you're
here you can see the poor little thing is still as white as a
sheet. She needs looking after.'

'Then why hev you set her to work?'

'This isn't work. She wanted to help me.' Becca poured
the tea and pushed a cup over to Ellen. 'I don't know
what's got into you, Ellen, coming here and making such
a set to and palaver.'

She pushed the cup back. 'I don't want that. I want my
daughter. Go and get your things, Rose.'

'What things? I ain't got no things,' Rosie said. She
lifted her chin. 'Anyway, I ain't coming home. I'm staying
with Aunt Becca. I'm ill.' She began to cough. She coughed
till she was blue in the face and frightened even her
mother.

'Well, p'raps another few days,' Ellen said, reluctantly

climbing down as Rosie lay gasping in the chair. She reached for the tea she had pushed away. 'We don't want her passing that cough on to the littl'uns.' She drank her tea in silence, then got up to go. 'But as soon as she's better she's to come home. Dolly can do with a bit of help and Rosie's seven now, old enough to be handy.'

After Ellen had gone Becca went back into the room. Rosie had her head in the box of china, making sure it was all unpacked. 'That was rather naughty, Rosie,' Becca said.

'What was?' She looked up, the picture of innocence.

'You know very well what I mean. That coughing fit. I wonder you didn't make yourself sick.'

Rosie grinned. 'I nearly did. I tried to.' She sat down in Jethro's armchair and swung her legs. 'Well, I didn't want to go home with Mum. I like it here. So I showed her what a bad cough I'd got.'

Becca sighed. She couldn't blame the child, there was precious little comfort in her own home and Ellen was clearly only interested in her capacity to work. Yet Rosie couldn't stay indefinitely, sharing Kate's room – although Rosie now slept on the made-up bed and Kate had her own bed back – and even more importantly, jeopardising the fragile goodwill that had been gradually building up between Becca and Ellen. It was quite a problem.

In the end, Becca kept her for another week, promising as the child clung to her when her father came to take her back that she could visit as often as she liked. But Rosie didn't come. Becca tried to tell herself that it was a long walk for a seven-year-old girl with a wracking cough but she knew it was not that. She knew Ellen wouldn't let her come. She knew, too, that the fragile friendship she had begun to rebuild with her sister was again in ruins because Ellen would never forgive her for winning a place in Rosie's affections.

Chapter Sixteen

Albert and Henry, the twins, left school and began working on the farm on their thirteenth birthday. They hardly noticed any difference. Ever since they were old enough to pick a stone or tell the difference between a weed and a turnip their schooling had taken second place to a day's work on the farm. The school authorities complained but what was the use? Farm labourers' wages were abysmally low and their families needed every extra copper that could be earned. Food in the belly was more important than facts in the head, learned parrot fashion from an older child briefed an hour earlier. It made little difference to the children of Wessingford – or any other farming village, either – that New York was the capital city of America, they were never likely to go there. Nor did it matter to them that 'I am hungry' was part of the verb 'to hunger'. To them it was part of everyday life. They were always hungry.

It was ironic that the twins were legitimately working on the farm for less than a year before they were both sacked. For a disaster in which they were only indirectly to blame.

George had taken some young bullocks into Colchester market. Before he left he looked for the twins, and when he couldn't find them asked Shorty the pigman to tell them to watch out for the cows on the marsh because it was possible there would be a high tide and they would need to be moved.

Unfortunately, Shorty passed the message on to Albert, who forgot, instead of Henry, who would have remembered.

And things might have been even worse if it hadn't been for the Miller children.

Kate had been sent to her aunt's house with a can of stew left over from dinner. In spite of the coolness between the sisters Becca often sent a can of stew or a bread pudding along to Ellen, who although she hated accepting it, and did so with a bad grace, was always glad of anything to supplement her children's diet.

When she'd been told about the errand Kate had made a face, then she brightened up. 'Do you reckon I'll be able to see the new baby?'

Becca smiled. 'I shouldn't be surprised.' She made a clicking sound with her tongue. 'Winnifred! What a name to give a little mite. I 'spect she got it out of one of them penny romances she's for ever got her head in. Well, go on then, put your hat and coat on and be off with you. Wrap up warm because thass a lazy wind out there, that don't stop to go round you, that'll go straight through. Oh, and call in at the cottage on your way back and see if Granny and Granpa want anything. You can take Lucy with you, too. It'll do her good to hev a walk and it'll keep her out of my way while I finish polishing the table in the workshop for your dad.'

There were sounds of hammering from the workshop. Jethro was making a coffin for Owd Grimble. He had died sitting in his corner at The Whalebone, quietly and without fuss. Nobody knew how old he had been but it was reckoned he was not far short of a hundred. Of course he had no money so there had been a whip-round at The Whalebone and Brock Badger had made up the difference to buy the wood for the coffin and Jethro was making it for nothing so the old man shouldn't have a pauper's funeral. Jethro was too kind-hearted for his own good, Becca sometimes thought. But she was wise enough not to say so.

Kate and Lucy played hop, skip and jump along the lane to the Askews' cottage, where the gate, still open and half off its hinges, had ivy growing over it. The younger children were playing in the dirt by the back door with an old wheel they were using as a hoop. Kate greeted them briefly and left Lucy watching them with her thumb in her mouth. There was no danger that she would play in the dirt with them. Lucy couldn't bear to be dirty.

Kate went into the wash house, where clouds of steam were issuing from the door and window. Through the steam she could see her cousin Dolly, in an overall three sizes too big, lifting sheets out of the copper in the corner with the aid of a long stick and a bucket. Her hair was plastered to her forehead and the sweat was running in rivulets down her face. Under the overall her frock had burst under the arms, partly because it was too tight and partly because it was rotten.

'Mum sent this stew. If you add a few more vegetables there should be enough for all of you,' said Kate. She felt somehow guilty that she and Lucy had warm coats – even though she knew Mum had made them from a blanket she bought at the sale room – while their cousins outside shivered in threadbare jerseys.

Dolly's pale blue eyes sparkled. 'Mmm. Smells lovely. Thank Aunt Becca kindly. But will you help me put these sheets out on the line afore we take it indoors, Kate? There's a good blow today so they on't take long to dry. They're Mrs Green's. Mum had to go to bed afore she could get to them and they'll be hollerin' for 'em up at the farm if they ain't back by Friday.' Pale, fair-haired Dolly was always good-natured and showed no trace of the discomfort that Kate felt at their different situations.

She helped Dolly spread the heavy sheets on to the piece of rope stretched between the house and a post half-way up the garden path. The garden was full of weeds except for a patch at the top where Uncle George had begun to dig it ready for potatoes. The whole place had an air of decay and neglect, unlike her own home, which was warm and cosy, the garden well tended and full of vegetables.

She followed Dolly into the house. 'Miss Holmes asked why you weren't at school? I said you'd got a new sister so you'd had to stay at home at look after the others,' she said importantly.

Dolly shrugged. 'I shan't be going back anyway,' she said, poking the fire into life and setting the can of stew beside it. 'I shall be thirteen next month and I'm to go into service as kitchen maid at the farm.' She tried

288

unsuccessfully to keep the pride and excitement out of her voice. 'Granny put in a word for me and Mrs Green said I could start as soon as I'd had me birthday. Mum'll be up and about by then so I can be spared.' She turned to Kate, her eyes shining. 'I dessay I shall hev a room all to meself! Jest think of that!'

Kate didn't know what to say. She loved school and couldn't imagine anyone being anxious to leave, especially to go and work as a kitchen maid at Tenpenny Farm. Mrs Green looked rather stern and fierce, even though she was very beautiful and wore clothes that came from London. No, Kate didn't envy Dolly one little bit. And yet . . . she looked round the room. There was very little furniture: a scrubbed table with an assortment of chairs and stools round it, a rag rug on the bare earth floor and a wooden armchair by the side of the fire. On the corner of the mantelpiece, displacing half a dozen cheap ornaments, there was a pile of well-thumbed novelettes. Across the ceiling a string of neatly ironed washing was airing.

Dolly followed her gaze. 'That lot's ready to go back to Mrs Badger at The Whalebone. I got up as soon as it was light and ironed it this morning.'

Kate smiled at her cousin. Anything must be better than living like this. 'I hope you'll enjoy working at the Greens',' she said.

'At least I'll get plenty to eat and me keep.' Dolly grinned cheerfully. She nodded towards the stairs. 'You can go up and see the new baby if you want.'

Kate went to the back door and called Lucy and together they went up the stairs. The bedroom was not

289

very big. As well as the double bed, where Aunt Ellen lay reading, there was a single iron bedstead along one wall and a cot along another. A chest of drawers stood jammed between the foot of the bed and the wall and Kate wondered how they ever managed to open the drawers.

Aunt Ellen looked up without smiling. She was pale, thin-faced and thin-lipped, and looked ten years older than her age. Kate never quite knew what to say to her.

'Come to see the littl'un, hev you?' She uncovered the bundle at her side and Kate dragged Lucy forward to peep at the tiny, red, screwed-up creature. As they peered at her the baby began to yell, but whether it was from hunger or fury that Fate hadn't given her a better deal in life it was impossible to say.

'Winnifred. Thass a nice name,' Kate said, for something to say.

'Yes. Thass the name of the girl in a book I jest read.' Aunt Ellen covered the ugly little face up again, ignoring the yelling, and picked up her novelette.

'Mum sent me along with some stew,' Kate said, for something to say.

Aunt Ellen's head shot up. 'Oh, did she! I s'pose she think we can't fend for ourselves.'

'Oh, no, it wasn't that. There was some left over . . .' Kate's voice trailed off. That was even worse. Now Aunt Ellen would think she'd been sent the leavings. 'We'd better be going. Come on, Lucy, we've got to get back. Goodbye, Aunt Ellen.' Kate caught Lucy's hand and pulled her out of the room. Sometimes it was hard to believe that Mum and Aunt Ellen were sisters.

Ellen threw her book down on the bed. She hated it

290

when Becca sent things. She didn't want her sister's charity and wished she could throw it back in her face. But the truth was it was only the cast-offs from Becca's children that kept hers even half decently clothed. And she couldn't deny she'd been grateful for all that china she had given her. There was still quite a lot of it left.

A delicious smell wafted up the stairs. 'Dolly!' she screeched. 'You can bring me a plate of that stew. I can't be expected to feed a baby on an empty belly.'

Kate and Lucy were glad to leave their aunt's house and they ran down the lane to Granny and Granpa's cottage. Granny was sitting on one side of the fire, busy knitting something for the new baby, grinding her gums together as she worked and making her face look all squashy. She'd only got one tooth left, a long yellow fang that got caught on her lip sometimes. Granpa called it her pickle-chaser, but Kate privately thought it must get in the way and she'd be better off without it. Her gums were so hard she could bite an apple with them.

Granpa was dozing in his wheeled chair opposite. He was very fat and had a bad heart. Mum said it was because his rheumaticks didn't let him move about much. He woke up when Kate and Lucy walked in.

'Is it still blowing half a gale?' he asked, looking at their rosy cheeks, as bright red as the woolly hats pulled down over their ears.

'Not as bad as it was yesterday, Granpa, but it's cold.' Kate went over to warm her hands by the fire while Lucy clambered on to Granny's lap for a cuddle.

'I reckon there'll be a rare high tide, what with this nor' east wind bringing the water down the coast and the sun

291

crossing the line – there's olwuss a rare high tide when the sun crosses the line. Thass the on'y time rat island get covered.'

'What do you mean, Granpa, the sun crossing the line. What line?'

'Why the Equator, child. Twenty-first o' March and twenty-first o' September is when the sun crosses the line and thass when we get the equinockshull tides.' He leaned back in his chair and felt in the big pocket at the side for his pipe. 'And if I ain't very much mistaken this wind'll whip the water up even further.'

Granny rocked Lucy. 'Don't take no notice of him, gals. He's an old Jonah. Olwuss looking for trouble.' But she gave him an affectionate smile, her single tooth sticking up like a tombstone in her shrunken gums.

Granpa nodded sagely as he stoked his pipe. 'Them as live longest'll see most, but I reckon if you was to go and take a look you'd find I was right.' He closed his eyes to savour his private bonfire. 'I didn't work on the land in all weathers for forty years and more 'ithout knowing what weather signs to look out for,' he added, speaking more to himself than anybody.

'We'll go and see,' Kate decided. 'We can go home over the fields and through the wood, it's not much further. If it's a big tide we'll come back and tell you, Granpa.'

Joe Stansgate shook his head. 'No need, my gal. I know very well there'll be a big tide.'

Kate and Lucy left. They went out through the back garden and across the meadow; over the stile where their mother and father had met, and across another field where the winter wheat was already green, to a meadow which sloped down to lush marshland enclosed by a sea wall where the cows were often put to graze. Beyond the sea wall, saltings bordered a wide creek which opened out into the river, winding away in the distance. With the brown sails of fishing smacks and the big stack barges it was a pretty sight. But not today. Today it was difficult to see where the creek ended and the river began. A wide expanse of churning water stretched from the bottom of the meadow almost as far as the eye could see.

Tim and Ash came running across the meadow. 'Have you come to see it, too?' Tim called. 'We've never seen anything like this before, have you?'

Kate stopped in her tracks. 'No. Golly gosh, Granpa was right. He said there'd be an enormous tide. Look, the saltings and the marsh have completely disappeared.' Her eyes were wide. 'Look, you can see the water creeping through at the bottom of the meadow, just down there! I've never, ever seen the tide as high as this before.' She shaded her eyes and looked across the wide expanse to Wyford. 'And look over there! You can't see Wyford quay at all! It's up to the window sills on the houses over there!'

'I reckon Owd Sharpie'll charge double to ferry people across, with the river this high,' Tim laughed.

Kate shook her head. 'It's no laughing matter. What about those poor people whose houses are all flooded?' she said, shuddering. 'It must be dreadful.'

'Well, at least it won't happen to us,' he said cheerfully. 'We live at the top of a hill.'

'I want to go and see the water coming up the meadow.' Lucy was jigging up and down excitedly and tugging at Kate's hand.

Tim grinned down at her. 'Off you go, then, Lucy loose-legs. You go and tell us how deep it is.'

'No, Lucy. Wait for me!' Kate ran after the little girl, calling over her shoulder, 'You should know better, Timothy Miller. You haven't any idea how deep that water is down there. She could drown.'

'I'll ketch her, Katie.' Ash loped down the slope, stumbling over his long legs, and Kate scooped Lucy up in her arms as all three reached the bottom together and stood looking as the insidious waves lapped further into the meadow. Tim followed and they all stood looking at the great sheet of dirty, muddy water that covered the entire marsh to such a depth that the river wall had completely disappeared, and only the tops of the scrubby trees and bushes that grew on the marsh itself were visible.

Kate screwed her face up. 'Doesn't Uncle George put his cows on this marsh to graze sometimes?'

Tim grinned. 'If he did they won't be very happy today. Hey, look! Along there!'

'Where?' Kate craned her neck.

'On the other side of the hedge, along there to your right. Up there, look, on the other side of that oak tree. There, can't you see the splashing? Isn't that a cow's head bobbing about? And look, there's another. And another! What the . . .'

'They're all trying to get into the meadow, but they can't get through the hedge because there's a ditch beside it and it's too deep.' Kate clutched his arm. 'Tim, the cows *were* on the marsh. They'll all drown if we don't do something!'

'Oh, poor cows.' Ash frowned at the plight of the animals. 'They're frightened.'

They all ran along the bottom of the meadow, where the water, though at this point not deep, lapped relentlessly up through the tufty grass, until they reached the place where some twenty cows were floundering and bellowing in fright.

'It's no use. We can't do anything ourselves, we must get help,' Tim said, taking control. 'Kate, you take Lucy home. Tell Dad what's happened. Tell him he might be needed. I'll run to the farm. It's probably quicker if I go by the fields rather than the road and there's always the chance I might see Uncle George on the way. He'd know what to do. Or the twins . . . they could help.' He turned to Ash. 'You stay and talk to the cows, Ash. You're good with animals.'

Tim ran off in one direction and Kate took Lucy's hand and hurried back home through the wood. As they emerged on to the road they ran straight into Mr Teddy, Edward Green's son. At twenty he had grown into a tall, slender man, with clean-cut features like his father, and wavy black hair that he wore longer than was fashionable and which he had a habit of tossing back. He was always immaculately, if not very conventionally, dressed. Today he was wearing a long camel-haired overcoat under which were stone-coloured trousers and a wine corduroy jacket. His checked shirt matched both and his cravat was pink and floppy. He was carrying an easel and portfolio, obviously on his way to the wood to paint, despite the cold wind, and was having difficulty in keeping his widebrimmed felt hat on his head as he walked.

'Oh, Mr Teddy!' Kate panted, although she wouldn't normally have dared to speak to him. 'Something dreadful's happened.'

Mr Teddy stopped and looked down at her, surprised at being accosted by the girl he vaguely recognised as young Ash Miller's sister. 'Something dreadful? And what might that be, child?' He tossed his hair back, just catching his hat before it blew away.

'Uncle George's . . . Mr Green's . . . the farmer's cows, sir – they're all on the marsh!'

'Nothing unusual in that, is there? I believe the cowman often grazes them there.'

'Yes, but don't you see? It's all flooded. They'll drown. I've never seen the tide so high. All the houses on the other side of the river are flooded . . .'

'*All* of them?' Mr Teddy smiled slightly. 'Surely that's an exaggeration?'

'All the ones on the quay.' Kate waved her hand impatiently. 'But the cows, don't you see? They can't get off the marsh because of the ditch and the hedge and they're all floundering about . . .' She was almost in tears with anxiety. 'They'll drown if something isn't done. My brother's gone for help.'

Mr Teddy nodded. 'Stout fellow.' He looked at the equipment under his arm and sighed. 'Well, I suppose I'd better take this home and then go and see what I can do to assist.' He fingered his cravat. 'Stupid creatures, cows.'

'But it's not their fault they're trapped, sir.'

'No, I suppose not.' He shuddered. 'Ugh! They'll be all wet and covered with unmentionable . . . but I suppose I'd better show willing.'

'Oh, yes, thank you.' Kate could have died with gratitude although she didn't know why. She hurried on home, turning round once to see that although Mr Teddy had turned back towards the farm he didn't seem to be walking very quickly.

The day Farmer Green's cows drowned was something of a milestone in the life of the village. For one thing, nobody had ever known the river to come up so high, either before or since, and for another, every family in Wessingford received a joint of beef from the bloated and butchered carcasses. Because nearly half the herd perished that day.

As the Miller children ran about raising the alarm everybody rallied round. George Askew's brother Sid, who had taken over from his father as blacksmith, left his forge as soon as he heard and came still wearing his leather apron; Johnny Groves the farrier arrived with ropes and tackle; Jethro left his workshop in such a hurry that a pot of glue boiled dry on the stove while he was gone; men from the other farms and from Old Mr Green's estate came running, armed with pitch forks, rakes, ropes, anything they thought might be remotely useful. The women followed behind, to wring their hands and weep for the poor helpless struggling animals. Becca came too. Frowning anxiously, she looked for George. The cows were his responsibility, so where was he? Why had he left them to drown on the marsh? Surely he couldn't be slaking his thirst – which was becoming legendary – yet again in The Whalebone? Appalled at the scene, yet knowing there was nothing she could do to help, Becca went home again. Unlike the other women, watching the sad spectacle was not her idea of entertainment.

It was indeed a sad sight, and one young Kate never forgot. Years later she could still recall the noise – the shouted and contradictory orders from the men to each other, the bellowing of the cattle and the splashing and thrashing about in the water. Some of the men got a rope round the horns of one cow but she was stuck fast in the soft marshy mud and as they pulled her neck snapped with a sound like the crack of a whip. They managed to make a sling to slip under the belly of another so that the men on the other side of the hedge could haul her to safety but she struggled so much that the sling snapped and she fell back, breaking her legs.

The way parted for Mr Edward when he arrived. He strode anxiously up and down, cursing George Askew, never where he was needed, at the same time doing lightning calculations in his head. Felicity had recently persuaded him to buy one of the new Minerva motor cars, which had cost him over a hundred pounds that he could ill afford, and he wasn't sure now that he liked it better than the old one. And only last month his favourite hunter had jibbed at a hedge and fallen, breaking a leg so it had to be shot. Now, with this disaster on top of it all, he could see nothing but ruin ahead. As he dashed the tears of fury and frustration from his eyes the village folk regarded him sympathetically, guilty to think they had misjudged him in thinking he didn't care for anything except having a good time.

The last of the bullocks had just sold – and for a reasonable price – when the news reached George at the market.

Tears ran down his face when he learned of the plight of his beloved cows. 'But I left word with my boys to fetch 'em back if the water looked like comin' up overly high. I wouldn't hev put them down there at all but the marsh grass is sweet and there ain't that much else about this time o' year,' he said as he was brought home on the back of Jeg Nelson's cart. 'But I 'spect the Gaffer counter-manded me an' sent the boys orf to do suthin' else so they couldn't watch out for 'em. He's olwuss doin' that sort o' thing. Olwuss chuckin' his weight about. Not like his father. The Owd Gaffer's a real gentleman.' He climbed out of the cart and ran down the meadow beside the wood to see what was going on.

'Thass no use, bors,' he shouted, white-faced and waving his arms. 'You're doing' more harm than good, a-pullin' at 'em like that. You'll break their bloody necks, the lot of 'em.'

'Where were you? Why weren't you here? Why were the cattle put there in the first place?' Edward Green, white with financial worry, turned on George.

'Jest leave me be a minute and let me think what's best to be done,' George said absently, frowning and summing up the scene. His face began to clear. 'Yes, look, young Nooncey Miller's got the right idea. Thass right, bor, lead 'em to that little hump where the ground is higher.'

It was fortunate that Becca hadn't stayed, because Ash had wriggled through the hedge into the icy water and was half wading, half swimming round the frightened cows, gently talking to them, calming them and persuad-ing them towards the hummock of higher ground. Here they could at least stand safely and he stayed with them,

299

quietly rubbing their backs and talking to them, waiting for the swirling waters to recede. Ash coaxed nine of the cows to safety; the frightened animals seemed to trust his gentle voice where the shouts and sticks of the men, and even George himself, only seemed to terrify them even more. Everyone knew Daft Ash had a way with animals, but this was nothing short of a miracle. In spite of the icy water round his thighs the boy wouldn't leave the cows until the tide had receded sufficiently for them to be led safely through to the dry ground of the meadow. At the end of the day only twelve cows out of the herd of twenty survived, the nine Ash had looked after and three others.

'That boy'll ketch the new-monia.' Men shook their heads as they watched. 'Why don't you fetch him outa that water, Jethro? He'll ketch his death.'

Jethro shook his head. He was as anxious as anybody about his son. 'He wouldn't come,' he said. 'He won't leave the cows.'

'I'd say bugger the cows,' someone was heard to mutter.

Jethro paced restlessly up and down, his eyes never leaving his son. Suddenly he caught sight of Kate. 'Run home to your mother, Kate. Tell her to get plenty of water hot an' put a hot brick in the boy's bed. We'll shove him in a mustard bath soon as we get him home and then put him to bed with some hot milk and I'll fetch a drop o' whisky from Brock's to put in it. That way, please God, he shouldn't take no harm.'

'Strikes me I'd have done better to trust the cows to young Nooncey Miller than to you two silly little buggers,' George said to the twins later, when the cows that remained had been brought back to the farm and examined by the vet – at further expense. 'I told you to be sure and keep an eye open for the water comin' over the marsh. Why didn't you do as I said?'

'The Gaffer sent us up to Middle Field stone pickin',' Albert said sullenly.

'Well, you shoulda told him you'd gotta watch out for the cows.'

'I forgot.'

George turned his attention to the other twin. 'Well, you shouldn't hev forgot, Harry, even if that silly little sod did.'

'I never knew nothin' about any message,' he said smugly. 'Nobody told me nothin' about watchin' out for no cows. I ain't to blame.' He gave a shrug.

George's face darkened at the sight of his two unrepentant sons. In spite of being twins, with a marked similarity in their features, they were far from identical. Both had grey eyes, Albert's were shifty, Henry's were calculating; both had brown hair, Albert's an untidy mop, his cap perched rakishly on it, Henry's always neatly brushed – what you could see of it – because he wore his cap squarely and pulled down nearly to his ears; both had square, stubby hands, Albert's with dirty, broken fingernails, Henry's bitten down to the quick. Albert had a smile that bordered on a sneer, Henry rarely smiled at all. They both had short, stocky, underfed figures and were always seen together, largely because nobody else wanted their company. People didn't trust the Askew twins; Albert because of his untrustworthy appearance, Henry because of what people suspected might be lurking, hidden, under his cold determined expression.

'Don't you realise what you've done, you daft buggers?' said George. 'You're s'posed to be larnin' and makin' yerselves useful about the farm! 'Stead of that you've lost me half me cows. If I ain't mistaken you'll both get the sack termorrer an' I shan't be far behind you. *Somebody*'ll hev to carry the can for all this, you mark my words.

'But the Gaffer can't blame us. That was him what sent us . . . ,' Albert whined.

'I know that. But you shoulda told him what I'd said about the marsh. He'd hev knowed that was more important.'

'You can't blame me. It wasn't my fault. I didn't know nothin' about it,' Henry said woodenly.

'Oh, get outa my sight.' George waved his sons away in disgust. 'I'm off down the pub. Tell your mother I shall be late.' He started off down the lane towards The Whalebone. He hadn't gone many paces before he turned back. 'Either of you got tuppence I can borry?'

They both shook their heads, Albert for once telling the truth, Henry less honest. He was determined not to let his father tip the few coppers he'd managed to hoard out of his wages down his neck.

Chapter Seventeen

The twins went off in the other direction towards home. 'I don't care if I do get the sack,' Albert said, slouching along, his hands in his pockets, kicking a stone into the hedge as he went. 'I never wanted to be a bloody cowman, anyway.'

'Nor did I.' By contrast, Henry marched beside him, his back straight, his hands clasped behind him.

Albert looked round at him. 'What do you want to be, then?'

'A builder.' The answer came with no hesitation.

'A builder? You can't be a builder. You don't know nothing about building.' Albert was scathing.

'I can learn, can't I?' Henry gave an enormous sniff. 'I dessay I'll start off being a bricklayer and work me way up.'

'Can't see what you wanta do that for.' Albert spat copiously.

Henry shrugged. 'Thass better'n bein' a cowman. An' better'n muckin' out pigs. What do you wanta be?'

It was Albert's turn to shrug. 'Dunno.'

Henry took off his cap, scratched his head and then rammed his cap back squarely between his ears. 'Well, I know what I'm gonna do. I'm goin' to Sprocket's the builder's tomorrer to see if I can get a job there. Then if Owd Greeny give me the sack, I can say I was gonna leave anyway.'

'I might as well come with you.' Albert kicked another stone into the hedge.

Henry thought for a minute. 'No. Let me go first. See how I get on. Once I'm in, I'll put in a word for you.' He wasn't going to let his brother spoil any chance he might have of a job with the local builder.

'OK.' Another stone flew into the hedge. 'Never thought about bein' a bricklayer, but I s'pose thass as good as anything else.' He dragged his sleeve across his nose. 'Wonder if there'll be any o' that nice stew at home Aunt Becca send up sometimes? My belly's flappin' against my backbone.'

Ralph Sprocket liked the look of the well-scrubbed, eager young lad who presented himself at the building site the next morning, even though the boy did have the backside out of his trousers. Being a pillar of the Chapel Ralph prided himself on always being willing to give the under-privileged a chance – and not entirely because they were usually happy to take lower wages. And when, after a week's highly satisfactory work, during which he'd been eager to learn and eager to please, young Askew asked if there might be a job for his twin brother Albert, Ralph Sprocket made the understandable mistake of thinking that being twins they would be alike in temperament and agreed to take him on. It only took him a week to realise his mistake.

For the second time in less than ten days Albert was sacked. Because it had been as Henry predicted: both boys were sacked from the farm. Or at least, Albert was, Henry wasn't even there. He was too busy fixing himself up with Ralph Sprocket. But somebody's head had to roll for the events on the marsh and naturally Edward wasn't prepared to shoulder the blame himself even though Shorty Johnson the pigman had told him Joe Stansgate had forecast flooding – and Joe had never been known to be wrong in forecasting such things. Edward, although he would never have admitted it, had known the cows were on the marsh and hadn't given a thought to getting them moved . . .

He couldn't spare George Askew, either. He was the best cowman in the district. Not that George was in any way to blame. He'd put the cows there in good faith, with – as he thought – the boys to keep an eye on them in case of the expected floods. After all, there would be six hours' good grazing between tides. No, he couldn't fault George. But those twins of his . . .

Edward was glad of the excuse to get rid of them on two counts; for one thing they were a useful scapegoat, and for another they would save him the two shillings a week wages he had to pay them. He begrudged their wages although Henry was quite a good worker. But young Albert was more trouble than he was worth. Young Nooncey Miller would be more use on the farm than that lazy young sod. He'd done very well, young Miller, calming the cows the way he had. Everyone said he had a way with animals and it would seem they were right. Even George Askew hadn't been able to handle them the way that boy had done. Edward frowned. It might be an idea to offer to take him on; probably wouldn't need to pay him much as he wasn't all there. He'd have to think about it. Wouldn't do to offer yet, though. After what had happened his father might think he was worth more than Edward was prepared to pay him.

In fact, Jethro was more concerned that nobody had been near to enquire whether Ash had taken any harm from being in the icy water for all that time.

'He coulda caught his death,' he complained to Becca, 'but there's never been even a message from the farm, nor a drop of milk to say thankee to the boy.'

Becca was sitting on a low stool in the workshop, re-caning a chair. She looked up. 'I ain't worried about that,' she said. 'I'm jest thankful he didn't take any harm. When I saw what he was like when you brought him home – blue with cold right up to his armpits – I was afraid he'd never get over it, him not being very strong at the best of times.'

Jethro chuckled as he carefully cut a sliver of veneer to fit into the top of a little marquetry side table. 'Not very strong! He must hev the constitution of a ox, that boy! Why, he never even took a cold!'

'He never look very strong, though,' Becca persisted. 'Thass why we've always thought he was delicate and cosseted him, ever since he was a baby. He must be tougher than we think.' She went back to her caning. 'I regret not giving you a son – a proper son, so you could

306

put JETHRO MILLER AND SON up on your board, Jethro,' she said, her head bent so that her face was half hidden.

He said nothing. He finished fitting in the sliver of veneer, then he went over to her and squatted down on his haunches, lifting her face to his. 'I don't never want to hear you talk like that again, Becca,' he said quietly. 'Young Ash is our son, and he's a proper son. If he ain't bright enough to do the kind of work I do, well, never mind it. He look after owd Blossom out on the pightle and the owd donkey, too, like a good'un. And he keep the cart washed and shiny, too. He's a good boy and we love him. And we're lucky we've got young Tim. He may not be of our getting but he's a good boy too, and we love him as if he was. He's beginning to show quite an interest in the workshop, too. I shall encourage him, see how he shapes up.' He smiled. 'You never know, I might still be able to put AND SON up on the sign later on.'

'But would that be right, Jethro? Would it be allowed?' Becca frowned anxiously. 'I mean, he isn't *really* our son. Not our *proper* son. It might be against the law.'

Jethro put his finger over her lips. 'Thass all history. He don't know that, nor do the other children, and nor do many other people. And there's no reason why they should. We've never made no difference between him and the rest of the family, hev we?'

'No.' Becca gave a little smile. 'Even the people in the village seem to have forgotten what happened.'

'Ten years is a long time, Becca. In fact, thass over ten years now. People's memories fade. Not that many of them knew the truth of it all at the time.'

307

'No, although I don't know why Mum and Dad were so anxious to hev it all hushed up the way it was. After all, there was nothing to be ashamed of, the girl had her marriage lines and everything. But with you making the coffin and the parson being agreeable to an early morning burial there weren't many as knew the truth. In fact, most folks thought the baby'd belonged to Ellen and we'd taken him off her hands because he came so soon after little Rosie. She was on'y jest over eight months old when he was born, if you remember.'

'There y'are, then. Anyway, he's as much ours now as if he'd come from us. And we're lucky to hev him. He's a rare fine boy. And I shall be proud to put him up on the board as my son when the time come.'

He got to his feet and went back to his work and Becca resumed her caning. The thought went through her mind as it had done many times over the years she had been married: Jethro was a good man. He was honest and upright and hardworking, although he lacked ambition. And if their marriage lacked that spark of – what? – excitement? – passion? – love? – would she have found it with George Askew, who drank too much and kept poor Ellen almost permanently pregnant? And was she deluding herself in imagining that George would have been a different man if she had been his wife instead of Ellen . . . She shook her head. There was no sense in dwelling on what might have been.

A few weeks after the episode with the cows, on a warm April afternoon, Teddy Green, the farmer's son, was sitting comfortably with his sketch pad in his favourite clearing in the wood. It was quite a large clearing, with a stand of five pine trees in the middle where he could sit quietly unobserved and draw or paint the squirrels and birds going about their business. Like his father, he was not at all interested in farming, but whereas Edward Green preferred the company of his hunting and card-sharping friends, Teddy liked to study quietly and paint nature. His mother encouraged him in this, convinced he had great talent, and had somehow persuaded his father to hire a tutor who gave him lessons twice a week. His hours with Adrian Benedict were the happiest of Teddy's life; he admired the man more than anyone he had ever met and thought his paintings worthy of being hung in the Academy, which made Adrian laugh.

Today, Teddy was making brief pencil sketches of squirrels – sitting bolt upright and nibbling at last year's acorns clutched between tiny paws; scuttling across the clearing; chasing each other up a nearby oak tree. He had nearly enough detail to begin the proper drawing Adrian had suggested when he heard the snap of a twig and the tall, pale figure of Ash Miller slipped quietly through the undergrowth into the clearing and sat down at Teddy's feet, his long legs sticking out.

'I thought you'd be along. But watch out with those legs, you'll knock the easel over.' Teddy smiled affection-ately down at the boy as he spoke. He liked the simple Miller lad. Ash was always interested in hearing about the birds and woodland creatures, and in listening to the stories Teddy made up about them. Once he had brought a bird with an injured wing that he had found, thinking Teddy could charm it back to health, which he had found quite touching. Perhaps that was why he was fond of the boy, because Ash respected him and looked up to him – hero-worshipped him, almost – in a way that nobody else did. That in itself made him feel good. 'Have you come into the wood to escape family strife like me, Ash?' he asked, ruffling the boy's hair affectionately.

Ash looked up at him, trying to understand. 'I don't think so. I don't know what you mean by family strife. I've come to see you. Like I do sometimes.'

Teddy gave a little laugh. 'Yes, of course you have. And you wouldn't know what family strife is because you come from a devoted and loving family, don't you? Your parents aren't continually at loggerheads. You don't have to escape to get away from it all.' He turned back to his sketching, his mouth twisting bitterly. 'God, this last little episode's been enough to drive a fellow insane! At the moment I feel I never want to see or hear of another cow as long as I live.'

'Some of them died. On the marsh,' Ash said, latching on to something he understood. 'I saved some of them, but I couldn't save them all. I tried. But they got drownded.' He shook his head, sighing.

'Yes, yes, I know all about that,' Teddy said with a trace of impatience. 'It's all I've heard about from my father ever since it happened. And as for my mother . . .' He raised his eyes. 'Well, you'd think Pa was personally responsible for the whole business.'

Ash sat up. 'Did you see the water, Mr Teddy? It came right over the marshes and right through into the meadow.' He shuddered. 'It was very cold.'

'No, Ash, I didn't see it, although I heard you were the

310

hero of the day.' He smiled at the boy, then went on putting the finishing touches to a squirrel's tail. 'I came to the top of the meadow but there were so many people about I thought they could do without me, so I came back home. I don't like being caught amongst crowds of sweaty bodies.' He gave a discreet shudder. 'And I certainly didn't want to see what happened to the cows.' He shuddered again. 'Mind you, I guess it's all put Pater in Queer Street, especially as he's just bought this smart new car, which I know he only got to keep Mama quiet. Mind you, I must say he really cuts quite a dash in it, even though I think it's noisier and smellier than the old one.'

He sighed. 'They are always, but always, rowing about money, my parents. Can't understand it myself. As long as Pa pays my art tutor and I have enough for my materials and clothes for my back, I ask nothing more. But Mater . . .' He sighed again. 'Not only does she want everything she sees, but she's always got her head stuck in some catalogue or other to make sure she hasn't missed anything new that's come out.' He paused to look at what he'd done. 'Oh, and speaking of anything new, isn't the new maid that's just appeared at home some relative of yours? Dolly, I think she's called?' He looked questioningly at Ash.

Ash nodded importantly. 'Cousin Dolly. Aunt Ellen's girl.'

'Ah, I thought there was some tie-up. She seems a likely enough girl, very willing. Got good bone structure, too, apart from her legs, of course. They look a bit rickety to me, but perhaps it's just the way she walks.' He sighed and continued with his sketching. 'There was

311

a row over her, too. Mater insisted that now Old Daisy can't work as much she needed someone younger to take her place and Pa said he couldn't afford it. But after the usual tantrum and hullabaloo Mater got her own way like she always does.'

'It's always been the same, I've never known my parents live in peace and harmony. I can remember crying myself to sleep at night because I was so afraid one of them – either of them – would go off and leave me. I was never quite sure whether I didn't want one to go or whether I didn't want to be left with the other. I still don't know, really.' He was talking as much to himself as to Ash, much of the time through a pencil held between his teeth.

He sat back to survey the sketch again, took the pencil from his mouth, then leaned forward and carried on, 'My father was determined to "make a man" of me. Kept trying to make me play shooting games with tin soldiers, which I hated. He bought me boxing gloves and nearly killed me trying to show me how to use them. I hated that, too. But I hated it even more when he ignored me, which he did when he wasn't trying to "make a man" of me.'

'And my mother was as bad, always either weeping over me and calling me her heart's darling or telling Nanny to "remove the child" out of her sight.' He looked briefly down at Ash, who was watching a caterpillar make its way up a blade of grass. 'I seem to remember your father did a lot of work for her at one time, Ash, but that stopped suddenly. Then there was a man who kept coming to redecorate the rooms. There was always one room

312

being decorated and she would spend hours with – what was his name? – Mr Handsome, that's right. He *was* quite handsome, too. Mater was always choosing colour schemes and changing her mind a dozen times. I had to be kept out of the way, of course. But as I got older I got sly and would hide behind curtains and watch.'

He surveyed his drawing through half-closed eyes then carried on, 'I can tell you this, Ash, Mr Handsome didn't spend all his time with a paint brush in his hand. In fact, he spent a good deal of it in my mother's arms. I could never feel the same about her after that. It was all so sordid. And a terrible shock to discover that my own mother was nothing more than a . . . well, perhaps not quite as bad as that. But I don't care any more. I go my own way. I do what I like, when I like. As long as Pa pays my allowance regularly I ask for nothing more. I have my painting lessons, Adrian says I'm quite good, and I look forward to them every Wednesday and Friday.'

He looked down at Ash again. 'Adrian's a wonderful man, Ash. You'll have to meet him one day. He's taught me all I know but I'll never be as good as he is, not if I live to be a hundred, which of course I shan't. Oh, damn, that's not right. I'll have to start again.' He tore the sheet from his pad and screwed it up.

'I found a weasel,' Ash said. Obviously he hadn't been listening to a word Teddy had said. It was as well.

'What?' Teddy frowned, dragging his attention back to Ash.

'I found a weasel.'

'Did you? Was it alive?'

'Yes.'

'Sure it wasn't a stoat?'

'Yes. It had a black tip to its tail.'

'What did you do with it?'

Ash frowned and shook his head. 'I never done nuffin with it. It ran off down its hole.'

'Oh, I see.'

'No, you never didn't. You wasn't there.' Ash was quite indignant.

Teddy smiled. 'I meant that I understood what you were telling me, Ash.'

'Oh.'

'Do you think you can find the bank where the primroses grow, Ash? I want a few to press. I'll show you how to press flowers, too, if you like.'

'Yes, I know where they grow.' He scrambled to his feet.

'Well, don't bring armfuls. Just a few.'

Ash went off and Teddy began another drawing. Everywhere was very quiet except for the collared doves cooing in the branches and he sketched busily for some time. He liked young Ash. He could tell him all his troubles and he knew Ash wouldn't say anything, probably because he didn't understand. He was lucky.

Ellen viewed Dolly's move to Tenpenny Farm with mixed feelings. She was glad to think that there would be a little more room and one less mouth to feed in their already overcrowded cottage and looked forward to the shilling a month wages Dolly would receive – and pass over – in addition to her keep. On the other hand Dolly was a good worker and never ran off to do other things when she was asked to sweep the floor or do the ironing like young Rosie did. Rosie wasn't near so biddable. She hated looking after the baby, and said so, and contrived never to be there when she was wanted. She wasn't all that strong, either, with a nasty, dry cough that Ellen didn't like the sound of. Ellen was fond of Rosie in the slap-happy way she was fond of all her children, but she knew she was going to miss Dolly.

As for Dolly, she had never been so happy in the whole of her short life. She had a room up under the eaves, with a single iron bedstead and a flock mattress with sheets and blankets and a feather pillow. All to herself. Under the window there was a chest of drawers to keep her things in – not that she had much – and a chair beside the bed and a rag rug on the floor. Added to that she had plenty to eat and a uniform consisting of a pretty lilac dress that wasn't all that much too big and a large white apron. In the morning she wore a mob cap to keep her hair tidy and in the afternoon changed it for a little white cap with streamers which perched on the top of her head and had to be carefully pinned to her hair so that it didn't slip.

Dolly was popular. She was popular with Cook because she wasn't afraid of hard work and never minded what she did; she was popular with Mrs Felicity because she took trouble over ironing her ruffles and was quick and neat with her needle; she was popular with Mr Edward because she was quiet and unobtrusive; and she was popular with Mr Teddy because she cleaned his room without disturbing things and would cheerfully bring his food on a tray if he didn't want to go downstairs.

'She's got good bone structure. Hasn't she got good bone structure, Adrian?' he asked when she took tea to him and his art tutor.

'Mmm.' Adrian Benedict took a step back and put his head on one side in what Dolly thought was rather an exaggerated way. He put his finger under her chin and lifted it a little. 'Yes, in a rough and ready kind of way I suppose you might say that.' He turned away, losing interest.

'I thought I might paint her,' Teddy said eagerly.

'Oh, my dear! Really?' Adrian gave him a playful pat on the arm and laughed, an unnatural high-pitched sort of giggle which Dolly found irritating. 'What are you thinking of calling it: "Girl With a Slop Bucket"? He went into peals of laughter.

Teddy flushed. 'Well, if you don't think it's a good idea, Adrian . . .'

'Oh, it's all experience, dear boy. You haven't tried portraits yet, have you? Nor nudes. How about painting her nude?' He gave a discreet shudder. 'If you could bear to.'

Dolly finished pouring the tea, put the teapot down heavily and left the room, closing the door with what might have been construed as a bang if she hadn't been a servant.

'Oh, my, do you think we've offended our little rustic?' she heard Adrian remark. She didn't wait to hear Teddy's reply.

After that she avoided going into Master Teddy's studio when she knew that Adrian would be there. There was something about the man that gave her the creeps, and it wasn't simply the purple trousers and bright green smock that he wore. And Teddy said no more about painting her, for which she was glad. Not that she would have minded sitting for Teddy – although she would never, ever have taken her clothes off to be painted, the very thought made her blush to the roots of her hair. But the idea of Adrian Benedict looking at a portrait of her that Teddy had drawn, touching it, criticising it, laughing – oh, not at the painting but at her, the sitter – made her flesh crawl. It was a good thing that Teddy never asked her because she would have lost her place at the farm rather than accept. And that would have broken her heart.

Chapter Eighteen

Just before Christmas in the year 1906 Granpa Joe died. Everyone knew he was ill, he had been ill for as long as most of the children could remember, but he had always been there, sitting in his wheeled chair, smoking his pipe and offering his wisdom, and it was unthinkable that he should be dead and his chair empty.

Strangely, it was Daisy, the one who had lost most, who seemed troubled least. In her solid, countrywoman's way she accepted Joe's death as part of the inevitable cycle of life. She had done the best she could for him whilst he was alive so she had nothing to reproach herself for in his death, therefore she felt none of the remorse that stems from guilt. And Joe was out of all his pain. She had no reason to grieve. Grieving was a luxury, very akin to self-pity. If she shed a tear, no one saw it.

Jethro and George followed the coffin to the grave-yard, with Shorty Johnson and the other farm hands walking behind, Brock Badger from The Whalebone with them. Brock had sent a keg of beer to Daisy for the 'do'

318

after the funeral as a token of his respect for the old man and she, with Becca's help, had prepared the food: a joint of ham that Becca had provided, with pickled cabbage and beetroot and pickled onions. 'Thass what he liked best,' Daisy said, spreading her good white cloth on the table, adding with a wry smile, 'pity he ain't here to enjoy it. He loved a good get-together.'

'Who's to say he ain't watching over it all?' Becca said gently. 'Who's to say he ain't sitting in his chair there, only we jest can't see him?'

Daisy rounded on her. 'Thass heathen talk. Your dad was a good man. He's gone to meet his Maker. Setting in his chair, indeed.' She shook her head disapprovingly and jerked her thumb towards the ceiling. 'He's up there, with the Good Lord, where he belong. God rest his soul.' She banged the jar of pickled onions down on the table.

'Sorry, Mum, I didn't mean no disrespect,' Becca said quietly.

The men returned, beating their arms across their chests to restore some warmth after standing round the grave in the windswept churchyard.

'Did it all go off all right?' Daisy looked anxiously at Jethro.

'Aye. We sang "Abide with Me" round the grave and Parson said the service.' Jethro sat down by the fire and eased his starched collar where it had begun to chafe his neck. 'You don't need to worry, missus, we see that he was buried all proper and decent.'

'Thass all right, then.' Daisy's gaunt shoulders seemed to relax slightly.

'Brock said he'd sent up a drop o' beer,' George said,

319

looking round for it. He was still in his working clothes because he hadn't any others.

'Can't you wait!' hissed Ellen.

'I on'y said...' George looked bewildered. 'I was gonna offer to fetch it in.'

'Well, Becca's gone to do that, so sit down and shut up.'

The five of them sat round the table eating ham and pickle and drinking Brock's beer. The children were all in the wash house, eating jam sandwiches. Dolly and the twins had been given the afternoon off out of respect for their grandfather, but it had not been thought proper for them to eat with the adults so Becca had lit the copper fire for warmth and they sat happily enough on sacks and upturned buckets, the young ones being looked after by the older ones.

'I ain't heard nothing from Owd Mr Green,' Daisy said, mangling a slice of ham thoughtfully between her gums.

'Did you expect to?' Ellen asked. 'Come to that, I thought Mr Edward mighta followed the coffin but he never, did he, George?'

He shook his head. 'Too busy with the Hunt. Every Thursday, come wind, come weather. Mebbe if we'd buried Joe on a Friday...'

The others nodded. They all knew Edward Green.

Daisy sighed. 'Well, I reckon I shall hear from the owd chap afore long. I doubt he won't let me stay here now Joe's gone.' She took a drink of beer. 'Bah, I don't like this stuff, never hev. I'll make a nice cuppa tea. You want a cuppa tea, Becca? Ellen?'

'Yes, please.' Becca looked at Jethro, her eyebrows raised. Almost imperceptibly he nodded. 'Are you afraid Old Mr Green'll turn you outa this cottage because he's bin paying the rent all these years, Mum?' she asked.

'Why, yes.' Daisy swirled hot water round in the teapot to warm it. 'I can't expect him to carry on now Joe's gone, can I?' She turned away and spooned tea into the pot. 'I dessay I'll hev to go to the Spike. That won't be so bad for me. I shall get on all right. Joe wouldn't hev liked it, o' course, but thank God he didn't hev to go there.'

'Oh, Mum.' Ellen put her hand out. 'You wouldn't like it, neither.'

Daisy shrugged her off. ' 'Course I shan't like it.' She squared her shoulders, 'But I can put up with anything, if I hev to.' She sniffed. 'On me own, that is. I couldn't hev bore to see your dad shut up there.'

Becca stood up and put her arm round her mother. 'Thass all right, Mum, you don't hev to worry about going to the Spike. Nobody's gonna turn you outa this cottage.'

Daisy looked up at her. 'How do you know? Hev you seen Owd Mr Green?'

'Thass got nothing to do with Mr Green,' Becca explained gently. 'He ain't bin paying the rent on this place. Jethro's bin paying it. Ever since Dad was took ill.'

Daisy's jaw dropped open and Ellen turned a dull red. 'I never knew that!' Daisy said.

'And you wouldn't hev knowed it now if it wasn't to set your mind at rest,' Jethro said, looking uncomfortable.

Daisy sat down. 'Well, I never. All these years. Well, I never.'

'Thass what comes of heving a rich son-in-law,' Ellen said, her voice brittle.

'I wouldn't say that, Ellen,' Jethro said mildly. 'I ain't a rich man, by any means.'

'Well, you ain't short if you can go chucking it about like that.' Ellen tossed her head.

'Keeping a roof over Mum and Dad's head ain't exackly what you'd call chucking money about,' Becca said, her voice ominously low. 'Jethro ain't one for doing that. But he don't go chucking it down his throat, neither. Mebbe if George . . .'

He got up, scraping his chair back on the stone floor. 'I ain't staying here to be told what to do and what not to do.'

'Oh, sit down, George,' Ellen said irritably. 'Don't take no notice of Lady Muck.'

'I'll thank you all to keep a civil tongue in your head,' Daisy said sharply. 'Remember, this is your dad's funeral. If you can't be civil to one another today of all days you oughta be ashamed of yerselves.' She turned to Jethro, and for the first time there was a glint of a tear in her eye. 'Thankee, Jethro, bor, for what you done for us all these years. You saved us from ending our days in the Spike. Time was when I never thought I'd say the words but I bless the day Becca took up with ye.' She leaned over and kissed his whiskery cheek.

He patted her hand, embarrassed. 'Well, you don't need to fret, missus. You won't never be turned outa this house, not while I can find the few coppers for the rent.' He turned to George. 'And I'll hev a drop more of that beer since you've got it in your hand, bor. While there's still some left.'

Out in the wash house the children had eaten all the jam sandwiches and drunk the jug full of lemonade. Now they were taking it in turns to tell stories. Dolly was sitting on a bucket nursing little Winnie and Georgie was sitting on Kate's lap. Rosie was teaching Lucy to play cat's cradle and Joey and Arthur were playing five stones. The twins were exploring the darker corners of the wash house, slightly bored but unwilling to leave in case they missed anything.

'Look here, Harry,' Albert said. He had squeezed himself between the mangle and the tin bath. 'There's a cask here with some of Granny's home-made wine in it. Anybody want a drink?'

'What sort is it?' Henry asked.

'Dunno.' Albert put his finger under the spigot and turned it on. 'Mangold, I think. Or p'raps it's parsnip. Thass a drop o' good, whatever it is. Got a cup, anybody?'

Dolly produced the cups they had all the drunk the lemonade from and Albert filled them.

'Do you think the littl'uns oughta hev any?' Dolly asked anxiously. 'That might make them bad.'

'We won't give them much. Jest half a cupful,' Henry decided.

Albert doled out the wine and they all sat down to drink. 'Thass a little bit on the sharp side,' Henry said, trying to make out he knew what he was talking about.

'I don't like it,' Joey said.

'Give it to me, then. I'll drink it.' Albert held out his hand.

They all sat round, sipping the home-made wine and feeling very grown-up.

323

'I'll tell you a secret, if you like,' Dolly said, when her cup was half empty. She gave a little giggle. 'Although I shouldn't really . . .'

'Go on, you'll hev to tell us now,' Kate nudged her. She held her cup to Albert. 'I wouldn't mind a drop more, Bert, thass quite nice. More for you, Dolly?'

'Well, jest a drop.' She waited till Albert had re-filled her cup, then she began. 'You know we always call Mrs Edward "the Lady Felicity", don't you?'

'Well, she is. She's a titled lady,' Rosie said. She had a little difficulty with the word 'titled', it came out as 'tilted', she didn't know why.

'Ah, thass jest it.' Dolly looked owlishly round at them. 'She ain't tiled . . . tilted . . . titled at all.'

'You're heving us on.' Henry held out his cup to Albert for more wine. 'Everybody knows she come from London.'

'I never said she didn't come from London,' Dolly said. 'All I said was, she wasn't a tilted lady.' She didn't bother to correct her mispronunciation.

'Who is she, then?' Albert was getting bored. He drained his cup for the third time and refilled it from the cask. When Dolly finished telling this silly story, he'd get them all singing 'One Man Went to Mow'. He knew some good words to it and felt like singing. 'Come on, hurry up with your yarn.'

'She was an actress!' Dolly paused dramatically to let her words sink in. Everybody knew that actresses were 'no better than they should be'. None of them knew quite what that phrase meant except that it was something said about people who were not quite respectable.

'I don't believe you,' Kate breathed.

324

'Thass true. Thass as true as I'm sitting here.' Dolly nearly fell off the bucket as she spoke.

'How do you know?' Rosie asked. 'Who told you?'

'I heard her and the master rowing – well, they're always rowing – and I heard him say "Do you think I'd have married you, either, Maudie Sadler, if I'd known you'd been on the stage?" Well, I couldn't believe my ears – I was brushing down the stairs at the time so I couldn't help listening – and then Mr Teddy came along. "Well, now you know all our family secrets, Dolly," he say.

' "I'm sure I don't Mr Teddy," I told him. "I don't know what you're talking about." Well, I didn't. I didn't understand. Not really. So he set himself down on the stairs then and there and told me all about it.'

They were all wide-eyed now, even the twins, so Dolly went on, 'Mr Teddy told me that the Lady Felicity's real name was Maudie Sadler. But when Mr Edward first met her he was at some "do" in London – and she was introduced to him as the Lady Felicity Arbuthnot' – Dolly had trouble with that – 'which was the part she'd been playing on the stage. But Mr Edward didn't know that – Mr Teddy says he reckons he'd had too much to drink – because he thought it was her real name!'

'Fancy that!' Kate breathed.

'Well, Mr Teddy said, Mr Edward quite fancied being married to a titled lady so *he* told *her* his father owned a great big house and a lot of land.'

'Well, the Manor House is quite big,' Rosie said.

'Not as big as he made out,' Dolly laughed. Once she'd started laughing she couldn't stop and that made them all laugh. They laughed until their sides ached, then they calmed down and had another drink of the wine and Dolly continued. 'Well, *she* fancied being married to a rich landowner, so she never put him right on what her real name was . . .'

'Maudie Sadler?' Kate gave a little hiccup. She was having trouble keeping her eyes open now, what with the wine and the stuffy atmosphere of the wash house. 'Are you sure thass right?' she asked.

' 'Course I'm sure. Mr Teddy told me. He said she never stop going on at him because she's landed up living in a muck yard. And I know that bit's right, 'cause I've heard her say it.'

Kate frowned. 'Why should Mr Teddy tell you all this?' she asked suspiciously, trying to marshal her thoughts.

Dolly blushed and bridled a little. 'Well, me and Mr Teddy . . . well, Mr Teddy like to talk to me . . . he often tell me things.'

'Do you think he like you? I mean, you know, *like* you?' Rosie asked.

'Well, thass not for me to say, is it?' Dolly said coyly. 'But, well,' the words came out in a rush, 'he said he wouldn't mind painting me.'

'What colour?' Albert said from beside the wine cask and they all went into further fits of laughter.

'Paint my picture, stupid,' Dolly said, annoyed that her brother should make fun of her.

'I think you're in love with him,' Rosie stated. She had already begun to read her mother's novelettes.

Dolly blushed to the roots of her hair. 'Don't be daft.'

'Well, I never. So the Lady Felicity ain't the Lady Felicity at all? She's plain old Maudie Sadler. Well, I never.' Kate leaned back against the wall of the wash house and closed her eyes and Dolly, exhausted from her efforts at story-telling, did the same. The little ones were already asleep, curled up on the sacks.

Albert, in charge of the wine, poured Henry another half cupful. 'Ain't much left,' he said. 'You prop the cask up and I'll lay underneath and let it drip into me mouth. Don't wanta waste any.'

None of them ever forgot Granpa's funeral. Or the day after.

It was several weeks before Kate plucked up the courage to mention Dolly's story to her mother. 'Thass gossip,' Becca said sternly. 'You shouldn't listen to gossip and you certainly shouldn't repeat it. In any case, Dolly wasn't . . . well, she wasn't quite herself, that day. And neither were you, come to that.'

But if Kate had known it Becca didn't practise what she had preached. That night in the big bed she repeated Kate's tale to Jethro. 'Do you think thass true?' she whispered.

Jethro stared up into the darkness, remembering the trouble he'd had with Edward Green's wife a few years back. Dolly's revelations would explain a lot.

'I don't see that matter to us one way or the other, Becca,' he said after a while. 'That ain't none of our business, is it?'

'No,' she said thoughtfully, 'but somehow that ain't quite the same to see Maudie Sadler go sweeping about the village in a motor car. That don't command quite the same respect as the Lady Felicity.' She gave a little

327

giggle. 'Fancy Mr Teddy telling Dolly. I wonder why he did that?'

'Yes, I wonder,' Jethro agreed sleepily. But he clearly didn't wonder for long because soon he began to snore.

Henry worked hard for Ralph Sprocket, the builder, quickly learning the right way to lay bricks: get the mortar mix right, not too sloppy, not too dry; put sufficient on to set the brick but not too much; keep checking the level. He had his eye on Ralph's only child, Maisie, too, a plump girl of fourteen who bulged in all the right places and knew it. Henry went out of his way to wink at her and give her admiring glances. He reckoned he was a bit young to start courting in earnest but there was no harm in letting her know he had his eye on her – well, one eye anyway. The other was on Ralph's business. He saved what money he could and began to smarten himself up.

Albert, having been sacked both from the farm and from Sprocket's the builders was now working for his Uncle Sid at the blacksmith's forge. He would have been sacked from there if he hadn't been family, but Sid kept him on for his brother George's sake, although he was often heard to say that the lazy little bugger was neither use nor ornament.

Dolly worked hard like her brother Henry, but for a different reason. She thought she must be the luckiest girl alive. She loved living at Tenpenny Farm and having her own room; she loved her lilac dress and the stiffly starched apron that went with it; and when she took off her mob cap and put on her 'afternoon' cap with its long stream-ers, she felt like a queen in her crown. She saw little of Mr

Edward, he was often out early in the morning and always home late at night. Dolly could always tell how his gambling had gone. If he had won he would be full of high spirits and calling for bread and cheese to have with his nightcap. But if he had lost he would slam the doors and shut himself in his study to drown his sorrows, often continuing to drink into the small hours, when he had to crawl up the stairs on his hands and knees.

Mrs Felicity – Dolly couldn't bring herself to think of her in any other way – was alternately complaining and kind. Often she would show Dolly samples of material that had been sent from London and ask her which she thought would suit her best. Dolly had no idea, she thought they were all beautiful, but she would choose one, knowing Mrs Felicity wouldn't take her advice and only asked her so she could show off the lovely brocades and taffetas and shot silks. But Dolly didn't care. All she cared about was Mr Teddy. She thought he was the most handsome man she had ever seen in her whole life, with his long black wavy hair and his full-sleeved, colourful shirts. It made her heart turn over when he flicked his hair back or ran his fingers through it. Oh, how she would have loved to run *her* fingers through it! The thought made her feel all funny inside.

He hadn't said any more about painting her picture, but he often smiled at her and would stop and talk to her if he met her on the stairs. One day their hands touched on the banister and she had the feeling that he might have engineered it. A thrill ran right up her arm at his touch and left her all funny and breathless.

She noticed other little things too, like the way he

would ask her to bring his tea up to the studio and then keep her there, talking, and she began to wonder, to hope, that he was beginning to feel for her a little of what she felt for him. It had been known for the son of the house to marry a servant in real life. It didn't always happen in story books.

So she sang about her work and Mr Teddy said, 'You've got a very nice voice, Dolly. I like to hear you sing, it shows you're happy.' And that made her even happier and she sang even louder, until Mrs Felicity told her to stop the noise because she'd got a headache. Then Dolly would think, Blow you, Maudie Sadler! and go to another part of the house where Felicity couldn't hear her, and go on singing. The landing outside Mr Teddy's studio and bedroom was kept well dusted and polished.

Dolly wasn't so happy on the days that Mr Teddy's art tutor came to the house, because then he was so wrapped up in his painting that he had no time to talk to her. As soon as she saw Adrian Benedict's bicycle her heart would sink, although she knew exactly which days he was due and that on those days tea didn't have to be taken to the studio until after he had gone because it would interrupt their concentration. When Adrian had gone Mr Teddy would be flushed and happy because his tutor had praised his work, which Dolly could see was very good, even though she didn't understand this stuff they called abstract – it looked like a lot of daubing to her. Once when Mr Teddy asked her what she thought he should call one of these paintings – it was all orange and black and bright blue and red swirls – she had put her head on one side and said it looked for all the world like a headache to her, because that was how her head felt inside when she had a headache. But Mr Teddy hadn't understood and he had been offended and hadn't asked her opinion again.

It was Wednesday, the day Adrian Benedict was due. Dolly watched for his bicycle, that was her cue to keep well out of the way so that she didn't meet him on the stairs. But at three o'clock the bicycle hadn't arrived so she made up a tray like she did on the other days of the week and took it upstairs to the studio, tapping at the door before she went in.

The room appeared to be empty. The easel, with some creation in yellow and purple with dark green lines like prison bars on it, stood by the window – Teddy's painting was being spoiled by that man, Dolly thought. She liked his drawings of the little woodland creatures best, the squirrels and rabbits and birds. But they were the ones that Adrian dismissed as 'amateurish'. She looked round for somewhere to put the tray. The studio was littered with tubes of paint, brushes, and bits of rag, with no surface clear enough to set the tray down on. She went over to put it on a chair by the bedroom door, which only had an old towel thrown on it, when through the open doorway she saw Teddy. And Adrian. They were on the bed, their clothes in a heap on the floor. For a moment she stared, frozen, like a rabbit caught in a bright light, unable to comprehend or believe what she was witnessing. Then, with a little whimper, she turned and rushed out of the room, catching the tray on the door post as she went. It slipped from her hands and crashed to the floor but she didn't stop. She rushed upstairs to her bedroom in the attic and threw herself on the bed, stark with horror and confusion. She didn't understand . . . she couldn't believe . . . But she knew she had seen something she shouldn't have seen.

After a long time she came to her senses, realising that nobody had seen her, and that if she could get the tea tray cleared away nobody need ever know she had been anywhere near. She crept down the stairs, feeling sick with guilt and a kind of terror. Terror of Adrian Benedict, who had always given her the creeps, although he wore bright, flamboyant clothes and floppy hats. Somehow he was not like any of the other men she knew; her father, brothers, Uncle Jethro, even Mr Edward. She prayed fervently as she crept along the corridor that Mr Teddy's art tutor wouldn't come out of the room while she was clearing up the mess. She couldn't think how she had missed seeing his bicycle because he always left it in the same place under the hedge. She was not to know that he had walked to Wessingford that day because his bicycle had a puncture.

She reached the studio door. To her amazement the tea tray had gone, the spilled tea all mopped up. The door was open and Teddy was standing at his easel. There was no sign of Adrian Benedict. Teddy looked up and smiled at her, for all the world as if today was just like any other day. 'Ah, Dolly, fetch a chap a cup of tea, will you? There's a dear. I'm as dry as a chip.'

'Certainly, Mr Teddy.' She scuttled down to the kitchen and fetched the tea. There was no sign of any broken crockery and Cook said nothing. Puzzled, Dolly took the fresh tea to Mr Teddy.

'Ah, good girl. Put it down over there, will you?' He

put his head on one side to regard his painting. 'You don't think this one looks like a headache, do you, Dolly?' he asked with another smile.

'No, Mr Teddy. It's very nice.' She couldn't meet his eyes as she answered.

'Good. We'll educate you in art appreciation yet. You can poor me a cup, Dolly.'

She poured the tea and left the room. And that was how it was. Nothing was ever said. Never by so much as a flicker of an eyelid did Teddy hint that he knew Dolly had seen anything she shouldn't have done. In fact, after a while, she would have wondered if she had imagined the whole episode were it not for the fact that Adrian Benedict never came to the house again. Teddy bought himself a bicycle and cycled into Colchester for his painting lessons.

As far as Dolly was concerned that was much better. It meant she never had to run the risk of seeing that creepy man again. And better still, sometimes when Mr Teddy came back he would give her a little present – a bar of nice soap or a little trinket he'd seen in Woolworth's that he thought she might like. Her hopes soared.

Chapter Nineteen

Six months later Dolly's world fell apart.

It was September and she had been allowed time off from her household duties to help with the harvest. She enjoyed this, because it meant she could spend long days in the late-summer sunshine with the women and girls from the village, hearing all the news and catching up on all the gossip. Gathering up the sheaves was hard work, but Dolly didn't mind. She had been used to hard work all her life and it was good to be there with her little brothers and sisters and not feel totally responsible for them. Rosie was supposed to look after them these days, although she seemed to take her responsibilities far more lightly than Dolly had ever done, spending much of her time larking with the boys and leaving the little ones to their own devices.

An added pleasure for Dolly was the fact that her cousin Kate, who had gone to work as live-in nursemaid to a family in Colchester, had a few days' holiday and had also come to help. Kate had three little boys in her charge and told Dolly that she loved her work. Dolly couldn't understand this, since she herself had been glad and thankful to get away from small children – much though she loved her little brothers and sisters – and the last thing she would have wanted was a job as nursemaid.

'Do you know what homo-sex-uality means?' Kate asked, whispering the unfamiliar word very carefully as they worked side by side in the field.

'Homo – what?' Dolly frowned.

'Homo-sex-uality.' Kate said the word again, slowly. 'Yes, I'm sure I've got it right. Homo-sex-uality.'

Dolly hunched her shoulders. 'No. I've never heard of it. Why? What is it?'

'I dunno. They were all talking about it in the servants' hall at Lexden Hall – well, the men were. When us girls came into the room the housekeeper snatched the newspaper away and shut them up, quick.'

'What were they saying?'

'Something about somebody being taken to court for homo . . . whatever it is.'

'Oh.' Dolly wasn't interested. She didn't know what Kate was talking about. 'Look, do you like my brooch?' She pointed to the little paste butterfly pinned on her dress.

'Yes. Thass pretty. Where did you get it?'

Dolly blushed. 'Mr Teddy give it to me.' She gave a shy smile. 'He often give me little bits.'

'What for?' Kate frowned.

'I dunno.' Dolly gave a little smirk. 'Cause he like me, I s'pose.'

'Oh.' Kate went back to her previous topic. 'Well, I looked it up in the *Essex Standard*.'

'Looked what up?'

'What I was saying. Homo-sex-uality. I had a job to find it but there was a little bit at the bottom of the page. It didn't *say* thass what it was but it said somebody had got had up in court for being caught breaking the law with another man, and the name was the same as the butler had said. And do you know who it was?'

'Don't see how I should.' Dolly straightened up and rubbed her back. 'Anyway, I dunno what you're talking about.' She went back to work.

But Kate was not to be put off. 'It was a man called Adrian Benedict,' she said. 'I remembered the name because wasn't that the name of the man who was your Mr Teddy's art tutor?'

'Yes, it was.' Dolly shuddered. 'I didn't like him. He gave me the creeps. I was glad when he stopped coming to the house.'

'Well, the paper said something about offences with art students. I think he's being sent to prison.'

Dolly was silent, mulling over this information. Mr Teddy was one of Adrian Benedict's art students. She wondered if he knew anything about all this. Then, suddenly, the scene she had witnessed in his bedroom came back to her. At the time, although she had been shocked by what she had seen, she hadn't quite realised . . . after all, her brothers always shared a bed, though they always kept their shirts on and they never went to bed in the middle of the day. In a flash of understanding the little trinkets from Woolworth's, the nice soap that she kept among her underwear, and the bottles of cheap scent all took on a new, somehow sinister significance.

336

Strangely, her immediate feelings of disgust and revulsion towards Adrian Benedict were weaker than the flood of compassion that swept over her for Teddy Green. She was sure it couldn't have been his fault and she was saddened beyond words to think that Mr Teddy didn't trust her. Surely he must know she loved him and would never, ever betray him, whatever he did?

She tried to think of a way in which she could let him know that he need never fear, that she would die rather than betray his trust. In the end she left a note on his pillow, where he would be sure to find it. It said simply, 'Dear Mr Teddy, You can trust me. Love from Dolly.' She had agonized over whether to put 'love' or whether that would be too forward, deciding in the end that it would do no harm to let him know what her feelings for him were. Sometimes men needed a little encouragement.

She need not have worried. Teddy Green never read her note. It came too late. By the time she wrote it he had disappeared. Three days later his body was washed up and left half submerged in the mud at low tide on the other side of the river at Wyford. The thought of facing his father had been more than he could bear. Dolly retrieved her note, devastated.

As for Edward Green, his grief at the loss of his son needed an outlet and blame was the obvious one. He wanted to hurt someone else the way he had been hurt. 'It was all your fault,' he told his weeping wife. 'He would never have got involved with that art fellow if you hadn't turned him into such a namby-pamby nancy boy.'

'Teddy wasn't a nancy boy!' Felicity shouted back, her

face ravaged with tears. 'He was sensitive, that's all. And that's something you would never understand.'

'Then why was his name brought forward at the trial as one of those who . . . ?' Edward put his head in his hands. 'Oh, my God, the shame of it. To think that a son of mine . . .' He dragged himself to his feet and went over to the window. 'Of course that's why he killed himself. He couldn't bear to think of the shame it would bring on the family name. In a way I admire him for that.' He swung round and pointed a finger at Felicity, sitting at her dressing table, her head in her hands. 'Of course, it was all your fault,' he repeated. You're the one who insisted that he had artistic abilities. You're the one who hired that . . . that . . . creature to teach him. I never liked the man – man? What am I saying? He was a travesty of a man if ever there was one.'

'Oh, yes.' Felicity lifted her head and her mouth twisted bitterly as she looked at him through the mirror. 'You'd have to blame somebody, wouldn't you? You couldn't bear to believe it might be your fault that he turned to that poor unfortunate man for affection because of the way you treated him. Making him play war games with tin soldiers, buying him boxing gloves and making him fight. He hated that. Hated it! Couldn't you see he was a gentle, sensitive boy?'

'Gentle! Sensitive! He was nothing more than a namby-pamby mother's darling. And *you* did that for him. You turned him into a nancy boy.' He raised his fist above his head. 'My God, to think the only son you could give me was only half a man.'

And so it went on. Dolly went about her duties shocked

and heartbroken, trying not to listen. How could they argue about Mr Teddy in that cold-blooded, selfish way? All they thought about was themselves. They hadn't spared so much as a thought about Teddy's feelings and the agony he must have gone through to take his own life, knowing that he would have to be buried in unconsecrated ground. Tears streamed down Dolly's plain little face. Didn't they care that he would never go to heaven? Poor Mr Teddy. It was not his fault he was born gentle and didn't like fighting. He was always kind, which was more than could be said about his father. Or his mother. She dashed the tears away from her face with her sleeve and got on with her polishing.

The quarrelling went on for three weeks. Then one day Dolly was called to pack Mrs Felicity's luggage. 'I'm not staying here a moment longer,' she said, pacing up and down her room, her red hair escaping from its pins in her agitation. 'I shall return to London. I have friends there. Which is more than I can say of this place,' she added vindictively. She sniffed and wiped away a tear. 'I would have gone years ago if it hadn't been for my darling boy, but now he's . . . gone . . . there's nothing to keep me here in this God-forsaken hole. Nothing at all.'

Felicity left, ordering a taxi-cab on the recently installed telephone to come all the way from Colchester to fetch her.

After she had gone the house seemed deadly quiet. Dolly still crept miserably about the house, unable to get over Teddy's death. It seemed such a waste, and him with such talent, so much to live for. And she missed him so much.

Mr Edward was not himself, either. He would sit for

long periods in his study, staring at the wall, an untouched glass of whisky at his elbow. He didn't gamble and when the time came he refused to go hunting. Meals were sent back to the kitchen only half eaten and if the servants tried to talk to him he simply barked at them and sent them away. It was a long, hard winter at Tenpenny Farm. Nobody knew, because he would allow nobody near enough to talk to him, whether he grieved more for his son or his wife; whether he was eaten up with remorse, self-pity or anger. It was doubtful whether he knew himself.

Christmas came and went. Dolly alone understood what her employer was going through because she was suffering, too. But she didn't know how to help him. In the end one evening she plucked up courage and took him in a pile of tasty sandwiches. 'Come now, Mr Edward. You hev to eat a bit more than you do,' she said firmly, although she was quivering inside. 'I made these sandwiches meself. You mustn't let them go to waste. And I've brought you a nice mug of milk, too. That'll help you sleep.'

'I can't sleep, Dolly. I don't believe I shall ever sleep again.' He raised haggard eyes to her. 'I never thought I should miss Maudie the way I do.' He shook his head. 'And Teddy. It wasn't his fault. He couldn't help . . . But was it mine? Did I make him the way he was? Was it my fault? It goes round and round in my head. No wonder I can't sleep.'

'I don't sleep very well, either, sir,' she said quietly.

He looked up at her. 'You were very fond of Teddy, weren't you, Dolly?'

She bit her lip and nodded, not trusting herself to speak.

340

He pushed the sandwiches towards her. 'You have one. You've lost weight.'

'Oh, I couldn't . . .'

'Nonsense. We'll both have one.'

Uncomfortably, she stood on the other side of his desk, nibbling a chicken sandwich, whist he polished off the rest. When she had finished it she said, 'I'll fetch a hot brick and put it in your bed, sir. You really should try and get some sleep.'

He sighed. 'All right, Dolly. I'll do as you say.' He got to his feet, dashing his hand across his eyes. 'Yes, you're right. I must try and pull myself together. After all, life goes on.' He gave her a lop-sided smile that was almost sheepish. 'You're a tough little thing, aren't you, Dolly? None of the other servants would have talked to me like you have.'

Dolly flushed. 'Oh, sir. I hope I hevn't spoke out of place.'

'No, no,' he waved his hand, 'not at all.'

That night, as she lay in her own narrow little bed, Dolly thought about her employer. He wasn't nearly so fierce as people thought. A bit like her dad, really. If you stood up to him he was all right. You could twist him round your little finger.

From then on her relationship with her employer changed subtly. Dolly couldn't put a finger on how exactly, except that he noticed her and didn't treat her as part of the furniture as he did the other servants. Sometimes, if she encountered him on the stairs or in the hall, he would even smile at her. His smile was a little like Mr Teddy's.

'Are you sleeping better, sir?' she asked as she took him in his dinner one evening. She had taken it upon herself to wait on him at meal times and would stand over him until he had finished.

'Not much. I have these awful nightmares.' He shuddered and pushed his plate away.

'Come on, you hevn't finished, sir. And cook did the mutton jest the way you like it.' She put the plate back in front of him.

Obediently, he ate the rest.

That night as she lay staring up into the darkness her door opened and Mr Edward slipped in, wearing his nightshirt. 'I can't sleep, Dolly,' he whispered, 'and when I do I have these awful nightmares.' He sat down on the side of her bed and put his head in his hands. 'It's terrible. I see my son rising up out of the river all covered in that horrible slimy mud and he's holding out his arms to me. But I can't reach him. I can't help him.' He gave a funny little whimper. 'I can't bear it. Oh, Dolly, I can't bear it.' He began to cry.

'Oh, sir.' Without thinking, she hopped out of bed and cradled his head to her breast. Soon his tears had soaked her white calico nightgown. When he was calmer he lifted his head. 'Now look what I've done,' he whispered, 'I've made your nightgown all wet. I'm sorry, Dolly.'

'Never mind it, sir,' she said, her voice not quite steady. 'As long as you're feeling better now.' She shivered in the cold night air.

'I am, Dolly. I am.' He released her. 'Get back into bed. You're half frozen with cold.'

'So are you, sir,' she said as he held the bedclothes for her to slide back into her hard little bed.

'Yes, Dolly, I am.' It seemed the most natural thing in the world that he should get in beside her.

'You don't mind, Dolly, do you?' he whispered in her ear as he drew her nightgown aside.

For a brief moment she stiffened. Then she wound her arms round his neck. 'Oh, no, sir, I don't mind a bit.'

The drowning of Teddy Green followed so closely by his mother going away was the talk of Wessingford for several months. Nobody thought Felicity would stay away for long but time went by and there was no sign of her returning. By and by people got fed up with watching for her and the whole affair receded into village history.

Becca was busy in the workshop with Jethro one Friday afternoon just before Easter when there was a knock at the front door. Polly answered it and came scuttling through like a frightened mouse. 'There's a man, says he's come to see you, Mum,' she said, her eyes wide. 'He look a bit fierce, Mum,' she whispered. 'I should take the poker if I was you.'

Puzzled, Becca left what she was doing and went through to the front door. A tall, heavily built man, with thick black hair and a bushy beard and a face the colour of old mahogany stood there. There was a gold earring in one ear and a livid scar ran the length of his cheek. For a moment Becca stared at him, almost as scared as Polly had been. Then recognition dawned and she flung her arms round him.

'Tommy! Thass the boy Tommy! Jethro!' she called, breathless from the bear hug he was giving her. 'Come and see. Thass the boy Tommy. At long last he's come home from the sea.'

Jethro came through, wiping his hands on his canvas apron. 'Tommy, bor, thass good to see you,' he said, shaking him by the hand. 'Come and set you down and we'll hev a drop of beer.'

Jethro poured the beer and Tommy sat down at the table with Becca. 'Where've you bin all these years, boy?' she asked, hardly able to take her eyes from him in case he should disappear. 'Running away like that and then never so much as a word from you. Mercy me, you went away a boy and come back a man but I'd hev reckernised you anywhere.' She wiped the corner of her eye on her apron. 'Oh, thass good to see you home, boy.'

'Yes, your owd mum'll be something pleased.' Jethro pushed a tankard of beer over to him.

'I reckon she will.' Tommy took a long draught. 'I reckon she'll be right pleased to know we're settling in Wyford, jest across the river, too.'

'We?' Becca raised her eyebrows.

'Me and the fam'ly.' He grinned. 'There's Alice, the wife, and the four children; Selina, she's going on fourteen, Johnny's ten, Willy's six and 'Liza's jest gone two.' He counted them off proudly on his fingers before emptying his tankard and pushing it across to Jethro to be refilled. 'I bin all round the world two or three times. I reckon thass time I dropped anchor.' He took another drink and sucked the froth off his beard.

'What's China like?' Becca leaned forward, her elbows on the table.

'China? Thass one place I ain't never bin to.' Tommy slapped his knee. 'But never mind that. Wass happened here since I bin gone?' He looked round. 'You and Jethro seem well enough set up here. And I can see you got a little maid out there.' He nodded out of the window, where Lucy was playing with her doll and the doll's pram Jethro had made her.

Becca nodded. 'Yes, she's our youngest. Kate, the eldest, she's in service in Colchester. Then Ashley – we call him Ash . . .'

'He look after the horse,' Jethro cut in quickly. 'He's inclined to be a bit on the slow side, but good with animals. But young Tim's the one who's gonna take after me in the business. He can do near anything with a bit of wood.'

Becca shot Jethro a puzzled glance, but he seemed not to notice.

'So you've got two boys and two girls? And what about Ellen?' Tommy grinned. 'Or shouldn't I ask?'

Becca shrugged. 'Ask if you like. Better still, go and see for yourself.'

'Her and George still live in Racky Harris's cottage,' Jethro said, 'with their nine.'

'Nine?' Tommy raised his eyebrows.

'Yes. And the cottage is still in much about the same condition as that was afore you left. George ain't much of a one for looking after things,' Becca added. Her voice softened. 'Dad's gone, o'course. He died about eighteen months ago. He never forgot you, Tommy. Never stopped talking about you and hoping you'd walk through the door. Why didn't you even drop a line, bor?'

He shrugged. 'You know I wasn't never one for putting things down on paper. But I thought about them. I thought about all of ye.'

'We wasn't to know that, Tommy,' she said 'Not without a word from you. I think you going away like that near broke Mum's heart.'

'Is Mum still . . . ?'

'She's still at home.'

Tommy nodded. 'I'll go and see her.' He stood up. He was even taller than Jethro and had to duck his head under the beams. 'Ellen, too. I'll call and tell you how I get on on the way back.'

After Tommy had gone Becca said, 'You were very quick to say that about Tim, Jethro. After all, Tommy's got a right to know . . .'

Jethro shook his head. 'I ain't so sure that might not be better to let sleeping dogs lie. You heard what he said, didn't you?'

'What?'

'His oldest daughter is going on fourteen. Now young Tim was fourteen last December so . . .' He nodded sagely.

Becca frowned as she tried to calculate. 'You mean this wife – Alice, had already fallen for the girl – what was her name? Selina – when Tim was born?'

'If my calcylations ain't amiss that seem very like it to me.' Jethro nodded.

'Then what are you saying?'

'I ain't saying nothing. All I think is we should bide our time before we start raking up history.'

Becca frowned. 'I only hope Mum and Ellen will do the same.'

'They won't say nothing,' Jethro said. 'They won't consider it their place. Tim's our boy, so it's up to us. Thass what they'll think.'

346

She nodded. 'Reckon you're right, Jethro. Oh, I'd like to see Mum's face when the boy Tommy walk in.' Suddenly, her own face lit up. 'We could hev a party, Jethro. Out on the pightle. Spring is here so the weather's warmed up. Tommy could bring his family over and we could all celebrate together. What do you think?

Jethro chewed his beard for a few moments. Then he nodded. 'I think thass a very good idea. I've got some trestles and planks, I can soon rig up a table and benches . . .'

'And there's a big white tablecloth that belonged to your aunt in the chest of drawers. Now, what shall we hev?'

Becca and Jethro were still planning Tommy's home-coming party when he called in on his way back to Wyford. He thought the party was an excellent idea and promised to bring his family over to tea on Easter Monday.

The party was a huge success. Becca had boiled a ham and cooked a hen that was egg-bound and Daisy had made an extra batch of bread and brought pickles and vegetables salted over the winter. Polly, who had become an expert pastry-maker, had made great fruit pies and George had brought two big jugs of cream from the dairy at Tenpenny Farm. Three days earlier Jethro had fetched a cask of Daisy's home-made dandelion wine so that it would have time to 'settle' before it was broached.

Everyone was in great high spirits. Daisy was quite overcome with happiness to see all her family together, her three children and seventeen grandchildren round one big table. 'I jest wish your dad coulda bin here to see this day,' she said, wiping away a tear. She couldn't take her eyes off the big, swarthy man who had returned in place of her gangling young son and he paid her exaggerated attention, watched by his wife Alice, a cheerful, well-built girl who looked as if she knew how to look after herself and had probably had to during her husband's trips abroad.

'Would you like to see Dad's grave?' Becca asked quietly when everyone had eaten their fill and was dozing in the late April sunshine while the children talked in groups or ran about the pightle playing 'last touch'.

Tommy yawned and stretched. 'Yes. Why not? I get restless if I set too long in one place.'

He accompanied Becca to the church yard and together they stood beside the mound that was all that remained of Joe's earthly life.

'You shoulda written,' she said. 'You broke Mum and Dad's heart, never so much as sending them a post card to say whether you was alive or dead.'

He shrugged. 'I told you, I was never much of a one for pen and paper. You know that, Becca.'

'Mind you, we did hev news of you,' she said slowly, leading the way to another grave. She and Jethro had talked this over and after some argument he had agreed that Tommy ought to be told about Tim's mother.

'What's this, then?' Tommy asked, as they stood by a stone that simply read JENNY STANSGATE 1874–1894 in letters partly obscured by moss.

Becca watched him. 'Thass your wife's grave, Tommy.'

She saw him pale under his tan. 'My wife? What do you mean?'

'Jenny. Don't you remember Jenny?'

He sat down on a nearby tombstone and put his head in his hands.

'She was your wife, Tommy, wasn't she?'

He nodded without raising his head. After a while he looked up. 'How did you know? How did she come to be buried here?'

'She was buried here because she died here,' Becca said. 'She got here jest in time to give birth to your son. She'd walked all the way from London, sleeping in ditches and picking up food where she could. She had rags round her feet and she was half-starved.' Becca spoke in a flat, unemotional voice.

'But I found her lodgings,' Tommy said, bewildered.

'Yes, but you never sent her any more money to pay the rent, did you? And landlords don't take kindly to people who don't pay their rent. They turn them out in the street.'

'I did send her more. It must have arrived after she'd left.' He shook his head.

'Thass as maybe. But she hadn't got nowhere to go so she decided the best thing to do was to find her way to Wessingford because thass where your family lived. Your son was born in Mum's front parlour and thass where your wife died. She said you'd had to take a boat to China because her brother threatened to kill you.' Becca sighed. 'But that wasn't true, was it, Tommy? You told me the other day you'd never bin to China.'

He kicked at a tussock of grass. 'No, that wasn't true.'

'I guess the truth of the matter was that you'd got another girl into trouble by this time, Tommy. Am I right?'

349

He nodded without looking up.

'And I guess you married her, too.'

He nodded again.

'Well, Tommy, boy, that seems you've bin a bit of a rake in your day.' Becca had never raised her voice as she was speaking. 'How many more girls hev you got in the family way and married?'

He gave a ghost of a grin. 'I ain't married any others, Becca.' Now he did look up. 'What about the boy? What about Jenny's son?'

'Jenny's son is our Timothy. And by my reckoning he's about six months younger than your Selina. Did Alice know you already had a wife when you married her?'

'Don't be daft, 'course she didn't.' He gave an impatient shake of his head.

'How far was she gone when you was wed?'

'Three months.'

'Then least said soonest mended, because at that time you'd still got a wife. For all you knew you'd *still* got a wife to this day. Hevn't that worried you?' Becca looked at him accusingly.

'Thass worried me all me life,' he said. 'I was forever looking over me shoulder and thass the truth of it. In fact,' he fingered the scar on his cheek, 'Alice think I got this in a pub brawl, but I didn't. Jenny's brother found me – he always said he would – and he did it. I wonder the bugger didn't kill me. It wasn't his fault he didn't.'

'I dessay he wanted to know what you'd done with his sister. And you couldn't tell him 'cause you'd cast her off like an old shoe.'

'I wouldn't put it quite like that,' Tommy protested.

350

'Wouldn't you? How would you put it, then? Telling her you were off to China for two years. All I can say is, you may be my flesh and blood, Tommy Stansgate, but whatever Jenny's brother did to you was no more than you deserve, treating the poor girl the way you did. She was a lovely girl, too.' Becca regarded her brother accusingly. 'You've bin a real tearaway, Tommy, and I 'spect thass why you've come to settle over the river at Wyford, ain't it? To get away from Jenny's brother?'

He nodded. 'Partly. I met a bloke on the fishing smacks that come into Barking. He said there'd be a job if I was to come this way.' He took a deep breath. 'So I've come to make a fresh start, Becca.'

'Good.' She watched him as he took off his cap and scratched his head and then replaced it. Then he kicked another tussock of grass. She knew what he wanted to say but she was determined to give him no help. 'Shall we go back now?' she asked.

'No. Wait a minute.' He scratched his head again. 'I'd be glad, Becca . . .' he began. He started again. 'Young Tim . . .'

'Yes?' She raised her eyebrows.

'I wouldn't want to take him from you, Becca, even though he is my rightful son.'

'I didn't think you would, Tommy. But I'm glad to hear you say it.'

'And like you say, least said, soonest mended, don't you think? Does anybody else know?'

'Nobody who's likely to say anything,' Becca answered. 'Your secret's safe enough.'

'It's for Alice's sake, you understand.'

351

'Oh, I understand, Tommy. But Jethro and me thought it was only right that you should know.' Becca began to walk towards the gate. Her feelings were mixed. Tommy was her young brother; she loved him and had always tried to make excuses for the way he had treated his parents. But she couldn't excuse the way he had treated Jenny and she was disappointed in him. There was no getting away from the fact that he was selfish and irresponsible.

'Yes. Yes, of course. Thankee for telling me. And thankee for looking after my son all these years.'

'Your son?' Becca looked at him in surprise. 'Didn't you say you were happy for Tim to remain Jethro's and my son? And nobody any the wiser?'

Tommy nodded, chastened.

When they got back to the others Becca noticed Tommy looking searchingly at Tim. But he was busy talking to Selina and the other new cousins and took not the slightest notice of his uncle.

Chapter Twenty

Becca liked Alice, her new sister-in-law. She was a large, capable girl who knew how to handle Tommy, drunk or sober. They had managed to rent a little cottage in Sun Yard, not far from the river, but they had precious little furniture to put in it because in London, Alice told her, their rented rooms had been furnished, albeit sparsely. So Jethro sorted out a few pieces from his store and he took Tommy to Mr Letch's emporium to buy two or three secondhand beds which they transported home on the cart. Becca helped out with some odd pieces of china.

'I wonder you don't start up a shop,' Alice laughed, gratefully unpacking what Becca had brought, 'you seem to hev plenty of stock.'

'Oh, you don't know jest how much I should like to,' Becca said with a sigh. 'In fact, I keep on at Jethro to hev one but he won't hev anything to do with the idea.'

'Keep on at me? I should think she do!' Jethro looked up from helping Tommy fix the iron bedstead together.

'Well, that ain't as if we couldn't afford it,' Becca said, half under her breath, giving him a sideways look.

'I never said it was. But I say we should be content with well-doing. We're comfortable enough the way we are and I don't see no need to alter our ways.' Jethro straightened up and rubbed his back.

'I see there's an empty place on the corner of Anchor Hill,' Tommy teased. 'That'd do you all right, Jethro.'

'Don't you start,' he growled good-naturedly. 'I hev quite enough to contend with, the way Becca carry on.' He looked at the clock on the mantelpiece – it was one of the things Tommy and Alice had brought with them, he'd picked it up in India. 'Is there anything else on the cart? If there is we oughta shift it because thass time we was thinking about getting back. Thass half hour after low water now and we shan't ford the river if we don't make haste. And we don't want poor owd Blossom to hev to cart us all round by Colchester to get home, for the sake of a few minutes.'

They took their leave of Tommy and his family and climbed up on to the cart. The river was easy to ford at low water, with a good solid hard on both banks, and it was only in the very middle that Blossom was nearly up to her fetlocks. 'Only jest did it in time,' Jethro said as they pulled out on to the further shore. 'But Blossom never mind getting her feet wet, do you, gal?' He gave a gentle slap with the reins.

Becca didn't answer. She was busy with her own thoughts. 'What do you think about it, Jethro?' she asked.

'Think about what?'

'This shop.'

'I don't think about it at all, Becca. You know my views. I've towd you time and time again.'

She was silent for some time. Then she said, 'I've a mind to go into it meself.'

He turned and stared at her. 'Whatever do you mean?'

'I've saved up quite a lot of money from my china, Jethro,' she said with a lift of her head. 'I dessay I've got enough put by to pay the rent for several weeks. I could take the shop and sell my china there. Thass what I've always wanted to do, as you very well know.'

By this time Blossom was labouring up Ferry Hill, spurred on by the knowledge that her stable was not far off. Jethro slackened the reins and let her go at her own pace between the hedgerows white with may blossom, broken here and there by workmen's cottages. 'Now listen to me, Becca,' he said in a tone he might have used to a child. 'How ever do you think you could make a go of a shop selling china in Wyford? Thass only a small place. Whoever do you think would buy it?'

'I grant you that might be easier in Colchester,' she agreed, 'but that would cost a lot more'n I could afford. So I'd be content to start small. As to who might come and buy – well, even the poorest folks need cups and plates and I often get bits I could sell off cheap. The better stuff, well, once I get meself 'stablished, I dessay I can advertise and you never know, I might get people coming on the train to see what I've got.' She was quiet for a while. Then she said, ''Course, that would be better if you was to come in with me, but since you ain't interested I'd be happy to sell a few of your bits in the shop, but you'd hev to pay me commission.'

'You've got it all worked out, hevn't you?' There was a certain grudging admiration in Jethro's voice.

'Yes, I hev.' Becca said no more because they had reached the pightle and she had to get down and open the gate. She had spoken largely out of bravado, because truth to tell she wasn't at all sure that she could make a success of a china shop in a small place like Wyford, but she knew she had given Jethro something to think about.

Dolly's stays got so tight that in the end she had to leave them off. She knew what the trouble was. She had missed three times and felt permanently sick. Her mother had had these symptoms enough times for Dolly to be in no doubt that she was pregnant. When she had first suspected this might be the case she had stolen some of her mother's gin but that had only given her a headache and now she was at her wit's end, especially as she had noticed Cook eyeing her thickening waist. Every night when she said her prayers she asked God to tell her what to do, but he didn't seem to be listening. So she crept about her work, worried and frightened, not daring to speak to anyone of her predicament.

'The Master want to speak to you in his study,' Cook said one morning. Her tone was smug and knowing. She was a fat, beady-eyed woman with a bitter tongue. The rumour was that she'd been crossed in love when she was young and had never got over it. Dolly had never liked her much although Cook had never treated her badly.

'What, now?' Dolly was still wearing the sacking apron she wore over her uniform to blacklead the grates.

'Yes. Now. So you'd better clean yerself up.'

Dolly untied the sack apron and washed her hands before hurrying along to the study. Mr Edward didn't usually single her out for attention during the day, but ignored her much as he did the other servants. It was only at night that he made her feel she was someone special, and even then he often didn't speak to her.

She knocked at the door and entered. He was standing looking out of the window with his back to her. 'Is there anything wrong, Dolly?' he asked, his voice cold. 'Cook tells me you haven't been yourself lately.' He turned and eyed her up and down, his gaze coming to rest on her dress where it strained over her full breasts. He sniffed. 'She also says you seem to be putting on weight in a certain place. I hope this doesn't mean you've been tumbling with farm hands.'

Dolly's head shot up and she blushed fiery red. 'Of course not, sir. I'm a respectable girl.'

'You mean you're not ... er ... pregnant?' He lifted his eyebrows and Dolly imagined she saw his shoulders relax slightly.

'Er, no, sir.' Dolly hung her head. Then she said in a rush, 'At least, yes, sir. I fear I might be.'

He swung round. 'You're pregnant?' he interrupted. 'Then Cook was right in her observations.' He shook his head sternly. 'I must say I'm surprised at you, Dolly. I didn't think you were a girl like that.'

'But, sir . . .' Dolly looked at him in surprise. 'You know it's only you that comes to . . .'

'Enough! I'll have none of your impertinence. There is no excuse for your immorality. If you choose to behave like a slut then you must take the consequences.' He went over

357

to his desk and took out a sovereign. 'Here, take this and go. And that's more than you deserve. I've said repeatedly, I will not tolerate loose morals among my staff.'

'But sir . . . ?' Dolly couldn't believe her ears. How could he say such things, this man who had come to her bed nearly every night for the past four months. It was his child she carried, he must know that. 'Sir, the child . . .'

'Don't stand there and argue with me, girl.' He was white with anger. 'If you know who the father is, which I very much doubt, perhaps he can be persuaded to marry you? Do you know who it is? No, I thought not,' he went on, without giving her the chance to answer, 'your sort never does. It could be any of half a dozen, I dare say.'

'That's not true, sir. I'm a good girl.' She lifted her head and looked straight at him although the tears were streaming down her face.

He turned away. 'You're no better than a common whore. Pack your bags and go. I never want to see you near this house again.' He swung round. 'And don't go running to your father with a pack of lies either, if you want him to keep a roof over his head. Let me tell you there are plenty of cowmen in the district looking for work. Well, go on, what are you waiting for?' as she remained where she stood, staring at him in utter disbelief. 'Get out of my sight. And out of my house. I'll give you half an hour.'

Utterly shattered at the way this man, to whom she had given everything, was treating her, Dolly went upstairs and gathered her things together. She didn't have much because she left the pretty lilac uniform on the bed, but she was careful to pack the little box in which she kept

358

her most precious possessions, the cheap trinkets Mr Teddy had thought to buy her silence with. Then she didn't know what to do so she went home.

Rosie was helping her mother to fold sheets. Ellen dropped her end of the sheet as Dolly appeared at the door. 'What you doing home at this time of day, mawther?' she asked. 'You ill?'

'I bin turned out.' Dolly sank down on the nearest chair, too numb even to cry.

'Why, for goodness' sake?'

'Because I'm in the fam'ly way.'

'Oh, my God.' Ellen sat down with a thump. She looked at Dolly with disgust. 'You little slut! Who you bin larking around with? I'll send your father after him, whoever he is. He'll hev to marry you.'

Dolly shook her head. 'He won't never marry me,' she said in a flat voice. 'Thass the Master. Mr Edward. But he won't never admit it. He's trying to make out I bin tumbling with the farm hands.' She opened her palm. 'He give me this and told me to go. He said he never want to see me near his house again.' A tear rolled down her cheek. 'And I thought I was comforting him. I thought he needed me.'

'Hmm. They all say that,' Ellen said primly. 'But I dessay you led him on.' She looked her daughter up and down. 'How far gone are you?'

'Over three months.'

'Well, you needn't think you can stay here, mawther. We're a respectable household. We don't want shame brought on us.'

Dolly looked up, panic in her eyes. 'But, Mum, there ain't nowhere else for me! Where else can I go?'

'You should hev thought of that before you started playing around.'

'I *didn't* play around, Mum. It was the Master. If I'd refused he'd hev chucked me out.'

'You've bin chucked out anyway. At least you'd hev bin chucked out pure.' There was not a vestige of sympathy in Ellen's voice. She turned to Rosie. 'And you can take dreadful warning, my girl. If you ever bring trouble home here you'll get jest the same treatment.'

Rosie looked from Dolly to her mother and back again, not knowing what to think or say, so she kept quiet.

'Well?' Ellen glared at Dolly. 'What are you waiting for? There's the door.'

Slowly, Dolly picked up her bag and went out, rejected by all those she loved most. She didn't know what to do or where to go so she began to walk down the lane. As she passed her grandmother's gate she stopped. Granny would help her. Surely Granny would help her? She pushed open the gate and walked slowly up the path.

Aunt Becca was there with Granny. They were all warm and rosy from bread-making. Dolly took one look at their kind, loving faces and burst into tears.

A long time later, after an exhausting cry and two cups of tea, Dolly's story was told.

'Hypocrites! The whole lot of them. Hypocrites,' Becca said, her face set.

'What do you mean, Aunt Becca?' Dolly asked.

'Why, Farmer Green. To get you in the fam'ly way and then turn you out for being no better than you should be.' She gave a little snort. 'I don't s'pose you invited him into your bed. I dessay that was his idea, not yours.'

360

Dolly nodded, hanging her head. 'I said I didn't mind,' she admitted.

Granny sucked her gums. 'Poor little innocent.'

'And I don't know how Ellen could hev the gall to turn you out, neither,' Becca went on.

'She said she didn't want shame brought on her house,' Dolly said sadly. Her face crumpled again. 'And I should never hev told you that was Mr Edward. He said he'd turn Dad out if I told a pack of lies . . .'

'He meant if you told the truth,' Becca said, pursing her lips. 'I know his sort, they're all the same. They think they can treat servants like dirt. Thass all wrong. We'll all be the same when we stand before our Maker, when all's said and done.'

Dolly wasn't listening. She began to sob. 'Oh, Aunt Becca, Granny, what am I gonna do?'

Becca went and put her arms round her. 'We'll think of something, child, never fear. You won't be turned out to end up in the work'us.' She turned to Daisy. 'Will you watch the rest of the loaves, Mum? I'll take Dolly home. I think I oughta hev a word with Ellen.' Her tone was ominous.

'Be careful what you say,' Daisy warned. 'You know you can never speak a civil word to each other at the best of times. And the mood you're in . . .'

'Don't you worry, Mum. I shan't fall out with Ellen. Come on, Dolly.'

'I'd rather stay here with Granny,' she said. She was hunched up on a chair in the corner.

'Thass right. You stay here with me, mawther, and we'll hev another cuppa tea.' Granny pulled the kettle forward as she spoke.

'Yes. Maybe thass the best thing.' Becca nodded. She took off her apron and put on her hat and went off to Ellen's cottage. Her sister was sitting on a low chair by the fire with Winnie, now a skinny three year old, on her lap. Rosie was ironing sheets.

'I've jest seen Dolly,' Becca said, coming straight to the point.

'Little slut,' was Ellen's answer.

Becca turned to Rosie. 'Take young Winnie for a walk over the field, Rosie. I wanta talk to your mother,' she said.

Rosie willingly put the iron back in the hearth and took Winnie's hand. Becca watched them go, then sat down on a chair by the table and turned to Ellen. 'By what right do you condemn your own daughter for following in her mother's footsteps?' she asked quietly.

'I dunno what you're talking about,' Ellen said sulkily.

'You know very well what I'm talking about,' Becca said. 'Only, by all accounts, Dolly didn't hev much choice, whereas you wasn't forced to lift your skirts for George Askew. In your case you couldn't wait! By my reckoning that makes you a damn' sight more blameworthy than Dolly. Yet you hev the gall to get on your high horse and shut the door in her face when she come to you for help!' Becca hadn't raised her voice and she didn't now but her tone was ominous. 'Nobody turned you out, Ellen. In fact, when you got yerself in the fam'ly way, Mum and Dad were prepared to ruin my life so that you shouldn't suffer.'

'Things ain't turned out so bad for you,' Ellen flashed.

'No, I bin lucky. Jethro's a good man. But I hadn't even met him when you took George. I coulda bin an old maid

362

for the rest of me days for all you knew. Or cared. I coulda chucked meself in the river and drownded and that wouldn't hev worried you as long as you'd got George away from me. I know that and so do you, so there's no point denying it.' Becca smoothed the sheet that lay on the table with her hand. 'But thass all in the past. What I'm saying is, you should remember how you was treated and try and use a little Christian charity on your own girl. I reckon she's bin through the mill, one way and another.'

'But the shame . . .'

'More shame if you turn her out, I'd hev said.' Becca looked round at the muddly little room. 'One more mouth won't make that much difference, I wouldn't hev thought. And Dolly was always a good worker.'

'Thass true.' Ellen nodded thoughtfully. Rosie hadn't proved half as willing as her sister to take on the household chores. 'But I don't know what George'll hev to say about it all.'

'Don't know what George'll hev to say about what?' George came in, his face like thunder. 'About that girl? Where is she? I'll thrash the living daylights out of her. Thass what I'll do, never mind what I'll say.' He looked round, throwing his dirty old cap on to the table, on top of the clean sheet. 'Where is the dirty little bitch?'

'You know about it then, George? Who told you?'

'The Gaffer. He come to me and told me he'd sacked Dolly because she was in the fam'ly way.'

'Did he say who the father was, George?' Becca asked.

'No. What are you doing here, anyway?'

'Dolly came to Mum's after Ellen had turned her out.'

'Ah, good. You turned her out, Ellen. Thass saved me

the job. The Gaffer as much as said if I let her stay at home we'd be turned out of the cottage. So she couldn't hev stayed here even if we'd bin prepared to put up with the shame.'

Becca was open-mouthed with amazement. 'How could he? How could that man be so two-faced?'

'What do you mean?' George picked up his cap and settled it back on his head.

'Don't you realise, George? It was Mr Edward that put Dolly in the fam'ly way?'

His face turned purple. 'The dirty bugger! If thass true I'll knock his teeth down his bloody throat.' He turned to Ellen. 'Is it true, Ellen?'

'So Dolly say.' She sighed. 'And Dolly ain't one to lie, I'll give her that.'

George sat down. 'No wonder he said he'd turn us out if we kept her at home. Stands to reason he don't want to see his bastard running round. Bloody old ram!' He took off his cap again and banged it on his knee in frustration. Clouds of dust rose.

'So what about Dolly?' Becca asked.

'God knows.' George shook his head. 'Where is she now?'

'At Mum's. But she can't really stay there. We don't want Mum being turned out, do we?' Becca said. She stood up. 'I'll go home and have a word with Jethro. I don't know what good it'll do but he might be able to think of something.'

George nodded. 'Thankee, Becca.' He was silent for some time. Then he said, 'Poor little mawther.' He got up and began to pace round the room, then he stood looking out of the door for a long time. 'Thass no good,' he said finally, turning back into the room, 'I can't do it. I can't turn the poor little mawther out whatever happen, I'd never forgive meself. Becca, jest call in at Daisy's on the way home and tell Dolly we'll stand by her, will you? Thass right, Ellen, ain't it?'

She shook her head. 'I don't rightly know, George. We got the others to think about, when all's said and done. If you lose your job and we get turned out . . . Oh, I dunno, George. I dunno what to say.'

'P'raps the Gaffer'll change his mind,' he said hopefully.

'Not if what Dolly say is true. He on't want his by-blow running about to remind him.'

'P'raps she's making it up, thinking she'd get more sympathy that way?'

Ellen shook her head. 'Dolly ain't one to lie. Any case, I doubt she'd hev been clever enough to make up a story like that.'

'I still think we must stand by her,' George said.

'All right, if you say so. But God in his mercy know how we'll do it,' Ellen said, her shoulders sagging under the weight of worry.

Becca went home and when all the children were in bed she told Jethro the sorry story.

He spat into the fire. 'Thass always bin the same,' he said savagely, 'one law for the rich and another for the poor. I admire George and Ellen for standing by Dolly, but do they realise what that'll mean? As sure as eggs is eggs they'll be turned outa their cottage and George'll lose his job.' He sniffed and scratched his beard. 'They can't

365

do it, Becca. They got all the other children to consider. They can't do it.'

'Could you turn a child of yours out on to the street in a state like that then, Jethro?' she asked.

He shook his head wearily. 'No, I don't believe I could.'

'Well, then.'

He sighed. 'Thass a terrible job to know what to do for the best. Where is the gal now?'

'She's staying the night with Mum. But she won't be able to stay there many days, will she?'

'No. Gaffer Green'll turn Daisy out as soon as look at her if he think she's going against his wishes. Oh!' He took out his pipe and filled it, ramming the tobacco down. 'He's a two- faced bugger if ever I saw one. We shall hev to get young Dolly away from there right quick.'

'And then what?'

He lit his pipe and when it was drawing to his satisfaction he looked across at her. 'I'm buggered if I know, Becca.'

They both sat staring into the fire until long past their usual bedtime and it was with heavy hearts that they finally climbed the narrow stairs to bed.

Chapter Twenty-One

Becca had no chance to speak to Jethro the next morning because it was market day and he had to go into Colchester. It wasn't until the evening when the children were all in bed that they had an opportunity to talk. And what Jethro had to say had nothing to do with Dolly's predicament at all.

He fished in his pocket, looking extraordinarily pleased with himself, and drew out a key which he threw down on the table.

'Wass this?' she said, picking it up.

He grinned. 'Thass the key to our shop. The one at Wyford you was so set on.'

'What, the one on the corner of Anchor Hill?'

He nodded, smiling.

'Jethro!' She flung her arms round him. 'You mean to say you've bin and rented it?'

'Thass right.' He took her arms and held them. 'That is what you wanted, ain't it?'

'Yes. yes, you know it is. But what made you change your mind?'

'Jest get me a mug of beer and I'll tell you. I couldn't spit a tanner, I've done so much talking today.'

She fetched the beer and poured a mug for him and a small glass for herself, her hands trembling with excitement. 'Now,' she said, her eyes shining, 'tell me all about it.'

He drained his mug and pushed it over for more, sucking the froth off his beard. With ill-concealed impatience Becca re-filled his mug and pushed it across to him. He took another draught, then said, 'Well, I never wanted to start up a shop, you know that, Becca, but when it come to it I couldn't see no other way round it.'

'I don't see what you're getting at.'

'You will in a minute.' He took another swig of beer. 'Thass like this, you see. I laid awake best part of the night thinking about that poor little mawther, Dolly, and the fix she's in. Thass all very well for George to say he'll stand by her, but talk's easy. When they find they ain't got a roof over their head and no money coming in to feed the littl'uns, that'll be a different story. So I reckoned the best way was to think of some way of helping him. I thought about offering him to come and work for me but there wouldn't be that much for him to do. After all he's a cowman, not a chair mender. And I ain't exackly rolling in money that I could pay him jest to loaf about. So I had to hev another think.'

Becca sipped her beer, never taking her eyes off Jethro's face.

He went on, 'Well, now, one of my objections to heving a shop was that I couldn't be in two or three places at once. I couldn't fetch and carry stuff, repair it and see after the shop . . .'

'But I said, I'll see after the shop,' Becca interrupted.

He held up his hand. 'Let me finish. Anyway, on me way to market this morning I called in and had a word with George and put a proposition to him. Then I went to the bank. And the upshot is, I've took the shop in Wyford and George is coming to work for me.'

'George is coming to work for you! But what will he do? You jest said yourself he's a cowman, not a chair mender!'

'Why, don't you see? He'll do all my carting. He'll fetch and deliver, bring the stuff across the river to the shop when I've repaired it, deliver it to customers when thass sold, take stuff into Mr Letch for me – that sorta thing.'

'Can we afford it?'

'Thass what I went to the bank to find out.'

'So I'll be in the shop, you'll be over here doing up the furniture, and George'll do the running about?'

'Thass about the size of it.' He shrugged. 'Thass not exackly what I would hev chose to do, if I speak the truth, but I couldn't see no other way to get George outa the hole he's in. Anyway, Tim is getting to the age when he can give me a hand. And if Dolly is at home I shouldn't wonder if young Rosie might like to come and help in the shop. She took a rare interest in your china, didn't she?'

'Yes, she did.' Becca's eyes moistened. 'You're a good man, Jethro.' She leaned over and kissed his cheek. 'There's only one thing you don't seem to hev thought of. If George don't work for Edward Green, where will they live?'

'Thass where you're wrong, Becca.' He grinned. 'I've thought of that, too. There's an empty cottage halfway

369

down Ferry Hill. Owd Granny Merchant died last month so the cottage is up for rent. That ain't in bad nick, either. I looked it over when her son asked me to give the furniture the once-over to see if there was anything worth a bob or two. And thass another thing – if George come to work for me we can do house clearances. There's often a bit to be made there and you can pick up some nice pieces sometimes, if you know what you're looking for.'

'Will the cottage be big enough for the family?'

'Oh, yes. Thass a bit bigger than Racky Harris's place and that want a bit doing to it, but George can see to that. The rent's not too high, neither.'

'You're expecting a rare lot of George, Jethro.'

'Yes, I am. And I've told him so. *And* I've said if he come to work for me he's got to lay off the drink. I ain't heving him driving Blossom three sheets in the wind. There's something else, too.' Jethro stopped to drain his beer. 'Young Ash will be able to give George a hand. The lad ain't very bright, but he's as strong as a horse and he'll be able to help George with the heavy stuff. As long as he's got somebody to tell him what to do he can manage. It'll be good for him, and he can keep an eye on George and see he don't go off the rails.'

'And did George agree to all this?'

Jethro grinned. 'He shook me hand and swore he'd never touch another drop, he was that grateful.

'And what about Ellen? I reckon she'll have something to say.'

Jethro's grin widened. 'I ain't that brave. I've left George to tell her.'

'I wonder what she'll say?' Becca picked up the key and

turned it over in her hand, her eyes shining. 'A shop. Jest what I've always wanted. The day before we open we'll hev a party.'

Jethro smiled at her affectionately. 'You and your parties, Becca.'

As Becca had predicted, Ellen had plenty to say when George told her of Jethro's offer. 'You surely didn't agree to go and work for Jethro Miller!' She was shocked. 'You can't be serious. No, George, I ain't gonna kowtow to him for every penny. And I shoulda thought you'd got more self-respect than to agree to it.'

'I think Jethro's made a very generous offer,' George said loftily. 'I shall give him a good day's work and for that he'll pay me. I see no shame in that, even if he is your sister's husband.'

'Oh, don't you see? Don't you understand?' Ellen said impatiently. 'I don't want to be beholden to my sister for anything.'

'Oh, don't be so bloody daft,' George said. 'Can't you see, we ain't got no choice? Surely you wouldn't want me to work for that randy bugger at the farm any longer, because I won't! Not for Father Peter, I won't. But I gotta work somewhere else we'll starve. And this way we'll be able to see the gal Dolly all right. She'll be a good help to you in the house. Good God, woman, can't you see this is the answer to our prayers!'

He sat down and threw his cap on the table. 'Trouble with you, Ellen, is your damn' silly pride. Thass wass making you so bitter. You always seem to think Becca is trying to play the lady on you, but she ain't, you know.'

He chewed his beard. 'Not like you would if you was in her place. I reckon you'd be a right owd Lady Muck.' He nodded his head. 'Jethro and Becca hev made us an offer that'll get us out of a hole. Aside from the fact that I don't see no other solution, thass a very generous offer. I'm very grateful to them and I've towd Jethro as much. I jest hope, Ellen, you'll find it in your heart to show them enough generosity to accept it in the spirit it's given.' He sat back in his chair and scratched his belly.

She stared at him, open-mouthed. She had never heard him make such a long speech in the whole of her life before.

But he hadn't quite finished. 'After all,' he added, 'that on't cost you anything except your pride. I've got to give up the drink.'

Ellen's jaw dropped even further. 'What, altogether?'

George nodded miserably. 'If I work for Jethro, I've got to sign the pledge.'

Ellen shook her head from side to side. 'Well, I don't know. I've never heard the like in all me born days. But if you can sign the pledge, George Askew, I reckon I can swallow my pride.' She gave a deep sigh. 'I s'pose you're right, George. I've let pride and envy rule me for far too long.'

He gave her a smile and a fleeting change of expression, the nearest she could manage to a smile, flitted across her face.

'Thass better.' His smile widened. 'Come on now, put your hat on and I'll take you along and show you the new cottage. Then we'll call in and thank Jethro and Becca. I think we owe them that, don't you?'

372

Ellen struggled again to smile. 'Yes, I reckon we owe them more'n we can ever repay.' She jammed her hat on her head. It was one of Becca's cast-offs. She forced the hat pin home. It was not going to be easy.

A month later, George and his family were settled in the cottage on Ferry Hill. George had already given it a coat of paint. Ellen couldn't hide her excitement at moving to a bigger house and was at last making an effort to change her slatternly ways. Dolly, abject with gratitude that she was not being turned out, was ready to work her fingers to the bone and it wouldn't be long before Ellen would be quite happy to let her take over the running of the house while she played the lady, sitting under a tree reading her novelettes or riding high on the cart with George when he went to do his deliveries. But that was in the future. For the moment, whilst everything was fresh and new, she was happy to do her share.

Over the river in Wyford the shop was ready, its windows sparkling so that the furniture and china could easily be seen from the road. Becca had put a large advertisement in the local paper to say that The Corner Shop would be opening on the last Saturday in June, and on the Friday evening she invited the whole family to the shop to see it and to drink to its success.

While Jethro had gone to fetch Daisy, old and frail now, Becca took a last look round the little shop she had hankered after for such a long time. It was quite a hotchpotch of furniture and china. At the front were all the expensive things: a Sheraton bookcase, a pair of elegant elbow chairs, a sofa table – all things Jethro had found tucked away in the shed at the back of his workshop, bits that his uncle had collected, knowing that one day they would be worth money. Here, too, was the best of Becca's china: the Famille Rose plate on the wall, the Dresden teapot, the pair of Worcester vases. But in the large store-room at the back was the secondhand furniture that would provide the bread and butter sales. Jethro had insisted that the back room be given over to this because it was where most of their money would be made. Becca didn't agree with him but she was too happy to argue.

'Jest put a duster over that little table in the window, Rosie,' she said, anxiously looking round to make sure nothing was out of place. 'And are the glasses all ready?'

'Yes, Aunt Becca. They're all on the tray.' Rosie beamed as she carefully dusted the little table. She was doing what she had always dreamed of doing, helping Aunt Becca. Her cup of happiness overflowed and she tried to forget that there had been blood on her hanky when she'd coughed this morning.

Suddenly, the whole family were there, filling the shop with laughter, chatter and congratulations. Only Ellen's little Winnie and Tommy's Liza, who were being looked after by Polly at Tommy's house in Sun Yard, were missing. Becca looked round at them all. There was Daisy sitting gingerly in one of the spindly elbow chairs. She was old and toothless and less agile now, her bent back evidence of a life spent in hard work. She had suffered heartache and disappointment in her long life but today she was happy, with family gathered round her. Becca turned away to wipe a tear from her eye, uncertain as to why she should suddenly feel so emotional.

As she did so she noticed Albert, his face reddened from his work at the forge, slip something into his pocket and saw that the silver snuff box that had been on the shelf behind him was missing. She made a mental note not to let him go without turning out his pockets; she'd always suspected that he wasn't very honest. His twin, Henry was there with Maisie Sprocket, the builder's daughter. It was Ralph Sprocket who owned the shop and Becca smiled wryly at the thought of paying rent to her nephew in the distant future, because Henry and Maisie were walking out seriously together now. But maybe it wouldn't last. Maisie was already ordering him about, and them not even engaged yet.

In a corner, Kate and Selina were talking to Tim, Ash with them. Dolly, her pregnancy obvious now, was standing a little apart. Suddenly, Tim and Selina threw their heads back and laughed. Becca nodded with satisfaction. It was nice that the cousins got on well together. Then, for some unexplained reason, a faint stirring of apprehension passed through her as the thought crossed her mind, supposing Tim and Selina . . . She shook herself. Cousins didn't fall in love, the relationship was too close.

Lucy came up to her. 'Look, Mum, Ash is clumsy, he's made me spill wine down my new dress.'

'Never mind, dear, it's only a spot.' It was. Becca had difficulty in seeing it, but Lucy was fastidious and couldn't bear to have so much as a hair out of place. She was eight now, a pretty child, with a peaches and cream complexion and fair curls; her ambition was to marry a rich man and live in a big house. Becca had no doubt she would achieve it, for how could any man resist her?

Tommy got up on a stool. He had no need to, he already towered above everyone else, even Jethro. 'Now, everybody,' he called. 'I want you all to raise your glasses to the success of Jethro and Becca's Corner Shop. You deserve to prosper together, and I'm sure George and Ellen agree. Not to mention young Dolly here.' He smiled at his blushing niece as she tried to hide behind an aspidistra in a pot. 'Becca, Jethro, here's to your very good health and success.'

They all raised their glasses. Becca noticed George grimace with something like disgust at the pale lemonade in his glass, but he drank it cheerfully enough. Ellen was standing beside him, in her first new dress for years. For the first time in years, too, she had lost the pinched, discontented look that had etched ugly lines on her face. In fact, she looked quite happy and contented, and stood with her hand in the crook of George's arm. As she caught Becca's eye she managed to smile and as she raised her glass Becca could detect no sign of the old jealousy and rancour.

Jethro, standing beside Becca, put his arm round her. 'I'm glad we've bin able to do something for George and Ellen, Becca,' he said softly. 'After all, we owe them sech a lot.'

She twisted round to look up at him. 'What do you mean?'

'Well, if it hadn't bin for them getting married the way they did, you'd hev married George and you and me would never hev wed. So I can't put a price on what I owe to them.' He lifted his glass. 'Here's to you and me, Becca,' he said softly. 'Things ain't worked out so bad, hev they, even if we did get off to a bit of a shaky start? I remember saying to you that I was willing to chance me arm and get married if you were. I ain't never regretted it, Becca. Not for a single day. Hev you?'

She shook her head. 'No. I reckon I've bin very lucky, Jethro. You're a good man.' She raised her glass. 'Here's to our shop.' They both drank, then she said with a twinkle, 'I always said we'd hev a shop, didn't I, Jethro?'